ALL YOU NEED IS LOVE

JESSICA REDLAND

Boldwood

First published in Great Britain in 2021 by Boldwood Books Ltd.

A CIP catalogue record for this book is available from the British Library.

Paperback ISBN 978-1-80048-444-3

Large Print ISBN 978-1-80048-443-6

Hardback ISBN 978-1-80162-564-7

Ebook ISBN 978-1-80048-446-7

Kindle ISBN 978-1-80048-445-0

Audio CD ISBN 978-1-80048-438-2

MP3 CD ISBN 978-1-80048-439-9

Digital audio download ISBN 978-1-80048-441-2

Boldwood Books Ltd
23 Bowerdean Street
London SW6 3TN
www.boldwoodbooks.com

To my Auntie Jennifer, a beautiful woman taken too soon.

For all those who are affected by Parkinson's and dementia, and specifically to Auntie Jennifer's family with love xx

1

JEMMA

Three years ago – 21st May

'Mum!' I called up the stairs. 'Mum! The hearse is here.' I cocked my head to one side, listening for her reply. Nothing. What *was* she doing up there? She'd told me forty minutes ago that she was 'almost ready' and, as she isn't one of those women who spends hours teasing one strand of hair into place, there was no reason to disbelieve her. Of all the mornings to take forever, why choose today? Shaking my head, I opened the front door to Mum's cottage, Bear's Pad, before Mr Golding, the funeral director, had a chance to lift the grizzly-bear knocker.

'Good morning, Ms Browne.' He gave a reverential bow of his head. 'We're ready when you are.'

'Thank you. We'll be out in five minutes.' I glanced back towards the stairs. 'Actually, it could be ten. Do we have time?'

'Ten minutes is no problem.'

My throat tightened as I glanced past him to the black limousine parked on the sloped driveway and the hearse parked on the road. It was still hard to take in. This wasn't a day I'd expected to experience for several decades.

I tried not to curl my lip up at the orange and yellow floral lettering arrangement resting against the side of the coffin. I hated it but Logan, my seven-year-old brother, had requested it because his best friend Billy Thomas had apparently told him that people who didn't have one were mean and that the dead would come back to haunt them. I could have throttled Billy Thomas. Logan also wanted a floral teddy bear to thoroughly protect him against any risk of ghosts but Mum and I had managed to talk him out of that. The deceased would *not* have been impressed with a bear. He probably *would* have haunted us for that.

'Mum!' I called again after I'd closed the door. Still no answer. Just a lot of clattering and banging.

'What's Mum doing?' Logan looked up from where he was playing with his Lego on the lounge rug. 'She's being very noisy.'

'I've no idea, but I'm about to find out. Have you been to the toilet?'

'Not yet.'

'Can you do that while I check on Mum? And make sure you wash your hands.'

He put down his Lego and pouted. 'I always do.'

'Logan! What have we discussed about telling fibs?'

'Okay. I promise I'll wash them. You can smell them if you want.'

I smiled at him. 'Tempting, but I might pass on that.'

Logan headed past me and through the kitchen, giggling as he made a big show of sniffing at his hands. Happy that he was doing as asked, I kicked off my stilettos and ran up the stairs. I paused for a moment outside Mum's bedroom listening to the racket, punctuated with the occasional expletive, then pushed open the door and gasped.

'Oh my God! What's going on? Mum! Why aren't you ready?'

Wrapped in a fluffy cream towel, Mum turned to face me and blew a wisp of dark hair out of her face.

'I only bought them on Saturday,' she said, as if that explained why half the contents of her drawers were strewn all over the floor.

'Bought what on Saturday?'

'Black knickers. An M&S three-pack. But I can't find them, Jemma.'

'Where did you last have them?'

She planted her hands on her hips and rolled her eyes at me.

'Why do people always say that? If I knew the answer, then *this* wouldn't have happened, would it?' She waved her arm across the carnage.

'The hearse is here,' I said, equally unhelpfully.

Mum frowned. 'I thought they weren't due till 10.15.'

'It *is* 10.15. Well, near enough.'

She twisted round to look at her bedside clock. 'Crap! Why didn't you call me sooner?'

'Because you told me you were nearly ready forty minutes ago and because I was busy with Logan.'

'Logan? Oh my goodness, I'm so sorry, Jemma. Is he ready?'

'Yes. He's downstairs waiting. We need to go in about seven minutes. Can you manage without the knickers?'

Her eyes widened. 'Jemma-bear! Are you suggesting that I go commando to your father's funeral? I'm not sure that's appropriate.'

I laughed loudly – also not appropriate for a funeral. 'I didn't mean go without *any* knickers. I just meant without the new black ones.'

'Oh! That makes more sense. I suppose I'd better. I can't believe I lost track of time like that. Give me five minutes. Hair and make-up are done. It's just clothes I need.' She bent down and plucked a pair of scarlet lacy knickers from the pile on the floor. 'Sod it. I'll say goodbye in style.' She paused as she stared at the knickers in her hands. 'Do you know what? The last time I wore these was the night Logan was conceived. That was the end of our marriage and today's the end of everything for him. How apt.'

I didn't know what to say to that so I closed the door behind me and headed downstairs to check that Logan had washed his hands, hopefully without having to sniff them.

I'll never forget the day I discovered I was going to have a new brother or sister because it was the day that Dad packed up his stuff and moved out. I'd recently turned eighteen, had finished my A Levels and was working in Mum's shop, Bear With Me, before going away to university. It was a surprise to overhear her telling Dad that she was pregnant and a greater shock to hear that the baby was his because I'd been aware for a long time that my parents had a marriage in name only.

Growing up, I remembered them constantly arguing but then the arguments seemed to stop. Dad moved into the spare room and they somehow managed to co-exist in the same house while living completely separate lives. Dad acted more like a lodger than a husband or father. He spent all his time at work or the golf club, only venturing home to eat, shower, or sleep.

Dad had worked in a bank since leaving school – a steady, sensible career. Mum, on the other hand, had an amazingly exciting jet-setting career. When I was four, she'd set up a specialist teddy bear shop, Bear With Me, in the North Yorkshire seaside town of Whitsborough Bay where we lived. A genius with a sewing machine, she designed and made a range of jointed teddies called Ju-Sea Bears. Her talent was recognised with a stint as the guest bear artist for some of the leading collectible bear manufacturers. Her Ju-Sea Bears became highly sought-after which took her all over the world to exhibitions and shows. And as if that didn't keep her busy enough, she valued teddy bears for both a local and a national auction house.

For years – even the ones before they'd moved into separate bedrooms – my parents had holidayed apart, Dad going away with his golfing buddies and Mum and I travelling round Europe visiting bear manufacturers and retailers. Dad hated bears, Mum hated golf, and I was pretty certain they hated each other. I'd therefore never understood why they didn't just call it a day.

So how had she ended up expecting his baby? What's that phrase? Grief does funny things to you? It certainly did funny things to my parents. My grandma – Mum's mum – had sadly passed away during my exams. It turned out that the 'dodgy tummy' was actually terminal cancer. Grandma had known that her days were numbered yet she hadn't breathed a word to anyone. Mum had been very close to her and was devastated that she'd not known how ill she was. A few weeks after the funeral, I was having a sleepover at my best friend, Karen's, to celebrate the end of college. I'd registered the date too late: Grandma's birthday. Mum refused to let me cancel and insisted she'd be fine. She'd have a glass of wine and toast Grandma, then maybe design a new bear in her honour. Only the glass of wine turned into a full bottle. She was an emotional mess when Dad arrived home from partaking in a few too many at the nineteenth hole. Surprisingly, he'd been a great comfort. A bit too much of a comfort. The consequences changed everything.

Mum had thought that I was in my room when she told him she was pregnant but I'd been thirsty and was on my way to the kitchen when I stopped dead on the stairs, my jaw dropping at what I'd just heard. I crouched down and peered through the bannister.

Mum was on the sofa but I could only see her legs, not her face. Dad was facing the fireplace, gripping onto the mantlepiece. Even from my hiding place, I could feel the tension emanating from him. He turned round to face Mum.

'Are you planning on keeping the baby?' It came across more like an accusation than a question.

'Of course.' She sounded surprised that he'd even ask.

His fists clenched in his hair. 'Despite the fact that we barely have a relationship, let alone a marriage?'

'It's not the baby's fault.' Mum's voice was gentle which I knew would rattle him even more.

'And it's not my fault either!'

I could imagine Mum raising her eyebrows at him.

'Look, Jules, you can do what the hell you want, but I don't want another baby. Ever.' He pointed an accusing finger at her. 'If I was to offer you an ultimatum of me or the baby, we both know what the answer would be, don't we? Which begs the question: why the hell are we still married?'

I assume Mum had no answer to that – or perhaps she simply shrugged – because it went quiet. Then Dad folded his arms, shook his head and said in a much calmer voice, 'I guess it's goodbye, then.'

'I guess it is.'

Scurrying back up the stairs, I sat on my bed and hugged my pillow to my chest while I listened to Dad moving around in the next bedroom, presumably packing the essentials.

When the front door slammed, Mum sought me out and told me her news. I feigned surprise, choosing not to add to her pain by telling her that I'd seen his reaction for myself. It must have taken a lot of restraint to speak with empathy as to why Dad had chosen to move on instead of painting him in his true colours.

He came back at the weekend and collected the rest of his belongings. He didn't even say goodbye.

Mum put the house on the market and, four months later, with my university place deferred for a year, the two of us moved to the cottage in Little Sandby – a village ten minutes west of Whitsborough Bay – where we prepared for the arrival of my baby brother.

She tried to make excuses for my dad refusing to attend the scans. I hated keeping things from her so I confessed that I'd overheard the baby conversation and there was never any need to protect him – I knew exactly who he was and I wouldn't think badly of her if she ever wanted to vent. Mum hugged me and admitted she should have left Dad years before. I agreed.

'Why did you stay?' I asked.

She shrugged. 'Habit? Laziness? Too embarrassed to admit I'd made a mistake?'

'Did you love him?'

'I thought I did. I quickly realised I didn't, but I was already pregnant with you. He was a good man. He was steady and reliable and he took charge. I needed those qualities in him back then but they stifled me as the years progressed. When you meet someone, Jemma, make sure he makes your heart sing and your tummy fizz. I never had that with your dad, or at least not after the first few dates.'

Life in Little Sandby without Dad was like a breath of fresh air. A new hairdo and a fresh style of clothes changed Mum's physical appearance, but her whole personality seemed to change too. She was more relaxed, full of fun and laughter, and constantly singing.

Dad had always tried to control me: what I was wearing, who my friends were, when I did my homework, and how I should 'get a proper job instead of playing with teddies all day like your mum'. I hadn't realised how much he'd tried – and succeeded – to control Mum too. I don't think she had either.

But now he was dead.

'Are those hands washed?' I asked Logan, who'd returned to his Lego by the time I got back downstairs.

'You want to smell them?'

I shook my head. 'I'm going to trust you. Let's get your shoes on. Mum will be down in a few minutes, then we'll be going.'

Logan picked up his black school shoes, plonked himself down on the sofa, and fumbled with the laces. 'Jemma...' he pleaded, exasperation in his voice. I knelt down and fastened them for him.

'All done, Logan-paws.'

He usually smiled at his pet name, but his little face looked very serious when I stood up again.

'Jemma?'

'Yes.'

'Is today a sad day?'

I sat down beside him. 'Yes. It is.'

'I don't feel very sad. Billy Thomas said people cry when people die. Should I be crying?'

Tears pricked my eyes as I put my arm round him and cuddled him against me. I took a moment to compose myself so he didn't hear any wobble in my voice. 'Billy Thomas is right. When someone dies, people *do* often cry because they're sad that they won't see that person again and they'll miss them.'

'Oh! I didn't see Daddy much and I never missed him when he wasn't here. Not like I miss you when you go back to London. Is that why I'm not sad?'

'Probably.' I cuddled him even more tightly against me.

For all he'd tried to control my life and Mum's, Dad had been completely the opposite with Logan. It hadn't just been the baby years he wasn't interested in. He hadn't wanted *any* of the years with his son.

He made a token effort to see him around his birthday or Christmas and gave him a gift that was usually age-inappropriate or something he already had. He'd maybe see him two or three other times during the year, but only if I was home for the weekend, and he'd spend all the time talking at me and still trying to control me. He'd only acknowledge Logan to tell him to: be quiet, stop talking with his mouth full, get his elbows off the table, stop playing with his food. For the first time, I realised that perhaps he had been trying to control Logan too.

Logan looked up at me, his eyes big and sad, his voice tentative. 'Will Mum be sad if I don't cry?'

'Of course not!'

'Will *you* cry?'

'I don't know.'

'Are you sad that Daddy's gone to heaven?'

I swallowed hard on the lump in my throat. Was I? I didn't want to lie to Logan but the truth was that Dad and I weren't close. We had been when I was little, but the minute I showed interest in Mum's passion for bears rather than his passion for golf, he seemed to lose interest in me. You'd have thought he'd have been proud of his daughter for securing her first job aged fourteen but he'd always resented Mum for the success of Bear With Me so he just rolled his eyes when I told him I had a Saturday job as Assistant Bear Keeper.

Looking down at my brother, I chose my words carefully. 'It's always sad when someone dies, especially when it's unexpected.'

'Will the drunk man go to prison?'

'I hope so, Logan.'

A creature of habit, Dad always took a flask of coffee and *The Sunday Times* to a bench on a quiet country lane just outside Cranton where he'd settled. He'd been killed instantly when, despite it being late-morning, a drunk driver misjudged a bend and ploughed straight into the bench... and Dad.

'Billy Thomas says that the drunk man wasn't allowed to drive a car. He says he was dequal... decoll...' He wriggled free of my hug. 'I can't remember the word.'

I stood up. 'It's disqualified. Billy Thomas says lots of things, doesn't he?'

'His daddy drives an ambulance. He tried to fix our daddy, but he couldn't.'

Oh crikey! I hadn't known that.

'He said Daddy didn't stand a chance. What does that mean?'

What had Billy's dad been thinking, having so much to say about the situation in Billy's presence? 'It means that it was a horrible accident and Daddy could have done nothing to stop it. He probably didn't even see the car coming and he won't have felt anything.' I hoped. An image sprung to mind of Dad seeing the car veering towards him, helpless to move, then... I shuddered. I couldn't bear to think about it.

The sound of Mum running down the stairs brought me out of the dark place my mind was heading towards. She appeared in the lounge doorway, looking calm, relaxed, and stunning. She didn't look like someone who, minutes earlier, had been wrapped in a towel surrounded by piles of knickers and bras. Her layered shoulder-length dark hair with streaks of red and copper in it was flicked out at the sides and back in her trademark style. She wore a simple black shift dress with capped sleeves and a thin red belt. Pulling on a black fitted jacket, she smiled at us both. 'Ready?'

'You look amazing, Mum.'

'I couldn't resist a splash of colour.' Mum pointed to her belt then winked and pointed lower. 'Make that two splashes of colour.'

* * *

The church was busier than I expected. 'Who *are* all of these people?' I whispered to Mum as we took our reserved pew at the front.

'Work colleagues and golf club members,' she whispered back. 'Either that or they're random strangers who are here for the free vol-au-vents and Pringles.'

Several of them stood up and gave emotional eulogies. Each one enveloped me with guilt as I realised that I hadn't known my dad at all.

It seemed that many of the traits I disliked in him were admired among others. His desire for control had turned the golf club's finances from dire into healthy. His fondness for structure and processes made him a role model at work and meant his branch consistently topped league tables. His calm and quiet demeanour meant he was the person they all confided in during troubled times. Who knew? Certainly not me!

And I did cry. I tried to be strong for Logan, but something snapped inside me as I watched the coffin disappear behind the red velvet curtains before being lowered into the crematorium below. My dad was gone. We may not have been close, unlike Mum and I, but I still cared about him. In a funny way, I'd actually miss our awkward, stilted conversations. Over the past few years, he'd finally seemed to accept that he couldn't control my career and, instead, feigned interest in my job as curator for the children's section of the Past Lives Museum in London. In return, I feigned interest in the bank or golf, trying to stop my eyes from glazing over as he talked about ISAs, pensions, irons and handicaps. We always avoided talking about Bear With Me. And Mum. And Logan. It's amazing how many conversations a person can have about the weather.

* * *

Logan fell asleep in the car on the way home from the wake. He was completely out of it so Mum carried him into Bear's Pad.

'Baileys?' I whispered, removing Logan's shoes as Mum kicked off her heels.

'Gosh, yes! A huge one with lots of ice.'

She carried Logan upstairs while I poured two generous measures of Baileys then opened the freezer. As I pulled open the drawer that usually contained the ice cube trays, I frowned. What the hell was that? I lifted the packet out of the drawer, brushed a few flakes of ice off it, and stared at the item in my hand: a three-pack of M&S black knickers.

2

SAM

Three years ago – 21st May

I sat in my car on Sea View Drive, staring out the windscreen at the waves rolling onto North Bay at the bottom of the cliff. Surfers bobbed on the swell, occasionally catching a wave then wiping out – some in spectacular style – before they hit the beach. Dogs scampered across the sand chasing balls, tugging at pieces of seaweed or leaping into rock pools.

The evening was warm with a gentle breeze, perfect for a romantic stroll along the beach followed by a pint outside Blue Savannah, which I assume was Nicole's plan given that she'd suggested meeting outside The Surf Shack on North Bay Corner.

Running my hand across my freshly-shaved chin, I shook my head. Shit! I couldn't do it. I'd told Jack I wasn't ready and the stupid twat hadn't listened. I picked up my mobile and called him.

'Don't tell me she hasn't turned up,' he said, connecting the call after the first ring.

'I don't know. I'm not there.'

'You can't be stuck in traffic. There isn't any at this time of night.'

'No, I'm not. But I'm not going. I shouldn't have let you talk me into this.'

'Sam! You can't just not turn up.'

'I wasn't going to. I'm not a total git. I want you to call her and tell her I'm not coming.'

'No can do, bro. I don't have her number.'

I shook my head. 'That's bullshit, Jack, and you know it. I was with you when she texted you with the time and place.'

He laughed. 'Busted! Let me ask you one question. Are you backing out because of Kirsty?'

My stomach twisted at the mention of her name. 'Yes,' I muttered after a pause. 'Because, like I said to you when you came up with this stupid blind date idea, it's too soon.'

'Too soon? Christ, Sam, it's not like she's dead. She's very much alive and still shagging her way round all our colleagues.'

'Thanks for the reminder.'

'You're welcome. Look, Sammy–'

'Don't call me that.'

'Mum does.'

'And you're not Mum.'

Jack laughed again. 'Okay, *Sam,* what harm is there in going on one little blind date? One date. *One!* I'm not asking you to marry Nicole. I'm not asking you to jump into bed with her. Actually, maybe that would be a good plan. If you shag her, you might get Kirsty out of your system. I want to hear all about it, though. Remember I'm not getting any so I need to live vicariously through you.'

I swear that, most of the time, my brother acted about ten years younger than me instead of four years older. His wife, Millie, was six months pregnant and had put a ban on sex a couple of months ago citing vomiting, exhaustion, and 'a general feeling of ickiness' as three pretty good reasons for abstinence. It was killing him.

'And I'm not cancelling your date,' he added.

'You are.'

'I'm not.'

'You *are!*'

'Bye, Sam.'

'Don't hang up on—'

But he'd already disconnected. I tried to call him back but, predictably, it went straight to voicemail. Wanker. He knew that there was no way I'd stand anyone up, especially someone who worked at the same hospital as Jack and me. He also knew that I wouldn't be able to meet her then tell her I wasn't staying in case she thought it was because I'd taken one look at her and didn't like what I saw.

Cursing, I started the car and drove down Hearnshaw Hill to park in one of the spaces on the seafront. I'd get him back for this.

I slammed the car door shut, crossed the road, and slowly made my way towards North Bay Corner. I was already late, but I couldn't seem to make my legs move any faster.

Why the hell had Jack brought up Kirsty? He was right, though. It *was* because of her. I needed more time to get over what she'd done to me... to us. I should have known what to expect, though. She'd been seeing someone else when we met at the hospital's Christmas do. Jack had warned me that the vivacious, beautiful Nurse Kirsty Griggs had already worked her way through several of the doctors and consultants in the two years she'd been working at Whitsborough Bay General. I didn't listen. I thought I was different. I believed her when she told me she loved me and that the others had been casual flings until the right man came along. She told me she'd had to kiss a few frogs before she found her prince. Okay, so she'd kissed a whole swamp full of frogs but who was I to judge? It wasn't like I hadn't had other partners.

Just over two years we'd been together. Two exciting, passionate, amazing years. She was feisty and I was stubborn so we had some horrendous arguments where we shouted and screamed at each other but the make-up sex was worth the angst. Her many frogs had certainly taught her a thing or two!

But it turned out they were still teaching her and I hadn't a clue. If my meeting hadn't been cancelled that February evening, I might have still been with her, completely oblivious. I don't think that image of opening the lounge door of our rented flat to the sight of my girlfriend on all fours on our new IKEA rug with one of the junior doctors will ever leave me.

Kirsty, all her crap, and the IKEA rug moved out that evening.

* * *

My stomach did a somersault as I got closer to The Surf Shack. Christ, I'd do anything to avoid doing this.

I looked at my watch. Bollocks. Fifteen minutes late. Nice first impression. I scanned left and right as I approached but I couldn't see anyone waiting on their own. Several couples and groups were seated on the metal chairs outside Blue Savannah enjoying their tea or a few drinks but there was no 'tall lass with dark hair and a nice arse' to give Jack's description of her.

A dark-haired woman came into view and paused outside The Surf Shack. She wasn't short but she certainly wasn't what I'd call tall. Could she be Nicole? A toddler with an ice-cream in his hand ran up to her followed by a man and the three of them disappeared down the steps to the beach. Not Nicole, then.

The only other brunette I could see was holding a surfboard, wearing a wet suit, and standing outside The Surf Shack chatting to one of the beach lifeguards. Clearly not Nicole either. She'd obviously gone and I couldn't blame her. I wished bloody Jack had called her when I asked so she hadn't gone home believing she'd been stood up.

Sighing, I leaned against the wall at the top of the steps looking out towards the twinkling sea. I pulled out my phone to ring Jack.

'You're late,' came a woman's voice.

I spun round and came face to face with the brunette in the wetsuit. 'Me?'

'You are Sam, aren't you?'

'Yes. Are you Nicole?'

She smiled and her blue eyes twinkled like the sea behind me. Her shoulder-length hair was wet and slicked back, with streaks of sand in it. Her face was tanned with a spattering of freckles across the bridge of her nose and the tops of her cheeks. She was beautiful in a very natural way; such a contrast to Kirsty who was always caked in a mountain of make-up.

'That's right, although I prefer Nikki. Two Ks. No Y.' She wrinkled her nose at me. 'Do I have seaweed stuck to my face?'

I realised I was staring and quickly blinked. 'No. Sorry. How did you know it was me?'

'Jack said you were the exact opposite of him in build and colouring and that you look like Chris Hemsworth and I'd have to agree. Are you two *really* brothers?'

'Unfortunately, yes. He takes after our mum and I look more like our dad, although I'm liking the comparison to Chris Hemsworth. You can call me Thor if you like.'

I inwardly cringed at such a crap line but she threw her head back and laughed a loud belly laugh. 'Thor it is! Which means I'm going to have to call your brother Loki from now on.'

'He'll hate me for that.'

'Tough. So, Thor, do you surf?'

'No. Thor does not surf,' I said in a caveman-type voice. No idea where that came from. In the films, he speaks with a posh English accent!

'Ever tried it?'

'No. Thor's hammer gets in the way.'

She laughed loudly once more and I found myself laughing with her.

'That's the first time I've heard it referred to as that.' Her eyes sparkled with mischief. 'Seriously, though, have you ever wanted to try surfing?'

'Erm...'

'Well now's your chance whether you want to or not. I know it's not exactly a typical first-date activity but I figured that if your brother had lied about you and had set me up with a loser, at least I'd spend the evening doing something I love and it wouldn't be completely wasted. No offence.'

'Refreshingly honest. No offence taken.'

She crossed her arms and cocked her head to one side, staring at me for a moment. 'I will say, though, that Dr Jack isn't in my bad books... yet. First impressions are good... apart from the *incredibly* rude late show of course.'

'Sorry about that. I just, erm...'

'You were going to bottle it. I know. Jack *did* call me to warn me. He said he was sure that you were too much of a gent to stand me up but wanted to warn me just in case you went against type.'

'I'm sorry. It wasn't personal.'

'I know. But if you ask me, you're better off without her.'

'He told you about Kirsty?'

'He did, but before you get mad at him, I already knew. I'm afraid it's common knowledge at the hospital. If it makes you feel better, I could tell you that the junior doctor you caught her with was my boyfriend.'

'You're kidding me?'

She stared at me for a moment, deadly serious. 'I wish I was. We have a little boy and we were going to get married and...' She stopped and belly laughed again. 'Sorry. Yes, I *am* kidding you! Truth is, I don't know the guy and I don't want to. I do know Kirsty, though, and all I can say is it's her loss. If I'd captured the heart of the Ruler of Asgard, I'm not sure I'd let him go.'

She grabbed my hand and pulled me towards The Surf Shack. 'Come on, Thor. Let's get you changed into something more practical for the North Sea. If you manage to stand on your board, the drinks are on me. Assuming you don't still want to do a runner, that is.'

I looked down at our intertwined hands and, at the moment, I knew I'd never want to do a runner. It wasn't just a physical thing. Yes, she was beautiful, but there was something else about her that was captivating. Her sense of humour? Her sense of adventure? Her sense of knowing who she was and not caring if she wore no make-up and had sand in her hair? Whatever it was, it had me completely hooked. Jack could get things spectacularly wrong but somehow the boy had done good. Turns out he wasn't such a tosser after all.

3

JEMMA

Present Day – 24th June

'Scott! Sorry I lost you,' I said, as the train approached Whitsborough Bay Station. 'Bad signal. Where are you?'

There was a pause before he said, 'Still in Manchester.'

My heart sank. 'Manchester? No! Why?' He'd assured me that his meeting would be finished at lunchtime, giving him loads of time to drive to Whitsborough Bay ready for my birthday meal this evening.

'I'm sorry, Jem. I thought we'd have been finished by lunch but they wanted to discuss a new design.'

'Didn't you tell them you had plans?' I cringed at the whiney tone in my voice.

'I know you're disappointed but what could I do? Refuse to discuss a half a million pound business deal because it's my girlfriend's birthday? I'd have lost my job. And then all the nights and weekends apart would have been for nothing.'

He was right. He needed the work. Scott worked for a company that... well, I'm not really sure what they did. He'd told me when we met but it had been completely over my head. Something to do with renewable energy and engineering but that's about as far as my understanding went. His job took him all over the country during the week to meet clients, and had him working most weekends at exhibitions and trade shows to generate interest and hopefully secure some business. As such, time together over the past seventeen months had been rare and precious. Scott assured me that it would only be for a couple more years, at which point the company would have expanded, he'd get promoted, and he wouldn't have to travel so much.

'I know it's not your fault,' I assured him. 'I'm just dying to see you, and I was excited about finally being able to introduce you to Karen.' Scott had been home with me twice before so he'd met Mum and Logan, but Karen had been away for the weekend both times. Every time she'd been down to London to visit me, it seemed to coincide with a weekend that Scott was working and I hated it that my best friend and my boyfriend had never met – not even in the virtual world because Scott refused to engage with social media, saying life was too short to spend it looking at pictures of what people had eaten for lunch.

'I'll still get to meet her,' he said. 'I'll probably be there at about nine.'

I could hear voices in the background and the clinking of mugs. 'Sorry, Jemma. Coffee break's over. Have an amazing meal and I'll be there as soon as I can. I love you only.'

'I love you always.'

* * *

At Whitsborough Bay Station, I spotted Karen immediately. Even if it hadn't been for the large metallic helium balloons in the shape of the number twenty-eight, it was impossible to miss the short flared summer dress adorned with large yellow and turquoise flowers. Living in lycra leggings, T-shirts and trainers for her job as co-owner of Bay Fitness – a bootcamp and personal training business she ran with her fiancé, Ryan, and a friend of theirs, Steff – she tended to favour bold patterns and bright colours when she wasn't working.

'Happy birthday!' she squealed.

I braced myself for one of her power-hugs that could knock you off your feet if you weren't ready for them. Sure enough, she hurled herself at me. 'I've missed you.'

'I've missed you too.'

'The car's outside and I'm free all afternoon to do whatever you want. What's the plan, Jemma Browne with an 'e' on the end?'

I laughed at our little saying. We'd become friends when we met at senior school and united over both having colours for surnames spelt with an 'e' on the end; something which our fellow students and even our teachers seemed to struggle to get their heads round.

'Back to Mum's so I can get changed, Karen Greene with an 'e' on the end. Maybe a drink in The White Horse? Mum and Logan should be home at about four.'

We walked towards the car park. Mum had wanted to meet me but Logan and a few of his classmates had won the regional heats in a school science project and there was a presentation to which parents were invited. Since Dad died three years ago, Mum had gone out of her way to try to be there for Logan at anything like this, trying to make up for him only having one parent. I didn't like to point out that Logan was used to only having one parent around given Dad's lack of interest when he'd been alive.

'I'm looking forward to meeting the elusive Scott,' Karen said. 'I was beginning to think you'd created a fake boyfriend.'

'A fake boyfriend? Do people do that?'

'You'd be amazed. One of my clients told me she wanted to lose weight and get fit for her wedding in four months' time. The big day came and went and, when I asked about photos, she started crying and admitted that she didn't have any because she hadn't got married. I felt terrible. Thought she'd been jilted. Turns out she didn't even have a boyfriend. Her sole reason for getting in shape was that she wanted to find one, but she'd been too embarrassed to admit that, so this whole wedding lie just spilled out.'

'No!'

Karen nodded. 'I know. It's sad, isn't it? We talked about how she should get into shape for *her* and not because she thinks a person she's never met will like her that way. She *did* meet someone who liked her for being her, lumps and bumps and everything, and they got married last month. I saw the pictures this time.'

I smiled. 'Aw, I like a happy ending. Well, Scott is definitely real and he's definitely coming but he's stuck in Manchester so he won't make it until after we've eaten.'

'Bummer.'

'I know. Leah, Tiff and Drew are all still coming up though.' My three flatmates had insisted on catching the train up from London to celebrate. They said it was the perfect excuse for a trip to the seaside.

'Excellent. Any chance that the gorgeous Drew Short for Andrew has renounced his love of men?'

I shook my head. 'Sorry. Drew Short for Andrew is still very gorgeous and still very gay. And you're still very engaged, are you not?'

She glanced at her ring. 'I am and disgustingly happy with it. A girl just likes to know what her options are in case a freak wave wipes out her fiancé in the middle of a beach bootcamp and she needs to find a man with an equally amazing six-pack to immediately take his place.'

We reached Karen's car and loaded my case and the giant balloon into the boot.

'I still can't believe you pulled a stranger on a tube platform and it turned out to be love,' Karen said once she'd pulled out of the car park. 'That's seriously impressive.'

It had been a freezing cold evening in mid-January last year when I met Scott. A fierce wind and ice-cold driving rain meant the streets were eerily deserted. I'd been working late at the museum and ran for the tube but the doors closed a split second before I could reach them. Karen's favourite curse – 'arse' – slipped out and I laughed as I heard a man's voice say 'bollocks' at the same time. I glanced down the platform to see a tall dark-haired man in a suit who'd also missed catching the same tube. Our eyes met and my tummy fizzed. He opened his mouth but whatever he said was blocked out by an announcement that, due to signalling failure caused by frozen electrics or something like that, our line would be temporarily suspended and, as there were already problems with two other lines too, passengers were advised to make alternative arrangements for their journey.

'Bollocks,' I cursed as he said, 'Arse,' and we both laughed.

'Were you heading far?' he asked, taking a few steps closer to me.

We discussed stops and it turned out that he was staying in a hotel very close to where I lived.

'Looks like it's going to have to be a cab,' I said. 'I don't suppose you fancy going halves on the fare, assuming you're not a mad axe-murderer, that is?'

He laughed. 'I'm Scott. Scott Hastings. And I only murder people on weekends. Thursdays are my "be nice to humanity" days so you're in luck. Unless you were specifically looking for a mad axe-murderer in which case Thursday is close enough to the weekend that I could make an exception.'

I laughed too. 'I'm Jemma Browne with an 'e' on the end, and I've got far too much work to do before Saturday to pretend the weekend has started already so you can keep your axe locked away for now.'

Fifteen minutes later we were both shivering from the cold after zero success in flagging down a black cab and no sign of availability on any apps.

Scott turned to me with a smile. 'Jemma Browne with an 'e' on the end, I don't suppose you fancy going halves on dinner instead of a cab? Scrub that. Can I buy you dinner?'

I didn't even need to think about it. In the short time we'd spent together so far, my stomach hadn't stopped fizzing. My feet and fingers were numb, I couldn't feel my cheeks anymore, but my heart was singing.

Scott took my hand and we ran through puddles and rivers of rain to the nearest restaurant so we could dry out and warm up.

As I sat opposite him in La Vecchia Scuola, shivering and dripping rain from my long dark curls into my wine, I felt so grateful that the tubes had been cancelled because I suspected that I might have just found love.

* * *

⌕ From Mum
About to leave Logan's school. Are you at home? Xx

⌕ To Mum
Hope it went well. Karen and I are in The White
Horse. We'll finish our drinks and meet you at
home xx

Our timing couldn't have been more perfect. Mum pulled onto the drive of Bear's Pad the moment I'd unlocked the front door. Logan waved frantically from the front passenger seat and Mum shouted 'Jemma-bear!' out of the window. My heart leapt. I loved my life in London but I missed my small family and Karen so much while I was away. London was vibrant and exciting, I adored my flatmates, I had some other great friends there too, and I had an amazing job, but I still thought of Whitsborough Bay and Bear's Pad as home. I couldn't help it. Home is where the heart is and my heart was with Mum, Logan and Karen. Always had been, always would be.

'Jemma-bear!' Logan cried, running round the car to get to me.

'Logan-paws!'

He grabbed me in a bear hug, singing happy birthday to me.

'Are you taller than me now?' I asked, winking at him when we pulled apart.

'Everyone's taller than you.'

'Cheeky!' At five foot five, I was the same height as Mum, but it looked as though Logan was going to have Dad's genes. I suspected he'd end up being over six feet.

'Oi! Shift over, Logan,' Mum said. 'It's my turn. Happy birthday,

Jemma-bear.' Her eyes glistened as she reached her arms out for me. 'I'm so glad you wanted to come home to share it with us.'

'I wouldn't want to be anywhere else.'

We giggled as both Logan and Karen hurled themselves at us for a group hug.

'Let's go in and get some presents opened,' Mum suggested.

* * *

Karen cracked open a bottle of wine while Logan changed out of his school uniform, then we made our way onto the deck.

I loved it out the back of Bear's Pad. Located on the outskirts of Little Sandby, the cottage was at the end of a quiet street of properties, each one unique in design. Occupying an elevated position and backing onto open fields, Mum's had a stunning sea view.

The back garden was surprisingly large, even for a four-bedroom property. It had been an overgrown mess when we'd moved in and we'd cleared it over the years but, when Dad died, Mum was shocked to discover that he'd made provisions in his will for her; more evidence of that caring side that we'd never seen. She paid off the outstanding mortgage, had the kitchen and dining room knocked through and refitted, then had the garden professionally landscaped into terraces. The top terrace was the deck with a large barbeque area, approached through fully folding doors off the new kitchen diner. The next level was a vegetable plot and herb garden, which my green-fingered brother took great pride in maintaining. The next few levels had different types of flower, shrub and water features and a couple of small seating areas, before reaching a grand paved terrace at the bottom with a patio heater and comfy seating. Along the side of the house, completely private from the road, there was a summerhouse and a hot tub with a view.

'What *is* your mum doing?' Karen asked when we'd both made it halfway down our wine with no sign of her. 'I'm dying to give you your pressie.'

'I'll go and find her,' Logan said.

I stood up. 'It's okay. I'll do it.' I headed into the house. 'Mum?' Silence. 'Mum?'

Stepping into the hall, I could hear her pacing around upstairs.

'Mum? Where are you?'

I found her in her bedroom, opening and closing drawers and cupboards, sighing before she shut them. It took me back to the day of Dad's funeral when she'd been searching for her knickers. Thankfully this time she hadn't emptied everything over the floor.

'Are you okay?'

She jumped. 'You scared me!'

'Sorry. What are you looking for?'

'Your birthday card. I've found your presents.' She pointed to a selection of colourful gift bags on the bed. 'Your card isn't with them, though. It's huge and it's in a bright pink envelope so it should be easy to spot.'

'Can I help?'

She shook her head. 'It could be anywhere. You go downstairs. I'll do one more check in my workshop then I'll be out. If it's not there, I'll buy you a new one tomorrow.'

'There's no need.'

'But it's your birthday.'

I smiled. 'Cards are lovely and you know I'd be lying if I said I didn't love pressies, but the most important thing is being with three of the four people I care most about. Right now, one of them is rummaging in her wardrobes when she should be on the terrace drinking wine with the others.'

She planted her hands on her hips and pretended to look shocked. 'You've given your brother wine?'

I laughed. 'Make that drinking wine or Irn-Bru.'

'Phew! Five minutes. I promise.'

'What was she doing?' Logan asked when I returned to the terrace.

'She couldn't find my birthday card.'

'Oh.' The smile slipped from his face and he suddenly seemed very interested in his feet.

'Logan? What aren't you telling me?'

'It's nothing.' He wouldn't raise his eyes.

'It's clearly something.'

He shrugged. 'Mum often forgets where she puts stuff.'

I laughed. 'I hate to say it, but it happens to us all. It'll happen to you when you're older. I'm always putting things in a *safe* place then forgetting where they are.'

He shrugged again. 'She couldn't remember where she'd put my football boots but we found them in the oven. And she couldn't find the cauliflower I'd picked for Sunday dinner. It was in the airing cupboard. It stunk.' He looked up and I could see how worried he was. The poor lad was ten. He should be worrying about his voice breaking – not whether his mum was losing the plot. Butterflies danced in my stomach as I thought about the knickers in the freezer.

I smiled brightly and hoped it looked more genuine than it felt. 'We all do dippy things when we're busy or tired and Mum's both at the moment. When the next auction's over, I bet things will be back to normal. Don't worry, Logan. It'll be fine.'

But even as I said the words, I knew it wouldn't be. Something was wrong. Very wrong.

4

JEMMA

'To Jemma!' cried Drew later that evening. After our meal, we'd moved onto Minty's, a cosy bar at the top of town. He waved his pint in the air, sloshing beer over his hands. 'Hurry up and turn thirty like the rest of us cos you're making me feel old! Happy birthday, gorgeous girl.'

Karen, Leah, Tiff and Mum echoed his toast, raising glasses of prosecco in the air.

Logan, Karen's mum Rachel and Karen's younger sister Eden, had joined us for the meal then said goodnight. Logan was staying with Rachel and Eden overnight so Mum could stay out for a few drinks.

Mum and Rachel were as close as Karen and me, which I loved. When Mum was working away, Logan usually stayed with 'Auntie Rachel' which he loved because, with only a year between them, he was great friends with Eden.

'Thank you,' I said, toasting them in return. 'And thanks so much for being here.'

I was genuinely touched that Leah, Tiff and Drew had travelled north when we could easily have gone out for a meal in London instead after my birthday. They really were the best.

I'd met Leah through work. She was a financial accountant but volunteered as a tour guide at the museum during weekends. Shortly after Dad died, I'd been leaving the museum with her one Saturday evening when my landlord rang to tell me that he was selling up and emigrating to New Zealand. I went into full panic-mode about where I was going to live and Leah insisted I accompany her to the pub before rushing into any renting decisions I might regret, especially as her twin sister and their cousin – who she was meeting for a drink – might be able to help with my predicament.

The three of them shared a four-bedroom flat that Drew had inherited from an auntie on the other side of the family. They'd recently said goodbye to their fourth flatmate – an acquaintance of Drew's who stole their food, smoked in the flat, used all the hot water, refused to do any cleaning and generally epitomised the most irritating flatmate ever – and were half-heartedly looking for a replacement so they could afford to re-fit the kitchen. As soon as I met them, it was like being among old friends. They insisted I see the flat before I agreed to move in but I already knew that I wanted them as flatmates, even if the flat was a bit rough round the edges, and it had been the best decision ever. There was always laughter and banter in our flat, just like there'd always been in Bear's Pad after Dad left and we moved to Little Sandby.

'What time's lover boy finally planning to put in an appearance?' Drew asked.

He didn't like Scott and, unfortunately, the feeling was mutual. They'd stared at each other over breakfast the morning after I met Scott (the meal had gone *very* well!) before Drew retired to his bedroom with his cereal, not re-appearing until Scott had left.

I asked him about the strange atmosphere but he said he couldn't put his finger on what was wrong other than that he didn't trust Scott. It unnerved me because Drew was usually a good judge of character, but then I'd reminded myself that he'd thought that my predecessor would make a great flatmate when he clearly hadn't.

I confronted Scott too but he said he'd only been off with Drew because Drew had been giving him the evils which was true. I decided to accept it as one of those things and hope that they'd tolerate each other, even if they never became friends.

'Scott will be here at about nine,' I said. 'Play nicely.'

'I *always* play nicely.'

'You do *not!*' cried Tiff. 'You either blank him or you give him the Spanish Inquisition!'

Drew pulled a shocked and hurt expression. 'Me?'

'So how's it going with Dr Indiana Jones?' I asked Tiff and Drew, keen to change the subject. They were nurses at the same hospital and a new doctor had started there recently whose name really was Dr Jones. They couldn't resist the Indiana Jones connection, which I suspected the poor guy had been ribbed about ever since he'd qualified. They both had a crush on him, but weren't sure whether he was straight or gay. Personally, I think they were more interested in the mystery than the actual man because they'd told me on several occasions that they'd never date a doctor.

'I nearly spoke to him on Tuesday,' Tiff said.

'Nearly? Wow! That's great progress.'

'He spoke to me yesterday,' Drew announced, grinning.

'Bullshit!' Tiff cried, punching him lightly on the arm.

'He did!'

'He said "thanks" when you picked up the pen he'd dropped. That's hardly a meaningful conversation.'

Drew held his hands up in surrender. 'Who mentioned a meaningful conversation? I just said he spoke to me. Which is a million times better than *nearly* speaking to him. What's *nearly* speaking to someone anyway?'

I sipped on my prosecco and laughed as the banter continued. Leah retold the story of a disastrous blind date that one of her accountancy colleagues had arranged for her earlier in the week with a tax accountant called Ernie who turned out to be in his fifties; something the colleague had failed to mention. Karen told us about a couple of elderly gents who proposed to her every time she ran an over-sixties fitness class at her local community centre. One of them had offered to feed arsenic to his wife if she said yes, and she suspected he was deadly serious. Then Mum told us about her 'friendly stalker' – a man in his fifties called Terrence who popped into the shop at least once a week, refusing to speak to anyone but Mum, and leaving with his tail between his legs if she wasn't working that day or was running a bear-making class and couldn't say hello.

I looked round at my friends and family and realised that it was thanks to them that time apart from Scott wasn't nearly as difficult as it could have been. They always cheered me up if I was feeling melancholy.

'Is there someone in here celebrating a birthday?'

I turned round and jumped up from my chair, nearly upturning it. 'Scott!'

He put down the gift bag he was carrying and pulled me into his arms, kissing me until we were blasted with cries of, 'Get a room!'

'Sorry I couldn't get away earlier. I missed you.'

'I missed you too.'

'I love you only.'

'I love you always.'

I giggled when Karen started making vomiting noises. 'Let me introduce you to my very rude friend, Karen.'

'Let's get you a drink,' I suggested once he'd had a chance to say hello to everyone and Karen had prodded him to check he wasn't an apparition. 'Are you in the car?'

'Nope. Already dropped it off at your mum's and got a taxi in.'

'Thank you.'

He was so thoughtful. For obvious reasons, I felt very strongly about drinking and driving. For me, it was either drink and don't drive or drive and don't drink. I didn't care that there was a legal limit because I knew from personal experience that I could have three glasses of wine and feel perfectly in control, or have three sips and feel tiddly and unsteady. So why risk it? Just abstain! Scott was always supportive about it.

'I reckon it's my round as a forfeit for being late,' Scott said. 'What's everyone having?'

He disappeared with instructions to get another bottle of prosecco and a pint for Drew.

'So that was the elusive Scott,' Karen said when I sat down next to her again. 'He *is* real after all.'

'I can't believe you prodded him to confirm it. That's outrageous! What do you think of him?' I knew that Mum and Logan had really taken to him, but it was important to me that he also had Karen's approval.

'Marks out of two? I'd give him one.'

'Karen!' cried Mum, as Karen and I creased up at the phrase we'd picked up in our late teens.

'Sorry, Julie,' Karen said. 'I think he's lovely, Jem. Very gorgeous and obviously completely smitten with you. I approve.'

Mum leaned across the table. 'I meant to ask you this before. Scott always says he loves you only...?'

'Oh yeah! I noticed that.' Karen frowned. 'He loves you only amongst his harem of twenty?'

'There's a context. I promise. After we'd been together for a month or so, I decided it was time to properly induct him into the world of teddy bears so I introduced him to the hug.'

'The hug?' Tiff asked.

'It's the term given to a collection of teddy bears,' Leah said. 'Don't you listen to anything we tell you about bears?'

From the colouring of Tiff's cheeks, she obviously didn't, but that was fine. They weren't everyone's cup of tea.

'Do continue,' Mum prompted.

'I explained the differences between the fabrics, joints, eyes etc. and probably bored him senseless. I kept going on about how much I loved different bears. He picked one up and said he loved the expression it had, but what he really loved was me.'

A chorus of 'Aww' went round the table.

'It was the first time he'd told me he loved me. I told him I loved him too, but I'd never said that to anyone before so I got all embarrassed and started saying the names of different bears I also loved. He stopped me and said, "Well, I love you only." It kind of stuck and, because I felt I needed something to say in return, "I love you always" became my thing.'

Mum nodded. 'That makes perfect sense now.'

Karen pointed to the gift bag that Scott had left on the floor. 'What do you think's in the bag? Bit big for an engagement ring.'

'Engagement? You don't think he'd...?'

She shrugged. 'I don't know. Coming up to eighteen months together. Birthday. Could be the perfect occasion.'

I looked towards Mum, but she just smiled and looked away. I stared at the sparkly silver bag. 'No. He wouldn't. As you say, it's too big to be an engagement ring.' But now that she'd planted the thought in my mind, it wouldn't go away. I tracked back to recent conversations trying to find clues in anything he'd said or done, but there was nothing to suggest a proposal was on the cards.

I felt stupidly nervous when Scott reappeared. He gave Drew his pint, topped up our glasses with the prosecco, then raised a toast. 'To my gorgeous girlfriend, Jemma. Happy twenty-eighth birthday! I'm sorry I missed the meal but I've bought a pretty special gift that will hopefully make up for it.' He handed me the gift bag. 'Happy birthday.'

I knew what was in there immediately. I'd handled too many bears over the years not to recognise the feel of them, even encased in a bag. The exciting part was what sort he'd have chosen. Old? New? Artist? I gently peeled back the sticky tape and peered inside, grinning.

'What is it?' Karen asked.

'A bear.'

'A real one?' Drew asked.

'Ha ha.' I reached my hands into the bag and carefully lifted him out. 'Oh my God! Scott! He's one of Mum's!'

Drew frowned and looked at Mum, then me. 'Scott's given you one of your mum's teddies? Why?'

'Not literally one of Mum's bears. It's a Ju-Sea Bear. Remember I told you Mum designs them? This is one of her designs. He's absolutely gorgeous, Mum. Thank you so much, Scott. I love him.'

Checking the table wasn't wet, I sat him down. He was a traditional-looking bear, about 35cm high when seated, wearing a really cute waistcoat, the front of which was made out of small grey and blue patchwork diamonds.

'What's his name?' Karen asked. Mum gave all the bears a name. Karen and I had named several over the years when Mum was stuck for inspiration.

I looked at his tag. 'Diamond. Aw, cute. Is that because of the diamonds on his waistcoat?'

'Partly,' Scott said. 'And partly because of what he's got in his pocket.'

I caught Karen's eyes across the table and knew that she was thinking about the conversation we'd just had. My heart raced as I reached my fingers into the pocket of Diamond's waistcoat and lifted out a simple platinum ring with a small square diamond held in place by four claws.

Scott got down on a bended knee beside my chair as the others gasped. 'I love you only, Jemma, and I want to marry you. Excuse the pun, but do you think you could *bear* to spend the rest of your life with me?'

Could I? Nothing would make me happier! Eyes glistening, I nodded, handed him the ring, and held out my shaky left hand.

'Is that a yes?' he asked.

'Yes!' I squealed.

He slipped the ring onto my finger, stood up, and wrapped his arms round me. This time, there were no shouts about getting a room. His lips met mine for a warm, tender kiss and I melted against him. I'd never felt so happy as I did at that moment. I could feel the love emanating from him with every kiss and every touch.

'Did you know?' I asked Mum after everyone had admired the ring and given hugs.

'Yes. He asked my permission.'

'Aw, that's so traditional and so sweet.'

She hugged me once more. 'I'm so happy for you. You two are just perfect for each other.'

I gazed across at him laughing with Tiff and Leah, my heart aglow. I really had found love that day at the tube station and, unlike Mum and Dad, I'd found someone who still made my tummy fizz and my heart sing nearly eighteen months down the line. It was going to be forever.

5

SAM

Present Day – 24th June

'You didn't have to come,' I said, picking up my half-empty pint and taking a gulp.

Jack dropped an overnight bag onto the floor, pulled out a stool, and sat down opposite me in a gloomy corner of my local, The Hero & Hammer. The irony of the pub's name wasn't lost on me.

'Of course I was going to come. How are you?'

I gulped down the rest of my drink and held the glass out to him. 'Get me another one of these and I'll tell you.'

'How many have you had?'

'What are you? The bereavement police?' I slammed the glass down on the table.

'No. Just a concerned brother.' He stood up and grabbed the empty glass.

'Dark Anvil,' I muttered.

'What?'

'It's a real ale. Dark Anvil.'

With a sigh, he turned and headed towards the bar.

I leaned back on the cushioned bench, resting my head against the panelled wall, cursing under my breath. He was only trying to help and I'd snapped at him, but surely he'd have expected it. I was hardly going to be a laugh a minute this weekend.

'Pint of Dark Anvil,' he said, placing two glasses on the table. 'Thought I'd give it a try too.'

'It's good.'

He took a sip. 'It *is* good. Millie sends her love. Actually, she instructed me to give you a huge hug but maybe later.'

'Depends on how many of these I've had as to whether I let you.'

We sat in silence for a few minutes, sipping our drinks, until Jack cracked. 'Sorry, bro. I'm crap at this stuff. Millie would have been so much better than me. I still can't believe Nikki's gone.'

'It's been seven months, thirteen days and...' I glanced at my watch. 'Nearly two hours.'

Jack sighed and shook his head, at a loss for words for once.

'She was my life, Jack. It's so unfair. We should have grown old together but she never even made it to our wedding day.'

* * *

The drinks had been on me that first night together. Who knew surfing was so damn hard? Lying on the board on the sand and manoeuvring to a standing position had seemed easy. Lying on the water and doing the same? Jesus! Nikki had been an amazingly patient teacher but a couple of hours in the sea definitely wasn't enough to master it. At one point, though, I did manage to ride a wave kneeling and I got why surfers became hooked on it. The adrenaline rush of surging forward towards the beach was like nothing I'd experienced before.

And being with Nikki was like nothing I'd experienced before either. She was so different to Kirsty that I found myself unable to think of a single reason why I'd stayed with Kirsty for so long. Nikki and I had so much in common and I loved making her laugh that loud belly laugh of hers.

It turned out that Nikki was getting over a cheating ex too so we agreed to take things slowly, just as friends, both keen not to jump into a rebound thing. But I couldn't stop thinking about her. She was a radiographer and I hadn't spotted her around the hospital before, but suddenly she seemed to be everywhere. I found it harder and harder to do the friends thing when all I wanted to do was pull her into the nearest store cupboard and kiss her like there was no tomorrow.

On my third surfing lesson, a couple of weeks after we'd met, we were the last ones bobbing about on the swell as the final streaks of the most stunning sunset faded into darkness.

'Last wave then we need to call it a day,' she said. 'Ready?'

And, finally, I made it upright on the board and rode that wave all the way to the shore, right beside Nikki. We pulled the boards out of the water and she threw her arms round me, squealing excitedly.

I don't know who moved first but the next moment we were kissing and thirty minutes later we were back at her rented flat, all thoughts of taking things slowly thrown completely out of the window.

* * *

'To Nikki?' Jack suggested, raising his glass.

I nodded and clinked mine against his. 'To Nikki. To the thirtieth birthday she never had and the wedding day we never shared.' The cold liquid felt like a lump of coal forcing its way down my throat.

It had seemed like a good idea planning our wedding for the same day as her birthday. Nikki said it would be the most amazing thirtieth party ever with double the celebration. Instead, it was double the pain. With the day before proving hard enough, I had no idea how I was going to get through tomorrow.

'She was one in a million,' Jack said.

'Too right. You knew what you were doing that day when you set us up, didn't you?'

He nodded. 'As soon as I met her, I could see her with you. You were perfect for each other.'

'Then why the hell did she leave me?' Each word carried my pain and anger.

'She'd never have chosen to.'

A pile of torn fragments of beer mat sat next to my pint. Had I just done that? I swept them onto the floor.

'How many of these do you think I need to forget?' I gulped down the remaining half pint in one.

'That's the answer, is it? Drink till you pass out?'

'Have you got a better idea? What would you have done on the weekend of your wedding if it had been Millie who'd dropped dead with a brain aneurysm seven-and-a-half months earlier?'

He stared at me for a moment, nodding slowly, then raised his glass and downed it in one. 'Same again?'

'Same again.'

He picked up the glasses and headed back to the bar. I hated myself for being so aggressive towards him, but I was angry and I had every bloody right to be.

Jack leaned on the bar with his head in his hands, taking deep breaths. I knew that pose well. It was how I started each day, hoping it was finally the day when the aching pain in my heart would ease a little and the desire to yell, 'fuck it' and join Nikki in the ever after would fade away. But that day never seemed to come.

Jack returned, pale-faced, and handed me my fresh pint. 'Can I ask you a question?'

'As long as it isn't "how are you?" again because I think we know the answer to that one.'

'The night of the blind date, you wanted me to cancel it. Knowing what you know now and feeling how you feel now, do you wish I'd listened to you and called it off?'

I shook my head. 'No. What's that cliché? Better to have loved and lost than never to have loved at all? I'd sell my soul to have her with me still and be marrying her tomorrow, but if all we could ever have was our two-and-a-half years, I'd rather have had that than never to have known her at all. You did the right thing, bro. You did the right thing.'

Jack released a shaky breath. 'I wondered if that was part of the reason why you'd moved to London. Because you were angry with me.'

'Christ, no! It was just too hard being in Whitsborough Bay without Nikki. She was everywhere. At home, at work, at the beach. I needed a break.'

Within a couple of months of getting together, we'd both given notice on our rented flats – no emotional loss as they were blighted by our exes and their indiscretions – and had bought a top floor apartment in a Victorian terrace overlooking North Bay. On the one-year anniversary of our blind date, we picked up the keys to a bright orange restored VW campervan and I handed them to Nikki. When she spotted the engagement ring dangling from a ribbon attached to the keyring, she squealed like she'd done the time I caught my first wave standing.

Four months ago, the day after my birthday, I handed over the keys of our flat to a property management company ready for my first tenant, then drove the campervan down to London ready to start afresh. New home, new hospital, new people. I'd genuinely thought that London – a place with no connection to Nikki – would be a good location to help me move on.

The relief on Jack's face was obvious. That thought must have been eating away at him for ages. It had never entered my head that he could be feeling guilty for my pain.

'Do you fancy giving surfing another go tomorrow?' I asked.

'Where?'

'Kent.'

He shrugged. 'Not really, but I will if that's what you want.'

'It is. And I think it's what Nikki would have wanted.'

'No laughing at me in a wetsuit this time. I'm not fit and toned like you.'

'Sorry, Loki, but Thor has few pleasures in his life at the moment. You can't take that away from him.'

Jack grimaced. 'I can't believe she got everyone at work to call me

Loki and you Thor. Abject humiliation! Okay, you win. You can laugh a bit, but then you need to show some respect for your elders. Deal?'

'Deal. You'll have to drive, though. I'll be way over the limit still.'

'No! That orange campervan thing? Oh God! Could it get any worse?'

I hoped not. Surely I'd already had the worst experience ever thrown at me. From now on, it had to get better. I just had to get through this weekend and I'd have survived four key occasions: my birthday and what would have been our three-year anniversary, her landmark birthday and our wedding day. It had to be up from there because I didn't think I had the strength to stop me from spiralling downwards.

6

JEMMA

I woke up on the morning after my engagement and reached across to Scott's side of the bed, but it was empty. I lay there for a few minutes gazing at the ring on my finger, which I hadn't been able to bring myself to remove when I climbed into bed. Scott had apologised for being unable to afford anything bigger or flashier. I didn't need flashy. It was the gesture that counted, not the extravagance.

I couldn't wait to get Scott to myself so we could start planning. If it was completely up to me, I'd choose the village church in Little Sandby, white dress and morning suits, not too big, and a fairly relaxed reception venue; perhaps a pub. I had no idea what would appeal to Scott, though. We'd never talked about anything like that. Neither of us had attended any weddings in the time we'd been together so the subject had never arisen. Ooh, and what about the honeymoon? The Caribbean? South Africa? Canada? So many possibilities.

Pulling on a thin cardigan over my nightie, I padded downstairs in search of my fiancé.

Mum emerged from the lounge with a mug in one hand and a copy of *Teddy Bear Times* in the other. She smiled up at me. 'Morning sleepy-bear.'

'What time is it?'

'About half eight.'

'Is Scott down here?'

She nodded. 'In the kitchen. I think he was trying to organise breakfast in bed for you, but Logan's been distracting him. I don't think he's got much further than pouring the juice. Has it sunk in?'

'Not yet. Still feels like a dream. I can't believe I'm getting married.'

'Neither can I. My baby girl's all grown up. It makes me feel old.'

'Well, you certainly don't look it.' She didn't. Mum could easily pass for a woman in her mid to late-thirties rather than forty-six. She'd always had a youthful face, a great figure and, now that Dad had no control over her wardrobe choices, she was very stylish.

'I may not look it, but I'm starting to feel it. I'm convinced my body stopped working properly the moment I passed forty-five. Some days climbing the stairs feels like conquering Everest. You might have to get me a stair lift for Christmas.'

'You should join Karen's yoga class. That would soon limber you up.'

'Karen suggested that too. I'm not sure I can see myself in a leotard with my legs behind my ears.'

I laughed. 'I don't think it's quite like that.'

'I know. It's finding the time, though. I feel as though I never have enough time for your brother as it is.'

'He could always go with you.'

Mum laughed loudly. 'Could you imagine Logan in a leopard-print leotard with his legs behind his ears?'

'Ew! Don't make me picture things like that!'

I looked into Mum's tired eyes. 'Seriously, though, are you okay, Mum? You look shattered.'

She shrugged. 'I'm not sleeping very well at the moment. I've got a doctor's appointment on Friday.'

'For not sleeping? Or is there something else?'

She paused. 'There are a few things.'

My hand gripped onto the banister and my heart started to race. 'Such as?'

Mum smiled. 'Don't look so worried, Jemma. I shouldn't have said anything.'

'Of course you should!'

'I'll tell you all about it later. For now, I want you to go into the kitchen and find your gorgeous fiancé, then I want us all to have a fabulous day at the races.'

'Mum!' We'd always talked about everything. 'No secrets' was our family motto – something that Mum insisted upon after we discovered Grandma's cover-up of stomach cancer.

As if reading my thoughts, Mum said, 'Honestly, Jemma. I'm not breaking the motto. I *will* tell you but now isn't the right time. Tomorrow.'

'Promise?'

'Promise. Now smile because you have lots to celebrate today.'

'You're sure you're okay?'

'I'm fine. But I'd be even better if I could have a hug.' She put her mug and magazine down on the hall table and stretched her arms out.

I stepped down into the hall and hugged Mum tightly. She'd lost weight. She'd always been slim but I could feel the bones in her back as I hugged her. I knew immediately that she wasn't okay and fear gripped me.

The door to the kitchen diner opened and Logan wandered out. 'What's going on?'

'Hugs with my baby girl.' Mum released her hold. 'Do you want one?'

'No. I need a poo.' He pushed past us and ran upstairs. Nice.

'Please don't worry about me,' Mum said, when we heard the bathroom door close. 'Enjoy your birthday weekend. Especially now that it's become an engagement weekend too.'

I squeezed her again then she gently nudged me towards the kitchen to find Scott.

It was pointless pushing. She'd always been strong-willed and the fact that she was going to tell me all about it tomorrow was going to have to be enough. If I pushed too hard, she might clam up completely and I didn't want to risk that. I needed to know because I was already imagining the worst-case scenario.

* * *

A day at the races wasn't something I'd done before but, when Leah and Tiff had discovered that it was York Races the weekend of my birthday, they'd got all excited about it and begged me to go. I wasn't sure about the betting aspect but I certainly liked the sound of getting all glammed up and drinking prosecco. When I'd mentioned it to Mum, she'd insisted on travelling in style and booked a stretch limo.

With no spare bedrooms at Mum's – her fourth bedroom being her workshop – Leah, Tiff and Drew had booked into a B&B in Whitsborough Bay so, after dropping Logan and Eden off for sleepovers with different friends, Karen picked my flatmates up and drove them over to Bear's Pad with her mum.

'Don't we all look a-may-zing!' Drew announced as we gathered on the deck for a quick drink before the limo arrived. We'd agreed to go for it with posh dresses and hats.

My stomach did a backflip at the sight of Scott in his dark two-piece suit. There's something about a man in a sharp suit and tie that absolutely does it for me. And I think that my outfit did it for him too judging by the twinkle in his eyes.

'I want to give you a hug but I don't want to rumple your dress,' he whispered, lightly kissing me on the cheek and lingering for a stomach-fizzing moment. 'Actually, I want to give you more than a hug. You look exceptional.'

'Thank you. So do you.' I leaned in for a kiss.

'Ew! Put him down,' Karen called.

Scott's phone rang a few minutes later. He rolled his eyes and excused himself, stepping into the kitchen diner. I sipped on my drink and asked Drew to explain how betting worked again. I swear my brain switched off every time he tried to explain the difference between win, place and each-way.

When Scott stepped out onto the deck five minutes later, I could tell from his expression that he was the bearer of bad news.

'I'm going to have to take the car,' he said. 'Sorry.'

My fingers tightened round my glass. 'Why?'

'That was my colleague, Adam. He's at a show in Sheffield. His wife's pregnant with twins and she's not well. Her sister's gone round to sit with her, but he might have to go home.'

I was aware of the silence on the deck and all eyes on our exchange. It wasn't his fault, but it was hard to keep the frustration out of my voice. 'And I'm assuming you need to cover for him?'

'I'm afraid so.'

'The garden's looking stunning, Jules,' Rachel said, making her way towards the steps. 'How about giving us all a tour?'

'Great idea, Mum,' Karen said, following her.

When we were alone, I took a deep breath and tried not to sound petulant as I said, 'You might as well leave for Sheffield now.'

Scott shook his head. 'Adam said there's no need. She's okay at the moment.'

'Yeah, but if she gets worse, Adam's going to need to leave immediately. You'll still have a ninety-minute drive from York. Wouldn't it make sense for you to pre-empt it and drive there now?'

He took a step closer to me and gently cupped my face, making me look into his eyes. I didn't want him to see the tears starting to pool in mine. I wanted to look supportive instead of upset. 'It *would* make sense,' he said, 'but I don't *want* to do that. I *want* to be with you. Assuming I'm still welcome, even if I have to abandon you mid-race.'

'Of course you are.'

He ran his fingers lightly under my eyes, catching the tears that had annoyingly refused to stay put. 'Please don't cry. If there was anyone else who could do it instead of me, I'd let them, but it has to be me.'

'I know. I understand.' And I did. I knew how important his work was and how stretched the company was. All the long hours and nights apart would be worth it in the end. 'But what about Adam and his wife? Put yourself in their shoes. I don't *want* you to go, but I think you should. If it was me who was pregnant and ill, I'd want my husband with me.'

Scott drew me into his arms and kissed the top of my head. 'That's one of the many things I love about you. Always putting others first. How about I set off at the same time as the limo and I give Adam a call on the hands-free as I approach York? If everything's still okay, I come to the races. If he needs me, I continue to Sheffield.'

It seemed like a reasonable compromise and I wasn't going to debate it further. Much as I felt for Adam's wife, I selfishly wanted my fiancé by my side.

* * *

We were only betting small amounts – and collectively losing more than winning – but it was fun. The tension that built into a cheering frenzy during each race was exciting although I could imagine it would feel exhilarating when winning big. I was far too cautious to splash the cash – a trait I hadn't realised I'd inherited from Dad.

I was more interested in soaking up the atmosphere and spending time with my loved ones than the races. I loved checking out the outfits and the hats in particular had me captivated. As did my fiancé.

'I love it that you can't take your eyes off him,' whispered Karen in my ear as I watched Scott waiting in the betting queue on the level below us. Adam had apparently insisted that he didn't need to leave, but asked Scott to check in with him every hour, just in case.

I turned to Karen and smiled. 'Sorry. I can't help it. Sometimes I can't believe my luck that he picked me.'

'Why shouldn't he? You're gorgeous and you're a lovely person. Strange obsession with teddy bears, perhaps, but I blame your mum for that.'

Scott must have been aware that I was watching him because he looked round, smiled and blew me a kiss. My stomach fizzed and so did other parts of me. I couldn't help it. I loved him so much and so did my body!

I'd had a few boyfriends before Scott but none of them had been serious or long-term. Most couldn't get their head around my passion for teddy bears. Paul had constantly taken the mickey out of me, calling me a child, so I childishly dumped him on Facebook. Andy said he was creeped out by their eyes watching him when we were in my bedroom and said it was the bears or him. No brainer. Nate took me for Sunday Lunch at his parents' house. Midway through our starter, his dad asked what I did for a living. Nate laughed and said, 'She plays with bears and dolls all day, but I'm sure she'll get a proper job soon.' Wow! He sounded exactly like my dad. How I resisted pouring my soup over his head, I'll never know. When he dropped me off at home later, I said, 'Seeing as I'm so busy playing with bears and dolls all day, I'm not going to be able to play with you anymore. Goodbye.' It had taken me the whole of the hour-long journey home to come up with that line but it felt so good delivering it!

Being with Scott was therefore incredibly refreshing. He was interested in my job, had no objection to the bears displayed round my bedroom, had come up with a few design ideas for my Ju-Sea Jem Bears – a miniature range of bears that I designed and made to complement Mum's larger bears – and had even asked for a guided tour of the museum. Definitely a keeper!

'Oh my God!' I grabbed Karen's arm, my pulse racing. 'He's got a pint! What's he got a pint for? He knows my views on drinking and driving.'

'He won't be over the limit with one pint.'

I shook my head. 'I know I'm overly sensitive about it because of Dad, but he usually indulges me and doesn't touch a drop.'

Karen shrugged. 'I'd say give him a break. He probably feels pretty crap for disrupting your plans and has a bit of a thirst.'

'I know, but...'

She sighed. 'If it bothers you that much, you could move in for a kiss and accidentally knock the drink out of his hand.'

'Knowing my luck, I'd spill it down my dress.'

Drew appeared by my side. 'Where's Scott?' he asked.

'Why?'

'So I can wrestle him to the ground in a show of manliness,' he quipped. He laughed at my astonished expression. 'Okay, I lied, although I'd like it to be noted that I'd definitely win if that happened.'

'I'm sure you would. And the real reason you want Scott is...?'

'He held my pint while I went for a dump. Enough information for you?'

I grimaced. 'More than enough. He's in the betting queue over there.' I pointed towards Scott, then Drew set off down the steps to retrieve his drink.

Karen nudged me. 'Things aren't always what they seem, you know.'

'I know. I feel really mean now.'

'Then make it up to him.' She winked at me then moved off to join in a conversation with Leah and Tiff.

Below us, Drew took the pint from Scott, laughed at something he said, then wandered along the line of betting kiosks, checking out their odds.

I made my way down the steps as Scott finished his transaction. He turned round, clutching his betting slip. 'This one's for you. £50 on Diamond Dancer in honour of our engagement and your new bear.'

'£50? Oh my God, Scott. That's a fortune!'

'At odds of 9:1 our winnings *will be* a fortune! Don't look so worried. I set myself a £50 budget for the whole day and I'm already £30 up. Do you fancy going closer to watch?'

Scott reached for my hand and, despite my panic at the money – I was clearly far too cautious with my £2 flutters here and there – I couldn't help but feel infected by his enthusiasm.

'I want to hear some proper cheering and whooping,' he said. 'Even if Diamond Dancer comes in last which, of course, he won't.'

He grabbed my hand and pulled me closer to the railings and we looked up at the giant screen as the horses moved into their starting stalls.

When an announcement came over the loudspeaker that Angel's

Glory was a non-runner, he turned to me, eyes shining. 'That's the favourite out of the race. Yes! I can taste the victory.'

The race started. 'Which colour?' I asked, staring at the twelve galloping horses.

'Purple and white. Fifth from the front.'

The cheers from the crowd steadily grew as the horse at the front dropped pace and a horse with red silks edged forward. It was overtaken by one in blue and the pair of them remained pretty much neck-and-neck.

'This is it!' Scott cried as Diamond Dancer increased his pace to fourth. Then third. The volume increased as the crowd cheered and screamed out the names of various horses.

With Scott by my side, leaping up and down like Logan on Christmas morning, I finally understood why some people loved the races for more than the dressing up and drinking. My heart pounded as I watched the horses galloping along the final stretch.

When Diamond Dancer galloped alongside the leader, I whooped and cheered and stamped my feet. As they flashed past us, I could feel the pounding of their hooves and felt like I was part of the race. What a thrill!

A photo finish literally had me shaking and when the commentator announced that Diamond Dancer had won, I actually screamed. So did Scott although his was more of a manly cheer. He grabbed me and spun me around, laughing, showering me with kisses.

As he lowered me to the ground, he gazed into my eyes. 'That's the first £500 for our wedding account.' He cupped my face in his hands but his smile slipped, replaced by a sombre, serious expression. 'I can't wait to spend the rest of my life with you, Jemma. I really do love you only.'

'And I love you always.'

He kissed me so tenderly that I felt quite weak when he pulled away.

'I'm really sorry again about the situation with Adam. He hasn't called yet, so—'

At that moment, his mobile started ringing and my heart sank.

Scott put his phone to his ear. 'Hello?' He listened for a moment and laughed. '*You* ask her.' He handed the phone to me and I frowned.

'Hello?'

'It's me!' cried Karen. 'Tiff's heading to the bar and she wants to know if you're still on the prosecco.'

'Yes, please.' I twisted round to see the group on the higher tier of the Grandstand. I waved at Karen and she waved back. 'Why didn't you phone me?'

She lifted up my handbag and I laughed.

'Stop snogging your fiancé and get back up here for some serious drinking.'

I disconnected the call and handed Scott his phone.

'How come Karen has my number?' he asked, frowning.

'You gave it to Leah a few months ago when my phone was playing up. Karen must have got it off her.'

'Ah yes. I remember. Shall we collect our winnings?'

Scott handed me the wad of notes ten minutes later. 'Take the money and open an account. I won't be able to do it without a fixed address. I don't think they'd accept Mum and Dad's address in Canada.'

Scott had given up his rented flat in Nottingham before I met him because he spent so much time on the road with work. If he wasn't away, he stayed with friends, me or even in a B&B saying it was cheaper than renting when he was hardly ever at home.

His parents had emigrated several years earlier but his dad had developed a few health problems that prevented him from flying. I'd therefore never met them although Scott had been over to Canada a couple of times since we'd met.

I stared at the bundle of notes in my hand. 'Are you sure?'

'I'm sure. I think I can trust you not to spend it on twenty bears. Actually, knowing your tastes, it would probably only be two or three bears for that amount.'

'You know me well. I promise not to spend it on bears. Besides,

Diamond has just joined the hug so he'll satisfy my bear-acquisition needs for a little while. Thank you. It's a lovely idea.'

We returned to the group where a glass of prosecco was thrust into one hand and my handbag into the other. I secured our winnings in a zipped compartment then snuggled against Scott's side as he shared the news of our victory.

Everyone was in such a fabulous mood. Even Scott and Drew seemed to have cast their animosity aside to laugh and joke together. What an amazing afternoon.

Then Scott's phone rang.

'Hi, how's it going?' He mouthed 'sorry' to me and wandered away from the group. My heart sank.

Drew put his arm round me and squeezed me to his side. 'He managed a few hours which is more than you expected, isn't it?'

'I know. I just wish he could have stayed all day.'

'So do I. And not just for you. I've actually had a good laugh with him today. It's the longest I've spent in his company and I've seen a different side to him.'

'You're not just saying that to cheer me up?'

Drew squeezed me again. 'I promise I'm not just saying it. I know we haven't exactly been the best of friends but I might have misjudged him. I thought he seemed like the sort who'd shag and go, but he's proved me wrong. He might be good enough for you, after all.'

Scott returned moments later and his expression said it all. 'They're taking Adam's wife to hospital. They might need to induce the birth. I'm sorry. I have to go.'

I smiled brightly. I didn't feel bright, but it wasn't Scott's fault. 'Okay. Can I walk you to the exit?'

He nodded, said goodbye to the rest of the group, hugged my mum and thanked her for being a great host, then took my hand as we walked through the crowds.

Another race was about to start so the entrance/exit lobby was fairly quiet. Scott gently pulled me to the side and took both my hands in his. 'If I could stay, I would.'

'I know.'

'This week's going to be crazy and I'm working at the weekend, but I'll be in London at the middle of the following week.' I could hear the regret in his voice and see it in his eyes too. 'We'll go out together – just the two of us – and talk weddings.'

I squeezed his hands. 'I'm not angry with you. I know this isn't your fault. It's just one of those things. But a night out alone would be amazing. We could go for a meal.'

'How about the same restaurant we went to when we met? La Vecchia Scuola, was it?'

I smiled. 'Well remembered. Sounds perfect. Like you.'

Scott bit his lip and lowered his eyes. 'I'm far from perfect, Jemma.'

'That's true. You fart in your sleep and you love Marmite. What's that all about?'

He looked up at me, a gentle smile on his lips. 'And you like gravy on your chips and drink real ale. What's that all about?'

Outside, the cheering of the crowd had built to a crescendo but, as Scott drew me into a passionate kiss, I could barely hear the noise. All I could focus on was this amazing man who loved me and wanted to marry me. I wanted to stay that way forever, locked in our own little world but it was only delaying the inevitable.

With great reluctance, I pulled away as the final cheer erupted and the winner was announced.

'Just as well we didn't bet on that one,' Scott said. 'We'd have lost.'

'The racing gods were obviously smiling down on us today.' I patted my handbag containing our winnings. 'You'd better go. I know you won't be able to phone me when you get there, but text if you can.'

'I'll try, but I think it will be a quick handover then straight into it. Adam has appointments all evening so it'll probably be tomorrow before I can get in touch. Don't panic if you don't hear from me.'

Scott was exceptionally reliable when it came to texting and phoning. He always contacted me when he said he would and he let me know if he might be delayed. I loved that he understood me being worried about him travelling so much.

'Jemma?'

'Yes?'

'When I see you next, there's something I need to tell you.'

I was about to make a joke, but he looked very serious. My stomach somersaulted. 'That sounds ominous. Can't you tell me now?'

With the race over, the lobby had become busy again and we were getting jostled. Scott looked round us and grimaced. 'It's not really the time or the place.'

'That sounds even more ominous. Oh my God! You're not ill, are you? Cancer or something?'

He quickly shook his head. 'God, no! It's nothing like that.'

'Then can't you tell me? I'm only going to worry about it for the next ten days if you don't.'

He took my hands in his once more. 'I'd rather wait so we can talk about it properly.'

'Scott! Please don't do this. Can't you give me a clue?'

He sighed. 'It's about the wedding.'

'Go on.'

'I... it's... I...' His eyes kept darting round the room and I could barely hear him for the rising noise.

'You're scaring me!'

He looked deep into my eyes then smiled. 'I'm sorry. I shouldn't have said anything. I've gone and made it into a big thing when it really isn't. It could have waited until I saw you and we were talking weddings.'

He was having to shout so he took my hand and led me through the lobby and we stepped outside.

'I was thinking that, with my dad not being well enough to travel, you having lost your dad, and neither of us having big families, maybe we could elope.'

My stomach did a massive somersault. 'Elope?'

'Run off to get married. Just the two of us.'

'I know what eloping means. I just...' I wanted to marry him so much but not like that. 'My mum and Logan have to be there. And I want Karen as a bridesmaid. And—'

Scott nodded. 'Of course you do! I'm being selfish. It's your day. We can do whatever you want.'

'It's *our* day, Scott, not *mine*. I'm happy to compromise on anything, but I don't think I can consider eloping. It would break Mum's heart. And mine. I'm happy to have a small wedding, but I want Mum and Logan there. And Karen and her family. They're like my extended family. It wouldn't feel right without them.'

He gave me a reassuring smile. 'I shouldn't have said anything. It was a stupid idea.'

'It wasn't stupid. I completely get where you're coming from. I know it's hard for you with your parents being abroad and your dad being poorly. Maybe we could go to Canada for our honeymoon? Visit your parents?'

'There you go again. Thinking of others all the time. What did I ever do to deserve someone as thoughtful as you?'

I clutched my hand to my heart. 'Thank God that's all you wanted to say. You had me panicking there.'

'Sorry. I didn't mean to worry you.'

'You'd better go.' I kissed him gently then he held me tightly.

'I love you only,' he whispered into my ear. 'Whatever happens, please never forget that.'

He released me, stepped back, and gave me one last lingering look as though he wanted to remember the moment forever. Then, without another word, he turned and ran across the road towards the car park.

I frowned as I watched him go. That was odd. Whatever happens? What made him say that? What could possibly happen?

As he disappeared from sight, I shook my head and smiled to myself. It was just a turn of phrase and I was reading far too much into it because, as he himself had said, he'd built something up unnecessarily and I'd managed to completely over-react to it and fear the worst. Everything was fine and I had my guests to get back to and a large prosecco with my name on it.

'I had a lovely time today,' Mum said that evening back at Bear's Pad. We'd had a meal in York after the races and the intention had been to have a few drinks in Whitsborough Bay but, as the limo journeyed back along the A64, it was obvious to me that everyone was flagging. The pile of discarded stilettos, including my own, suggested that a pub crawl really wasn't on the cards. I had to laugh at the grateful nods when I mooted the idea that our plans had been a little ambitious and perhaps it was time to call it a night.

I lowered my shoulders further down into the hot tub bubbles and wriggled my aching feet. 'I had a lovely time too and this is the perfect ending to it. I just wish Scott was here.'

Mum nodded. 'He texted, though?'

'Yes. Just a short one to say he got there safely. I probably won't hear from him for a couple of days now.' I looked at the pretty coloured lights strung across the fence and round various potted shrubs. It was so tranquil. I closed my eyes and breathed in deeply. When I opened them, I looked over to Mum. She was gazing into the darkness, a faraway expression on her face. 'So tell me about this doctor's appointment on Friday. What's going on, Mum?'

She sighed. 'You don't want to leave it until tomorrow?'

'I'd rather know now.'

'I thought you might. Where do I start?' She sighed again. 'You know how I joked this morning about my body falling apart and sometimes climbing the stairs feels like conquering Everest? Well, it wasn't a joke. Some days it really does feel like that. It started in March. Logan had gone to bed and I was in my workshop making a bear. I needed some thread for his nose so I stood up, walked towards the thread drawers and stopped. It was the weirdest thing.'

'What do you mean, you stopped?' I thought about her forgetfulness with the knickers, my birthday card, Logan's football boots in the oven, and goodness knows what else. Was that what she meant? 'You'd forgotten what you wanted?'

She shook her head. 'I knew exactly what I wanted and where to find it. I mean I stopped. Physically. I was walking. Then I wasn't walking. It was like someone had super glued my feet to the floor. I can remember looking down at my feet and willing them to move, but they wouldn't.'

'Oh my God! What did you do?'

She shrugged. 'Some time passed. Could have been seconds. Could have been minutes. My legs and feet started working again and that was that. I didn't bother getting the thread out. I figured it was my body's way of telling me it was time for bed.'

I frowned. 'You really just stopped moving? No warning or anything?'

'Completely still. It freaked me out at the time but I didn't think much about it until I was at the supermarket a week or so later. I was pushing the trolley back to the car when I stopped. Right in the middle of the zebra crossing. Cars started beeping at me and there was absolutely nothing I could do. My arms were fine but my legs wouldn't move. Everyone must have thought I'd gone a bit loopy, playing with the traffic like that, but I couldn't control my legs no matter how much I willed them to move. Then they came unstuck and I shuffled off the crossing as quickly as I could, threw my bags in the car, and made my escape. It kept happening. Not every day by any means but frequently enough to know something was wrong. Rachel insisted on me making a doctor's appointment and my doctor referred me to a consultant and, well, it turns out...'

'What is it?' I asked when she fell silent and lowered her eyes. My heart raced. I wasn't sure I wanted to hear the answer. 'What's wrong, Mum?'

'It's Parkinson's. I've got Parkinson's.'

'But...' I paused for a moment, trying to digest what she'd just said. 'But you can't have. People with Parkinson's shake. I've been around you all weekend and I haven't seen you shaking once.'

She smiled weakly. 'I said exactly the same to my doctor and to the specialist who diagnosed me. Apparently shaking's one of the most common symptoms and it's the one that most people associate with Parkinson's, but it's not the only symptom and some people don't shake at all. The other main symptoms are slow movement and rigidity... or stiffness if you like. I've got that. It's what makes me stop suddenly. I don't shake, though. Some days I can move but not at a normal pace. I find that I can't pick up my feet to walk properly so I shuffle along like an old lady instead. They're my bad days.'

'But I haven't seen you suddenly stopping or shuffling.'

Mum's eyes were full of sympathy as she watched me recall something that had seemed so insignificant earlier that day.

'At the races today,' I cried. 'We were on our way to the bar. You were in front and you suddenly stopped and we all crashed into you. You said you'd spotted someone you knew but you hadn't, had you?'

'My feet wouldn't move but how could I tell you that and ruin your day?'

'Rachel manoeuvred us round you, joking that the last to the bar had to pay.'

Mum nodded. 'I'd asked her to watch out for any incidents. She knew I was going to tell you this weekend, but that I wanted you to enjoy your special day out first.'

I put my hand over my mouth, tears rushing to my eyes. 'Oh my God! Parkinson's? Are they sure?'

'One hundred per cent. Hey, don't cry. I'm not about to die, you know. As my consultant, Dr Steadman, keeps telling me, it's a treatable condition that I need to learn to live with, not a life-threatening illness. Patronising git.'

I couldn't help it. Great big tears rolled down my cheeks and plopped into the water. Mum held out her arms and I bobbed across the hot tub for a cuddle while my body wracked with sobs. How could this have happened? Mum had always been so healthy and so active. How could someone so active suddenly have their body give up on them? My mind was racing. I knew so little about Parkinson's. Would she need a wheelchair? Would it reduce her life expectancy? Could she work? Would she be able to look after Logan? The more the questions flooded into my mind, the more I sobbed.

Mum whispered reassurances and I took several deep breaths as I tried to pull myself together.

'Sorry,' I whispered when the tears finally subsided and Mum was able to let go of me. 'Me turning into a blubbering mess is probably the last thing you need right now.'

'It's okay. I understand. I cried when they told me too.'

'I wish you'd told me about your appointment. I'd have booked time off and been there for you. You shouldn't have had to go through that on your own.'

'Thank you, but I wouldn't have expected you to do that and, of course, I didn't think it was going to be anything serious. I wondered if it was something to do with arthritis, like my mum had, but when my doctor suspected Parkinson's and referred me, Rachel came to see the consultant with me. She's been amazing, as always. I'm so glad you and Karen became friends because I don't know what I'd have done without her over the years.'

'What happens next?'

'I'm on medication and I should really do some exercise, but it's finding the time.'

'Does exercise help?'

'It's meant to.'

'Then you *definitely* need to do it.'

'But Logan—'

'—will understand if you explain why you're doing it. I take it he doesn't know?'

She shook her head. 'I wanted to tell you first and I don't want to worry him.'

'What about the stopping and the shuffling? Surely he's noticed that.'

'I've joked about me getting older and slowing down and I think he's accepted that. He's too young to realise that forty-six isn't exactly what you'd call old and that what's happening to me isn't typical for a woman of my age.'

'How often are the bad days?'

'More often than they used to be. I was fine on Friday and I've had a fairly good day today so I wouldn't be surprised if I have a bad one tomorrow.'

'Then tomorrow you rest and let me look after you.'

'You're meant to be doing touristy things with your flatmates.'

'They'll understand.'

'No, Jemma. I appreciate the offer, but your friends have travelled all the way up here to spend the weekend with you. I won't have you letting them down.'

'But—'

She raised a hand to silence me. 'It's not negotiable. Besides, if I'm having a *really* bad day, I'll want to rest and work on my latest Ju-Sea Bear so there's absolutely no point in you sticking around. You could do something for me, though. It was good of Billy Thomas's mum to have Logan today but I think two days in a row would be taking the mickey. If you could take your brother with you, that would be a tremendous help. If your friends don't mind, that is.'

'They won't mind at all.' It was the least we could do.

'Maybe you could take them all to the lido.'

I frowned. 'The what?'

'The lido. On South Bay.'

I hesitated, feeling uneasy. 'You mean Splash Down near North Bay. The indoor slide pool?'

'Er, no. I mean the outdoor pool on South Bay.'

'But there isn't an outdoor pool in Whitsborough Bay. Not anymore.'

'There is! Stop winding me up! It's on South Bay and it fills with seawater. We go down there every summer although I swear it's colder in there than the sea itself.' Mum shivered. 'Speaking of cold, I think it's time to get inside and go to bed. Are you coming in?'

I hesitated, my mind whirring. 'In a minute.'

'Okay. Sleep well.'

'And you. I'll see you in the morning.' I tried to keep my voice bright as I didn't want to alarm her.

I watched her clamber out of the hot tub and wrap a towel round her shoulders. I hadn't registered it earlier but, now that I knew about her diagnosis, I could see that her movements were slower and stiffer than usual. It was a worry but what was concerning me even more was the conversation we'd just had. Whitsborough Bay *did* have a seawater lido. But it had been closed down and filled in when I was seven.

8

SAM

I'll give Jack his due. He hadn't moaned *too* much about driving Thor to the Kent coast the following day, although I think he'd been hoping the hangover from hell would have changed my mind. No way. I needed to do this today. For Nikki. It wasn't the same as surfing in Whitsborough Bay but nothing about my life was the same anymore.

'Jesus, Sam! I can't even get to a crouching position when a wave hits.' Jack spat out a mouthful of water and heaved himself back onto his board for the umpteenth time. 'How are you so good at this?'

'Great teacher.'

He watched me look at my watch again. 'Is it time?'

I nodded, my throat tightening. 'We'd officially be husband and wife by now.'

'Aw, mate...'

'I know.' I looked behind me. 'I'm gonna catch this one.' I started to paddle before Jack could say anything else, jumping to my feet as the wave took the board.

Riding the wave towards the shore, I could picture her right by my side, her dark hair slicked back, eyes sparkling, laughing that infectious belly laugh of hers.

'Goodbye Nikki,' I whispered. 'I love you.'

* * *

'What happens now?' Jack asked as we sat on the beach that evening.

'We drink and drink some more and hope the temperature doesn't drop too much because I'm not cuddling up to you for warmth. You stink of garlic.'

After dinner in a local pub, I'd driven the campervan to a remote stretch of coast. We'd carried a crate of lager over the sand dunes and lit a fire, just like Nikki and I used to do.

'And a less flippant answer would be...?'

I shrugged. I'd tried hard not to think about the future, knowing Nikki wouldn't be in it. 'Throw myself into the job and hope that, one day, I'll wake up and the pain will have eased, even just slightly.'

'Do you think it was the right decision to move down here?'

I took a glug of lager. I wasn't going to admit that, in a city with a population of nearly nine million, I'd never felt so lonely. 'Early days. It was a good career move.'

Jack tossed another handful of sticks onto the fire. 'I agree. Brilliant career move. But was it the right move for *you*?'

I didn't respond.

'Why don't you move back?' Jack suggested. 'I understand that living in your flat would be too full of memories, but you could keep renting it out and find somewhere new, couldn't you?'

I could. Thanks to the life assurance policy that financially-astute Nikki had insisted we take out, I could buy a new place straight out. But I couldn't move back home. I may not have Nikki anymore but I still had a career and I had to give it at least a year in London, preferably two, to maintain any sort of credibility.

I gazed into the fire. 'Maybe one day.'

'If you do, you'd be welcome to stay with us while you're looking for somewhere new. Providing you can put up with screaming babies and the permanent stench of shitty nappies.'

I gave him a half-smile. 'You need to work on your sales technique.'

We sat in silence for a while, both watching the flames.

'Thanks for coming down this weekend,' I said eventually. 'I was dreading it.'

'It's the least I can do.'

'Let's stop talking about me. How are the girls?'

'Teaching Isla to talk was a big mistake. She's already got the attitude of a teenager. I think the terrible twos might last forever. Saffron is on Australian time – sleeps all day, screams all night. We've forgotten what sleep is. Millie hates me and has threatened to slice my balls off with a cleaver and serve them to me in an omelette if I ever get her pregnant again. She's demanding I get the snip.'

'Are you going to?'

'No! We always wanted a boy and a girl. We'd agreed to try again if baby number two was a girl.'

'What if she gets pregnant and it's another girl?'

Jack shrugged. 'Keep going till we get a boy.'

'And Millie agrees to that?'

He paused and took a swig of his lager. 'She will. Eventually.'

'Jack! What about when number four's a girl too? And number five? You should count yourself lucky that you've been able to have *two* kids, whatever their gender, when there are so many couples out there who can't have any.'

I pictured the look of longing in Nikki's eyes as she'd held Isla a few hours after she was born. We'd talked about having a family at some point and, that night, we decided it was time. But nature had other ideas. It was heartbreaking seeing the look of disappointment on her face as each month passed without good news.

'I'm sorry, mate. You and Nikki would have made great parents.'

I couldn't respond. Memories swirled round my mind, making me feel dizzy.

'You will come up to visit soon, won't you?' Jack said. 'Isla would love to see her Uncle Sammy and I'm sure Saffron would love to projectile vomit all over you. It's a pretty special bonding moment. I know being back in Whitsborough Bay is hard on you and I don't want to come across as the demanding big brother, but Millie's an only child and you're my only sibling so you're their only uncle. It would mean a lot to Millie and me if you could try and see a bit more of them. I know it's harder with you being in London now and...' He tailed off. 'I've said too much haven't I?' Shit! Millie told me not to say anything. She said you'll make up for it when the time's right for you.'

A tear slid down my cheek and I slumped forwards. The nearly-empty bottle of lager slipped from my hands and landed with a soft thud on the sand as sobs racked through me.

'Christ! Sam! I wasn't having a go at you!'

I tried to say, 'I know', but the words wouldn't come out. My whole body shook and alien agonised sounds kept spilling from my mouth.

'What did I say?' I could hear the panic in Jack's voice but I couldn't reply.

Oh shit! No! I somehow scrambled to my feet and managed to stagger a little way down the beach before I threw up.

Within seconds, Jack was by my side, with his arm round me as I sank to my knees in the sand, trembling. 'Sorry,' I muttered, wiping my mouth. 'Don't know what happened then. I've only had two drinks. Must be a delayed reaction from last night's skin-full.'

'That wasn't the drink. That was grief.'

I closed my eyes and breathed slowly in and out a few times, trying to calm my racing heart.

'Are you okay, Sam?'

I picked up a handful of sand in my right hand and let it slowly fall through my fingers. 'Of course I'm not okay. My fiancée's dead and...'

'And what?'

I looked up into his worried eyes. I couldn't tell him. I still couldn't say it. I shook my head. 'And I don't know if I'll ever be okay again.'

'Come on. Back to the fire.' Jack helped me to my feet, kicking some sand over the vomit. 'Let's get you warm.'

'Uh oh! Drinking alone on a school night?' Drew closed the door to our flat behind him on Wednesday evening and dropped his backpack onto the floor with a thud. 'This isn't a good sign.'

I shrugged and continued to stare at the TV on mute, my eyes flicking to my phone on the armrest of the chair every few seconds.

'Still no word from Scott?' Drew sat down on the wooden coffee table, eased the remote control out of my hand, and switched the TV off.

I shook my head. 'Not since this text from him on Sunday morning.' I tapped in my password then thrust my phone at Drew so he could read Scott's text and my reply. 'Why wouldn't he respond to this? I was being supportive, wasn't I?'

✉ From Scott
Adam's wife had twins yesterday. Boy and girl. 8 weeks early and not doing so well. Feel a bit help-less xx

✉ To Scott
Oh no! Poor little mites. Hope they're fighters.

Did he make it home in time for the births? Please
don't feel helpless. There's nothing you can do in
these circumstances except be there if he needs
you. If you can't make it down next week because
Adam needs to be with his family, I completely
understand. We can talk wedding plans when things
settle a bit. Thinking of you. I love you always
and can't wait to be your wife xx

'Obviously I tried to call him as soon as I got his text to make sure he was okay, but it went to voicemail so I sent that text instead. Haven't heard a peep out of him since. It's so unlike him. What if something's happened to him?'

Drew handed my phone back to me. I could almost hear his mind ticking.

'You *definitely* didn't have an argument before he left the races?'

'No! I've already told you that. I walked him to the exit and he told me that he was expecting a busy week at work so he wouldn't see me till next week. We agreed to go for a meal and talk about the wedding. He said he wanted to elope and I told him I didn't.'

'And you *definitely* didn't fall out about that?'

'He realised it was a daft idea because of how close I am to Mum, Logan and Karen.'

'And me.'

I gave Drew a half-smile. 'Yes, and you. I couldn't possibly get married without you there.'

'I should think not! Could his phone have been stolen?'

'It's possible. But he could have rung me at the museum. Or emailed me.'

Drew ran his hand across his stubble. 'You've tried him on Facebook? Twitter? Instagram? LinkedIn? WhatsApp?'

'He doesn't do social media.'

'He's not on *any* sites? What's wrong with him? How does he survive?' For someone who had a profile on every form of social media going, Drew's shocked reaction didn't surprise me.

'He's on Facebook. Sort of. I made him open an account so I could put photos of us together on it and we could post selfies when we were apart. He's rubbish at posting but he always likes my pictures. I think I'm the only friend he's got on it, though.'

'And you've tried to contact him on that?'

'Several times. Facebook and Messenger. I'm worried sick, Drew. I can't sleep, I can't eat, I keep bursting into tears.'

Drew sighed. 'I know you're thinking the worst but, if he'd been in an accident, you'd have heard something by now. His phone would have been found and they'd have looked at his call logs.'

'Assuming he had his phone with him...' I shook my head. 'No, I don't think it's an accident. They'd have contacted his parents and they'd have got in touch. Scott said he gave them my number in case of emergency. I don't know what else to do. Why hasn't he been in touch? Do you think he's having second thoughts about the wedding?'

With downcast eyes, Drew fiddled with the strap on his watch.

'Oh my God! You do, don't you? You think he's got cold feet?' I felt sick.

'No! I don't know. There's one possibility although I don't know why he'd have done it. Give me a second.' Drew stood up and disappeared into my bedroom, returning with my laptop. He handed it to me and perched on the arm of the chair. 'Bigger screen so we can both see. Log onto Facebook.'

I frowned but did as I was told. 'I'm in.'

'Now find Scott's profile.'

'Scott Hastings,' I muttered as I typed his name into the search bar. 'He's not there! Hang on.' I typed his name in again, just in case I'd mistyped it. There was a rugby player, some bloke who arranged loans in Australia, an electrician... but not *my* Scott. 'Where's she gone? He was there yesterday.'

'Log into your emails,' Drew suggested, his voice calm. 'Try sending him a short email.'

I shrugged but did as he suggested. 'That was quick!' I said a moment later when a reply popped up on my screen. 'Crap! It's an undeliverable. "Email address does not exist". What?' I looked up at Drew, my heart racing and my stomach churning.

Drew grimaced. 'I hate to say it, Jem, but I think you've been ghosted.'

'I've been what?'

'Ghosted.'

'What the hell's that?'

'When someone ends a relationship without properly ending it. They just stop communicating. They don't text, or call, or email. They unfriend or unfollow you on all the social media. All they leave behind is their ghost.'

I slumped back in the chair, feeling weak and dizzy. 'Scott wouldn't do that to me. He just proposed to me, for God's sake. You don't ask someone to marry you then cut them out your life days later.'

Drew remained silent.

My mind whirred. Ghosted? No. He wouldn't. Nobody would. It was a horrible thing to do. If you wanted to end a relationship there were loads of options. You didn't just disappear. Then I remembered what had happened my first Christmas in the flat. I sat forward.

'That bloke from Finland did this to you, didn't he? What was his name? Luka?'

'Luukas.' Drew sighed. 'I waited at Heathrow for seven hours on Christmas Eve before I finally accepted he wasn't going to take me home to meet his family. Eight months together then absolutely nothing. Wiped from social media. Gone.' He raised his hands and splayed his fingers like a magician to illustrate his point.

'And you never heard from him again?'

'Not a word. As far as I was concerned, the relationship was going brilliantly, we hadn't had any arguments and there was no reason for it to end. That's what gets me. I *still* don't know if I said or did something wrong. I don't know if he met someone else or if an ex came back on the scene. I'd have been devastated if he'd had the guts to actually dump me, but at least I'd have had closure. Ghosting just left me in limbo. Two-and-a-half years later and I still think about it and wonder what the hell happened. That's why I've avoided relationships ever since. I couldn't cope if the same thing happened again.'

'That's awful, Drew. It's so cruel.'

'I know.'

We both sat in silence for a while. I tossed round the idea of Scott ghosting me. Could he have done? No! He wouldn't do that. 'Scott asked me to marry him,' I said. 'Why would he do that if he was planning to dump me? It doesn't make sense. There must be another explanation.'

I could tell from Drew's expression that he didn't think so. 'Have you tried to call him at work?'

'I don't know the name of his company. Don't look at me like that! It's not like he works for a big household name.'

'What do they do? Maybe we could find it on that basis.'

'I don't know.' I felt my cheeks flush. What a crap fiancée I was. 'Stop looking so shocked!'

'I think we might have found the reason why he's ghosted you. You don't listen to a word he says.'

The laughter in his voice made me smile as I nudged him in the ribs. 'I *do* listen. He told me exactly what he does when we first met but I didn't understand it. It's got something to do with energy and renewables. I think. We have so little time together that we try not to waste it talking shop. And he's *not* ghosted me. He can't have.'

Drew gave me a look that clearly said, 'Yeah, and I thought the same about Luukas.' He picked up my laptop and moved onto the sofa. 'I'll Google energy companies. Where's it based?'

I cringed. 'I don't know that either. He's not based in an office. He goes all over the country. Maybe the Nottingham area because he used to live there.'

'Let's start with Nottingham, then, and work out from there.'

A couple of hours later, I'd scribbled down a list of companies in Nottinghamshire, Leicestershire, Derbyshire, their websites and their phone numbers, along with a back-up list for the West Midlands just in case.

'It's like looking for a needle in a haystack,' I said, staring at the list.

'It might even be the wrong haystack but at least it's a start. I can't think of anything better. Can you?'

'Phone the police and report him as a missing person?'

Drew closed my laptop and gently laid it on the coffee table. 'You've already done that, haven't you?'

I lowered my eyes, nodding.

'What did they tell you?'

'That it didn't sound like a police matter and... well, I think she was suggesting I'd been dumped but was too polite to say so.'

'Let's try the list, eh? I'm off tomorrow. I've got some stuff to do in the morning but I don't mind ringing round some places in the afternoon while you're at work.'

'Would you really do that for me?'

'I'd do anything to put a smile back on that gorgeous face of yours.'

A scrabbling outside the door, a clatter of keys, and peals of laughter suggested Leah and Tiff were back from their double date.

'That's absolutely the last time I meet up with someone off Tinder,' Leah cried, bursting through the door. 'From now on, it's swipe left to everyone.'

'Which means you might as well delete your Tinder account,' suggested Tiff.

'Oh yeah! Good point. No more Tinder for me.' Leah threw herself onto the sofa next to Drew.

'I take it the date didn't go well?' Drew asked.

'The only reason they wanted to date us was because we're twins,' Tiff called, heading for the kitchen area. 'Dirty gits fancied a foursome. Water, Leah?'

'Yes, please,' Leah said. 'Apparently we completely screwed up the fantasy by being non-identical twins although I'd have thought that was pretty obvious from our photos.'

Tiff returned from the kitchen and handed Leah a drink. 'I knew something was up when they kept asking Leah if she'd consider dying her hair blonde and having a streak put in it.'

'One of them asked if we ever dressed the same and, when they heard that Tiff was a nurse, they asked if I'd dress up in one of her spare uniforms.' Leah shuddered. 'Needless to say, we won't be seeing them again. What are you two up to?'

'Nothing much,' I said. 'Just a bit of detective work seeing as my fiancé might have ghosted me.'

Tiff sat down on the coffee table. 'No! Has he cut you off?'

I nodded, blinking back the ready tears.

'Why would he do that?' Leah cried. 'Why would he propose then dump you days later?'

'Your guess is as good as mine.' I stood up. I couldn't face going through it all again. 'I'm going to call it a night. See you in the morning.'

'Night, Jemma,' they chorused.

Drew caught my hand and gently squeezed it as I passed him. He'd been so supportive. I don't know what I'd have done without him.

As soon as I closed the door to the living area, I crumbled again. With Mum's Parkinson's diagnosis, if there was ever a time I needed Scott, it was right now. Yet, for whatever reason, he'd removed himself from my life and I felt completely and utterly bereft. Please let the company phone calls work because there was no way I could do what Drew had done and carry on for two-and-a-half years not knowing. I still felt like I had unfinished business with Dad, never getting to know who he really was – that caring side his colleagues and friends had seen – without having unfinished business with Scott too. Our relationship couldn't be over. It just couldn't be.

Yet it looked like it was, at least from his perspective, and I needed to know why.

* * *

My manager, Owen, sent me home the next day. He'd been out all morning so hadn't seen me until I met him for a meeting that afternoon about a large Steiff collection we'd been bequeathed. He took one look at my pale face and the bags under my eyes and said, 'Right, that's it! The meeting can wait until next week. You look like death warmed up. You need to get home and under your duvet right now.'

I protested that I wasn't ill – just worried about mum and a few other things. I couldn't bring myself to say I might have been ghosted, especially since I'd been bouncing off the walls with excitement on Monday as I flashed my engagement ring at all my colleagues.

'Worry can make us ill and we sometimes just need to rest,' Owen said. 'So off you go and I don't want to see you back until Monday. Go home and see your family again. Maybe accompany your mum to her doctor's appointment. And I don't expect you to take it as holiday. You've put in more than enough extra hours since you started here so let's call it a day and a bit in lieu.'

* * *

Walking through the door to the flat a little after 3.30 p.m., I found the list of companies we'd created last night on the coffee table along with a note from Drew:

Jemma
Sorry I missed you this morning. Hope you're OK.
Got called into work to cover sickness but managed to call the 1ˢᵗ 8 companies on the list before I left. Lots of bitchy receptionists playing 'gatekeeper' but I charmed the pants off them of course! None of them have a Scott Hastings working there. The numbers don't work for the 2 companies I've put a cross next to.
Sorry I couldn't do more, but I can probably call some more tomorrow after work.
Drew xx

I stood in the lounge with Drew's note in my hand. I liked the idea of going home again. If I tried some more numbers then packed, I'd miss the commuting crowd and would hopefully be able to bag a seat on the train.

Retrieving my laptop, a notepad, and a pen from my bedroom, I sat at the dining table and loaded up the first website while trying to psyche myself up to making the call. What would I say if I found the right company? *Hello, my name's Jemma Browne and the Scott Hastings who you've just said works for you asked me to marry him on Friday but seems to have deleted me from his life since then. Is there a way you can put me through to him so I find out what the hell's going on? Thank you so much for your help.*

Hmmm.

Sod it! I'd cross that bridge if it came to it. And it would never come to it if I didn't dial.

'Good afternoon, you're through to Energest Ltd, how may I help?' said a female in a sing-song tone when the first call connected.

'Hi, erm, yes, I wondered if you can help me. I'm trying to get hold of someone ... erm, someone I know... erm... Does a Scott Hastings work for you?'

'I'm sorry, but it's company policy that we don't give out the names of any staff members.'

'I'm not asking you to give out any names. I know his name. I just want to know if he works there.'

I could hear the sickly sweet smile in her tone and picture her rolling her eyes at a colleague or a visitor standing by the reception desk. 'I'm sorry, caller, but that's the same thing. I can't confirm or deny anyone works here.'

'That's ridiculous.'

'There are many very sensible reasons why we have this policy to safeguard our staff. Can I help you with anything else?'

'Yes. What would you have done if I'd asked straight out to be put through to Scott Hastings?'

'I'd have put you straight through if there was a Scott Hastings working here.'

'Then can you put me through to Scott Hastings please?'

'I'm sorry, we don't appear to have a Scott Hastings working here.'

'So why didn't you just say that in the first place?'

'Because I'm not permitted to give out staff names and you—'

I hung up. What a stupid, pointless conversation. But I'd learned a lesson. I brought up the next website and dialled the number.

'Hello, you're through to Atkinson and Associates, how may I direct your call?' It was a man this time.

'Hi, yes, erm... please can you put me through to Scott Hastings?'

'Scott Hastings?'

My stomach lurched. Was that a hint of recognition in his voice? 'Yes. Scott Hastings.'

'How are you spelling that?'

'Is there more than one way to spell it?'

'I don't think so, but I thought I'd better check. We've got a Scott Harris. He works out of our Dubai office. Is that who you're looking for?'

'No. Thank you anyway.'

I'd only called two companies and I was already losing the will to live. I owed Drew big time for getting through eight. I logged onto the next company website.

'Good morning... sorry... afternoon,' giggled a female with a Welsh accent. 'It's been a long day! The Kelshaw Group. Tegan speaking.'

'Hi. Can you put me through to Scott Hastings please?'

'One moment.' Some hideously tinny hold music started and so did the racing of my heart. Did that mean Tegan was about to put me through? Was I about to speak to Scott? What if he refused to take the call? What if he cut me off?

The music stopped. 'Sorry, what was that name again?'

My heart sank. 'Scott Hastings.'

'Bear with me a moment.'

I stared at my laptop as various photos scrolled on the company's website: buildings, pylons, waves, machines, tools, engineering drawings. Yawn!

The music stopped again. 'I'm sorry to keep you. I'm having a bit of a trouble finding a Scott Hastings, but I'm temping here. It's only my first day. Does he definitely work here?'

I hesitated then crossed my fingers. It was easier not to explain. 'Yes.'

'I'm looking down the list and he's not on it, but my colleague did say that it's a bit out of date. Has he worked here for long?'

'Quite a few years.'

'Oh. Then he should be on this list. Let me try one more place.' She didn't bother putting me on hold this time. I could hear her riffling through some papers and muttering under her breath. I continued to stare at the photos on the website. More pylons... lightning bolt (quite pretty that one) ... some sort of power station... Oh. My. God!

'That's him!' I squealed.

'What's him?' Tegan asked.

'On your website. Can you get your website up? There's a photo of two men at an exhibition. Scott's the one on the left. I've found him! He *definitely* works for you.' I clicked on the photo to stop it scrolling.

'Just a second. Let me get onto the right photo. One moment. Erm... Hilary? I've got a caller who wants to speak to Scott Hastings but I can't find him. She says he's in this picture.'

'Which picture?' said a muffled voice. 'Give me the phone a minute.' There were some scrabbling sounds as the phone was passed over. 'Hello, you're through to Hilary on reception. Can I help you?'

'Yes. I'm trying to get through to Scott Hastings but Tegan can't find him. He's in the picture on your website, though. The one at the exhibition.'

'I'm looking at it now. The one on the left or the right?'

'The one on the left as you look at it. The younger one.'

'That's Adam. Adam Hannigan.'

'No. Adam's Scott's colleague. Who's the other one?'

'That's Ian Pilsner. He left the company last year. Goodness, we must get this photo updated.'

'No. That can't be right. Are you looking at a photo of two men holding clipboards in front of a banner that says, "Into the Future"?'

'Yes.'

'The younger one with the dark hair and jacket is...?

'Adam Hannigan,' Hilary said.

'And the one with blond hair and no jacket is...?'

'Ian Pilsner.'

'You're absolutely sure the dark-haired one in the jacket isn't Scott Hastings?'

'I'm sorry, but I don't know a Scott Hastings. That's definitely Adam Hannigan. Did you want to speak to Adam?'

I felt sick. My mouth kept opening and closing but I couldn't form any words.

'Hello? Are you still there?'

'Yes,' I whispered.

'Did you want to speak to Adam...?'

I shook my head, which I knew was pointless over the phone, but I couldn't speak. Several phones were now ringing in the background.

'...because if you do, you're best leaving it a couple of weeks. You might find it easier to drop him an email. It's adam.hannigan@kelshawgroup.com. Is there anything else I can help you with?' The phones were still ringing and I could hear the urgency in Hilary's voice to get me off the phone.

'No. That's all.'

'Thanks for calling The Kelshaw Group. Goodbye.'

Adam Hannigan? ADAM HANNIGAN? What the hell was going on? There was only one way to find out.

To: Adam Hannigan
From: Jemma Browne
Subject: Important Question
Hi Scott ... or should it be Adam?

I'm sorry to contact you at work but, given that you seem to have cut contact through any other method, I don't think you've left me much choice.

I just have one question for you: WHY?

My mum has been diagnosed with Parkinson's. I needed you and you weren't here. I've got the message loud and clear that you don't want to be, but I think you owe it to me to explain why, including why you lied about your name. Don't you?

A reply came back instantly.

To: Jemma Browne
From: Adam Hannigan
Subject: Out of Office Response RE: Important Question
I'm on paternity leave for two weeks. Back on 11th July. Please contact John Eccles in my absence.

Oh! I guess that answered my question.

10

JEMMA

'Are you sure there's nothing wrong?' Mum flashed me a sideways concerned look as she drove us to her appointment with the consultant the following afternoon. 'You don't seem yourself. Whilst I'm thrilled to have you home for two weekends in a row, I can't help thinking it's because something's wrong.'

I *was* going to tell her – no secrets – but I wanted to focus on the appointment. If she knew about Scott, she'd suggest cancelling or, if it went ahead, she'd be distracted. We had the rest of Friday and the whole weekend ahead of us. I'd tell her when the timing was better.

Trying to smile when my world had fallen apart wasn't easy. 'I'm tired. Still recovering from last weekend. I don't think I can party as hard as I used to.'

Mum laughed. 'Lightweight. Wait till you hit my age. Then you'll *really* have something to complain about.'

She knew, of course. She knew I was lying, but she also knew me well enough to accept that I'd tell her when I was ready.

I stared out of the window, a lump constricting my throat, while she sang along to 'All You Need is Love' by The Beatles playing on Bay Radio. Of all the songs in the world, why did they have to play that one? Scott was a massive Beatles fan; this was his absolute favourite track of theirs. 'Pure pop perfection,' he called it. He often sang it to me then he'd say, 'Whatever life throws at us, all we need is love to get us through it.' We'd laugh at the cheesiness but I loved it when he said that. It made me feel really special.

Had he said exactly the same thing to the woman who'd given birth to his baby? Or babies perhaps. The more I thought about the last text he'd sent me before he ghosted me – *Adam's wife had twins yesterday. Boy and girl. 8 weeks early and not doing so well. Feel a bit helpless* – the more convinced I was that he'd been talking about himself. Maybe *Scott* loved me only, but Scott only existed in the imagination of some bloke called Adam who I didn't know from... er... Adam!

At the flat, I'd stared at the out of office email, my stomach doing somersaults. In a frenzy, I clicked onto LinkedIn – somewhere I'd never previously thought to look – just in case Hilary on reception had made a mistake. There he was: Scott Hastings staring back at me under the profile of Adam Hannigan. Dashing to the bathroom, I'd slumped over the toilet bowl, gasping for breath, but nothing came up. Somehow I found the strength to haul myself to my feet. I brushed my teeth, splashed some water over my face and, in auto-pilot, packed a bag for the weekend.

I'd half expected to find mismatched outfits and no knickers when I arrived at Mum's but somehow I'd managed to throw in enough clothes to avoid clashing colours or a patterns and patterns disaster.

Catching the tube to Kings Cross last night, I'd felt like I was in a dream. Faces seemed fuzzy, colours blended into each other, and noises were muffled as though I was underwater. On the train to York, I'd stared at the blurred fields and hedgerows through the window, replaying every single conversation I could remember having with Scott, trying to make sense of the lie I'd lived for the past eighteen months. I wanted to disbelieve it. I wanted that so badly but the photo-graphic and written evidence had been there.

I'd suggested going on holiday abroad on several occasions but he'd said he wanted to wait until he felt more financially stable at work. I'd offered to pay for us both but he'd refused. I'd thought that was about him wanting to pay his own way but it had clearly been because it was impossible for him to go on holiday with me. How would he have explained the passport in a different name? What would he have told his wife?

And no wonder I'd never been able to visit him. The story about him giving up his rented flat because he was always on the road had seemed so plausible yet it had obviously been exactly that: a story. Presumably he didn't travel nearly as much as I'd thought. All those times when he'd arranged to call me, he'd probably been sat in his car round the corner from his family home. No wonder he'd never wanted to FaceTime me from his 'hotel'; the game would have been up.

I thought back to that final conversation at the races when he'd said he had something he wanted to say to me. What if it hadn't been that he wanted to elope? What if he'd been planning to confess about his secret life as Adam Hannigan? What if he was going to tell me about the wife and twins but he'd chickened out? Because, let's face it, how do you tell the woman you've just proposed to that you can't actually get married to her because you're already married to someone else? Oh, and she won't become Mrs Hastings because that's not your name? And when he'd said that he wasn't perfect, had he been trying to tell me about his real identity then? Was it my fault? Had I not given him the opportunity to confess? No! I couldn't blame myself. This was all Scott. When I'd met him that stormy January evening, I hadn't said, 'Hi, my name's Jemma. What's your name, but please give me a fake name rather than your real one?'

'We're here,' Mum said, jolting me back to the present. 'It's party time!'

I knew she was worried despite the joviality. 'How are you feeling?' I asked as we walked across the car park towards the hospital entrance.

'Great.' She shook her head and sighed. 'Nervous. I've had a couple of bad days this week. They're getting more frequent. I'm worried he might tell me I can't drive.'

At the start of the week, in between bombarding Scott with emails, texts and voicemails, I'd spent my evenings researching Parkinson's and knew that the driving ban was a very real risk. 'Have you had any stiff-ening whilst driving?'

'Not yet, but I think it's only a matter of time. When I've got up and known it's a bad day, I've caught the bus to the shop. At the moment, there are more good days than bad, but I'm expecting that to change.'

'Today's a good day?'

'It's an okay day.'

'What's a bad day like?'

Mum stopped. 'You really want to know?'

I nodded. 'You joked that climbing the stairs feels like climbing Everest but, funnily enough, I've never done that. I'm guessing you mean it's slow and painful?'

Mum linked my arm and pulled gently on it to indicate we should continue walking. 'Remember that time you did cross country at school and you got cramp so badly when you were running across Moor View Farm that you couldn't stay on your feet? You said you've never been in so much pain in your life.'

Despite it being fifteen years ago, I could still remember that day clearly, writhing around on the grass in agony, clutching onto my leg. 'It's like that?'

'It can be. And, when it is, it's not just in one calf. It's like every muscle in my legs has tensed from my hips to my toes. It's like my joints are on fire. It's like my legs are about to explode which I hope they don't because that wouldn't be pretty.'

'Oh Mum!' My heart broke for her having to go through this.

'Other days, I don't have cramps, but I can barely move. It feels like my feet are encased in cement and I can't budge, like that first time in my workshop. Then there's the exhaustion. I get up and my whole body aches. You know that feeling you get if you've been decorating or gardening all day and your muscles feel tired and heavy? It's like that. Then there's the times when I get all fidgety and can't sit still. There's this feeling of restlessness throughout my body and I have to move. But when I move, it's slow. What's that all about? Do you want me to go on?'

We stopped again and a tear slipped down my cheek as I hugged her.

'Sorry, Jem,' she whispered into my hair, 'but you asked and we don't keep secrets in this family, so I hope you're going to tell me yours after my appointment.'

'I will. I promise. Let's focus on you for now, though.'

We set off towards the hospital again.

'Have you been okay at work?' I asked. 'Have you told Annie and Liv?' Annie worked full-time in Bear With Me and Liv worked weekends but also provided cover for when Mum was running workshops or working away.

'They both know and they've been really supportive. Liv has already said that, if I wake up and can't face it, I'm to give her a call and she can cover but I'm sure it won't come to that for a long time. It'll take more than a Parkinson's diagnosis to hold me back.'

Poor Mum. She was putting on a brave face and she'd even tried to sound upbeat as she'd described her condition, but this had knocked her for six and I could tell she was struggling to cope with it. She'd always been a bundle of energy, balancing her valuing roles, bear-making, travel, the shop, and being a mum. If Parkinson's was slowing her down, it followed that she was going to have to slow down her workload at some point. And she wasn't going to like that. At all. I suspected that things were about to get very difficult.

11

SAM

'Oh my God! I *love* Whitsborough Bay!' Tania exclaimed, eyes shining with excitement. She was one of the nurses from the neurology department and she'd insisted I join her table in the crowded pub. She'd done a round of introductions but I'd already forgotten most of the names. I hated being the new guy.

'My grandparents used to hire a static caravan there every summer and my brother and I would go and stay with them.' She grinned at me. 'You're so lucky to have lived there.'

Lucky? I had been when Nikki had been with me. I smiled politely. Whenever I mentioned being from Whitsborough Bay, the response was always the same – gushing childhood memories like Tania's or complete oblivion as to where it was.

'My grandparents used to do the same,' said another of the nurses. Ellen? Helen? Helena? Something like that. 'I remember there being this pool when I was little which filled with seawater. It was freezing in there.'

'I think it had closed down when we started going,' Tania said. 'I remember the slide pool, though.'

And then they were off, reminiscing about holidays spent in my hometown while I sat on the periphery wondering what the hell I was doing there.

It was a Friday night and nearly two weeks had passed since the wedding that wasn't. That had been one seriously tough weekend. I'd always be grateful to my brother for being there and helping support me through it. I'm not sure what I'd have done if I'd been on my own. I'd known it was going to be hard but the outpouring of grief had been unexpected and overwhelming. And probably long overdue.

On the Sunday night after Jack left, I lay down on the sofa holding onto a framed photo of Nikki and me that I'd taken with a selfie stick shortly after I proposed. Nikki was holding her hand up, flashing off her ring. The campervan was behind us and the sea behind that, capturing everything we loved in one shot. We adored that photo. We both looked so happy and in love which, of course, we were. After telling our immediate families, we'd used the photo to announce our engagement on social media, then had a copy printed and framed. We'd even discussed having a muted version of it as the background for the seating plan at our wedding.

Running my fingers lightly across her beautiful face, I realised one thing: Nikki would have been heartbroken to see me like this. She'd been such a vibrant person who'd embraced spontaneity and had lived every moment to the full. She'd have wanted me to continue to do the same and I *was* going to. It might take time and there'd be several setbacks, but I'd get there eventually.

The starting point was to stop turning down invitations from work colleagues. I was lonely in London but that was my fault. My colleagues had tried to get to know me and I'd turned away from them all. Not anymore. Which was why I was now surrounded by doctors, nurses, consultants and admin staff packed into The Dog and Duck round the corner from the hospital. One of the doctors was going on a one-year sabbatical to Africa. I didn't even know which doctor it was so felt like a right fraud attending their leaving do.

I finished my pint and wondered whether I could slip out quietly. I doubted anyone would notice. The conversation about Whitsborough

Bay continued round me but I wasn't part of it. To my right, a few colleagues were having a conversation about the latest Marvel film. A long-time fan, I itched to join in the discussion. But what if they started talking about Thor? What if one of them decided, like Nikki, that I looked like Chris Hemsworth. Would I be able to hold it together?

I picked up my empty glass and headed towards the bar, trying to convince myself to stay for one more. The queue was three people deep and there were only two very fraught-looking staff members serving. I looked back towards the seat I'd just vacated. Someone was already in it.

I recognised several colleagues but they were all engrossed in conversations with people I didn't know. Nikki would have barged in and started chatting, but I wasn't Nikki. I'd made a start. I'd accepted an invite out, and I'd had one drink. That would have to do for now. As I always told my patients, it was about making adjustments, one step at a time. I'd taken my first step.

Opening the heavy wooden door, I slipped outside, hoping nobody would notice and call me back. I was still looking back when I reached the corner and smacked straight into someone, knocking them to the ground.

'Shit! Sorry! Are you okay?' I dropped to my knees beside the young woman.

She looked up and smiled. I clocked the streak of cerise pink in her long blonde hair and recognised her as one of the nurses from the hospital. She reached out her hand and I gently helped her to her feet.

'Nothing broken,' she reassured me, brushing her uniform down. 'Although I reckon I'll have a huge bruise on my arse after that.'

'I'm really sorry. I wasn't looking where I was going.'

'No shit! Where were you off to in such a hurry? Pub's that way.' She pointed in the direction of The Dog and Duck.

I shrugged. 'I know. I've already been.'

She laughed. 'That good, was it?'

I wasn't sure how to respond.

'I'm Tiff, by the way. I've seen you around but there's never been the opportunity for a proper intro. Dr Jones, isn't it?'

She held out her hand which I shook. 'Yes, but please call me Sam.'

'Sam? That's a shame.'

'What is?'

She gave me a cheeky wink. 'I was kind of hoping it was Indiana. Oh God! You've probably heard that loads, haven't you?'

I smiled. 'Once or twice perhaps.'

Tiff visibly cringed. 'Sorry.'

'It's fine. It doesn't bother me. My brother's a consultant neurologist too and so was our dad before he retired so we have three Dr Jones's in our family. Makes me feel quite special having an action hero's name. The connections don't stop there, either. Sam Jones played Flash Gordon in the eighties classic and my fiancée thinks I look like Chris Hemsworth's Thor so I've—' I stopped dead. What was I saying? This was the longest non-medical conversation I'd had with anyone since moving to London and I'd just spoken about Nikki as though she was still alive.

'Are you okay?' Tiff asked.

I frowned and ran my hand over my stubble. 'I'm fine. Sorry. I've got to go. It was nice meeting you, Tiff.'

'And you. You're sure I can't tempt you back for another drink?'

'I'd love to but I'm meeting someone and I'm already late.'

'Your fiancée?'

'No... She's er...' I couldn't just blurt out that she was dead, especially after I'd just spoken as though she was very much with us.

'Another time then,' Tiff suggested before the silence became awkward. 'My cousin, Drew, and I like to make it our mission to help newbies settle in, especially when they're new to the big smoke. He's a nurse too. He's also a superhero geek and *Flash Gordon* is one of his favourite films so he's going to be gutted he missed you. Drinks another time?'

I nodded. 'Thanks. I might take you both up on that. See you.'

'See you, Indy.'

We set off in opposite directions. I stopped and turned round. 'Tiff,' I called. 'You want to know the real reason I left the pub early? It's full of snakes and I hate snakes.'

Tiff laughed at the film reference and waved.

I smiled as I made my way towards the tube station. Human interaction. A proper conversation. And a joke. Another small step.

12

JEMMA

I lay on the sofa on my back with my laptop resting on my stomach, staring at a slideshow of photos of Scott and selfies of us together. Every so often I paused the slideshow and clicked onto his company's website or LinkedIn, shaking my head at the photos of Adam.

It was nearly two weeks since his text announcing the birth of Adam's twins and just over a week since I'd discovered that he was actually Adam and concluded that the twins were his. I couldn't make sense of it. Who was the man I'd fallen in love with in January last year? The man I'd given my heart to? The man who I'd planned to spend the rest of my life with? Had any part of our time together been real or had I just been a bit of fun between work commitments? But if that was all I'd meant to him, why propose? Why take it to that next step?

Mum had stared at me, ashen-faced, when I'd told her my news after her appointment with the consultant. She kept saying, 'There must be some mistake.' I recognised the denial as I'd been there myself.

I logged onto Adam's LinkedIn profile and showed her. Feeling irritated that she still doubted it when I needed her to be focused on helping me get through this, I Googled 'Adam Hannigan' to see what else I could find. I wished I hadn't. It turned out my social media-hating ex-fiancé had a Facebook and Instagram account under his real identity and wasn't very careful with his privacy settings. I uncovered images of his house (pretty three-bedroom semi in a village outside Nottingham), his wife (Fiona, married for four years), his dog (a cute black pug called Bracken), and his new twins, as yet unnamed. I saw nights out with friends, holidays, and Christmases. When I clicked on a Facebook photo album entitled, 'Our Wedding', Mum leaned forward and closed my laptop. 'Enough, Jemma,' she said. 'I believe you. You don't need to torture yourself with those.' She'd wrapped her arms round me and we'd cried together.

A key turning in the lock jolted me back to the present. Leah was away for the weekend on a hen do, and Tiff and Drew had been out to a leaving do for a work colleague which had obviously been a good night given the late hour.

'How was it?' I asked, peeking over the top of the sofa.

'Jemma! You scared the life out of me.' Tiff snapped the light on as she pushed the flat door closed. 'What are you sitting in the dark for?'

I shrugged. 'Thinking.'

She headed into the kitchen area and flicked the kettle on. 'About your lovely mum or about that lying, deceiving, two-timing twat?'

I put my laptop down and sat up properly so I could see her. 'Both.'

She spooned coffee into a mug and held up the jar and spoon as a question, but I shook my head. I was finding it hard enough sleeping as it was without giving myself a caffeine rush at 1.00 a.m.

'No Drew?' I asked.

'Lucky bugger pulled. He's gone clubbing.'

'It wasn't Dr Jones, was it?'

She laughed. 'He wishes, but the gorgeous Dr Jones has a fiancée.'

'You've been doing some detective work?'

'Nope. Didn't have to. Got it straight from the horse's mouth.'

'He was there? You spoke to him?'

'Only because he ran into me and knocked me flying.'

'Seriously?'

'Seriously. I have a bruise and everything. Anyway, we had a brief chat and first impressions are good.'

'Shame about the fiancée thing.'

Tiff shrugged as she poured boiling water into her mug. 'I'm not bothered. As I've said to you before, I wouldn't date anyone from work. It's not worth the hassle. Besides, Dr Jones may be hot but he's far too immaculate for me. Give me a beard, tattoos and piercings any day.'

She tossed the teaspoon towards the sink. It bounced off the rim and skidded along the worktop. Shaking her head at it, she left it where it was and joined me in the lounge area.

'So, your mum and the twat. Tell me more. I take it he hasn't been in touch.'

'No, although unless he's checking his work emails while he's on paternity leave, he won't know he's been rumbled.'

'And you've kept your promise not to get in touch on his real Facebook account? Because it won't come to any good if you do.'

'I know. And, yes, I've kept my promise.' I'd discussed it with my three flatmates and we'd collectively decided there was no point contacting him because he'd likely ignore my messages considering he'd already ghosted me. But my resolve was weakening.

'I still can't believe he lied to you like that.'

'Neither can I. I keep going back over conversations we've had, wondering if there were clues that he was living a double life but I can't think of anything. I'm so confused, Tiff. He seemed so genuine. I'm sure he loved me. There must be an explanation. I know we said he'd probably ignore me if I contact him on his real Facebook page but it's so tempting to try. I can't stand not knowing. Maybe he—'

'Jemma! Stop it!'

I flinched at Tiff's sharp tone.

'Sorry, but you seriously need to stop it. I know you loved him so this is going to sound really harsh but it has to be said. Scott or Adam or whatever his name is lied to you for eighteen months. He lied about his identity, he lied about where he lived, he lied about his wife, and he lied about her pregnancy. He seemed like the genuine article, but he wasn't. Stop trying to give him the benefit of the doubt. He lied to you about who he was, Jem, and he was good at it because he had us all fooled. And, much as I hate to say this, if he's that good an actor, it's highly possible that he lied to you about his feelings too.'

'Then why ask me to marry him?'

'Why not? In all likelihood, a proposal was a continuation of the fake world that he'd created. He was never going to leave his wife and twins for you. I've seen the photos. I've seen how happy they are together.'

I opened my laptop and clicked onto the slideshow, thrusting it into her eyeline. 'Are you saying we're not happy in these photos? That's not fake. It's real!'

Tiff sighed as she watched the photos scrolling. 'I don't know. The whole thing is pretty messed up if you ask me. Either he's acting with both of you, acting with one of you, or he actually loves you both. Whichever it is, he's not worth another minute of your time. Keep remembering that when you met him, he was married. He introduced himself to you under a fake name and he slept with you that night. It could have ended there and you'd never have known he wasn't really Scott Hastings, but he kept the lie going. Remember that all those texts and the occasional FaceTime conversation at very specific times weren't from hotel rooms. They could have been from his bedroom in the home he shared with his wife while she was watching telly in the lounge. He was having sex with you and he was having sex with her. He has to have been. Twins don't appear out of nowhere. I know you want answers, but you're not going to get them, Jem. If he did respond to you, is there anything he could possibly say to make this messed up shit better? Of course there isn't! Walk away knowing that *you* did nothing wrong but *he* set out to deceive both you and his wife from the outset. That's not a person you want or need in your life.'

I closed my laptop and placed it on the coffee table with shaky hands.

'I'm sorry.' Tiff affectionately patted my leg. 'I'm worried about you.'

'I know.' I couldn't bring myself to look at her.

'I don't mean to lecture you.'

'I know.'

'Tell me about your mum, instead. How's she doing?'

Tiff had upset me and I wanted to walk out the room, but I knew it was only because she cared. And she was right, even if I didn't want to admit it. Truth hurts.

'Good days and bad days,' I said, finally looking up. 'I didn't warm to her consultant and Mum can't stand him either. About the only helpful thing he did was giving her a lecture for not doing any exercise. He said that being too busy at work to find time for it would be an excuse she regretted when the symptoms worsened. I lectured her too, then Karen and Rachel came round and had a go. She's now doing yoga and Pilates with Karen several times a week. It's early days but Karen reckons it's already making a difference. The next step is convincing her to cut back on her time at Bear With Me but that will be like convincing her it would be a good idea to chop off her right arm. That place is her life. I know it'll be hard for her to ease back from it but, for the sake of her health, she needs to.'

Tiff stared at me for a moment, then smiled. 'It's hard when someone you care about needs to walk away but won't, isn't it?' She stood up. 'I'm off to bed. Night.'

'Night.'

I watched Tiff go through the door to the bedrooms and nodded. She was right. I should walk away from Scott and put the sorry episode behind me filed under 'serious case of misdirected trust'.

But I wasn't sure if I could.

13

'Are you expecting an important call?' Owen paused by the display of early twentieth century teddy bears I was stock-taking, cleaning, and rearranging on Monday morning.

I stepped down from the kick-stool, my heart racing. Had Scott called the museum? 'Why? Has someone phoned?'

'No. But I've walked through here several times this morning and you've been checking your phone every time.'

'Oh my God! Have I? I didn't realise. I'm so sorry, Owen. I'll stay late.'

He shook his head. 'You're not in trouble and I don't expect you to stay late. I'm just a concerned boss and friend. Is your mum okay?'

I blushed. 'Yes and no. It's not Mum, though. It's…' I shook my head and lowered my eyes. 'It's Scott.'

'That waste of space? What are you in touch with him for?' I'd told Owen my sorry tale last week after returning from my weekend in Whitsborough Bay. I'd removed my engagement ring and he was the sort who'd have noticed so I'd wanted to get in there first with the explanation.

'I'm not in touch with him,' I said. 'He's ghosted me, remember? The thing is, he'll be back from paternity leave today. He'll have picked up my email to him at work and know that I've discovered his true identity. I'm not expecting a call, but I'm half-expecting a text or an email from him.'

Owen's expression softened. 'From what you've told me, I don't think you'll hear from him again. I'm sorry, Jemma.'

I nodded. 'I know. You're right. That's why I'm only *half*-expecting it.'

'If he did text or email, what are you hoping he'll say?'

Good question. 'I suppose the daydream is that it's all been a big mistake and he really is Scott Hastings, but that's not going to happen is it? Maybe an explanation? Or an apology? Or both?'

A small group of visitors entered the room. 'Don't get your hopes up,' Owen whispered, heading off in the opposite direction.

'Easier said than done,' I muttered under my breath.

I moved the kick-stool aside so the visitors could see the display more clearly and hovered nearby, answering a few questions about the various bears.

'You're so lucky working here,' said an elderly lady with a Cornish accent. 'Although I'd never get any work done if it were me. I'd be stroking the bears all day, I would.'

I smiled. 'Oh, I do that too! It's in my job description. And hugging them. They get upset otherwise.'

'It would be my dream job,' gushed her friend. 'I don't think anything would get me down if I was surrounded by bears all day.'

Thanking me for answering their questions, they disappeared into the next room ten minutes later, leaving me pondering on their comments. Yes, I was lucky. I had my dream job working with something I'd been passionate about since childhood. I often put in long hours but it never felt like work. But since Scott had disappeared from my life, the joy had gone. I'd stopped looking at the bears and had just been getting on with my work on autopilot while my mind flitted from the lie that the last eighteen months of my life had been, to worries about the future and what that meant for Mum.

I *would* get the joy back. As hurtful as it was, I needed to put my time with Scott behind me, accept it was over, and stop trying to find an explanation for what he'd done. Tiff was right. Was there ever going to be an explanation that would be acceptable for his infidelity and justify the fake identity from the outset?

I shook my head. Scott meant nothing to me. He wasn't worth another minute of my time. Owen was right. Leah, Drew, Mum and Karen were right. He was clearly a very cruel person and it was fortunate that it had come to light so I could move on. From now on, I was going to focus on the important things in life: my job, my friends, and my family. Although Mum assured me she was coping with the Parkinson's and was finally exercising, I couldn't shake this feeling that there was something else going on with her and being there for her and for Logan absolutely had to be my number one priority.

* * *

Throwing myself into my work for the rest of the day, I finished the display I'd been working on by mid-afternoon then caught up with some paperwork in the office. My phone stayed in my drawer, out of sight and out of mind. I could do this.

Bidding goodnight to Owen, I flicked through my emails on my phone as I left the building. It was part of my going-home routine, deleting all the marketing emails that had materialised throughout the day.

As I reached for the final internal door, I stopped dead. Oh my God! He'd emailed.

To: Jemma Browne
From: Adam Hannigan
Subject: Sorry

I've started and deleted this email so many times. I'm so sorry, Jemma. It seems such an inadequate word for what I've done to you but please know that I wasn't lying when I said that I love you only. I still do and I always will. Please forgive me.

I'm sorry to hear about your mum. I hope she responds well to treatment. Thinking of you all and missing you like crazy xxx

What the hell was he playing at? He loved me only? He still did? Kisses? As my stomach churned and my heart raced, I was back to square one. Despite everything he'd done, he still meant the world to me and I missed him like crazy too.

14

'What do you fancy seeing?' Leah asked as we stood in the cinema lobby checking out the viewing times on Thursday evening.

'Anything but romance.'

'Still no word since Monday's email?'

'No. All quiet again. Do you think it's my fault? Should I have emailed him back?'

'Of course not! Unless it was to give him a mouthful. He's a lying, cheating... Seriously, Jemma, he's not someone you want or need in your life. You've got your apology. You've got your closure. Move on.'

'I don't know if I can.' I shuffled over to a nearby leather sofa, suddenly feeling quite weak. 'I still don't know why he did it. And he says he still loves me.'

Leah plonked herself down beside me. 'Listen to me, Jemma Browne. I know you loved him, I know you'd planned to spend the rest of your life with him, and I know you're hurting like hell right now, but you won't always feel this way. There are loads of clichés about time healing and the reason there are loads of them is because it's true. The pain goes and people move on with their lives. Most of us get our hearts broken at some point. Sometimes several times. Hello!' She pointed both her thumbs towards her chest to indicate her unlucky-in-love status. Leah didn't do steady burn. She either didn't feel the chemistry and moved on immediately before allowing anything to develop, or she felt the fizz and fell big time. Usually it wasn't reciprocal.

I picked at a loose thread dangling from the hem of my coat. 'What if I still love him?'

'Do you?'

'I might do.'

'DO YOU?'

I shrunk in my seat, trying to avoid the gazes Leah's shout had attracted. 'Yes. Don't get mad with me. I can't help it. I hate him for what he's done to me and his wife, but I still love him. There's no switch to magically turn off my feelings.'

Leah put her arm round me and I rested my head on her shoulder. 'What are we going to do with you?'

'Give me time, I suppose.'

She squeezed my arm then helped me to my feet. 'Come on. We'll do horror. Maybe we can scare those feelings out of you.'

Five minutes later, we'd purchased our tickets and were in the queue for snacks. Leah refused to watch a film without popcorn and a large Sprite.

I delved into my bag as my phone started ringing. 'Hi Tiff.'

'Where are you?'

'At the cinema with Leah, queuing for popcorn.'

'You need to come home.'

'Are you okay? Is Drew?'

Leah raised her eyebrows questioningly. I shrugged.

'It's Scott,' Tiff said. 'He's here.'

'At the flat?' I grabbed Leah's arm and pulled her out of the queue.

'Yes.'

'What does he want?'

'To beg you to run away to a Mormon community in America and set up home with his many wives and children? I don't bloody know.

Funnily enough, I didn't fancy a cup of tea, a garibaldi biscuit, and a nice chat with him.' I winced at her sarcasm.

'We're leaving now.' I pulled Leah towards the door. 'I'm sorry, Tiff. Are you going to be okay on your own with him?' We set off in the direction of the flat.

'I'm not with him. Drew is.'

'Is he giving him a hard time?'

'He wanted to but he decided that's your place so, instead, he's staring him out and refusing to speak to him.'

I could imagine Scott sitting on the chair with Drew on the coffee table, legs almost touching, intimidating the hell out of him.

'Is Scott drunk?' I asked.

'I don't think so.'

'What do you think I should do?'

'Push the twat out of the kitchen window and hope he doesn't bounce.'

Despite my anxiety, I couldn't help but laugh. 'And a sensible suggestion would be...?'

'Send him packing, of course. Jemma! You're not seriously thinking of taking him back, are you?'

I paused for a moment. Was I? When I'd been talking to Leah earlier, Scott had gone silent on me again so it wasn't a possibility. But if he was at the flat...? 'I don't know what to think about anything at the moment. I'm so confused.'

'You loved *Scott,* Jemma, but *Scott* doesn't exist. He's a figment of Adam's imagination. You don't love Adam. You don't even *know* Adam, for God's sake. And Adam's the one who's real. Unfortunately.'

I didn't want to argue with her. 'I'll see you shortly.'

'Don't take him back. He's a liar. From the minute you met him, he's deceived you. Don't lose sight of that.'

* * *

Scott – I couldn't think of him as Adam – and Drew both stood up when I pushed open the door to the flat.

'Jemma!' Scott sheepishly held up a bunch of flowers.

As Leah and I had raced back to the flat, I'd wondered how I was going to react when I came face to face with him. Would I burst into tears and rush to hug him? Would I feel numb? Sick? Angry? Really, really angry. Looking at him now with his pathetic peace-offering, I saw red.

'You really think a paltry bunch of supermarket flowers can make up for what you've done?'

He looked down at them, shamefaced. 'There were no proper florist shops open.'

'Oh my God, Scott! You're missing the point. It's the flowers, not the origin. After what you've done, you seriously expect a bunch of flowers to fix it?'

'No, but...'

Drew walked towards me, and touched my arm. 'Do you want me to stay?'

I shook my head. 'Thanks, though.'

'We're in our rooms if you need us.' He rubbed my arm, then turned round to face Scott. 'You!' He pointed two fingers towards his eyes then towards Scott. Very childish but I appreciated the gesture.

My three flatmates headed to their rooms. I dropped my bag on the floor, shrugged off my coat and hung it up on one of the hooks by the door while trying to slow my racing heart. Why did he have to be so damned gorgeous? He was wearing his charcoal grey suit and a sky blue shirt – the outfit he knew I found sexiest. He wasn't playing fair.

I strode into the lounge area and sat down on the armchair opposite him.

'You look amazing, Jemma,' he said.

'Yes, well, I was out on a date when I got Tiff's call.'

He looked pretty devastated. Good. 'You're seeing someone else?'

It was so tempting to keep it up, but I wasn't a liar like him. I sighed. 'No. I think you'll find it's you who's seeing someone else, not me. Do you really think I could move on that quickly? This happens to be what I wore to work today and I was at the cinema with Leah just now.'

He nodded, a clear expression of relief on his face.

Silence.

I stared at him, an eyebrow raised slightly in question. I wasn't going to make this easy for him.

He gulped. 'How's your mum? I was so sorry to hear about the Parkinson's.'

'Not good, but shit happens. And speaking of shit happening, why are you here?' I sounded more confident than I felt. My stomach was in knots.

He visibly squirmed. 'I've made a huge mistake.'

'Just the one?'

'No. Loads of them. I don't know what I was thinking.'

'Neither do I. I'm so tempted to kick you out of here, but the part of me that needs to know why you did what you did won't let me. Let's start at the beginning, shall we? You're married. Tell me about that. The truth this time.'

He nodded slowly. 'Yes, I'm married. Her name's Fiona and we were mates at school.'

'And? You need to give me a bit more than that. Not *too* detailed, though. I don't want to hear the graphic stuff.'

'I wouldn't do that to you.'

'Yeah, well, I thought you wouldn't cheat on me but life's full of surprises, isn't it?'

He shrugged. 'I guess so. So, Fi and I hung out at school. Just as friends. When she was eighteen, she moved in with this really rough bloke, Begsey, who didn't believe that men and women could be friends and kept accusing me of trying it on with *his* woman. My girlfriend at the time was jealous of Fi too so we drifted apart to save our relationships. A couple of years later, I bumped into Fi. She'd lost weight, she had a black eye, and she looked awful. She told me she'd walked into a kitchen cupboard she'd left open, but I wasn't buying it. She'd never been a good liar.'

'Unlike you.' I couldn't help myself.

He stared at me for a moment then nodded. 'I deserved that but I promise what I'm telling you tonight is the absolute truth.'

'We'll see. Go on...'

'We went for a coffee. Long story short, Begsey was beating her up but had managed to convince her that it was all her fault for not cooking his dinner or not keeping the house tidy or for dressing the wrong way. I begged her to leave him but she wouldn't. She said she loved him and he'd promised her he'd change. A couple of months later, she discovered she was pregnant. The beatings hadn't stopped and she was scared of losing the baby. I helped her to move out and into my spare room. Unfortunately she *did* lose the baby. It could have been one of those things but it could have been Begsey's fault. I convinced her to report him and helped her through the court case.'

A huge lump formed in my throat at the thought of him falling in love with and marrying someone else. And, much as I wanted to hate his wife, my heart went out to her... if he wasn't lying again.

'How long have you been married?' I already knew from his real Facebook profile but I wanted to hear it from him.

'Four years. Our friendship developed and, after a couple of rough relationships myself, I mistook it for love and I asked her to marry me. It's been good but, after I met you, I realised that—'

'Why the false name?' I snapped. I wasn't ready to hear the, 'I don't love her, I love you,' spiel which was clearly where this was heading. 'Were you worried I'd find you on Facebook and discover you were really married?'

He shook his head. 'It was nothing like that. It's so stupid. Fi and I went through this phase at school where we had to introduce ourselves to strangers using the name of a character from a cartoon, film or TV series. It was obvious stuff like Mickey Mouse or Luke Skywalker. After we got married, we started it up again but with slightly more obscure characters. If the stranger recognised the name and mentioned it you lost and had to do the ironing for a month. If you got away with it, the other one had to do the ironing.' His cheeks flushed.

'So you're telling me that Scott Hastings literally is a fictional character?'

He nodded. 'Fi loves *Strictly Come Dancing* and a friend introduced her to this Australian film from the nineties called *Strictly Ballroom*. Have you seen it?'

'I think so. Years ago.'

'Scott Hastings is the name of the male lead. When I met you, I'd had the challenge for months and hadn't had the opportunity to use it so it just came out. You were a stranger on a tube platform and I thought it wouldn't matter. I wasn't expecting things to progress with us and, when they did, how could I tell you that I'd lied about my name?'

'Plus, it meant I wasn't going to find out about your wife online, didn't it?'

He shrugged. 'I suppose so but I didn't set out to do it. You have to believe me.'

I stared at him, my emotions in turmoil. It all sounded very plausible – one of those moments where you say or do something that you think will have no impact yet it actually does. But he'd still lied about being married.

I stood up. 'I need a drink. Do you want anything?'

'I'd love a coffee.'

'Stay here.'

I headed into the kitchen area and busied myself boiling the kettle for Scott and pouring a glass of wine for me. I gulped it down then poured another large one.

Returning to the lounge area, I handed him his drink and returned to the armchair, far away from him. 'I can see how the Scott Hastings thing happened and I can see how awkward it would be telling me you'd made it up. But what I can't see is how you slept with me that night when you were married.'

'Isn't it obvious?'

I shrugged. 'No. Ooh, don't tell me. You'd had an argument with your wife and you couldn't help yourself. Or perhaps she didn't understand you like I did, or whatever excuse it is that men use to justify their infidelity.'

He put his mug down on the coffee table and stayed leaning forwards. 'Why did *you* sleep with me that first night?'

'What?'

'It's not a trick question. There must have been a reason because, let's face it, I was a stranger who you might never see again, and I know that you'd never had a one-night-stand. I remember you telling me that it usually took weeks, if not months, before you took that step with a boyfriend. So, why did you sleep with me that first night?'

My cheeks flushed as I muttered, 'Because I fell in love with you.'

Scott gazed at me, a soft smile on his lips. 'Same here. It was unexpected and crazy but I knew I had to continue seeing you. I *hadn't* had an argument with Fi. We *weren't* going through a rough patch. She *did* understand me. I wasn't looking for anyone else so it made no sense but there you were and it was like being struck by a lightning bolt. What I had with you was so exciting and passionate and completely different to what I had with Fi or any other girlfriends before her and I couldn't get enough of you.'

'But you were married. Surely you knew that what you were doing was wrong?'

'This is going to sound awful but I barely gave Fi a second thought that night. I was mesmerised by you, Jemma. As soon as I met you, I knew what real love looked like and that I'd made a huge mistake marrying Fi. I didn't love her. Not in that way.'

Butterflies swarmed in my stomach and I felt a rush of love for him, but I had to push my feelings aside. This was about getting an explanation. It was absolutely *not* about forgiving him and trying again. 'If you didn't love her, why did you marry her?'

'I mistook friendship for love. I had this overwhelming need to protect her after what she'd been through with Begsey and I got carried away. We both did. We should never have taken things beyond friendship. When I woke up with you by my side, I knew I had to be with you forever instead of Fi. I knew it would be painful but I was going to tell her the truth and end it when I got home, tell you all about the Scott Hastings thing, and hope that you forgave me for what genuinely had been a little white lie.'

'So what happened when you got home because clearly you didn't leave your wife for me and I had no idea you were really called Adam?'

Scott slumped back in his chair. 'Crap timing, which has become a bit of a theme. I got home to find her in tears. She'd started a new job a few months before, which she absolutely loved, but her manager had told her he was letting her go. Begsey had cornered him one night and had asked if he had good insurance because, if he didn't sack Fi within a week, he might find he needed to claim on the fire policy. If he went to the police, the same would happen to his home. Fi was devastated that she'd lost her job, but she was even more devastated that Begsey still had a hold over her.'

'Then why didn't you do the right thing and end it with me?'

'The right thing for who? For Fi? Because it certainly wouldn't have been the right thing for me, or for you.'

'But you were married, Scott! Shit! I mean Adam! Being married meant it wasn't *right* for any of us.'

'I never set out to hurt either of you.'

'Maybe not, but you've managed to.'

'I know and I hate myself for it, but I can't live without you, Jem. I wasn't lying when I said I love you only. I do love Fi but it's a deep friendship thing. With you, it's the *real* thing. I've tried to tell you the truth so many times, but I've bottled it because I couldn't bear the thought of losing you. I've vowed to end it with Fi so many times, but the timing's never seemed right.'

'The timing's never right to dump someone. Especially your wife.' I downed the rest of my wine and took a deep breath. 'Tell me about the twins. A wife was a hell of a surprise. Twin babies took it into another stratosphere.'

He closed his eyes for a moment and the strain this had taken on him was obvious from the slump of his shoulders. I could see he was broken and I wanted to reach out and hold him but I couldn't do that.

If I held him, there was no way I'd be able to let him go because, as I'd told Leah earlier, I couldn't just switch off my feelings. I still loved him.

He opened his eyes and gave a weary sigh. 'I knew I'd let it go too far and that there'd never be a good time to tell Fi so I'd just have to blurt it out. I'd been working away and I marched through the front door announcing that there was something I had to tell her. But she said she had to give me her news first. She was pregnant. She'd already had another two miscarriages by that point and she was under strict orders to take things easy and avoid any stress. I cursed myself for not having the guts to end it before because, obviously, I couldn't tell her about you at that point. I couldn't risk being the cause of another miscarriage.'

He looked as though he was expecting me to agree with him but the enormous lump in my throat prevented me from getting any words out.

'She had a tough pregnancy and the twins were premature. They're still in hospital but they're doing well. For any normal couple, it would be an exciting time but our life isn't normal. All I can think about is you and how much I love you and miss you. I tried to cut you out my life, but I can't let you go. I still want to marry you and to have a family of our own.'

'What about your twins? You're a dad now. Are you saying you'd abandon your children so you could start a family with me?'

'No. I couldn't do that. I'm already smitten with them and it's hardly their fault I don't love their mother. What I really want is to have them in my life and to have you.'

His eyes lit up as he mentioned being smitten with the twins and tears stung my eyes at the thought of the man I loved with his perfect little family. 'Yes, well, we don't always get what we want, do we?'

'It doesn't have to be like that.' Scott left his chair and knelt on the floor beside me. 'What do you want, Jem?'

I stared at the floor, unable to bring myself to look at him as I lied. 'I want you out of my life. I wish I'd never met you.' I'd hoped the words would come out loud and strong but I could hear the lack of conviction in every single one.

'You don't mean that. Look at me, Jem. I *know* you don't mean that.'

He gently lifted my face and my heart pounded at his touch. I knew that the right thing was to pull away and order him to leave but I'd spent the best part of three weeks dreaming of a moment like this. Except in my fantasy, there wasn't a wife and kids waiting in the wings. It was just the two of us.

'I do mean it. I hate you. You've ruined my life.'

'You don't hate me. You hate what I've done to you... to us... but you don't hate *me*.'

I leapt up, needing some distance, and crossed the room before turning on him. 'I don't *know* you!'

He stood up, facing me. 'You do! Nothing else I've told you has been a lie. The person you fell in love with is still the real me. The person you agreed to marry is still me. I know I'm a shit for leaving Fi but I'd be even more of a shit if I stayed, knowing I could never love her the way I love you. I'll always be there for the twins but I can't be Fiona's husband because you're in here, Jemma.' He pointed to his head. 'And in here.' He pointed to his heart. 'From the moment you sat opposite me in La Vecchia Scuola with the rain dripping off your hair into your wine, laughing that infectious laugh of yours, I knew it was going to be you forever.'

The tears I'd managed to keep at bay spilled down my cheeks. 'How do I know this isn't more lies? Have you actually left your wife?'

'Not yet.'

'Scott!'

'It's not like that. After I got your email, I tried to be strong and stay away no matter how much it broke my heart. Then I got sent down here with work. I wasn't meant to be down south again until the week after next but there was a series of bizarre coincidences that brought me here. I couldn't help thinking it was meant to be like the time we met on the tube platform. I was never meant to be there that day either.

I had to face the truth – that it was time to stop living a lie and be with you properly.'

He sounded so sincere and I wanted so desperately to believe him. My resolve crumbled with every word.

'I *will* end it with Fi but not over the phone. It's something I have to do face to face but I am going to do it. I've made an appointment with a divorce solicitor and I've worked out my finances to see how I can support Fi and the twins and still marry you. I know we'll have a stack of logistics to work out but I'm serious about this. I'm definitely leaving Fi, even if you say no to taking me back.'

'Why didn't you end it first, before you came to London? Worried I'll say no and you'll be homeless?'

Scott crossed the room and took my hands in his, sending a zip of electricity throughout my body. 'Because it was only when I got away from home that my head cleared and I knew what I had to do. I could have waited until I got home again and ended it then before coming to find you, but I couldn't bear to be away from you for another minute. I had to see you and explain. It really is over with Fi, whatever the outcome with you. I can't continue to play happy families when my heart belongs to someone else.'

He kissed the back of my hand gently, sending another ripple of excitement through me.

'I'm at a conference in Brighton for the next three days. If you'll let me, I'd like to get the train up to see you tomorrow night and again on Saturday night so we can really talk. But I promise you, whatever you decide about our future, I'll go home on Sunday and confess everything to Fi.'

'What if it's bad timing again? You said you'd tried to tell her before and it never worked out. What if you go home and one of the twins is poorly or your wife's upset about something? Oh my God! What am I saying?' I snatched my hand away. 'You have a wife and two babies. You should be with them. Not me. This isn't right.'

'It's difficult but it *is* right. I choose you, Jem.' Scott led me to the sofa and sat down beside me, knees touching, hands clasped. 'I need you and I know you need me. We're meant to be together. It's always been you.'

He tilted my head towards him and gently kissed my tears away. I tried to pull back but who was I kidding? I hated what he'd done but I still loved him and I still wanted him. Badly.

'I love you, Jemma,' he murmured, as his fingers entwined my hair and his kisses trailed round my neck.

'I love you too,' I whispered back as my lips found his. And I meant it. I hated myself for being so weak, but I couldn't bear to let him go.

15

'I wish I didn't have to go to Brighton.' Scott grabbed the belt of my dressing gown and pulled me towards him by the front door early the following morning. 'I'd rather stay in bed all day showing you how sorry I am.'

My legs felt like jelly at the thought of it. 'Didn't you show me enough times last night?' I'd heard Tiff and Leah talk about how amazing make-up sex could be, but I'd never had an argument with Scott, or any other boyfriend for that matter, so I'd never experienced it. Oh my God! It had been absolutely incredible. Passionate. Intense. Inventive. Attentive. *Very* attentive. Talk about being completely focussed on me. I swear my body was still having aftershocks!

'I have a lot of making up to do,' he said, undoing my dressing gown belt and slipping his hand inside to cup my breast.

I moaned as I melted into his kiss.

'Don't mind me,' came a gruff voice.

'Leah! Sorry.' I pulled my dressing gown tightly round me and refastened my belt. 'Scott's just leaving.'

'I expected him to have done that last night.'

'I'd better go,' Scott whispered, kissing me lightly. 'I'll see you tonight. La Vecchia Scuola at half seven. And thank you for giving me a second chance. I'll spend the rest of my life making it up to you. I promise.'

'Don't forget to reactivate your email and Facebook so I can stay in touch with you.'

'I'll do it on the train.'

I closed the door behind him and walked slowly towards Leah who was making a hell of a noise in the kitchen, clattering her cereal bowl and spoon down on the worktop, and slamming cupboard doors shut.

'I know what you're thinking.'

'I'll bet you do. I don't know what *you're* thinking, though.'

'I love him, Leah. I can't help it.'

She shook her head as she poured muesli into her bowl. 'I always thought you were made of stronger stuff than that. I never saw you as someone who so desperately needed a man in her life that she'd welcome back a cheat and a liar.'

'Leah! I—'

She spun round to face me and blew her fringe out of her face. 'You don't need to justify yourself to me, Jemma. It's your life and it's up to you what you do with it, but don't expect me to be pleased for you because I'm not. I've lived with you for the past few weeks. I've seen what he's done to you.' She yanked open the fridge door and grabbed the milk. 'In my opinion, you've made a huge mistake letting him worm his way back into your life and your bed. But it's your mistake to make and, because I love you, I'll be here for you when it all goes wrong which it absolutely will do.' She poured the milk into her bowl, splashing it all over the worktop.

'You don't know that,' I protested.

'Wake up! I'd *love* him to prove me wrong, but I know he's going to break your heart again. I wouldn't be surprised if nothing's changed and he's still playing the family man with his wife and twins.'

She grabbed her bowl and spoon and headed past me towards the bedrooms but stopped by the door and turned to face me. 'I'm sorry if I sound harsh, but it's only because I care. Be careful, Jem. People who play with fire tend to get burned.'

* * *

⌧ To Scott
Hope you got to Brighton safely. Sorry about Leah
this morning. She's worried you're going to hurt me
again xx

⌧ From Scott
Then I'll have to work extra hard at proving her
wrong. You're my forever, Jemma. I know I've messed
up spectacularly but I will make it up to you. It's
over with Fiona and I'll tell her on Sunday no
matter what you decide over the next 2 nights. I
love you xx

⌧ To Scott
I love you too. Can't wait to see you tonight xx

'What are you grinning at?' Owen asked, placing a mug of coffee on my desk.

I put my phone down. 'If I tell you, will you promise not to lecture me?'

He sat on the spare chair opposite me. 'If it makes you smile but it might make me lecture you, would I be right in guessing that a certain young man is back in your life?'

I nodded. 'He turned up last night.' I gave Owen the edited highlights.

When I finished, he shrugged and sighed. 'I'd love to be excited for you. I really would.'

'But you can't.'

Owen stood up and sighed again. 'Sorry, Jemma. In my experience, leopards don't change their spots, but if you do decide to give him another chance, I hope he proves me wrong. I want him to. I really do.'

⊠ To Scott
Just told Owen. He was as enthusiastic as Leah

⊠ From Scott
Don't let them get you down. Grab some of those
bears and give them a hug. I'll prove them all
wrong. I promise xx

Moments later, a notification came through from his Scott Facebook account and showed a selfie of him blowing me a kiss. It filled my heart with joy but I glanced across at Owen and thought about Leah earlier and the doubts returned.

Despite Scott's reassurances and a few lovely messages and photos on his Facebook profile across the morning, my stomach was still in knots. Had I done the right thing? Nobody else seemed to think so. Leah had obviously passed on the 'good news' to Tiff and Drew because I'd had texts from both of them. While stopping short of lecturing me, they didn't exactly convey excitement at my news.

Needing reassurance from someone I phoned Karen at lunchtime hoping to catch her on a break between clients.

'You think I'm making a mistake too, don't you?' I asked when she remained silent after I'd told her about Scott's reappearance. 'It's okay. You can say it. Leah, Tiff, Drew and Owen have all made it clear that I must have a screw loose.'

'I'm trying to put myself in your shoes,' she said. 'How would I feel if I'd just discovered that Ryan wasn't really called Ryan, that he was married and had been since way before we met so had basically been unfaithful to me the whole time we were together and, on top of that, his wife had given birth to premature twins who he'd just walked out on? Would I consider him to be a catch? Would he still be the one I wanted to spend the rest of my life with? Could I trust him not to meet some other random stranger on a train platform, give her a false name, have an affair with her, and walk out on me and our kids a few years down the line? With an attractive proposition like that, it's *certainly* a dilemma.'

I sighed and slumped back in my chair. 'When you put it like that, it makes me seem so pathetic.'

'No. It makes *him* seem pathetic. Not you. I'm just not convinced he's going to leave his wife and kids and, if he does, what sort of man is he? Honestly, Jemma, who abandons their newborn babies like that?'

'He's not going to abandon them. He'll still see them and support them.'

'And how's that going to work? Will he continue to live in the family home, allegedly living separate lives? Because, if he wants to be a proper dad, he sure as hell can't move to London to be with you when his kids are in Nottinghamshire.'

There was a pause and I couldn't find any words. My head thumped and my stomach felt like it was on spin cycle.

'Sorry for having a go,' Karen said gently. 'But you *did* ask.'

'I know. And I wanted the truth.'

'And you knew you'd get it from me.'

True. But I'd also wanted reassurances and was sure I'd have been able to rely on Karen to understand and see it from my point of view. It was worth one more push. 'You do understand why I'm willing to explore giving him another chance, don't you?'

Silence for a moment, then a big sigh. 'I do. I wish I didn't, but I do. If it had been Ryan, I know how hard it would be to walk away when I love that dopey idiot so much.'

'So you'd give him another try if you were in my shoes?'

'I honestly don't know. I'd certainly talk about it and I know I'd want to try again but infidelity is infidelity and I don't know if I could forgive and forget if push came to shove. I know how much you love Scott and I know you too well too. If you walk away now, without even discussing things, you'll spend the rest of your life wondering what if, so I'll admit that it's probably the right decision for you to spend some time getting answers.'

'I knew you'd get it.'

She sighed. 'I get it but that doesn't mean I like it. You've got two evenings together, Jem. That's a lot of hours to talk. Use that time. Don't tumble into bed again. Stay focused and give him a bloody hard time. He deserves it. And if, after you've interrogated him, you're absolutely 100 per cent sure you have a future together, then I guess you have my support if that's what you want.'

Relief flowed through me. 'It is. Thank you.'

'Please don't be mad with me for saying this but I can't help hoping you decide not to let him back in. I'm so sorry. I *will* support you but it worries me. Talking to him is the right decision for you but as to whether trying again would turn out to be the right decision, the jury's out on that one.'

I felt deflated again. They all thought I should walk away. I didn't want to lose my friends over this, though. Best end the conversation on something more positive. 'How are things with you? Good week?'

'Great. Did I tell you Ryan and Steff have got a place on the London Marathon next year?'

'No. I remember you saying he'd entered, but I didn't know he'd heard.'

'Yeah, last week I think it was. He's always wanted to do it. So has Steff.'

'You didn't fancy taking part? All three owners running together.'

'Not my thing. I love running, obviously, but that distance just doesn't do it for me. Anyway, I've set up a running club as a spin-off to the bootcamp and PT and it's doing really well.'

'World domination next?'

Karen laughed. 'Something like that. Look, I've got to go. I've got a PT session in ten minutes. Let me know how it goes this weekend.'

'I will. Thanks, Karen.'

'Stay strong. Only let him back in if you're 100 per cent convinced. If there's even a tiny fraction of doubt...'

'I promise. I'll speak to you later.'

I disconnected the call and breathed in deeply. Thank God someone was on my side. No, that wasn't fair. They were all on my side, which was why they were so negative about Scott. I was a big girl, though, and if Scott was a mistake, then he was a mistake I wanted and needed to make.

* * *

The moment I stepped inside La Vecchia Scuola that evening, it was like stepping back in time to that first night with Scott. I looked over towards the cosy table for two where we'd fallen in love by candlelight and my stomach fizzed. I could still remember everything about that unexpected evening. I'd known back then that meeting Scott would change my life. I just hadn't expected it to play out like this.

I was a little early and he hadn't arrived but the waiter said it wasn't a problem and directed me to the same cosy table for two. Was it coincidence or had Scott specifically requested it?

The restaurant was busy with only a couple of empty tables and there was that definite 'the weekend has arrived' buzz in the laughter and chatter. I ordered a glass of wine and scrolled through my phone while I waited.

Across the morning, Scott had posted a series of photos on his Facebook feed for my eyes only: a sad face as he waited at the station because he was missing me, the one of him blowing me a kiss, and a work pamphlet with 'I love Jemma' in a heart written in marker pen.

My favourite was the final image that he'd posted late this morning. He was standing on Brighton beach. Behind him was the sea and the silhouette of the burned-down pier. He was beaming at the camera. The caption read: *Quick tea break before it gets too busy. Can't wait to see you tonight. You've made me the happiest man alive. The pier behind me might be in ruins and I'm praying our future together isn't. I promise you won't regret it if you give me another chance. I'll never lie again and I'll never, ever let you down. Counting down the hours xxx*

Smiling, I ran my finger lightly over his image while butterflies danced in my stomach. This weekend was going to be the most important weekend of my life. Karen was right. By the end of it, I had to be

100 per cent convinced that Scott was being honest with me. I absolutely believed he loved me and wanted to marry me. The unknown was whether I believed he'd finally leave Fiona. Wanting to do it and actually doing it were two very different things. He hadn't managed it so far and the stakes were so much higher now that he was a dad. And, of course, I had to be sure that, if we did try again, I could forgive him and I could trust him because, if I couldn't, we didn't stand a chance.

Feeling nauseous, I put my phone down. If only there weren't children involved. Scott told me last night that he didn't think Fiona would be bothered about him ending their marriage because she'd got what she wanted out of it – children – but it wasn't that straightforward. Even if, like he said, she only loved him as a friend and was prepared to let go of him as her husband, he was tied to her as the father of her children. Would she really be prepared to bring up twins on her own? And would he be prepared to be a holidays and weekends dad? The Scott I knew would want to be fully hands-on and that was the right thing to do. But where did that leave me? Discussing that was going to be one of the most difficult parts of the weekend.

For tonight, we'd keep the conversation light over dinner but I'd take it steady on the wine so we could talk back at the flat without alcohol clouding things. Or that would be the plan if he turned up. He was fifteen minutes late and I'd had no texts from him although, if his train was running late and he was now on the underground, he'd have no signal.

Half an hour later and there was still no word. Stomach churning, I rang, I texted, I messaged. No answer. Was my ghost back?

The restaurant was full and there was a queue. I felt like everyone was staring at me, willing me to vacate my table. I asked one of the waiters if I should leave but he insisted I stay.

Two hours I waited. Two long, painful hours during which my imagination took me to hell and back. I imagined illness, accident, death. I pictured everything from emergency surgery on the twins, through to him and Fiona curled up on the sofa laughing at me for thinking Scott Hastings was a real person and how I'd fallen for his lies yet again.

I necked back the last dribble of wine in my third glass and popped the last black olive into my mouth before catching the eye of the waiter who'd told me to stay.

'I make you some spaghetti?' he suggested, his expression one of sympathy. He knew. Of course he knew. Everyone in La Vecchia Scuola knew that I'd been stood up.

'Just the bill please.'

He shook his head. 'Olives are not enough. You waste away.'

'Thanks, but I'm not hungry anymore. Sorry. Just the bill.'

'He have wrong time? Your boyfriend. He mixed up? Wrong time? Wrong day?'

Oh yes, he was certainly wrong. For me, for us, for his family. He'd made his decision and I shouldn't be surprised especially when, deep down, I knew it was the right one.

I placed a generous tip on the table then left the restaurant, trying to hold my head high, trying to will the tears back. It was over. My friends had all been right about the inevitable outcome which had come a little sooner than expected.

Bloody Scott Hastings had broken my heart yet again. And I'd let him.

* * *

The tube home was heaving. A hen party of young women wearing angel wings and halos tottered up and down the carriage on impractical heels. I found my mind drifting to what I'd have done for my hen do. I'd always fancied a weekend away in Dublin. Would that be good for a hen do? Or I could stay in London and do a meal and show. Or what about...?

I had to stop myself. What was I doing? Scott and I were never going to make it down the aisle. Even if he wasn't already married to someone else, the no-show this evening, the unanswered calls, the ignored texts all sent out a very clear message. I hoped desperately that nothing had happened to the twins but, whether it had or not, I knew I couldn't do this. I couldn't be the other woman. It wasn't fair to her, the twins, or me. When – if – he came crawling back to me, I had to be strong. I had to say no.

But as I swayed from side to side, clinging onto a metal pole, all I could picture were the good times. When – if – he came crawling back to me, I wasn't sure I could be that strong.

* * *

It was a little after 11.00 p.m. when the text came through:

✉ From Scott
I can't do this. I don't know what I was thinking.
I have a wife and two beautiful babies who need me.
I choose them. We should never have got together.
It wasn't fair on anyone. I'm sorry for all the
hurt I've caused you and my wife. You need to
forget about me and get on with your life without
me in it. Please don't make it harder on us all by
getting in touch again. It really is over. It was
fun while it lasted but I have responsibilities to
my family now and you need to let me fulfil them.
Goodbye.

OCTOBER

16

SAM

'Ah! Dr Jones. We meet again. Fancy some company, Billy No Mates?'

I looked up from my lunch to see Tiff standing over me, holding a packet of sandwiches and a banana.

I smiled as I indicated for her to join me. 'I actually did have company but he had to take a call.'

'Whatever you say. I've got a favour to ask you.'

'What sort of favour?'

'Nothing illegal or immoral, I promise.'

'Sounds a bit dull then.'

Tiff laughed. 'Actually, it's not even for me. It's for my flatmate, Jemma. You work in neurological sciences, yeah? Parkinson's?'

I nodded. 'That's my specialism. Why?'

'Jemma's mum's been diagnosed with Parkinson's. She's seeing a consultant but Jemma's worried that there's something else going on with her – something more than the Parkinson's – and I reckon she could do with speaking to someone who knows what they're talking about because Googling it is making her panic.'

'Why doesn't she just talk to her mum's consultant?'

'Her mum's not local so she can't go and see him. She tried to call him but he wouldn't speak to her without her mum's permission. She doesn't want to ask her mum for permission because she doesn't want to let on that she's worried about her and that she thinks there's something other than the Parkinson's going on. Vicious circle.'

I pushed the remnants of my shepherd's pie aside and took a sip from my bottle of water. It wasn't the normal way of doing things and there were charities that Tiff's flatmate could contact if she wanted to learn more. But I'd promised myself that I'd make more of an effort to get to know some people in London and here was an opportunity for another small step.

Tiff cocked her head on one side. 'I'm being a bit too cheeky, aren't I? You spend all day talking to people about this stuff. I bet the last thing you want to do is spend an evening doing the same, especially when you're not even being paid for it. Although, I promise there won't be any snakes.'

I smiled at her. 'Well, if there's definitely no snakes...'

Her eyes widened. 'You'll do it? You'll meet Jemma?'

I nodded.

'Oh my God! That's fantastic. She's had such a crap time of it recently and she could do without stressing about this as well. Can we swap numbers?'

She tapped my number into her phone. 'Thanks Indy. No rest for the wicked. If you're free mid to late next week, that would be awesome.'

'I'm sure I can manage something.'

Tiff grinned and blew me a kiss. 'You superstar. By the way, I'm thinking we can do better than the occasional catch-up over a canteen coffee. Why don't I introduce you to my cousin, Drew, and the three of us can go for drinks after work one night?'

Small steps... 'Sounds good.'

'The only rule is that you can't talk shop. I'll tell you about my latest Tinder disasters, Drew will witter on about comics and you can tell us about your fiancée. We need a proper getting to know you night out.'

I had to do it. It was the perfect moment. Okay, it wasn't really as we were in the canteen at work surrounded by colleagues who might overhear. I didn't want the sympathy vote for being the doctor who fled to London because he couldn't cope with living in the town that reminded him too much of his dead fiancée. But it *was* a moment and I needed to take it. I took a deep breath. 'About that—'

'Shit! Is that the time?' Tiff leapt to her feet and grabbed her food and phone off the table. 'I'm late. Sorry, Sam. Can you tell me later?' Without waiting for an answer, she power-walked out of the canteen.

Bollocks. Another moment lost. I just hoped she didn't think I'd been lying to her when I did finally get the opportunity to confess. I couldn't bear people who lied, like my ex, Kirsty, who'd lied to me throughout our relationship. I wasn't *that* guy. I had to set the record straight next time I saw Tiff. Top priority.

17

JEMMA

I'd no sooner got off the train on Thursday evening, ready for a long weekend at home, when I was jumped on. 'Whoa! Logan-paws! You nearly knocked me over.' I wrapped my arms round my little brother. 'Are you okay?'

'I've missed you,' he said, clinging onto me like a limpet.

'Where's Mum?'

'Waiting in the car park. There weren't any spaces.'

'How is she?'

Logan just squeezed me tighter and I kissed the top of his head. 'Don't worry. I'm home for four days. We'll have plenty of time to talk.'

It was already dark so I couldn't tell whether Mum looked tired or strained as she drove towards Bear's Pad. I asked her how she was, but all I got was a quick 'fine' before she fired a stack of questions at me about my day at work and the journey home; a clear sign that she didn't want to talk. Hopefully it was only in front of Logan and she'd open up when he'd gone to bed. Something had definitely happened, though, because the atmosphere in the car was seriously tense.

* * *

'Logan's in bed, my phone's on silent, the TV's off, I've made the drinks and you have my undivided attention.' I handed Mum her favourite teddy bear mug and curled up on the sofa with a cold can of Lilt later that evening.

Guilt was plastered all over her face as she sighed. 'There was an incident with Logan. He's pretty upset about it.' She wouldn't look me in the eye. 'It was nothing, really. Just a silly misunderstanding.'

'Go on...'

She wrapped both hands round her mug and blew on her tea. 'His cub pack are having a sleepover in the Scout hut and he needed to pay a tenner towards it. School are doing a couple of trips and he needed a tenner for them too. He'd been nagging me for ages, saying the deadline was due, but I kept forgetting to bring any cash home.'

Mum fell silent and stared into her tea. I took a sip from my can, wondering where the story was going because, so far, it all seemed pretty normal. Mum *never* had any cash on her and I remembered always having to nag her for bus fares and school dinner money when I was a kid. Perhaps she'd snapped at him for going on about it too much. Logan could be pretty persistent about stuff but, then again, couldn't most ten-year-olds?

Finally looking up, she said, 'I left Bear With Me early one evening to do the banking but I bumped into someone I knew on the way, got chatting, and the bank had closed by the time I got there. I left the money in my bag in the usual place in the hall. When I got round to trying again at the bank a couple of days later, I was £50 short. Next thing I know, Logan's handing me slips confirming payment for the sleepover and the school trips.'

I gasped. 'You think he stole £50? Logan wouldn't do that.'

She stared into her tea again.

'Oh, Mum! Don't say you actually accused him of stealing.'

'What else could I do? He's nagging me for £20 then, next minute, the trips are paid for and I'm £50 short. It *had* to be him.'

'But Logan's never done anything like that. He wouldn't.'

She nodded. 'I know. And I now know that it wasn't him.'

'How?'

'I told Liv about it at work. Her two boys are older than Logan but I wondered whether either of them had done anything similar, thinking maybe it was a phase that little boys went through. Anyway, she reminded me that I'd spotted her at the bus stop the night I missed the bank. Her bus hadn't turned up and it had started raining so I offered her a lift home. The fuel light came on so I stopped off at Sainsbury's to fill up because it's on the way to Liv's. I realised I'd left my purse at Bear With Me, but it didn't matter because I had the banking with me.'

'And you put £50 of petrol in the car?' I tried not to sound angry with her as I said it, but I felt pretty aggrieved on behalf of my poor little brother, being accused of stealing so much money.

'Yes. I still had the receipt in my bag with the banking.'

'What about the sleepover and trips?'

'It turns out I paid by cheque. I found the stubs in my cheque book.'

'Oh, Mum! When was this?'

'Middle of last week. I told Logan the truth, of course, and apologised to him, but I think he's still sulking. I can't say I blame him.' She looked up again, biting her lip. 'I shouted, Jemma. *Really* shouted. I didn't recognise myself.'

I nodded slowly as I let the information sink in. I couldn't recall a single occasion when I'd heard Mum shout. She'd never raised her voice when I was a child, not even when I'd cut up an expensive piece of her bear-making mohair because I thought it would make nice rugs for my Barbie house. She'd argued with Dad, but I'd never heard her shout at him and he'd certainly given her just cause over the years, especially when it came to his attitude towards Logan.

'What sort of day had you been having?' I asked.

'Not a good one, but not the worst. Definitely not the worst. I don't know what happened. I don't know why I forgot about spending the money myself, or paying for the trips by cheque, and I don't know what made me accuse my baby boy of stealing.'

'Mum, I hate to say this, but do you think there could be something else? Other than the Parkinson's, I mean.'

She frowned. 'I'm not with you.'

'Making you forget things. Could it be...?' I paused. I couldn't bring myself to say the word that had been haunting me since that evening in the hot tub when Mum had talked about the lido. 'I don't know. A side effect maybe? Could it be worth mentioning something to Dr Steadman next time you see him?'

She rolled her eyes at me. 'I doubt it. He didn't show much empathy about the Parkinson's so I don't think he'll give a damn about a couple of instances of forgetfulness.'

'But it hasn't just been a couple of instances.'

'It has.'

'It hasn't, Mum. There was the thing with your knickers at Dad's funeral and you put Logan's football boots in the oven and a cauliflower somewhere else. You couldn't find my birthday card, and then you talked about going to the lido on South Bay and now... What?'

Mum was looking at me, head cocked to one side, a bewildered expression on her face. 'I admit to the knickers and the birthday card, but I think Logan's winding you up about his football boots and the cauliflower. And I have no idea what you mean about the lido. I think it might be you who's having memory problems, not me.' She winced as she pulled herself to her feet. 'I'm going to have to call it a night. Are you okay to lock up?'

'I thought you'd already done that earlier.'

She frowned and shrugged. 'No harm in double-checking, is there?'

I smiled back and tried to keep my voice light. 'No. No harm at all. I'll check. Night, Mum.'

'Night, Jemma-bear.'

I pressed my head against the sofa cushions with my eyes closed, listening to her slowly pull herself up the stairs while my heart broke into a thousand pieces. It was getting worse. She'd locked up. Definitely. She'd announced she was going to do it after we'd eaten. We'd even had a conversation about whether she'd rather put her feet up while I did it, but she'd insisted that exercise – no matter how little – helped her. I'd watched her head out to the back. Unless she'd got distracted...

I picked up our mugs and headed into the kitchen diner. The sliding doors to the deck were not only unlocked, they were partially open. Oh God! It was worse than I thought.

⊠ To Tiff
Getting more worried about Mum by the minute. If you're sure that your new pal Dr Jones doesn't mind meeting with me outside of work, I'd really appreciate it. Can do any night next week except Monday. Thanks xx

⊠ From Tiff
Crap! Sorry to hear it. He's happy to meet you. I don't think he gets out and about much. It'll do him good xx

⊠ To Tiff
He doesn't think it's a date, does he?

⊠ From Tiff
Panic not. He's got a fiancée. He's just being friendly and helpful

⊠ To Tiff
Phew! Thanks. Really appreciate it xx

⊠ From Tiff
Any time. Drew says you have an objective for your evening with Dr Jones. As well as finding out about your mum, you have to find out if the fiancée is

male or female. He says I've assumed female. He
never talks about her and I don't know her name so
Drew's still convinced the lovely Dr Jones is gay
and would ditch his partner if he got to know Drew
a bit better. He loves the idea of dating Indiana
Jones! My cousin is a tart! Xx

✉ To Tiff
I'll see what I can do but, after questioning Mum
tonight and crashing and burning with it, I think
sleuthing is NOT my area of expertise

✉ From Tiff
Hang on in there. I'm at the end of the phone if
you want to talk about it before you're back xx

18

I rubbed my sweaty palms down my jeans yet again. Why the hell was I nervous? It wasn't a date. It was some advice and guidance for a friend of a friend. Day job stuff. Easy.

My phone buzzed in my pocket.

✉ From Unknown
Hi. It's Jemma! Hope you don't mind but Tiff gave me your number. I got held up at work and I'm going to be about 10 mins late. Don't want you to think I'm a no-show when you're doing me a huge favour! Don't know if Tiff told you what I look like but I've got long, dark hair and I'm wearing a burgundy dress and black boots. What do you look like? Tiff unhelpfully told me you'll be wearing a fedora, carrying a whip and hiding from snakes! Will be there asap. Thank you

✉ To Jemma
Ha ha ha! Tiff is hilarious. Not! Sadly, I look nothing like Harrison Ford or his alter ego. I'm

blond and wearing a grey T-shirt and jeans. I'm only a few minutes away so will grab a table. See you later

I put my phone away and breathed out slowly, wondering why I was so nervous. It was the blind date thing, wasn't it? Although it wasn't actually a date with Jemma, I *was* about to meet a stranger who I knew very little about which echoed of that first meeting with Nikki. Little had I known back then that a blind date that I'd tried so hard to wriggle out of would change my life forever. At least this Jemma person wasn't going to have that sort of impact on me although, if she was as much fun as Tiff, maybe I'd have another friend in London and could gradually start building up a new life. Without Nikki in it.

* * *

The door to The George and Dragon burst open twenty minutes later, blowing a swirl of leaves into the pub and Jemma Browne into my life. She pushed her windswept hair out of her face, looked round the pub, and beamed directly at me. I wondered how she knew it was me from my sparse description, but then I realised that the only other punters were an old man perched on a bar stool clutching a pint, a young couple snogging in the corner, a group of students, and an elderly couple seated side by side, staring into space.

'Sam!' she said, walking towards me with her hand outstretched. 'I'm so grateful to you.'

I shook her hand. 'It's no problem. Can I get you a drink?'

'No! Let me get you one. You're doing me a huge favour and I'll have to walk out and go home if you don't at least let me buy the drinks.'

'Honestly, you don't have to do that.'

'Yes I do and, if you don't let me, I'll dig my pet snake out of my bag.' She winked cheekily and I liked her immediately. It was the same instant warmth I'd felt towards Tiff

'Okay,' I said reluctantly. 'But if we have a second drink, it's on me. Deal?'

She pursed her lips for a moment then laughed. 'You drive a tough bargain, but okay.'

Drinks purchased, we settled back into the corner booth where I'd been sitting before. She shuffled in her seat and bit her lip. The haunted expression and awkward mannerisms were reminiscent of so many relatives of patients who clearly wanted to ask questions but weren't sure whether they should, especially in front of the patient. Even though her mum wasn't present, Jemma probably felt just as uncomfortable.

'Your mum's been diagnosed with Parkinson's, right? Why don't you tell me a bit about her?'

'She's amazing, but I'm so worried about her. What do you want me to tell you?'

'Anything you want to share with me. For example, her age, her job, her home life, her health until the diagnosis. Focus on your mum as you know her for the moment and then we'll talk about what led up to the diagnosis.' I indicated a pen and notepad on the table. 'Do you mind if I make a few notes?'

She shook her head. 'That's fine. She's called Julie and she's forty-six. She'll be forty-seven in March. She's divorced. My dad left her when he found out that she was expecting my little brother. I was eighteen at the time. Logan's ten now.'

I nodded. That made her twenty-eight, then – six years younger than me.

'Dad didn't want another child so Mum brought Logan up single-handedly. Dad isn't around anymore. He was killed by a drunk driver three years ago.' She paused and took a deep breath.

'I'm sorry to hear that.'

'It's been tough. He was a difficult man, but he was still my dad and... well, that's a different story and not relevant here. Let's get back to Mum, eh?'

I nodded, feeling empathy towards someone who'd also suffered loss. I knew all about the guilt that went with it.

'She's got her own shop selling collectible teddy bears. It's called Bear With Me and it's fantastic. She makes bears and runs workshops for anyone interested in learning how to make them, or for people who just want to learn how to sew. She values bears for a couple of auction houses so she travels a lot and Logan stays with my best friend's mum.' She paused. 'Too much detail?'

'No. It's all good. It gives me a picture of her lifestyle which sounds pretty hectic.'

'You could say that!'

'Tell me about her health. Any problems before the diagnosis?'

Jemma shook her head. 'Nothing significant. She's never regularly exercised because her work hasn't allowed her to get into a routine, but she's pretty fit. She's on her feet all day and up and down two flights of stairs loads of times. She's slim and she has a good diet.'

'And what about the diagnosis?'

I listened, scribbling the occasional note, while Jemma told me all about her mum's rigidity, the frequency of what she called 'bad days' and how it was affecting her everyday life.

'It's not the Parkinson's I'm worried about, though.' She twiddled with a spare beer mat. 'That's a lie. I *am* worried about the Parkinson's. Of course I am. It's just that I'm worried that there's something else and Mum's consultant is being an awkward twat. He says I'm not his patient so he won't take my calls. My question is this: does Parkinson's cause memory loss?'

I put my pen down. 'Not directly. Parkinson's is a neurological condition so it *does* affect the brain, but it's the part of the brain that controls movement, *not* the part that deals with memory. That's why patients experience slowness, rigidity, tremors and so on. These are all about movement. However, it's possible to have another condition alongside Parkinson's which *does* affect memory, like de—'

'Don't say it,' she cried, grabbing my forearm across the table and squeezing hard. She released her grip and shook her head. 'I'm so sorry. I didn't mean to dig my nails in.'

'Believe me, relatives of patients have done worse. I've actually been punched before when presenting a diagnosis that someone's husband didn't want to hear.'

'No!'

'Yes! I looked really professional wandering around with a black eye.' I took a sip of my drink and gave her my finely-honed empathetic smile. 'I have to say the word, Jemma. You're worried she might have dementia, aren't you?'

She lowered her eyes and nodded. I wanted to reach across and hug her and tell her it was going to be all right, but years of medical training coupled with my own personal experiences told me that it often wasn't.

'First thing to say is don't jump to conclusions. I'm assuming your mum has been demonstrating unusual patterns of behaviour for you to have gone down this path, but it's possible that it's just a bit of forget-fulness brought on from the stress of the diagnosis.'

'I wish it was.'

'Can you give me some examples?'

She reached into her bag and pulled out a notepad. 'I thought you might ask me that so I wrote them down as I was bound to miss one out otherwise.'

Her voice shook and I could see she was on the brink of tears. I wanted to give her a moment to gather herself. 'How about I get us another drink, then you could run through the examples for me?'

While I stood at the bar waiting for our drinks, I hoped that she was going to run through a list of everyday stuff that happens to us all like losing keys or walking into a room to get something then completely forgetting why you'd gone in there. I'd be able to smile and reassure her that there was nothing to be concerned about and these things often happened more with age.

Unfortunately, when she ran through her list, I couldn't give her those reassurances. The stealing example and the knickers in the freezer were worrying incidents, although they didn't necessarily signify dementia.

'It gets worse,' she said. 'Some friends joined me back home for my birthday in June. Mum was tired and asked me to look after my brother. She suggested we went to the lido, but it closed when I was little. I asked her if she meant the slide pool on North Bay but she insisted she meant the lido on South Bay and she was talking as though it was still there and... What's up?'

I stared at Jemma, mouth open, my mind racing. Jesus Christ! What were the odds? 'You're from Whitsborough Bay!'

Her eyes widened. 'How did you know that?'

'The lido. The bear shop. I'm from there! Your mum's consultant is Dr Steadman, right?'

Jemma nodded.

'He was my replacement when I moved down here. And I've met your mum. She's lovely. My fiancée and I had a bear from her when we got engaged – a Ju-Sea Bear I think it was called – and she made a Hawaiian shirt and a surfboard for him because we were surfers.'

'Oh my God! I remember that bear! She was so chuffed with how he turned out. She sent me loads of photos of him. He was gorgeous. Wow! Small world.'

'You're not wrong there.' I shook my head in disbelief.

'I wonder why Tiff didn't make the connection.'

'I don't think she knows where I'm from. It never came up. We've only had coffee a handful of times and it's always been daft banter or work chat.'

'So what made you and your fiancée move down to London? Not many places to surf round here.'

Oh shit! I'd walked into that one. No lies. No misunderstandings. I'd tell her straight out.

'Bit of a story there,' I started, wondering whether to blurt it out and be done with it or whether I should steer the conversation back to her mum because I'd spectacularly hijacked it away from the one thing she wanted to ask me about. Bollocks. I was such a chicken. I couldn't seem to say the words. 'How about we focus on your mum for now and, if you're not sick of the sound of my voice by then, I'll tell you how I ended up in London?'

'I hope you don't think I'm prying,' she said, blushing slightly.

'Not at all. I just don't want to make the evening all about me when you wanted to ask me about your mum.'

Jemma smiled. 'Thank you. I do want to talk about Mum, but I'm also interested in hearing all about a fellow Whitsborough Bay resident and how you ended up making the move to London like me. I'll tell you my story too, if we've got time.'

'It's a deal. Right. Focus. From what you've told me about your mum, I suspect that–'

I jumped when 'Ring Ring' by Abba started playing.

Jemma groaned. 'I'll kill my little brother. He keeps changing the ring tone to songs that are phone-related. He thinks it's hilarious.' She delved into her bag. 'Sorry. Might be Mum or Logan.' She frowned as she looked at the screen and mouthed 'Tiff' to me.

'Hi Tiff, what's up? ... Oh my God! No! ... When? ... How's Drew taking it? ... I'm not surprised... No, you finish getting ready for work. I'll come straight home.' She stood up and attempted to wind her scarf round her neck, getting it tangled round her arm instead. 'After everything he's done for me, I can't not be there... Yeah, I know... Look, I'm leaving now. I'll be home as soon as I can. Have you rung work to say you'll be late? ... Okay. See you soon.'

Jemma disconnected the call and tossed her phone into her bag with an angry little cry before yanking her tangled scarf from her arm and dropping it on her seat.

'Everything alright?' Clearly it wasn't.

'I'm really sorry, Sam. I'm going to have to bail.' She pulled on her coat. 'That was Tiff. We share a flat with her twin sister, Leah, and their cousin, Drew. It would appear that Drew's ex has just come back on the scene after ghosting him a few years ago.' She grimaced and took a deep breath as she draped her scarf round her neck. 'Drew never got over it and he's apparently in a right state. Tiff has to go to work and

Leah's away at a conference so I need to be there to make sure he doesn't leave the flat looking for a fight or something. He's a big lad so he could do some damage.' She flung her bag over her shoulder. 'Sorry.'

I grabbed my pad and coat. 'I'll walk you to the tube.'

'Okay. Thanks. You can give me your take on the situation on the way. Have you ever heard of being ghosted?'

'Is that like being haunted?'

'No. Don't worry. I hadn't heard of it either until it happened to me.'

We exited the pub and headed in the direction of the tube, while Jemma told me about how both she and Drew had been ghosted by men who they'd thought loved them. Some sleuthing on her part had discovered the reason why her fiancé, Scott, had ghosted her although she said it was a long story and she didn't have time to give me any more detail than that. Drew, on the other hand, had never found out why his relationship had ended and it had eaten away at him for years which was why the ex being back on the scene was a big deal.

We stopped outside the tube station. 'This is me,' Jemma said.

'You said that Drew is a big lad. How big?'

'He's about 6' 2" and works out a lot.'

'No offence, but if he decides he's going out, I don't think there's much you'll be able to do to stop him.'

Her face fell. She clearly hadn't thought about that.

'I'm coming home with you.' I took my Oyster card out of my pocket. 'You're not doing this alone.'

Jemma headed towards the barriers. 'Come on then. Hopefully it won't get nasty.'

'If it does, Thor's here to protect you.' I don't know why I said it. It just slipped out.

Jemma stopped and narrowed her eyes for a moment, then shook her head and ran towards the steps. I ran after her. Seriously? What the hell had I said that for? The last thing I needed was to start the Thor connection again and carry more memories of Nikki with me.

19

JEMMA

'I've just got off the tube,' I said as soon as Tiff answered my call. 'I won't be long. What's he doing?'

'The good news is he's stopped drinking lager.'

'And the bad news?'

'He's moved onto the vodka.'

'Arse!' I sped up. 'With you in five.'

Tiff was waiting at the top of the stairs, propping open the door to our flat with her body, her arms folded across her chest.

'I thought I might need reinforcements,' I said, taking in her surprised expression.

She nodded. 'Good idea. Hi, Sam. Sorry to abandon you both.'

'It's fine,' I said. 'We can manage it. Get to work and I'll text you later.'

'Hi! Bye!' Sam said as she dashed past us and down the stairs.

I raised my eyebrows at Sam. 'Time to introduce you to Drew.'

'Jemma! My cuddly little bear-maker!' Drew rose from one of the armchairs, staggered a bit, then sat down again. 'My ghost's back.'

'So I hear.' I swiftly removed my coat and hung it on the hook, indicating to Sam that he could do the same. 'This is—'

Drew's jaw had dropped open. 'The delectable Dr Indiana Jones. Can I call you Indy?'

'I prefer Sam, if that's okay with you.' Sam walked into the lounge area, hand outstretched to shake Drew's.

'Sam Jones?' Drew sat up straight. 'Seriously? I thought Tiff was joking. Sam Jones as in Flash Gordon?'

Sam nodded. 'Well, I'm not actually *him,* but I have the same name. And the blond hair. Sadly not the six pack or the rocket cycle.'

Drew laughed a little too loudly. 'You know the film?'

'I *love* the film.'

'Then you're welcome in our home at any time.' Drew raised his glass in a toast then necked it and leaned forward to pour another. Obviously remembering his manners, he offered the bottle to Sam.

'Maybe a lager if you have one?' Sam suggested.

'I'll get you one.' I stood up and headed towards the kitchen area.

I grabbed us both a bottle of lager from the fridge then sat down next to Sam on the sofa.

'What happened, Drew?'

'You know my mate, Evan? The one who draws the cartoons? He was at an engagement party last night for a mate of his – some Dane called Laust who I've never met. He put the pictures up today of the happy couple and guess who Laust is bloody well getting married to.'

'No! Oh, Drew.'

Drew took another swig of vodka. 'Luukas and Laust. How sickeningly alliterative. There's photos of them everywhere. Facebook, Twitter, Instagram. Everywhere. They're even on bloody TikTok.'

'Couldn't Evan have warned you?'

'He didn't know Luukas was my ex. I met Evan afterwards. I probably mentioned him, but Evan wouldn't have made the connection.'

'At least you weren't at the party. Imagine how awkward that would have been.'

Drew didn't respond. He necked the remains of the vodka and placed the empty glass on the coffee table then sat back in the chair. Phew! No top-up. Or at least not yet.

'I might have sent him a friend request on Facebook...'

'No! Why?'

'I couldn't help myself. I wondered if he'd accept. He did. I followed him on Twitter and Instagram too. He followed me back.' He screwed up his nose. 'And then I sent him a message.'

'You didn't! Drew!'

'It was *his* fault. What did he expect? He must have known I'd have questions.'

'Dare I ask what was in your message?'

'Nothing bad. I might have politely enquired as to whether there was a reason why he left me waiting for him at the airport without a word of apology.'

My heart went out to him and I thought about the hurt email I sent to Scott when I tracked him down to his workplace and realised he was really Adam. 'By "politely enquired", I'm guessing you mean rudely demanded?'

'He deserved it. Bloody cheek. Nearly three years, Jem. Three years without a word.'

'Did he reply?' Sam asked.

'Oh yes. Shall I read it to you?' Without waiting for either of us to answer, Drew picked up his phone and mimicked what I have to assume was meant to be Luukas's Finnish accent as he read it out:

Hi Drew, I think the years have caused you some memory fade. I would like to remind you that my name is Luukas and not "worthless piece of shit." I had left the UK because my father took ill but he is well now, thank you for your sympathy. I am moving back to London. I thought we might reconnect as I do remember you being fun but now I think perhaps not. I will not pass on your wishes to my future husband for him to be attacked by a plague of vampire bats. I am sure you will understand why this is not a good conversation to have with the person you love. You disappoint me, Drew. It would appear that you still have not grown up in the three years since we were together. Grown men do not obsess about comic book heroes. This is why I could not be with you before. Grown men do not call each other names. This is why I cannot have you in my life now. It has been three years, Drew. THREE YEARS! Please move on with your life and get over it. It is my regret that I did not tell you we were over. I do not remember now why I did not. I am sad to have caused you so much pain for you to write such an angry message to me. Is this enough to put closure on our acquaintance? Good luck with your future life. Regards, Luukas.

Drew's voice, slurred and wobbly throughout the reading, broke on the last sentence and he slumped back in his chair, sobbing, as the phone slipped from his hand.

I'd never seen Drew cry. Ever. I leapt up and hugged him, indicating to Sam to get rid of the bottle of vodka. He nodded and quickly hid it behind a cushion. I dreaded to think what Drew actually wrote to Luukas to result in such a response, but it had obviously been pretty vicious. It wouldn't help for me to point that out, especially after Luukas had well and truly chastised him.

'At least you know why he ended it,' I suggested, stroking Drew's back as though he was a baby. 'I know being into comic books is a crap reason, but at least it's a reason.'

The sobs slowed down until Drew was able to let go of me.

'Sorry,' he said, sitting back in the chair and wiping his eyes with his sleeve. 'I don't know where that came from. I never cry.'

'Not even when he first ghosted you?' Sam asked.

'Never.'

Sam nodded. 'Grief. You've bottled it up for three years. It has just found its release.'

Drew ran his fingers through his dishevelled hair. 'I had no idea he hated the comic book thing.' He looked at Sam. 'You're into all that, right?'

'Not really the comics, but I love the movies. Marvel or DC Comics. It's all good.'

'You don't think it's just for kids, though?'

Sam shook his head. 'I don't think anyone has a right to pigeonhole anyone's hobbies or interests. They're what makes us unique, whatever age we develop them and however long we continue them. Don't you think so, Jemma?'

'Hey, you're looking at the woman who plays with bears for a living,' I said, 'although I dumped the guy who introduced me to his parents as that.' I looked at Drew. 'You really had no idea he didn't like comic books and superheroes?'

'Nope. Not a clue. We watched loads of films together. On my birthday, his gifts included a Captain America T-shirt and a set of Marvel Top Trumps, which he insisted we play strip Top Trumps with. I thought he was into it. Not a geek like me, but certainly a fan. Apparently not. Why didn't he just say something? I wouldn't have stopped liking it but I wouldn't have talked about it around him.'

Sam put his empty bottle of lager down on the coffee table. 'There's nothing you said or did just before it ended that could have been a step too far for him? Like booking a weekend away at a convention and insisting you both attend in lycra Spidey outfits?'

Drew laughed. 'Nothing like that but, for the record, this body could so pull off a lycra Spidey outfit.'

It was good to see him laughing again and, he was right, he'd look amazing in lycra. He had one seriously fit body. Scott had often commented on how weedy and inferior he felt next to Drew.

'Oh shit!' Drew exclaimed. 'I don't believe it. There *was* something like that.'

'What?' Sam and I asked together.

Drew put his hand to his mouth. 'Oh my God! But he seemed really into the idea. Plus, it was only a suggestion. I didn't even have an outfit.'

'WHAT?' we cried again.

He bit his lip. 'It's a bit embarrassing but, sod it, I've had enough vodka to not care. Where *is* my vodka, by the way?'

'Don't get mad but I got Sam to hide it. Trying to save you from the hangover from hell.'

He shrugged. 'You may be too late for that. So I asked Luukas if he'd dress up as Thor for me. He had blond hair and muscles and...' He paused and looked at Sam. 'Oh my God! You're him. I mean you look like him. Like Chris Hemsworth. You've got it all! Flash Gordon, Indiana Jones and Thor all wrapped into one.'

Sam stiffened next to me. I'd been about to agree with Drew that Sam did, indeed, look like Chris Hemsworth, but something about his set jaw and stiff posture told me not to go there. I looked at Drew instead. 'You think that's what put him off?'

Drew nodded. 'He had a go at my passion for comic books in the message I read to you, didn't he? Why mention that three years down the line if it hadn't bothered him? It's either the dressing up thing that pushed him away or our eight months together was so insignificant to him that he's just come up with any old crap as an excuse for ending it.'

'Put that thought out of your head right now, Andrew Baxter,' I said. 'Nobody could spend eight *hours* with you and not be left with a lasting positive impression, never mind eight months.'

'Thanks, Jem. What would I do without you looking after me?' He rolled his shoulders a couple of times. 'I'm whacked. Can't deal with this emotional bullshit. I'm going to bed to watch *Avenger's Assemble* for the millionth time and bollocks to Luukas. Laust is welcome to him, the stupid uncommunicative twat. If he didn't want to do the Thor thing, all he needed to do was say so.' He stood up and stretched. 'You're not going to tell me where that vodka is, are you?'

'No, and you're not going via the kitchen to get something else instead.'

He nodded. 'Probably a good idea. Nice to meet you Dr Sam Jones Flash Gordon Thor.'

Sam stiffened again. 'And you. Night.'

'Night, Jem.

I stood up and Drew hugged me. 'Thank you,' he whispered.

'Any time.' We pulled apart. 'Do you think you'll be able to move on now that you've got a reason, albeit a crap one?'

'Maybe.'

'There's one thing I think you should do before you put the film on.'

'Drink a pint of water?'

I smiled. 'Yes, but I was going to say unfriend him and unfollow him. Sever all your connections with him. As several wise people have repeatedly told me over the past few months, you don't need someone like that in your life.'

Drew hugged me once more. 'We'll get there together, Jem. Fresh start. Both of us.'

He went via the kitchen area for a pint of water then disappeared into the bedroom corridor.

'Are you okay? I asked Sam. 'You look like you're miles away.'

'Sorry. I was.'

'Asgard by any chance?'

Sam quickly stood up. 'I don't think you're going to have any trouble with Drew trying to leave the flat. He seems pretty calm. I think I'll head off.' He marched towards the door and lifted his coat off the hooks.

I leaned on the back of the sofa, watching him. 'You can tell me to mind my own business, but there's something about Thor that upsets you, isn't there?'

He paused for a moment with his back to me, arm partway through his sleeve. He sighed then finished pulling it on. 'It's a long story.'

He still had his back to me so I got off the sofa and walked over to him. 'I don't have any plans for the rest of the evening.'

Sam turned round and looked at me, clearly battling with something, although I couldn't imagine what. 'Another time.'

He held my gaze for a while, then smiled and seemed to relax. 'Thanks, though. You've got my number. As I said, Drew seems calm now, but if he loses it again, call me and I'll be straight over.' He leaned in and gave me a gentle kiss on the cheek. 'It was great meeting you tonight. I'm not sure we finished our discussion about your mum so text me with some dates when you're free again.'

'You're sure you don't mind?'

'Happy to help. Maybe without the drama next time, though. I'm not sure I can handle so much excitement on a school night.'

I laughed. 'Thanks for everything tonight, at the pub, and here.'

'I'm glad Drew got his closure. It's hard to let go otherwise.' That distant look was back again for a moment before he smiled. 'Night, Jemma.'

'Night, Sam.'

I stood at the top of the stairs, leaning against the door, exactly where Tiff had stood earlier, and watched Sam trot down the steps, looking up and waving on the bend.

Closure. I nodded. Everyone needed closure. I closed the door and reached in my bag for my phone. In his final text to me, Scott had said not to get in touch but sod him. I needed to do this for me. Curling up on the settee, I started typing:

✉ To Scott

It's been 3 months since you left me all alone in our restaurant. When you ghosted me that first time, I'd never felt so lost and confused. It seemed like such a cruel thing to do, especially to someone you were supposed to love. Then I found out you had a wife and a family. If I'd been hurting before, it was nothing like the pain I felt at discovering our life together had been a lie. I did at least understand why you couldn't continue with our relationship. You were living 2 lives and one of those lives had 3 people depending on you. As angry as I was for what you'd done to me and to your family, I never stopped missing you or loving you. When you turned up at the flat begging me to forgive you, I didn't want to. You'd lied to me and your family and I shouldn't need you in my life. Yet I did. I still loved you as much as ever and I believed you when you said you'd chosen me. I hated the hurt it would cause your family but I couldn't let you go. Then you stood me up. You chose them and I understand why. Much as it breaks my heart,

it was absolutely the right decision which, believe
it or not, makes me love you even more. Maybe if
you'd stayed with me that weekend, it's the conclusion we'd have reached together. I hope you spend
the rest of your life making it up to your wife,
that you're always there for your children, and
that you never betray them ever again. I think you
have the potential to be an incredible husband and
a wonderful father. I'm only sorry I won't get to
experience that. I love you always but I need to
say goodbye. I want to return the money you won on
the horses as it obviously isn't needed for our
wedding. I'll send a cheque to you at work and
leave the payee blank. You can either keep the
money, give it to the twins, or you can donate it
to the hospital where they were looked after. I'd
like the latter, but it's your money so it's up to
you. Be happy. I'm certainly going to try to be xx

I read it through several times and nearly deleted it. He'd got his
closure, though, and I hadn't. Sod it. Send. Then I went to my bedroom
and dug out my cheque book. Giving up the money was easy. Giving up
Scott still hurt so badly.

20

JEMMA

✉ From Sam

I assume Drew was OK after I left. Hope his head isn't too bad this morning. I'm available to talk about your mum when you're ready. Sam x

✉ To Sam

No incidents although he got upset again so I was up till the early hours with him. He sunk a few more beers. I told him he'd be sorry. Sure enough, he's looking green this morning! I've got a day off tomorrow and am heading home for a long weekend. How does Monday or Tuesday sound? X

✉ From Sam

Monday 7pm? Same place? Have a great weekend at home 🙂

✉ To Sam

Hope you have a good weekend too. See you on
Monday. We can catch up on our Whitsborough Bay
gossip too. Probably need it after the heavy stuff!
😊

* * *

At lunchtime on Friday, I felt ridiculously nervous as I stepped out of
Whitsborough Bay Train Station, pulling my weekend case behind me.
I'd had several texts from Logan across the week telling me that Mum
kept shouting at him, so I knew that things had deteriorated and that
the next few days were going to be hard.

It was a bright mid-October day with a blue sky but a nip on the
breeze. Yellow and gold leaves whipped round my feet as I crossed the
station forecourt and headed down the precinct towards Castle Street.

Bear With Me was only a short walk from the station – five or six
minutes – and, despite my nerves, it did feel good to be home. Town
was busy but not packed. The holidaymakers had long-gone although
they'd be back the week after next for October half-term.

Castle Street was about two thirds of the way down the pedestri-
anised precinct on the right hand side and it always felt like stepping
into a different world. The main street was paved and home to chain
shops and banks but Castle Street was cobbled and full of independent
shops and cafés. In my eyes, it was the heart of the town.

Mum's shop was a double-fronted premises a few doors down on
the right, opposite the florist shop, Seaside Blooms. I smiled at the
old fashioned wooden sign with the picture of a traditional teddy
bear on it, swaying gently, then pushed open the door to Bear
With Me.

I paused inside, taking in the activity around me. Liv was at the till,
boxing up a Steiff bear for a customer. She gave me a nod and a smile.

An elderly woman was staring at the collection of Ju-Sea Bears and
Ju-Sea Jem Bears in a glass display cabinet, occasionally reaching out
to stroke one, and there was a younger woman with a plush teddy in

each hand, her head moving swiftly from one to the other, obviously debating which one to buy.

Mum had her back to me, chatting to a bald man with glasses who appeared to be in his mid to late-fifties. She kept laughing. That was a good sign. Hopefully.

I signalled to Liv that I'd be upstairs when Mum was free. I tucked my suitcase into a space under the stairwell and headed up to the kitchen/staffroom on the first floor, put the kettle on to boil, and helped myself to a piece of shortbread.

As well as the staffroom, the first floor of Bear With Me housed a large stock room, the staff toilet, and a second retail space full of bear-making supplies, costumes for teddies, bear-themed greetings cards and wrapping paper, as well as bear-themed stationery. The second floor was home to more storage and the bear-making workshop/sewing room.

'Jemma!' Over the racket from the world's loudest kettle, I hadn't heard Mum coming up the stairs. She gave me a brief hug before pulling out a seat. 'Ooh. That's better. Sorry about that. That was Terrence.'

She said the name as if it should mean something to me. I raised an eyebrow. 'Terrence?'

'My friendly stalker.'

I tossed teabags into the mugs, tears pricking in my eyes. She'd been telling us about him the day Scott proposed. Another lifetime ago.

'He didn't look very stalker-ish,' I said.

'He's completely harmless. A bit intense, but quite sweet. His sister has Parkinson's. She's fifty-one but she was diagnosed when she was the same age as me. She has rigidity, too, rather than shakes. He's going to put me in touch with her. It might be helpful.'

'Sounds good.' I placed a mug in front of her, hugged her, then sat down. 'You look tired, Mum.'

She shrugged. 'I'm fine. Busy morning. That's all.' She studied my face for a moment. 'If we were having a looking exhausted contest, I think I'd be taking second place. What's wrong, Jemma-bear? Scott hasn't been in touch, has he?' I'd never told her about Scott's reappearance then subsequent disappearance. There hadn't seemed any point in adding to her worries and Tiff, Leah, Drew and Karen had all been there to help me pick up the pieces, each managing to resist saying, 'I told you so'.

I blew on my tea. 'I don't think I'll ever hear from him again. Drew had an unexpected blast from the past, though, and he got a bit upset about it so I was up till the early hours yesterday morning consoling him. I'm still a bit tired from that.' *And I'm worried about you.* But I didn't add that. I wanted to finish my conversation with Sam before I broached the subject.

Mum reached across the table and squeezed my hand. 'You would tell me if Scott got in touch again, wouldn't you? The no secrets pact still counts. Just because I've got some health challenges at the moment, it doesn't stop me being your mum first and foremost. Parkinson's doesn't define me. You and Logan and this place are what defines me. And I know there's something you're not telling me about Scott. You've heard from him, haven't you?'

'Not recently.'

'But you *have* heard from him. No secrets.'

I sighed. 'Okay. I saw him. It was mid-July and he turned up at the flat...'

'And you've heard nothing since that text after his no-show at the restaurant?' Mum asked when I'd finished my sorry tale.

'Nothing.'

'How do you feel about him now?'

'I don't really know. Sometimes I'm in tears and I feel so lost without him and can't bear to face the future. Sometimes it feels like we're still together, still in love, and still getting married and that the double life thing was just a dream. Sometimes the overriding emotion is anger. How dare he betray me? How dare he come back to me and get me to fall for his lies all over again? How dare he choose them and not me? Then I feel unbelievably guilty because it's absolutely right that he did choose them.'

Mum squeezed my hand. 'It'll take time.'

'I know. A heck of a lot of time.'

* * *

The next day, Mum looked terrible. She shuffled into the kitchen barely able to prise her eyes open.

'Back to bed,' I ordered. 'I'll bring you some breakfast then I'll go to the shop.'

She didn't even attempt a feeble protest. She was obviously feeling horrendous.

'Logan?' she asked.

'I'll take him with me. It's about time he earned his keep.' I winked at her but she didn't even manage a weak smile in return.

Logan was a star. He didn't complain. He packed his tablet, DS, a sketchbook and some pencil crayons into his school bag and assured me he'd be fine on his own in the staffroom.

* * *

It felt strange preparing the till and getting ready to open up the shop. The last time I'd done that had been before I moved to London.

With ten minutes to go till opening time, I wandered round the ground floor, aiming to familiarise myself with where to find everything. Nothing much had changed, though. The designs differed and there were some new lines but everything had the same home as before. I was itching to re-merchandise some of the displays but I had to resist in case moving things round offended Mum.

Ten minutes after I'd opened up, Logan appeared downstairs and I braced myself for an, 'I'm bored' conversation, tensing at the thought of him traipsing up and down the stairs all day, moaning that there was nothing to do. Instead, he surprised me by asking if he could sort out the bear-making supplies because they 'look a bit messy'.

As soon as Annie arrived, I went upstairs with Logan to see what he meant. Messy was an understatement. Trashed was more like it. I agreed to let him tidy up, not expecting miracles but figuring it would be impossible to make them any worse than they already were. He put his headphones in and cracked on with it. When he'd finished sorting them out, he took a break to play on his DS then tackled the workshop too. It warmed my heart to see him so structured and organised. I thought of the vegetable garden at home and the pride he took in caring for it. He'd obviously inherited those traits from Dad, but executed them in a more casual, less controlling way.

Logan took some before and after photos on his tablet to show Mum what he'd been doing all day. When he showed her them after dinner back at Bear's Pad, she cried and hugged him. I don't think Logan understood why she was so upset but I was pretty certain that the photos proved to her that she needed help.

'Everything's slipping,' I said to Karen on FaceTime later that evening. 'The workshop was in chaos, the paperwork for the shop was all over the place and I mean literally. I found two invoices in the cupboard under the toilet sink and another one behind the toaster. It looks like she's ordered too many bears from one supplier and we've run out of bears from another so I'm going back in tomorrow to sort it out while the shop's closed. I'm worried. She can't do this on her own, no matter how much she wants to.'

'Will you speak to her about it this weekend?'

'No. I need to finish my conversation with Sam first, but then I'll have to tackle it. And I don't think it's going to go down very well.'

21

SAM

The George and Dragon came into view on Monday evening. Tonight was the night. I had to tell her. If Jemma and I were going to be mates – and I hoped we were – the truth needed to come out. I could do this.

As I pulled open the door to the pub and immediately clocked Jemma by the bar paying for a couple of drinks, my stomach did a somersault. She looked so relaxed and carefree as she laughed with the barman that I'd never have guessed that her life was in such turmoil. I was full of admiration for anyone who could do that. Over the years, I'd seen patients who always put on a brave face despite deteriorating health, and I'd seen others fall apart at the slightest of symptoms and become victims from that very moment.

Nikki had been like Jemma. She'd always put on a brave face to the outside world when things were tough. She'd tell me that, as long as she had me by her side, sharing her worries or simply listening to her whinge about a bad day, she could face the world with a grin and a laugh.

My stomach did another somersault as Jemma turned, locked eyes with me, and smiled widely. Uh oh! What the hell was going on? Why was I having that reaction to her? Then I checked myself. Idiot. It wasn't about Jemma. It was because I'd made the decision to tell her about Nikki. Phew! Because the last thing I needed right now was a childish crush on a potential new friend.

Jemma handed me a pint of real ale. 'No arguments. This is to say thank you for giving up your evening for me yet again.'

'Thanks, but it's no problem.'

She steered me towards the same corner table as before and dumped her bag on the floor. I slipped off my coat as she started to unbutton hers.

'I promise no major dramas this evening,' she said.

'How's Drew doing?'

She draped her coat and scarf over a spare stool then sat down. 'He's a bit up and down but he's coming to terms with it. I think that Luukas giving him such a poor reason for ghosting him has helped because Drew's starting to focus on all the negative stuff in their relationship. He's realised that he'd put Luukas on a pedestal. He'll get there. It takes time to get over losing someone you love, doesn't it?'

Oh God, yes! Confession time. A little earlier in the evening than I'd hoped, but best just to throw it out there.

I was grappling with how to word it when Jemma spoke again. 'I'm absolutely dying to chat about home, but would it be really rude if we finish talking about Mum first?'

Conversation closed. For now. I took out my notebook and pen. Hopefully I'd have another opportunity to tell her later. 'That's fine. It's what I'm here for.'

'Thank you.' She rummaged in her bag and, placing her phone on the table, she pulled a face. 'Sorry. Do you mind? I promise I'm not one of those phone-obsessed individuals but, with everything going on with Mum, I like to have it out, just in case.'

'I don't mind. Honestly. How was she at the weekend?'

'Not so good.' She shook her head as she brought me up to date and added in a few things she'd remembered since our last discussion.

I put my pen down on my open notebook when she'd finished. 'I know that you'd love me to give you a definite answer as to whether or not your mum has dementia, but I'm afraid I can't without actually meeting the patient and doing a proper evaluation.'

Her eyes immediately clouded with tears and she nodded her head slowly. I felt terrible.

'That doesn't mean we can't talk about dementia and what that might look like.'

'Okay.'

'Let's start with the science bit. When people think about dementia, they tend to think of Alzheimer's which, granted, is one of the most common forms and one of the most well-known. It's possible for a patient with Parkinson's to also have Alzheimer's. Both affect the neurological system but in different ways. There are also forms of dementia specifically linked to Parkinson's. There's something called Parkinson's dementia where the patient presents dementia symptoms a year or more *after* experiencing the motor symptoms – movement problems – and there's something called Lewy bodies which is where the dementia symptoms present at the same time or even before the movement problems. Does that make sense so far?'

Jemma took a sip of her wine and nodded.

'When most people think about Parkinson's, they think about people shaking but tremors aren't the only symptom and they're not something that happens to everyone.'

'Like Mum. She doesn't have any shakes. She has stiffness instead.'

'There you go, then. With dementia, it's the same in that there are several symptoms and not everyone with it will present with every symptom...'

Jemma sipped on her wine and listened intently as I talked about dementia and the different symptoms. She wrinkled her nose as I said each new one and I could tell she was thinking of something her mum had said or done which might suggest a display of that symptom.

'Do remember that your mum's only forty-six,' I added, 'and that developing dementia under the age of sixty-five is rare. It could be something else.'

Jemma finished her glass of wine. 'I hope so.'

'Another one?' I asked, nodding towards her empty glass.

'Yes please. I could certainly do with one.'

As I passed her, I gently squeezed her shoulder. 'It'll be alright.'

I stood at the bar, watching her slumped shoulders and hung head. Poor Jemma. The symptoms she'd described were certainly indicative of dementia but they were also indicative of other things like stress and depression. Julie's age was a big plus. She was very young for dementia, but that wasn't a reason to rule it out because there were exceptions to every medical 'norm'. Without meeting her, properly examining her medical history, and conducting tests, I couldn't give a diagnosis, no matter how much Jemma might want me to.

'Thanks,' she said when I returned to the table and handed her a large glass of wine. 'And I don't just mean for the drink. You've explained everything really well. I think we both know it's dementia but I understand that you're not allowed to say that without having met the patient.'

'I genuinely can't say it because, unless I've done a proper diagnosis, it's impossible to comment. It could be a number of things. It really could. Please don't convince yourself that it's dementia because, given her age, it's highly unlikely.'

'Really?'

'Really.'

Jemma smiled brightly and, in that moment, she looked like I'd lifted the weight of the world off her shoulders. 'Thank you so much, Sam. I can't tell you how helpful you've been.'

'Any time.'

'So, subject change time. Talk to me about home. Were you brought up in Whitsborough Bay?'

I nodded. 'Born and bred there and so was my dad. My mum's from Middlesbrough. We moved to York when I was three but my parents missed the sea too much so we were back within a year. What about you?'

'My dad was born in Whitby but his family moved to Whitsborough Bay before he started senior school, and Mum was brought up in

Great Sandby. We used to live in town but we moved out to Little Sandby when my parents split up. Mum loves it there and it's been great for Logan growing up in such a friendly village with loads of fields and woods to play in. I hope he still loves it when he hits the teen years and he can't see his mates on an evening because buses don't run.'

Small world. I'd been brought up in the next village to Little Sandby although I'd left home for medical school six years before Jemma had moved there. 'I was bought up in Settering so I know what that's like. My two best mates lived in Little Sandby, though, so I could cycle there easily.'

'Can I ask who? I might know them.'

'Stevie Barnes and Rob Harris. I've no idea if they still live there. We lost touch when we were eighteen. Well, I did. They're probably still mates.'

'Stevie Barnes and Rob Harris?' Jemma repeated their names a couple of times. 'Oh yes! I'm not sure about Rob but, if I'm on the right person, Stevie lives a couple of streets down from ours and he has a gorgeous Border Collie. How come you lost touch?'

'Stupid stuff. My fault. I didn't rate Stevie's fiancée but I wasn't mature enough to keep my opinions to myself.'

Stevie and Rob had been best mates since primary school but they'd never made me feel like the outsider when we met at senior school. For years, the three of us had been inseparable until I'd screwed it up. There was something about Maddy that didn't sit right with me. Stevie's parents had died and the way she behaved around him convinced me she was using him for his inheritance. It seemed a little too convenient when she fell pregnant so soon after they met and the plans for a rushed wedding didn't convince me otherwise. After too many drinks when we were out celebrating Rob's eighteenth, I stupidly shared my views. It got heated and nearly came to blows. I apologised when I sobered up but I couldn't take back what I'd said and I couldn't undo the damage.

I started medical school and made new friends but I was gutted that I'd lost touch with Rob and Stevie. It was a couple of years later when I discovered that the marriage had barely lasted five minutes. I'd been right about Maddy using Stevie but for the wrong reason. She wanted a baby and, when they lost it, she didn't want him anymore.

I thought about getting in touch but too much time had passed and I thought it would look like I was saying, 'I told you so.'

'Maddy sounds like a delight so I'm sure your comments were justified at the time,' Jemma said after I'd told her the story.

'Thanks, but you're being a bit generous. I was in the wrong and I regret that now.' It was only after I lost Nikki that I thought about Stevie again and felt the pain and loss he'd have felt at losing his parents, wife and baby. He could probably have used another friend and I hadn't been there. Nothing I could do about it now, though.

Clearly Jemma didn't think so. 'Then put it right. Get in touch with him.'

I raised my eyebrows at her. 'After sixteen years?'

'Why not? People reconnect through social media all the time after longer friendship gaps than that.'

It would be interesting to find out how he was doing and it would be good to say sorry again, but what was the point? If he forgave me, what would happen? We'd have a virtual friendship rather than a real one because I was looking for reasons to stay away from Whitsborough Bay rather than reasons to return. But Jemma had such an eager puppy-dog expression that I found myself saying, 'I'll think about it.'

'You do that.'

There was a pause in the conversation and I knew what the next line of questioning was going to be. It was inevitable. I decided to delay it and ask her instead. 'So what made you leave Whitsborough Bay for London?'

'No exciting story, I'm afraid. It was where the jobs were.' Jemma told me about her job as a museum curator, how she'd connected with her flatmates, and her love for London.

Her phone rang twice while she was talking and, with a shrug of an apology, she glanced at it each time then shook her head saying she didn't recognise the number before resuming our conversation.

'What about you?' she asked. 'What made you leave Whitsborough Bay?'

It was time. I had to say it. Jemma would be the first person in London, other than my boss, who knew. My stomach churned uneasily and I took a deep breath. 'I'd never planned to leave. I always thought I'd settle in Whitsborough Bay long-term. Get married. Have a family. Do lots more surfing.'

Jemma smiled. 'You've always been into surfing?'

'No. My fiancée, Nikki, got me into it. Her parents were surfers. Her dad said she could surf before she could walk. My brother, Jack, set us up on a blind date and she'd arranged for us to go surfing, figuring it wasn't a complete waste of an evening if I turned out to be a waste of space.'

'I like her thinking. Obviously she didn't think you were a waste of space.'

My throat tightened and I swallowed hard. 'Jack knew what he was doing when he set us up that day because I unexpectedly fell in love with Nikki and with surfing.'

'So here's an obvious question...'

I realised I was holding my breath.

'You're both really into surfing. Right?'

'Yes.'

'And you live in a seaside resort that's internationally recognised as a great place to surf. Right?'

'Yes.'

'So you move to London which isn't exactly renowned for surfing given that it's not by the sea.'

I slowly let out my breath, my heart racing. 'As I said before, London wasn't part of the plan but—'

Jemma's phone rang for the third time. She glanced down and frowned. 'It's the same number again.'

'Hadn't you better get it? They're obviously desperate to get hold of you.'

She sighed. 'I'm so sorry, Sam. If it wasn't for Mum, I really would have it switched on silent and away in my bag.'

'It's fine.' Plus, it delayed the confession. Why was it so hard to say the words? *My fiancée died. My fiancée's dead. My fiancée was walking next to me one minute making plans about the future and, five minutes later, she was dead in my arms.* I took a gulp on my pint, forcing it down over the lump in my throat. As soon as Jemma hung up, I'd just come out with it. Nikki's dead. Yeah. The minute she hung up...

22

JEMMA

'Jemma speaking.' I pulled an apologetic face at Sam. It was probably going to be a wrong number or some annoying salesperson trying to talk me into claiming for an accident that wasn't my fault.

There was a pause. 'Hi Jemma, it's Sarah Derbyshire.'

I frowned. Sarah Derbyshire? The name was familiar, but I couldn't place it. 'Sorry, I didn't quite catch that,' I said, hoping she'd give me a clue.

'Sarah Derbyshire. From Seaside Blooms.'

Of course! She ran the florist's over the road from Bear With Me. I'd chatted to her a few times but we'd never exchanged phone numbers so how and why was she calling me? 'Hi, Sarah, how are you?'

'I'm good, thanks. I hope you don't mind me calling you, but... well... I'm worried about your mum.'

My heart started to pound. 'Why? What's happened?'

'Probably nothing. It's just that I was working late and I noticed the lights were still on in Bear With Me. I figured your mum must be working late too so I came to the window to wave goodnight to her. And that's when I spotted that the door was ajar.'

'Oh my God! There's been a break-in?'

'I don't think so. There's a couple of police constables here now but they've had a good look round and there's nothing to suggest anyone's been in. The safe's still locked and the shelves seem to be fully-stocked.'

'And there's no sign of Mum?'

'No. I've tried phoning her but it goes to voicemail. I saw your number on the noticeboard in the staffroom so I thought I'd better call you. I didn't know what else to do.'

'You did the right thing. Thanks, Sarah. You say the police are still there?'

'Yes. Hang on a sec...' I heard muffled voices. 'Hi Jemma, I'm going to hand you over to one of the policemen.'

'Jemma Browne?'

'Yes.'

'My name's PC Gavin Haines. Am I right in thinking Bear With Me is your mother's business?'

'That's right.'

'I'm at the premises now. My colleague and I have searched all three floors. There's nobody in the building and there's no sign of anything being taken as far as I can tell. You're not aware of any reason why the premises would be left unlocked, are you?'

'No. Mum's always been vigilant about locking up. Some of the bears are worth a lot.'

'Yes, I noticed that. Do you have any idea where your mother might be? I'm keen to get hold of her so we can get the premises secured but the station have been unable to contact her by phone.'

What day was it? Monday? Was that her yoga or Pilates night? 'She could be at a yoga class with my friend Karen. I can try Karen's phone. Or she could be at Karen's mum's. Could you give me five minutes and I'll try their numbers? Should I call you back on the shop phone?'

There was another quick exchange of words.

'Sarah's going to stay for a bit. You can call me back on this mobile,' said PC Haines.

'Bad news?' Sam asked when I hung up.

I held my head in my hands for a moment, taking a few deep,

calming breaths then looked up at him. 'Mum's gone AWOL leaving the shop unlocked. The police are there and nobody can get hold of her. I need to try a few numbers. Sorry.' I scrolled through my phone for Karen's number.

'Is there anything I can do?' Sam asked.

I shook my head, holding the phone to my ear as it dialled Karen's number. 'Thanks but the numbers are all on my phone and... arse. Voicemail.' I scrolled through for Rachel's number, relief flowing through me when it connected after the third ring.

'Hi, Jemma.'

'Hi, Rachel. Is Mum with you?'

'Not yet.'

'You're expecting her, then?'

'Yes. Logan's here.'

'He's not listening, is he?'

'No. He's upstairs with Eden. They're having a competition to see who can build the highest Lego tower. Are you okay? Has something happened?'

I ignored her question. 'When's she due?'

'In about... Gosh, is that the time? She was due about half an hour ago. Should I be worried?'

I could feel the panic rising in me. 'I don't know. She left the shop unlocked and the police are there. They're trying to get hold of her. Is she doing yoga with Karen?'

'Sorry, no. Karen runs a bootcamp on Mondays.'

'Damn! I'd better hang up. I need to phone the police back then get hold of Liv or Annie to see if they can lock up. I think they've both got keys.'

'No need. I've always had a spare set in case of emergency. I can go and lock up now.'

'Thanks, Rachel, that would be amazing. One less thing to worry about. What about Logan and Eden?'

'I'll see if Alison's in next door. I'm sure she'll mind them if she is, otherwise I'll bring them with me. Don't worry. I won't say anything to Logan about Julie going missing.'

'Thanks again. Can you call me when you get back?'

'Yes. And I'll call you if I see or hear from her in the meantime. Try not to worry, Jemma. Your mum will be fine.'

That was easier said than done. Logan was safe and the shop was going to get locked up but Mum could be anywhere. What if she'd had one of her rigid moments when crossing a road and had been hit by a car? Could she have seized up when driving? Or what if it was her mind and she'd wandered off, confused? My breathing came rapidly and I could feel a scream building inside me as I stared at my phone. I was going to have to phone Sarah back and update her but I wasn't sure I could speak.

I'd forgotten about Sam being there until a pair of strong arms wrapped round me. 'It's okay. Just breathe. You've got this. Your mum will be alright. Breathe.'

As I rested my head against his chest, steadying my breathing in time with his, the panic eased and, for the first time in months, I felt calm.

* * *

Even though I was expecting a call, I still jumped when my phone rang shortly after 10 p.m. I looked at Sam who'd insisted on accompanying me back to the flat, especially when he'd heard that all my flatmates were out. He nodded encouragingly as I connected the call.

'Hello?'

'Jemma Browne?'

'Yes?'

'It's PC Gavin Haines. I wanted to let you know that we've found your mother.'

I gripped the arm of the sofa. 'Is she okay?'

'She's a bit confused but she's not hurt or anything.'

'Where was she?'

'Trying to get into a house in Fountain Street.'

'No! Why would she...?' I put my hand over my mouth as the street name registered. 'Was it number sixty-two?'

There was a pause and a rustle of paper. 'Yes, number sixty-two. I understand you used to live there.'

'Yes, but we moved to Little Sandby ten years ago. Was she really trying to break in?'

'Not quite. She had a set of keys out and, of course, they wouldn't fit so she rang the bell and the current owner answered. You won't believe who lives there.'

To be honest, with everything that had happened already, I'd have believed him if he'd told me that George Michael, David Bowie, Whitney Houston, Amy Winehouse and Michael Jackson were alive and well and had taken up residence there, working on new material for their super-group. 'Surprise me.'

'Sarah Derbyshire from the florist's.'

'No!'

'Her husband bought the house from your parents. He recognised your mother and, of course, Sarah knew to phone us.'

'Oh my God! I can't believe she went back to our old home.' I glanced at Sam who gave me a sympathetic look. 'Where is she now?'

'I'm at the hospital with her. She's getting checked over by a doctor.'

'What happens next? I'd come home but I'm in London. There aren't any trains running at this time of night and I don't have a car.'

'Assuming she's not admitted into hospital, is there somewhere she can go?'

'Rachel will look after her. She's the one who dropped the keys off earlier.'

'Good. She gave me her number so I'll get in touch with her. I know it's easier said than done but try not to worry. There's nothing you can do right now except get a good night's sleep and get home when you're able to.'

I thanked him for his help and hung up. I could feel the tears welling up but I needed to be strong. 'I'd better phone Rachel,' I muttered, scrolling for her number again.

After I'd spoken to her, though, I couldn't be strong anymore. Some sort of sniff/cough/hiccup sound erupted from me then hot tears coursed down my cheeks. In an instant, Sam was by my side, with strong, comforting arms round me once more.

'They've found her, Jemma. She's safe. She isn't hurt. Keep focusing on that. I know it's frightening, but she's in the best place to get the help she needs and, because of what's happened, Dr Steadman will have to re-assess her.'

When I'd finally calmed down, he gave me another reassuring squeeze, before releasing me.

Curling my legs up under me, I picked up one of Tiff's brightly coloured scatter cushions and hugged it to my chest. 'It's times like this when I wish I didn't live in London. I feel so far away and so helpless.'

Sam shifted his position slightly so he could face me on the other end of the sofa. 'I've got a car. Actually, I haven't. I've got a bright orange campervan but I can drive you home tonight if you like. I have to warn you that he isn't very fast. His maximum speed is about sixty and he drops to forty on the slightest incline.' He smiled. 'It always drove me mad that it took an eternity to get anywhere but Nikki used to say that the world was too full of people who spent their lives rushing around, and a slower journey made the arrival all the more delicious.'

I wiped my eyes and looked up at Sam but he'd broken eye contact and was staring into space, a wistful expression on his face. Had he just used the past tense when talking about Nikki or was it just a turn of phrase? Oh no! Had they split up? Was that why he'd moved to London? Maybe she'd met someone else. I decided to broach the subject carefully, aware that it was none of my business, but I really liked Sam. The connection to Whitsborough Bay probably helped, but he genuinely felt like a friend I'd known for years instead of a work colleague of my housemate, who I'd only just met.

'That's very generous but that's a hell of a long journey, especially at those speeds. It's late so you could fall asleep at the wheel, you've got work tomorrow, and we've been to the pub.'

'I wouldn't normally drive after having a drink but I barely touched that second pint and it's hours since the first. As for falling asleep, I doubt it. I hardly sleep these days. Work's a little trickier but I honestly don't mind.'

'You might not mind, but I bet Nikki would. I'm not sure I'd like my fiancé disappearing on a road trip with another woman he's only just met or throwing a sickie for her.'

'Nikki wouldn't have minded. She wasn't the jealous type.' He was still staring into space, but I noticed his jaw tighten and that was definitely two uses of the past tense. Crap. They *had* split up.

'Wasn't?' I asked, tentatively.

He swallowed a couple of times then turned to face me again. 'Nikki... erm... she...'

'Go on...' I readied myself for a tale of infidelity, knowing from personal experience exactly what that felt like.

'Nikki's not around anymore.'

'You split up?'

He shook his head slowly, biting on his lip.

I gasped. 'No! She's...?'

'It was meant to be our wedding in June. It would have been her thirtieth birthday that day too but she never made it out of her twenties. Aneurism. Last November.'

My eyes filled with tears. 'Oh my God, Sam! I had no idea. Tiff never said.'

'She doesn't know. Nobody at work knows except my manager and I asked him to keep it confidential. The plan was to start afresh, you know, away from the sympathetic looks, colleagues treading on eggshells, and all the memories.'

'I'm so sorry, Sam. That must have been horrendous.'

'It's been pretty tough.' He took a deep breath. 'Sorry, Jemma, this wasn't meant to be about me.'

'I'm listening...'

'We were on North Bay beach. It was an icy cold day with a biting wind. The sort of day that takes your breath away but it's so exhilarating being out in it.'

He looked at me and I nodded. I knew that sort of bracing weather and I loved it too.

'We'd been talking about our future together. Plans to do up the flat. The wedding. Suddenly she stopped walking and put her hand to her head. I asked if she was okay. She said her head hurt and joked that she wasn't as tough as she looked and would bring a hat next time. She took another step then dropped to the sand. Minutes later, she was gone.'

I clapped my hand over my mouth. 'Oh, Sam. That's awful. How are you coping?'

'Good days and bad days. I thought that moving away from Whitsborough Bay would help to ease the pain by taking me away from the places that remind me of Nikki. The problem is, I don't know anyone here so I've got lots of spare time to think. The more I think, the angrier I get that the life we should have had together was snatched away just like that.' He clicked his fingers.

The pain in his eyes and the grief in his voice was so raw that I couldn't stop the tears from coursing down my cheeks once more. I completely understood how it felt to have your future disappear just like that.

'Sorry Jemma, I didn't mean to make you cry again. I shouldn't have said anything.'

'I didn't give you much choice, did I?'

'I wasn't trying to keep it from you, you know. It's just that...'

I nodded. 'I know. Saying it makes it that bit more real, doesn't it? A bit like me saying the word "dementia". It's so hard.'

Sam put his arms out and I gratefully cuddled into him again, crying for him, for his lost fiancée, me facing the future without Scott, and for Mum, Logan, and what the future meant for our little family. When there were no more tears left, I didn't move, and neither did Sam. I lay against his chest, listening to his heartbeat, feeling safe.

23

SAM

I'm not sure what woke me up: stiff neck, the chill in the flat or the beep of Jemma's phone. Probably a combination of all three. It took me a moment to work out where the hell I was. That had been one seriously deep sleep. Better than I'd experienced since before Nikki died.

Jemma was sound asleep, slumped against me. Her phone beeped again and lit up on the coffee table. I could make out the name 'Rachel'. It was obviously about her mum so I needed to wake her up.

As I adjusted position so I could nudge her, Jemma slid down and rested against my chest. She mumbled something in her sleep, then put her arm round my waist, snuggling up to me. My breath caught. I'd given her a couple of comfort hugs this evening and had thought nothing of it but this was different. I hadn't held anyone like this since Nikki.

My heart raced as I looked down at her and felt the warmth of her body close against mine. Why did I have butterflies? It made no sense.

'Jemma!' I whispered. 'Jemma!' A bit louder.

A key turned in the lock and a woman with a striking resemblance to Tiff, but with a brunette bob rather than long blonde hair with a pink streak, entered the room. She stopped when she saw me looking over the sofa.

'Hello?'

'You must be Tiff's twin,' I whispered. 'I'm Sam. I work with your sister.'

She smiled, obvious relief on her face that I wasn't some random stranger in her home. 'Ah! Dr Jones! We meet at last. I thought we had squatters for a moment.' She removed her coat and hung it up. 'I'm Leah. The sensible one. Allegedly. Where's Jemma? And why are we whispering?'

I pointed towards my chest. Leah took a few paces forward and peeked over the sofa. 'Aw. Looks cosy.'

'She's had a tough night. Her mum went AWOL and left the shop unlocked, but the police found her.'

'Oh my God! Is she okay?'

'I think so.'

Leah wandered round the sofa and stood over us. 'She looks so peaceful. After everything she's been through recently, it seems a shame to wake her.'

'She's had a text from her mum's friend. I think she'd want to read it.'

Jemma wriggled in her sleep, resulting in her snuggling even closer to me. A tendril of hair dropped across her face and she wrinkled her nose as it tickled her. I gently moved it aside and tucked it behind her ear.

'What?' I whispered, looking up at Leah. 'Why are you looking at me like that?'

She shook her head. 'Nothing. You just look like a couple, snuggled up like that and what you did with her hair was so...' She sighed. 'Ignore me. Must stop reading romance novels.'

She crouched down and placed her hand on Jemma's shoulder, shaking her gently. 'Jem-ma, Jem-ma,' she said in a sing-song voice.

'Mum?' Jemma muttered, stirring.

'No. It's Leah. I'm here with Sam. You fell asleep.'

'What?'

'You fell asleep on Sam. You've got a text from...' Leah looked at me. 'Who's it from?'

'Rachel.'

'Rachel?' Jemma sat upright and grabbed her phone, rubbing her eyes with her other hand.

'It's nothing to worry about.' She looked up when she'd read it, the relief on her face obvious. 'Rachel's checked on Mum who's sound asleep and Logan's fine too. She'll ring me in the morning. I'd better reply to let her know I've got the message.'

Leah headed for the kitchen area and put the kettle on. I had no idea what time it was although, unless Leah's theatre trip had turned into drinks then a club, it couldn't be that late. I pulled my phone out of my pocket. 12.27 a.m. We could only have been asleep for about three quarters of an hour, yet I'd never felt more refreshed. I stretched and yawned.

'I should head home.'

Jemma sent her text then put her phone down. 'You don't have to go. I can get you a spare duvet and you can crash here if you want.'

'Thanks, but I'd have to be up early to get ready for work so I might as well head off now.' I stood up and Jemma followed me towards the door.

'Thanks for everything tonight,' she said. 'I don't think I'd have coped if I'd been on my own.'

'You're made of stronger stuff than you think but I'm glad I was here for you. Remember what you promised me at the start of the night?'

She frowned for a moment then smiled. 'Oh yeah, no drama. Epic fail! If you can stand to spend another evening in my company, hopefully it'll be third time lucky.'

'I'd like that,' I said, knowing that I genuinely would.

'I would too. I'd like to hear more about Nikki, if it doesn't hurt too much.'

'It hurts, but I think it would do me good. And you'll tell me about what happened with your fiancé. Scott was it?'

She nodded. 'We can be the lost fiancées club.' Her eyes widened and she gasped. 'I can't believe I just said that. Oh God! It sounds so... I don't know... so... so trite. I'm sorry. I didn't mean it like that.'

'Don't worry about it. I know what you meant. I think it would be helpful for both of us. Scott may not have died but you've still lost him and you're grieving that.'

She looked up at me, pain in her eyes. 'How do you get through each day?'

'Honestly? With great difficulty sometimes. The important thing is that you do get through it.'

I'm not sure who moved first but it seemed natural to hug again. It had been hard telling her about Nikki but I felt like I'd taken another one of those baby steps. Despite the empathy and understanding that my parents, Jack and Millie, and other well-meaning friends had shown, none of them had really understood. None of them had lost someone they loved. But Jemma had. Scott hadn't died but she'd certainly suffered a sudden and unexpected loss. And for a brief moment, much as I wasn't a believer in fate, I wondered if Jemma and I had been brought together for a reason. She needed me and I needed her.

* * *

A text came through while I was getting ready for work after a few surprisingly deep hours of sleep back at my flat; the most unbroken sleep I'd had since Nikki died:

✉ From Jemma

Hi Sam. Just wanted to let you know that I've spoken to Rachel this morning. Mum's OK but was in the shower so I haven't spoken to her yet. Owen's given me the rest of the week off so I'm getting the 10:30 train home. Back on Sunday. Thanks for being there when I needed you last night. You're my

knight in shining armour. I'm so sorry again about
Nikki. I'm here for you x

✉ To Jemma
Keep me posted about your mum and shout up if I can
give you any more advice. Thanks for listening. I
haven't told anyone down here about Nikki but
talking to you helped. I should probably tell Tiff
next x

✉ From Jemma
It might help. I won't say anything to any of them
in the meantime. It's your news for when you're
feeling ready x

✉ To Jemma
Thanks. Hope it goes well at home this week. I'm at
the end of a phone if you need me x

✉ From Jemma
Thanks. And sorry again about the lost fiancées
club comment. OMG! What was that?! *blushes*

She followed it up with a sticker of a cartoon panda's face with
bright red cheeks, which made me laugh. It was exactly the sort of
thing Nikki would have done. She'd always been able to make light of a
bad situation and not let it get her down. I was more of a thinker and
could really dwell on things. Nikki hadn't let me. She always made me
talk about it, learn from it, and move on. So what had I done since
she'd died? Refuse to talk about it, run away from it, and let it control
my life.

Until last night.

Opening up to Jemma felt like a weight had been lifted from me.
Plus there was an open invite to talk more. I wanted to. I felt like I could

talk to her about Nikki and not just because we were both in the 'lost fiancées club'. I would have and could have talked to her anyway.

Why had I bottled it up for so long? Not talking about Nikki wasn't going to suddenly magic her back to life. Not talking about her certainly hadn't stopped me thinking about her every waking hour and most of the hours I should have been sleeping too. Maybe talking about her would help me focus on the good times, stop beating myself up for not being able to do anything to help her, and give me the strength to face the next year, the next five years, the next ten years without her.

And who knows, maybe I would meet someone else one day and do the marriage and kids thing, although I doubted that I'd ever feel the same way about anyone else as I did about Nikki. Lightning wasn't supposed to strike twice, was it?

24

I felt drained as I caught the tube to work on Monday morning. The past week at home had been tough. Karen picked me up from the station on Tuesday afternoon and filled me in on Mum's mood swings as she drove me home. Rachel was at Bear's Pad with Mum who burst into tears the moment she saw me. When Logan got home from school, he ran to me and clung to me, sobbing, which set Mum off again.

It broke my heart to see Mum in such a state. The woman I'd looked up to all my life as a role model – single mum, entrepreneur, expert, creative genius – wasn't even a shadow of her former self. She seemed to move from anger and frustration to listless disinterest in the space of a day, and back again. It was like having a hormonal teenager in the house, lashing out at anyone and everything.

Liv and Annie at Bear With Me were incredible. They worked extra hours, stepped up to take on additional responsibilities. They suggested I spent more time at home than at the shop but, while I wanted to be at home for Mum, I knew I couldn't let things slip and risk adding financial difficulties to her mounting problems.

Fortunately Karen and Rachel were able to step in. They both spent as much time at Bear's Pad as they could during the week. Rachel's role as a freelance travel agent meant that she was predominantly home-based, giving her the flexibility to be with Mum or to have Logan round at hers. She worked on her laptop from Mum's dining table for a couple of days which meant I could focus on the shop knowing Mum wasn't alone.

Dr Steadman agreed to re-assess Mum on the Friday. I accompanied her and, as far as I could tell, he did nothing he hadn't already done. It was hard to believe that Sam had held that role previously and would have been Mum's consultant if he hadn't moved away. Comparing the two of them was like comparing strawberries to sprouts. Where Sam was warm, approachable and empathetic, Dr Steadman was cold, distant and uncaring. When I tried to explain some of the things Mum had said or forgotten, he actually told me to shush, accompanied by a finger over the mouth and a flash of the eyes. Unbelievable! Some of Mum's anger rubbed off on me and I fired off a feisty email to the Trust's complaints team when I got back to Bear's Pad.

It became pretty obvious that I was going to need to move back home. I talked it over with Rachel and Karen over a bottle of wine on Saturday night after Mum went to bed, and the three of us agreed that it would be better not to tell Mum my plans and to just get on with it, avoiding the stress and guilt Mum might experience while I worked my notice.

'So you're definitely going to do it? You're going to move back home?' Karen had asked.

'Looks like it. Just when you thought you'd got rid of me.'

She hugged me. 'I'd be lying if I said I wasn't delighted that you're finally coming home. I just wish it was under different circumstances.'

'Same here.'

'You're doing the right thing,' Rachel said. 'Plus, you love it here and you've always loved the shop so it's not like you're returning to a place you hate and a job you can't bear. Excuse the pun.'

We all giggled at that. 'It'll be fine,' I said, as much to convince me as anything else.

As I snuggled under my duvet that night after Karen and Rachel left, I started to compose my resignation letter in my head ready to give Owen when I returned to London. I loved my job and the museum so much that the thought of not working there actually hurt. I loved my housemates and my life in London and the thought of saying goodbye to them hurt too. But I loved my mum and my brother even more, and the thought of not being there when they needed me hurt the most.

* * *

'I had a feeling this would happen.' Owen sighed then slowly re-folded the letter and returned it to the envelope as we sat at his desk first thing with mugs of tea.

'I'm so sorry. You know how much I love this place and working for you, but I don't see that I have a choice. Mum needs me, even if she doesn't want to admit it. Logan needs me and he *has* admitted it. He's scared and confused which is hardly surprising. I'm twenty-eight and I'm finding it hard. The poor kid's only ten.'

'It won't be the same around here without you.' Owen gently placed his hand over mine.

'I'm scared,' I admitted, blinking back the tears. I was determined not to cry yet again. I felt like that's all I'd done lately. 'What if I'm not strong enough for them both?'

Owen patted my hand. 'You are. I know you are. You need to believe in yourself more. Do you want to leave immediately?'

'No.' I shook my head vigorously. 'That's not fair on you and it's not necessary either. I've got my stuff to pack and things to sort out. Plus, it's half-term and I'm certainly not going to leave you short this week. My contract says four weeks' notice but I'm still owed some holiday. If there's any chance I could do two weeks' notice, or even three, I'd be so grateful.'

He picked up a desk calendar and flicked between October and November, making funny shapes with his mouth. 'What about working until 29th October?'

'But that's the end of the week. Are you sure?'

'Jemma Browne, you're the best thing that's ever happened to the Past Lives Museum, and I'm devastated about losing you, but members of staff – even ones as amazing as you – *can* be replaced. Family *can't* be. Your family need you and you should be with them. Selfishly I also need you for half-term so I'd appreciate you doing this week but I'm only asking that because you said you have things to do and can't go home immediately anyway. If you'd needed to, we'd have managed somehow.'

'Thank you, Owen. That's so good of you. I'll stay late all week to finish off anything you need me to.'

'You'll do no such thing. This letting you off with only one week's notice comes with conditions.' He counted them off on his fingers. 'One: You'll work your normal hours and get your stuff packed and your life in order on the evenings. Two: You'll stay in touch. Three: You'll invite me to Whitsborough Bay to check out Bear With Me. I've heard loads about the place and I need to see it for myself and I would, of course, love to meet your mum. Four: You come to visit us if you're ever in London. Do we have a deal?'

'Yes, Boss. We have a deal.'

'Actually, I have one more condition. As you know, here at Past Lives Museum we pride ourselves on only displaying exquisitely made bears by extremely talented craftspeople from the past. We haven't specifically defined what *the past* means and as the museum will be in your past, my fifth condition is a commission for you to make two of your Ju-Sea Jem Bears. One is for my personal collection and one is to be displayed pride of place in the museum. I will pay for them, of course, and I don't expect them immediately as you have enough to deal with. Perhaps I can visit Whitsborough Bay at some point in the New Year and collect them personally?'

I felt my lip wobble and blinked back the tears. 'Have I ever told you that you're the best boss in the whole wide world? And a wonderful friend too. Thank you.'

Owen leaned across the desk and gave me a hug. 'No, Jemma. It's me who needs to thank you. You've turned this place around in the time you've been here. I never told you when you started here but the museum was struggling to stay afloat. It was a financial risk employing a curator but the knowledge and passion I saw in you convinced me it was a risk worth taking. If it wasn't for you, the museum would not exist today. You're more driven and much stronger than you realise. Don't ever forget it.'

'But I'm always crying. Look at me now.' I dabbed my eyes with a tissue.

'Crying isn't a sign of weakness. I personally think it means that you care deeply about something which is a good thing, isn't it?'

As I returned to my desk, I knew I'd done the right thing in resigning and I certainly felt boosted by Owen's words. Looking across at him now, laughing with another of my colleagues, I was so grateful for how understanding he'd been. It made a difficult situation so much easier. So that was it! One more week and I'd be moving back to Whitsborough Bay for good. It was definitely the right decision to move home but had we been right not to involve Mum in the discussion? Only time would tell.

☒ From Jemma
Really short notice but are you free tonight for a
catch up? Xx

☒ To Jemma
No plans. Usual place? X

☒ From Jemma
Any chance you could come to the flat? 7pm? We'll
get pizzas in

It was quite pathetic really. It was the Tuesday of October half-term but it could have been any night of the week – or the following week for that matter – and my reply would have been exactly the same: no plans. None. I seriously had to get myself some hobbies, some mates or both.

Thing is, I already had a hobby and I used to have a best mate to do it with. All I really wanted to do each night was throw the boards in the back of the campervan, drive the short distance from our flat to North

Bay, catch some waves with Nikki, and have a real ale in Blue Savannah while the sky melted from stunning purples and pinks into silky black.

But she was gone and so was the sea. Crawling along the M25 to the south coast to surf on my own didn't carry the same appeal.

I shovelled a forkful of salad into my mouth. What *was* I doing in London? I'd never wanted to live in a city. I could see what a great lifestyle it offered if you were into dining out, museums, theatres, wine bars, but I was a pie-and-a-pint-in-the-local kind of person who loved the outdoors. Who loved the sea. Not London material. Perhaps Jemma would change that for me. She'd settled really well so maybe she could show me round and convert me.

I still hadn't been back to Whitsborough Bay. Every time Mum and Dad or Jack phoned, they asked the same question: when are you coming home to visit? What they really meant was: when are you coming home for good? That unspoken question always hung in the air after the call ended, adding to my mountain of guilt.

'Dr Jones! What are you up to?' Tiff plonked herself down opposite me and ripped open the cellophane wrapping on a torpedo roll.

'This very second? Sending a text to Jemma. I'm coming to your flat tonight.' I pressed send on my message.

'Has she told you yet?'

I looked up from my phone. 'Told me what?

Tiff took a bite out of her roll and pulled faces whilst she tried to chew and swallow it quickly. 'She obviously hasn't. And if I'd got my brain in gear, I'd have realised that's why she's seeing you tonight.'

'She's won the lottery?' I suggested.

Tiff wrinkled her nose. 'I wish. No. She's moving back up north.'

I dropped my fork into my salad. 'To Whitsborough Bay?'

'Yes. But you didn't hear it from me. Act surprised, will you?' She grabbed my wrist and looked at my watch. 'No! Why am I always late? I'll see you at the flat later.' Clamping her mouth over her part-eaten roll like a dog carrying a bone, she dashed towards the exit.

I slump back in my chair. Jemma was leaving London? Shit! The only person I'd spent any time with outside of the hospital was shipping out. She wouldn't be showing me round, then.

Unable to face the rest of my lunch, I grabbed a coffee and headed back to my office instead. I pictured Jemma back in Whitsborough Bay with the squawk of gulls, the smell of salt in the air, and the stunning views of coast and countryside. Christ, I missed that. I missed the thrill of riding a wave, and the tranquillity of bobbing on my board in calmer seas. And I missed my family.

Back in my office, I called Mum.

'Sammy? Is everything okay?' The worry in her voice was obvious and I knew immediately it was because I never called her. Crap son. We'd always been close but I'd pushed her – and everyone else – away since Nikki died. I needed to rectify that.

'I'm fine. I was wondering if you and Dad had any plans this weekend.'

'Nothing much. Usual stuff. Bit of shopping. Jack and Millie's for Sunday lunch. Why?'

'I thought I might come home for the weekend. Would it be okay to stay with you?'

'That would be wonderful, Sammy. You know you're welcome any time.'

'I don't know if I'll come up on Friday or Saturday yet but I'll let you know later.'

'Will you stay for Sunday lunch? Shall I phone Jack for you?'

'It's okay. I'll phone him. I owe him a call.'

* * *

Jemma opened the door to her flat just after 7 p.m. and immediately hugged me. She held onto me tightly and I found myself doing the same. It was weird how quickly we'd formed an intense connection which made the idea of her leaving even more unpalatable.

'Thanks for coming round at such short notice,' she said when we parted.

'It was tricky but I managed to clear my diary. I wasn't really in the mood for dinner with the Mayor, a Royal Box at the theatre, and a private viewing of the latest Damien Hirst collection with the artist himself. They all begged me not to cancel but it's tough when you have such a demanding social life like me.'

Jemma raised an eyebrow. 'Ready meal for one and a *Game of Thrones* box set?'

'Am I that transparent?'

She laughed as she led me to the lounge. 'Drink?'

I sat down on the sofa. 'Lager if you've got one.'

'I have.' She raised her voice. 'Leah, Tiff, Drew! Sam's here. Time to order pizza.'

The flat became chaotic as they joined us, debating over what to order. Drew shook my hand as soon as he appeared and apologised for the previous week, but I told him not to worry about it.

'I still think you look like Thor,' he said. 'Don't you, Jem?'

I caught Jemma's eye and she nodded as though she understood that there was a connection to Nikki, even though I hadn't yet explained it.

'Give over, Drew,' she said. 'He's got blond hair and he's tall. You think all tall blonds look like Thor. Hurry up and order. I'm starving.'

Once the pizzas were ordered, they left us alone. Jemma turned to me as soon as the door to the bedrooms had closed. 'So, what's the deal with Thor? You got all funny the other night yet you mentioned something about Thor before we caught the tube here. I'm guessing there's a connection to Nikki.'

I nodded. 'Nikki said I looked like Chris Hemsworth the night we met...' I told her about the conversation. 'Nikki thought it would be a hilarious contradiction to christen our campervan Thor because he's slow and weak. I tried to talk her out of it but it kind of stuck.'

'That's classic. Do you want me to get Drew to quit it with the Thor thing?'

I shook my head. 'Actually, I quite like it. I know I flinched at first but it makes me smile. It's a happy memory.'

'It's good to hang onto the happy memories.'

She held my gaze for a moment and that understanding was definitely there.

'So how was your week at home?' I asked. Presumably things had deteriorated further with her mum if she was moving back.

Jemma grimaced. 'It's always good to be home but it was hard. Mum was in a bit of a state after going AWOL. Rachel and Karen are doing their best but they both have businesses to run and Rachel has an eleven-year-old daughter. They can't drop everything for Mum but I can. It's a huge decision but I know it's the right one. I'm moving back to Whitsborough Bay.' She narrowed her eyes at me. 'You don't look surprised. Tiff by any chance?

'Sorry. She saw me at lunch and accidentally let it slip. She made me promise to act surprised but I'm pretty crap at acting. When do you go?'

'Saturday. I handed in my notice yesterday and Owen's letting me leave on Friday so I just need to get my stuff packed and... crap... I forgot to phone the van hire place before it closed. Anyway, I've got to hire a van and move my stuff.'

'Have you got much to move?'

'Not really. I've always rented down here and it's been furnished flats so it's just boxes and a couple of shelving and storage units.'

'Would all your stuff fit in a campervan?'

Her eyes widened. 'Thor?'

'Yes. The campervan of Asgard. I decided a trip home was long overdue so I spoke to my mum this afternoon. I'm doing good son and brother duty for the weekend. If you don't mind the company, I'm more than happy to be your removals service.'

'Oh my God! Really? You don't mind?'

'You'd be doing me a favour. It's a long, boring journey on my own, especially at those speeds.'

Jemma grinned. 'Dr Jones, you're an absolute star and I owe you big time for this.'

'You don't owe me anything. Just helping out a friend and, as I said, doing myself a favour too. How's the packing going?'

'I've got as far as getting hold of some crates and boxes. Unfortunately there's nothing in them yet so I've got a few late nights ahead of me.'

'I don't mind helping.'

'I couldn't ask you to do that.'

'If you'd rather I didn't help, I understand. It's your stuff and some of it's going to be personal, but two pairs of hands would make light work for books and DVDs. And, let's face it, I've got sod all else to do, although I am about to start a new season of *Game of Thrones* and the last one ended on a cliffhanger.'

'You're on.'

Jemma grabbed me another drink. 'London really isn't you, is it?' she said as she sat down again.

'No. I'm not sure I'll ever feel settled here.'

'It can be a pretty lonely place despite being so full of people.'

It certainly was.

'So why don't you move back to Whitsborough Bay?'

It was a good question and one that I hadn't been able to stop thinking about since lunchtime. I shrugged. 'I can't. What would I do? Dr Steadman's got my job and there aren't any other vacancies. There aren't any jobs in York either. I've already looked. Not that I'd want to commute over an hour each way even if there were. I've rented out the apartment on a long lease too. No job. No home.'

'Yeah, but compare it to what you have here in London. Job? Yes. Home? Yes. Family? Friends? Sea? No to all. Which would you rather have?'

I took a swig of lager. Did I want to potentially harm the career that I'd spent so many years developing by walking away from my promotion? Without Nikki, my career was the main focus in my life. Should it be the only focus, though? It had been since moving to London, but only because I had nothing else. Jemma was right. If I moved back to

Whitsborough Bay, I'd have friends, family, and surfing. But I'd also be surrounded by places I'd been with Nikki, and it was those memories I'd fled from in the first place. I had a hell of a lot to think about while I was at home for the weekend.

26

I watched Sam's expression carefully. Had I said too much? It was obvious to me that he was exceptionally lonely in London. Tiff had told me that, if she saw him in the hospital canteen, he was either on his own or he was with colleagues but not really *with* them – more of a bystander to their conversation and banter.

The loneliness was easy to recognise because I'd experienced it first-hand when I'd moved to London six years ago. I'd phone Mum and Karen, making out that I had loads of new friends and an active social life when the reality was that I'd moved into a shared flat with the most anti-social group of individuals I'd ever encountered. I hated my job, my colleagues were an unwelcoming clique, and the only places I ever went were the supermarket, the library, or the cinema... on my own. Thankfully I secured the role at Past Lives Museum a few months later and, as soon as my lease was up, moved into a flat with friendly people, at which point I started to love my life in London. I'd loved it even more when I'd moved in with Tiff, Leah and Drew.

The door buzzer rang indicating the arrival of pizza and the flat burst into life. I watched the easy banter my flatmates had with each other and with Sam, smiling to myself. I was going to miss them so much but they'd promised lots of visits up north.

I could have happily stayed in the lounge chatting all evening but that wasn't going to get the packing done. They'd all offered to help me and I'd turned them down saying I had plenty of time but I didn't miss the raised eyebrows when I said Sam was staying to help.

'He's just a friend,' I told Leah as we took the empty pizza boxes down to the recycling bin.

'You say that, but remember I saw you two snuggled up on the sofa last week. Very cosy.'

'Behave! You know what he's been through.' He'd told Tiff about Nikki while I was away and had said she could tell the other two.

'I know. You've both had horrendous experiences which perhaps makes you kindred spirits.'

'The last thing on my mind right now is a new relationship and I'm sure Sam feels exactly the same.'

'We'll see.'

* * *

I put my hand on the knob to my bedroom door and turned to Sam. 'Before we go in, I should warn you that I have lots of bears. They're not everyone's cup of tea, but I love them.'

He looked round my bedroom in silence then slowly walked towards my bedside drawers. Bending down, he stared at Diamond for a moment. 'Did your mum make this one?'

'Yes. How did you know?' Mum sewed identification tags, a bit like washing instruction labels, into her bears. She always put them in their bottoms so they didn't spoil the look of the bear when he was seated.

'His face,' Sam said. 'He looks a lot like the one I bought for Nikki. I've spent hours staring at that bear since she died.'

I was about to ask him what she was like, but he turned away from Diamond. 'You said you make bears?'

'Mum makes Ju-Sea Bears, which tend to be medium to large. I make Ju-Sea Jem Bears, which are small to miniature.' I pointed to a shelf. 'I made those.'

'Can I pick one up?'

'Be my guest.'

He reached forward and picked up a miniature grey bear wearing a crocheted green scarf. 'Christ! What have you got in here? Weights?'

I laughed. 'It's steel shot. It weighs down their bums so they sit better.'

Sam sat the bear in the palm of his hand. 'You and your mum are extremely talented.'

'Mum's the talented one. I do my best.'

He put the grey bear down and picked up a miniature panda. 'Don't sell yourself short. These are exceptional.'

'Thank you.'

'Are these for sale or are they part of your collection?'

'For sale. I was going to put them on Etsy but they'll probably go in the shop instead now that I'm going home.'

'In that case, can I buy the panda and this purple one for my nieces? I've been a rubbish uncle since Nikki died and I feel I should go home with gifts. I'd rather get them something they can keep and appreciate when they're older than duplicate something they've already got.'

'How old are they?'

'Isla's three and Saffron's... crap. I don't actually know. She was born after Nikki died but it's a blur as to how long after.' He shook his head. 'I don't think I even got them a congratulations card, never mind a gift.'

'You had a lot to deal with.'

'Even so, it's not fair on Jack and Millie. Isla's definitely three because she had a birthday recently – which I also forgot – but Saffron could be anywhere up to ten months old. If Jack had his own way, they'd have another on the way, but Millie's put her foot down.'

'Three kids under school age? Wow! He's brave.'

I was relieved to see the serious expression slip from Sam's face as he smiled. 'Either that or bloody stupid. I haven't quite worked out which. How much do I owe you for these?'

'Nothing.'

He looked at me for a moment. 'Then they will have to go back on the shelf with their friends because I won't take them.'

'Sam! You have to. Call them a thank you for advice, the help with my packing, and the removals service. Please.'

Sam picked up the purple bear. 'What do you think, young Ju-Sea Jem Bear, should we accept her offer?' He held the bear up to his ear and nodded his head, then turned to me. 'Mr Purple Bear says okay as long as you let me take you out for a meal next time I'm back in Whitsborough Bay. Not this weekend as you'll have loads on and I don't think my family will let me out their sight after a very prolonged absence, but next time.'

I smiled. 'It's a deal. Now stop playing with my bears and help me pack.'

* * *

Sam had been right: two pairs of hands did make light work of it and, within a couple of hours, we'd packed away all of my books, CDs, DVDs, the hug, and various other bits and bobs, leaving me with mainly clothes and toiletries for tomorrow night.

As we worked, we chatted about growing up in Whitsborough Bay: favourite places, the schools we'd attended, people we knew, whether we preferred North or South Bay, whether we still visited the tourist attractions. It was lovely being able to chat and laugh about trivial things and I was pretty sure it was a relief to Sam too.

There was no avoiding the tough stuff, though, because the places we talked about were places he'd visited with Nikki, some were ones I'd visited with Scott, and all held memories of happy times with Mum.

Sam paused momentarily every time he mentioned Nikki and, if I stole a glance at him, he'd have stopped packing and have a distant look in his eyes. Then he'd smile and resume his story. It was heartbreaking to think about what he'd been through. I wished there was something I could say or do to take the pain away for Sam but what would help? Perhaps just being there and listening to him would make a difference, like it was doing for me.

A couple of hours later, I decided we'd done enough for now and grabbed us another couple of drinks. We sat together on my bed, leaning against the headboard, surrounded by boxes and crates.

'Thanks for helping.' I clinked my bottle against his.

'You're welcome.' He took a swig. 'Are you ready to tell me about Scott?'

'Okay. As ready as I'll ever be...'

* * *

Saturday morning arrived. Moving day. It didn't feel real. I'd said goodbye to Leah, Tiff and Drew on so many occasions – particularly in recent months to nip home for the weekend – but this time it was for good. The end of an era. Three-and-a-half years of tears and laughter, nights out, nights in, parties, movie nights, hangovers, illness, celebrations and commiserations with three of the best friends I could ever hope to meet had come to an end.

I wasn't the only one hurting. They might have been giggling like little kids and hurling abuse at each other about who was the strongest and how to hold a box properly, but I knew from the red eyes and the reassuring touches on the arm that they were finding this as hard as I was. They'd already collectively agreed not to replace me because I was irreplaceable. That had made me cry.

The three of them traipsed up and down two flights of stairs with my belongings, which Sam packed into Thor the campervan with astonishing precision. He'd emptied all the cupboards and under-seat storage for maximum removals capacity, which had been just as well because I'd have had to leave a few boxes behind for later transportation if he hadn't. I hadn't realised I'd accumulated quite so much stuff.

He slammed the door shut, stretched, then glanced at his watch. 'Ten to ten. Pretty good going.'

'All packed and ready to go?' Drew asked.

I nodded. 'I think so. I'll go in and do one last check then nip to the loo.'

A quick look round my bedroom, under the bed, and behind the door satisfied me that I definitely had everything. With a heavy heart, I closed the door for the last time.

Placing my key in a colourful dish on a bookshelf by the coat rack, I reached for my coat and scarf from the hooks and paused. This was it. Goodbye to my home, my friends, and life as I knew it. I knew I was doing the right thing for my family. I hoped Mum would see it that way too.

'You can't be hungry already,' Jemma exclaimed as I pulled into the car park of a McDonald's less than ten minutes away from her flat.

'I'm not.' Tiff had insisted we had a hearty breakfast before we could start loading up Thor and wouldn't let me lift any boxes until I'd eaten at least two bacon butties. No hardship.

'Then why are we stopping?'

'Because I've got something for you. Out you get.' I got out and walked round the campervan to meet Jemma.

'What's going on?' she asked.

'I think you need one of these.' I opened my arms wide and, without hesitation, Jemma snuggled against my chest, sobbing. I'd watched her trying to hold back the tears as she hugged her flatmates goodbye and made promises to stay in touch and visit each other regularly. I heard them telling her she was their family now and, even though she'd smiled, I could tell the words had broken her. As we set off, I could tell she was still trying to hold it together and it was pointless. We had a long drive ahead of us and she needed to let it go or she'd be on edge for the next four or five hours.

'Oh my goodness, I needed that,' she said, releasing me some time later. 'Thank you.'

'All part of the premium removals service.' I clambered back into the driver's seat and we continued on our way.

I could see that Jemma had visibly relaxed but she was still quiet, staring out of the window, probably trying to imprint the streets round her London home in her mind.

As if reading my thoughts, she said, 'I promise I will talk to you. I'm just taking it all in for one last time.'

'That's fine. You take your time.'

She was quiet for another five minutes or so, then she turned to me. 'How do you feel about going home? Did you say it'll be the first time since you moved down south?'

'Yes, which is really bad given that I moved here eight months ago.' I cringed as I said it. Jack had visited a couple of times, and so had my parents, so I had at least seen some of my family, but it was wrong of me not to have made an effort to see the others. 'I'm a bit nervous. No. Nervous isn't the right word. Or is it? I don't know. I feel guilty for staying away for so long. Embarrassed too. And, yes, probably nervous because I *think* I want to visit the spot of beach where it happened but I don't know whether that's going to be too hard to do.'

'What was she like? Or is it too painful to talk about?'

'No, I'd like to talk about her if you don't mind listening.'

'I'm not going anywhere for at least four hours.' She wriggled in her seat so she could face me a bit better.

I smiled. 'She was amazing. Absolutely amazing.'

For the first time, I opened up. I told Jemma the full details about how we met and how grateful I was to Jack for not letting me pull out. I talked about her passion for surfing and how she got me hooked, about buying the campervan and the dream we had of touring round the UK and visiting all the best surfing spots, our engagement, our wedding plans. And the day she dropped to the sand clutching her head and drew her last breath, cradled in my arms. My voice broke at that part and I had to blink back the tears. A loud sniff broke me from the vivid memory and I glanced at Jemma to see tears cascading down her cheeks again. She placed her hand gently on my arm as I concentrated on the road and on keeping my own emotions in check.

'I'm so sorry, Sam,' she whispered. 'I can't even begin to imagine how terrifying that must have been.'

'I remember people running towards us and me screaming out "somebody call an ambulance" but I knew it was too late. I begged her to stay with me but she was already gone. There was nothing that I or anyone else could have done to prevent it and, as Jack kept telling me afterwards, I had to keep focusing on the fact that I was with her, holding her, when she could easily have been alone. At the time, that didn't feel comforting because seeing the woman you love dying in front of your eyes is something I wouldn't wish on anyone, but I understand now what he meant by it and, while I obviously wish that it had never happened, I'm glad that I was with her when it did.'

'I wish I'd known her. She sounds like someone I'd have been friends with.'

'I think you would have been. I think she was a closet... what's that word?'

'What word?'

'For people who love bears.'

'Arctophile.'

'That's it. Strange word. It sounds rude.'

Jemma laughed. 'I know. It comes from the Greek words *arctos* meaning bear and *philos* meaning loving, so a lover or collector of bears is an arctophile.'

'Get you, Mrs Knowledgeable.'

She laughed again. 'Only about bears. Put me on a quiz team and I'm a liability.' She rummaged in her pocket for a tissue, blew her nose, and mopped her cheeks. 'You really think Nikki could have been an arctophile?'

'Judging by how long we spent in Bear With Me when we collected our surfer bear and how she kept pointing out which ones she liked best if I was ever stuck for birthday or Christmas gift ideas, I think so.'

Jemma was silent for a moment. 'You said you were on North Bay beach?'

'Yeah. Right at the north end just before the rock pools.'

'That's my favourite part.'

'It was ours too if we were out for a walk, although it was obviously the other end if we were surfing.'

* * *

We stopped at one of the service stations on the MI for a quick leg stretch and toilet break, although Jemma was nervous about leaving the campervan unattended so we took turns. She insisted on going second and returned, grinning, with a McFlurry in each hand, her purse tucked under her arm, and a big bag of wine gums dangling from between her teeth.

I took one of the ice-creams and released the sweets so she could settle herself back into the campervan. 'I knew you were up to something when you insisted I go first.'

'I know it's not exactly ice-cream weather but we're off to the seaside in a surfer's campervan so it feels right.'

We ate our treats then set off again.

'I have a question for you,' Jemma said when I'd pulled back onto the MI. 'You don't have to answer this if you think it's too intrusive.'

'I like your style. You wait until we're back on the motorway, trapped together, before you say that.' I glanced across and smiled at her. 'Fire away.'

'You said that you nearly backed out of your date with Nikki because it was too soon after your ex whose name I've completely blanked on.'

My jaw tightened. 'Kirsty.'

'You said that Kirsty had been unfaithful. What happened? Only if you don't mind telling me.'

'I don't mind. It would probably do me good to talk about her too because, like Nikki, I've bottled that up as well. Kirsty was... still is... a nurse at Whitsborough Bay General. I'd seen her around and she'd always given me this big grin and sometimes a cheeky wink when she passed me in the corridor, but we'd never had the opportunity to speak. Until the work Christmas party five years ago...'

Jemma listened as I told her how I couldn't take my eyes off Kirsty that night and despite Jack's warnings that she'd worked her way through most of the men at the hospital, I convinced myself that she simply hadn't found the right man yet. And, of course, I was that man.

'I'd like to think that there was a significant part of the two years we were together when it was just me she was seeing but, from what I discovered afterwards, I think it might have been as little as two weeks.'

'How did you find out?'

'I caught them at it. A meeting got cancelled and I came home early, hoping to surprise her, but it was me who got the surprise. I walked into what I can only describe as a scene from a porno film. They were both wearing these studded dog collar things, he wore a muzzle and she was attached to a lead.'

Jemma gasped. 'You're kidding!'

'I wish I was.' I shuddered as I pictured them. 'I'll just make it clear that I *never* did anything like that with her. I've no idea if it was some kinky little fantasy of hers that she thankfully never shared with me, or whether it was his thing and she was happy to go along with it. Either way, dressed up as dogs was some serious messed up shit.'

'I assume that was the end for you both?'

'Definitely. She moved out that night.'

'Wow! Completely different scenario to how I found out about Scott but equally grim. Did you love her?'

I thought for a moment. 'Yes. Or at least I thought I had until I met Nikki. No, I did. We had a very different relationship to the one I had with Nikki, which is inevitable as they were like chalk and cheese, but I did love Kirsty so I was pretty destroyed by what she did.'

'Would you have taken her back?'

'No. There was no way I could trust her after what I caught her doing and, without trust, there was no future for us. I'd have been questioning every text she sent, every phone call she made, every night out she supposedly had with the girls. I'd have worried about her at work too because plenty of gossip came to light afterwards about what she got up to in her breaks. If I'd taken her back, there'd have been jealousy, arguments, name-calling. It would have turned nasty.' I took a sideways glance at Jemma. Her brow was furrowed and I realised I might have put my foot in it as she'd taken Scott back. But they were very different situations.

'Kirsty begged me to take her back,' I continued. 'She walks her Nana's dog on North Bay every Sunday and I always seemed to bump into her when I was walking or running. It was a different technique each time from tears to seduction to pleading temporary insanity because she loved me so much and couldn't bear being away from me. I never understood that logic. If you miss someone, you send them a text, you look at a photo, you sniff their clothes. You don't play a game of hide the sausage dressed as a canine.'

Jemma started giggling. 'Sorry, Sam, I don't mean to laugh. It's just that...' She was laughing so much, she couldn't finish the sentence. Unlike Nikki's deep belly laugh, Jemma's laugh sounded more like a Smurf on helium, and it was unbelievably infectious. I had to concentrate so hard to keep the campervan in a straight line while I laughed along with her. Why hadn't I seen it before? It *was* hilarious when I thought about it.

When our hysterics subsided, Jemma gently placed her hand on my thigh. 'I promise I wasn't laughing *at* you. What she did was horrendous. It's just that the thought of her in a doggy gimp outfit is...' Then we were both off again.

'Christ, I needed that,' I said when we finally calmed down. 'I've barely laughed since Nikki died. I certainly haven't laughed like that. Thank you.'

'Thank you for sharing your shaggy dog tale with me,' Jemma said, wiping her eyes.

'Stop it!' But we were both off again. My head hurt, my stomach was in agony, but I felt like I'd taken another massive step forward. I'd finally laughed – the proper side-aching sort – and I'd found humour in the Kirsty situation when I'd previously only felt bitterness towards her. Jemma had definitely come into my life for a reason.

We travelled in contented silence for a while.

I glanced at Jemma, gazing out the window as we crawled along in the slow lane up a slight incline. 'What made you ask me about Kirsty? Was it because of what happened with Scott?'

She twisted in her seat to face me again. 'Kirsty was unfaithful and you stood your ground, refusing to take her back. Scott was unfaithful and I was so weak that I took him back the minute he apologised.'

I knew I'd put my foot in it. Idiot! 'It was different for the two of you.'

'How was it different? It's still discovering that someone that you love is having sex with someone else.'

I shrugged. It just seemed so different. 'He loved you. He was going to leave his wife for you. Kirsty wasn't planning on leaving me and, if she loved me, she had a funny way of showing it. She wanted to have her cake and eat it.'

Jemma's shoulders slumped. 'Yeah, but he didn't leave Fiona in the end, did he? What if he was just like Kirsty and wanted to have his cake and eat it? The only difference is that he was unfaithful with one person instead of a string of them. Or at least I assume there was only me. I should have been strong. I should have told him to get lost.'

She grabbed a wine gum and shoved it in her mouth then groaned. 'Green. Ew! I thought it was black. If I can't pick the right bloody wine gum, I've got no chance with picking the right bloke, have I?'

'I've just had a thought about why it was easier for me to say no to Kirsty,' I said. 'I caught her in the act. I had an adult only movie playing over and over again in my head. You only had whatever you let your imagination create for you and, if you had any sense, you wouldn't have gone down that route.' I glanced into the wine gums bag and spotted a black. I fished it out and handed it to Jemma.

'Thank you. You could be right about that. I saw photos of them and that hurt so I tried to avoid thinking about them together.'

'See. If I'd found out about Kirsty but hadn't seen it for myself, who knows whether I'd have fallen for one of those reconciliation attempts. I suspect I would have done. I don't think it would have lasted for long because so much came to light about all the others, but I do think that I'd have given her a second chance because that's what you do when you love someone. You want them to take that chance and prove you were right to give them it.'

'Which Scott absolutely didn't do.'

'Yeah, but he let you know this time, didn't he? I know he stood you up but he let you know his decision that night. He didn't ghost you again and he didn't string you along believing he was going to leave his wife when he wasn't going to. You should ask yourself this: If you'd sent Scott away without a second chance, would you have always wondered "what if?" I think you would.'

Jemma reached for another wine gum then paused before putting it in her mouth.

'Another green one?'

'No. Orange. They're good. It's just the green ones that offend me.' She chewed on her wine gum and I sensed she was also chewing over what I'd said.

'You know what you should do?' she said, when she'd finished her sweet.

'Remove all the green wine gums from the packet so you don't have to face that trauma again?'

She laughed. 'You *should* do that. But after that, you should leave London, return to Whitsborough Bay, and set yourself up as a mobile counsellor. You could fill Thor with soft cushions and boxes of tissues, and drive up and down the Yorkshire Coast giving out relationship advice or helping people come to terms with their relationship decisions.'

'Me? Give out relationship advice? With my track record of the extreme measures my last two girlfriends have taken to get away from me?'

'Seriously! Well, not really. I doubt it would pay much but you've just helped me loads.'

I stole a glance at Jemma to make sure she was being sincere.

'I mean it! I've been beating myself up for being weak as usual and letting him back into my life but you've just echoed what my best friend, Karen, said to me at the time and it's spot on. I *had* to take that chance. Who knows whether it would have worked out in the long run but I'd never have known if I hadn't tried.'

'You're not weak,' I assured her. 'I know we haven't known each other for long but I see a fighter. I see someone who picks herself up from all the knocks she gets. I see someone who's strong.'

'You really think I'm strong?'

'Christ, yes! I know you're devastated about Scott but you've picked yourself up and got on with life. And I know you're devastated about your mum's diagnosis too but you've just got on with that. You've not been happy with the advice you've been given so you've sought a second opinion. You've been home several times and assessed what's needed and, as a result, you've packed in the job and the life you love and you're going home to take control. That's what a fighter does. That's what you've done.'

As I said it, I realised she'd instilled some fighting spirit back into me too. I was going home for the first time since I'd run away to London, I'd made a decision to visit the spot where it happened, and I'd even started job hunting thanks to Jemma. She was right: London v home. No brainer. I wouldn't have had the courage to make any of those decisions if it hadn't been for the strength she'd shown.

✉ To Sam

Thanks again for moving me home. And for the advice
about Mum, the advice about Scott, supporting me
when Mum went AWOL, being there to help with Drew,
and bearing with me despite all the disruption I've
brought into your life. I can't believe we only met
17 days ago! Feels like I've known you for years.
You probably feel like you've aged 17 years after
all that drama! Flash Gordon/Thor/Indiana Jones?
No. I think you may actually be a real life superhero in your own right. I'd like to return one of
the many favours. You have a big challenge to face
while you're home. Visiting the spot where you lost
Nikki must be unbearably painful for you. I appreciate that this may be something you want to/need
to face alone but if you do need support — even if
that's someone waiting for you in Blue Savannah
with a pint and a listening ear after you've
visited the spot on your own — I'm here for you xx

⊠ From Sam
Hope you're settling in OK and your mum wasn't too
shocked to find you'd moved in when she got home
from work. Thanks for your offer. I think I need to
do it on my own but the idea of a pint and a
listening ear is appealing. You should work in
sales! Can I think about it overnight and text you
tomorrow? Xx

⊠ To Sam
Of course. This has to be what works for you. The
offer's there and you only need to accept it if
it's what you want/need. This is about you, not me.
Mum was stunned. She cried buckets. She lectured me
for leaving London but admitted she was relieved to
have me home. Phew! Sleep well and may or may not
see you tomorrow xx

* * *

I woke up on Sunday morning and lay still for several minutes, smiling
as I listened to the birds tweeting outside. No traffic. No shouting. No
sirens. Just peace.

'This is it,' I whispered to myself. 'Home for good.'

If I'd had any doubts, Logan's reaction last night had eclipsed them.
He squealed with excitement and clung onto me tightly. It felt good to
be needed.

Thank goodness the shop was closed on Sundays, although it
wouldn't be for much longer. Mum had tried opening seven days a
week throughout the year but had found that the Sunday trade outside
of the summer and Christmas seasons wasn't enough to justify the
salaries and overheads. The first Christmas Sunday opening was in two
weeks' time so the shop would soon be very full-on.

I couldn't stay in bed all day listening to the birds. I needed to unpack and work out what my new routine would look like. I'd also have a trip to the beach to fit in if Sam decided he wanted some company.

After a quick shower, I got dressed then went downstairs to make bacon butties as a special treat.

There was no sign of Mum or Logan when breakfast was ready so I loaded everything onto a tray and took it up to Mum's bedroom. She sat up and rubbed her eyes.

'I thought I could smell bacon,' she said, inhaling.

Logan appeared from his room, grabbed a butty, smothered it in ketchup, and started munching on it.

'Plate?' I questioned, watching a shower of crumbs drop onto the carpet.

He shrugged. 'Thought I'd save you the washing up.'

'By creating more vacuuming?' I raised an eyebrow at him.

'I'll do it. I like vacuuming.'

I looked at Mum doubtfully, but she nodded. 'He really does. He gets Henry the hoover out without me even asking, don't you Logan?'

Logan nodded. 'What are we doing today, Jemma-bear? Can we go bowling again?'

I grimaced. 'I'm not sure I can cope with being thrashed by a ten-year-old again.'

He giggled. 'You were rubbish.'

'I know! I don't need reminding. I think I need those barrier things they put up for the little kids and that slide thing for releasing my ball.'

'So can we?' He bounced up and down, dropping more crumbs.

'Why don't you give Jemma a chance to settle in?' Mum said, diplomatically. 'She's probably got unpacking to do and friends to catch up with.'

'Tell you what, Logan, how about I promise to take you bowling next Sunday if you let me catch up on a few things today. We'll see if Karen and Eden are free too. Would that be okay?'

'Promise?'

'Pinky promise.' I wrapped my little finger round his and regretted it immediately because his fingers were covered in sticky ketchup.

'Can I watch cartoons in my room, Mum?' he asked.

'Yes. Just not too loud.'

He grinned and ran out of the room, grabbing another butty first.

I pushed the tray to one side and sat down on the edge of Mum's bed. 'You two seem a lot happier around each other.'

She nodded. 'There've been no more incidents. The theft accusation seems to have been forgotten now.'

'That's a relief.' I placed a bacon butty on a plate and passed it to Mum, then took a bite of mine. We ate in companionable silence for a while, but my heart sank as I gazed round her room. I'd been aware that it was a bit messy when I walked in with the tray, but I'd been focussed on not spilling the drinks, then on Logan. Now that I could fully take it in, it was like being in an untidy teenager's room. Wardrobe doors were ajar with outfits thrown over the tops of them, clothes dangled from half-open drawers and there were heaps of dirty clothes on the floor. The bin in the corner was overflowing and discarded make-up wipes were strewn across the chest of drawers holding her mirror. Another part of her orderly life descending into chaos.

'I know it's a bit messy,' she said, obviously noticing my gaze.

'No, it's...' I shook my head, putting half my butty back down on the tray, appetite gone. 'Yes, it is. Can I help?'

'It's fine. I usually have a good tidy up on a Sunday. I'll do it later. What are your plans?'

'Hmm?'

'Jemma!' Mum said, sharply. 'Stop looking at the mess. I've said I'll sort it and I will. Remember who the parent is here.'

Thoroughly chastised, I focussed squarely back on her. 'Sorry. What did you ask me?'

'About your plans.'

'Oh, yeah. Well, I might be going out this morning or I might not. You know I told you about Sam, the one who brought me home yesterday? It's quite a sad story, really...'

Mum drank her coffee while I sipped on a cup of tea and told her about Sam and Nikki.

'You actually met them shortly after they got engaged. They bought a Ju-Sea Bear to celebrate. Must have been a couple of years ago.'

She shrugged and shook her head. 'For goodness sake, Jemma. I sell loads of bears. It could have been anyone.' She sounded exasperated.

'You made a surfboard and a Hawaiian shirt for him,' I prompted, trying to calm the nerves that swelled up every time Mum couldn't remember something. I couldn't let it go. She had to remember the surfing bear. She'd been so proud of him and had bombarded me with photos at the time.

Her face softened. 'Aw, no! It was them? They were a lovely couple. They were in the shop for ages. I think she'd have gone away with a full hug if she'd had her way.'

My churning stomach settled. She remembered. 'Sam said Nikki was pretty taken with the bears.'

'That's so sad. I remember her being so... what would the word be? Ooh! What's that word? When someone's full of life?'

'Bubbly?' I suggested.

'No. Erm... Ooh, I hate it when that happens.' She slapped her palm against her forehead, clearly frustrated. 'Full of life. Animated. Energetic. Begins with a v.'

'Vivacious?'

'That's it! Vivacious. That's what she was like. He seemed quieter, steadier.'

I hadn't seen any photos of Nikki yet but, from the conversations I'd had with Sam, I had a clear image in my mind of the sort of woman she'd been, both in looks and personality. Vivacious definitely fitted with that image.

'So, I may or may not be going to the beach with Sam,' I said. 'I've got some more unpacking to do but the most important thing is to talk about you, about me and what happens next.'

'What do you mean?'

'I'm home now and I'm here to help out but I don't want to take over. I want to understand what would work for you. It's your home and Bear With Me is your business.'

Silence.

'Obviously I'm out of work now so I'm kind of hoping I might be able to get my old job back as Assistant Bear-Keeper.'

Mum stared at me, her head on a slant, her eyes narrowed.

I knew I should have just shut up and let her speak. I knew it. Yet I didn't. Feeling unnerved, I continued wittering. 'I know you don't want things to change but surely you know they have to. When you went AWOL the other week, I was so worried about you. I'm still worried. I think you need to slow down. You've always taken on so much with the shop, the valuing, the bear-making, the workshops, and you've been this amazing woman who's balanced all those things, run the house, and been a great mum to Logan and me, but it's too much for you now. Everything's slipping.'

I didn't mean to do it, but I swept my hand round her bedroom to illustrate my point. 'I want to take on some hours at the shop for you, maybe run some workshops. You might want to let go of the valuation roles. There's too much pressure and too much travel for you. We could get a cleaner for here. One of Karen's PT clients runs a cleaning company. I could ask her for the details. What do you think?'

Silence.

'Mum?'

'What do I *think*? Bloody hell, Jemma! I *think* you might as well strap a boulder to my legs and push me off Lighthouse Point.'

I flinched at her angry tone. 'What do you mean?'

'I mean you've obviously thought it all through and you've got a master plan which doesn't feature me at all because you've already got me dead and buried. You want to take over my business, my job and my home. Do you want to play mum to Logan too because you're clearly a way better mother figure than me? You'd *never* accuse him of stealing, would you?'

I'd never seen her looking or sounding so mad and it was all my fault. 'That's not what I meant,' I said in a gentle voice, wishing I could take it all back. 'I'm sorry.'

Mum wasn't going to be appeased. 'But it's what you said, Jemma,' she cried. 'You started off by saying you didn't want to take over and you wanted to know what would work for me. Then you reeled off a list of what *you* want to do and what *you* don't want *me* to do. Clearly I don't have a say in this exciting new life you have planned.' She slapped her palm down on the duvet, making me jump.

'Mum...'

She narrowed her eyes at me. 'I should have known you'd be just like him.'

'Like who?'

'Your bloody father. Controlling. Demanding. Well you can just sod off back to London and leave me alone. It's *my* house and *my* business and I don't need you or your dad telling me what to do. I'm better off now that he's living in Cranton and I can manage perfectly well with you living in London. I don't need either of you interfering.'

My heart was pounding, making me feel sick and dizzy. 'Mum! That's not how I meant any of it.'

'Really? That's not what I heard and, to be honest, I've heard enough. It's time to leave.'

'Mum! We need to talk about this. Please.' She had a wild look in her eyes and her cheeks were aflame. It was new and scary and I was way out of my depth but I had to keep trying to reason with her.

'You do. I don't. Go away, Jemma.'

'Mum!'

'GET THE HELL OUT!'

With a frustrated cry, she hurled her mug towards the door. Coffee flew over the duvet and carpet. The mug chipped a chunk out of the wooden door as it smashed, splashing the remnants of drink down the walls and onto the floor.

I ran towards the door and, with shaking hands, carefully gathered the larger fragments in my palm. 'I'll get Henry,' I muttered through my tears.

'Stop trying to control everything. Leave it. Leave me. NOW!'

She didn't need to tell me again. Gulping back sobs, I dropped the pieces and fled.

* * *

'Here's the taxi,' I said to Logan as we stood on the front doorstep of Bear's Pad ten minutes later. 'Quickly fasten your laces.' I'd put sunglasses on so he couldn't see my red eyes. It was a bright day so I could at least get away with shades in October, avoiding any awkward questions.

He looked up from where he was bent over his trainers. 'Why am I going to Auntie Rachel's? I'm not meant to be seeing Eden until tomorrow.'

Good question. But not one with an easy answer.

Finishing his bow, he stood up. I cuddled him to my side and hoped he couldn't feel me still shaking. 'I need to go out, Logan-paws, and Mum isn't feeling very well so Auntie Rachel said she'd have you for a few hours. You don't mind, do you?'

He shook his head. 'I like it there. Mum doesn't feel very well most days.'

'I know, sweetheart, I know. But she's got some tablets and some nice doctors looking after her. It's just a bit difficult for her.'

'I heard her shouting at you. She never used to shout.'

I nodded as I squeezed him tighter. It had been too much to hope that he wouldn't have overheard. They'd probably heard at the bottom of the street.

I had no words of comfort for Logan and, even if I had, I couldn't speak. I gently pushed him in the direction of the taxi, which had now pulled onto the drive behind Mum's car.

I'd texted her to say I was going out and dropping Logan at Rachel's. I'd spotted her phone on her bedside drawers and figured she had more chance of seeing a text than a note downstairs. I hadn't dared open her door and tell her in person. I also hadn't dared take her car.

Using some of Dad's inheritance money to get a car of my own was going to have to be a priority tomorrow. Assuming I wasn't catching a train back to London.

'How about I take you bowling this afternoon after all?' I asked as the taxi backed off the drive.

Logan beamed at me. I hadn't made Mum happy but at least I could make my little brother happy.

He put his headphones in and concentrated on a game on his DS during the short journey to Rachel's so I grabbed the opportunity to send a text:

✉ To Sam
I don't know whether you need me this morning or
not but I need you. Had a horrendous run-in with
Mum just now and I don't know what to do. I'll be
at Blue Savannah from ten. If you can't make it, I
understand. I've already asked far too many favours
from you xx

✉ From Sam
I'll be there xx

* * *

It was shortly after ten when the taxi driver dropped me off near Blue Savannah having taken Logan to Rachel's. I'd quickly briefed her on my disastrous morning as soon as he disappeared upstairs with Eden.

I paused and breathed in the sea air as the taxi driver pulled away. Despite being the penultimate day of October, it was warm and sunny with the lightest of breezes. North Bay was already busy with children on scooters, families on bikes, dog walkers, and babies in buggies, all making the most of the last weekend of half-term.

Sam was coming out of the bar as I approached, carrying what looked like a coffee and an enormous hot chocolate piled high with cream. He placed them down on a metal table and waved at me.

'I thought it was a bit early for a pint of beer.' He lightly kissed me on the cheek after I'd taken the steps onto the terrace. 'But it's never too early for a pint of hot chocolate. I hope you like it with cream and marshmallows.'

'It's perfect. Thank you.'

We sat down, facing the beach. I dipped my finger in the cream and licked it. Yummy. 'Have you been to—?'

'Not yet,' he interrupted. 'I will, though. The last time I was here in Blue Savannah was with Nikki. It doesn't feel as strange as I thought it would.'

'Did you come here a lot?'

'Pretty much every time we went surfing. We liked to warm up with a coffee or chill out with a beer. They've usually got a couple of decent real ales on tap. They also do great pub grub and an amazing full English.'

I nodded. 'I brought Scott here for a full English the first time he stayed. Being on the road so much, he was a breakfast aficionado but even he admitted they did the best he'd ever had.'

We sat in silence for a moment, lost in our memories.

'So,' Sam said. 'You've got your hot chocolate and I've got my listening ear ready. What happened with your mum?'

'It was awful. Absolutely awful…'

Somehow I managed to relay the morning's events without crying although I still felt shaky.

'And, to top it all, she thinks my dad's still alive. There were two definite present tense comments about him. I don't know what to do.' At that point, my voice cracked and I couldn't say any more. Mum yelling at me and hurling her drink at the door had been terrifying but that was nothing compared to the idea that she'd regressed into a world where Dad was still with us.

29

SAM

I wished I could reassure Jemma. I wished I could get her to laugh it off. Say something like, 'Forget about it. She'd obviously woken up in a bad mood. I'm sure she'll be fine once she's had some more sleep.' But I couldn't give her those reassurances. It didn't sound fine at all.

Instead, I tried a different angle. 'Dr Steadman said that things were "inconclusive" with your mum?'

She nodded. 'Can you believe that? His patient turns up at a house she hasn't lived in for a decade and he says it's "inconclusive"? I'm beginning to think that he's got one of those degrees you can buy online because he clearly hasn't a clue.'

'I never met him but I can't say I'm impressed from what you've told me. He shouldn't be dragging his heels like that.'

Jemma fished a marshmallow from the bottom of her drink with her fingers. 'I wish you were Mum's consultant,' she said, before popping the marshmallow in her mouth and licking her fingers. 'Get him sacked and come back.'

'I wish it was that easy.'

Leaning forward in my chair, I watched the activity on the beach. In my immediate eyeline, a pair of spaniels were chasing each other in a circle, splashing through a pool of seawater, a retriever was steadily destroying an abandoned – yet pretty impressive – sandcastle, and a toddler had broken loose from his parents and was making a beeline for the sea. All round them were more dogs, children, families, couples, all soaking up the autumn sun on their faces, the feel of the sand beneath their feet, and the whisper of the breeze. I loved this place. What the hell had I been thinking, running away from all of this?

I turned my attention back to Jemma. 'What does your mum think of Dr Steadman?'

'She can't stand him.'

'Do you think she'd agree to a consultation with me? Completely off the record?'

Jemma's eyes lit up. 'You'd do that?'

'I want to help. I shouldn't interfere but you're obviously not getting anywhere with him and I'm wondering if the outbursts from your mum might be partly down to frustration at not getting the support she needs.'

She shrugged. 'It could be.'

'I don't think it would be a good idea to do it today. Not because I've got plans as I could easily change those, but because I think your Mum needs a chance to calm down a bit and settle into a routine now that you're home. How about I try to come up again next weekend?'

Jemma's eyes glistened with tears and she reached across the table and took my hand in hers, nodding. Poor lass obviously couldn't speak. This was tearing her apart and if I could help, I wanted to.

We sat for some time, still holding hands, watching over the beach. The silence between us was only perforated by the occasional burst of laughter, the cry of a child, a dog barking, a car horn beeping, and the clink of teaspoons.

In my peripheral vision, I watched Jemma's lips moving slightly as though she was rehearsing a speech – what she was going to say to her mum, perhaps? Or maybe she was going over their fight again. What if she wasn't thinking about her mum at all? What if she was thinking about Scott? She said she'd brought him to Blue Savannah. It certainly held plenty of memories for me but they weren't as painful as I'd expected.

I turned my gaze beyond Jemma to the steps in front of The Surf Shack where I'd first seen Nikki. The pain had definitely eased since I'd opened up to Jemma about what happened.

The sun disappeared behind a large grey cloud and the gentle breeze picked up. Jemma shivered and tightened her grip on my hand.

'Cold?' I asked.

'I wasn't, but I am now.' She nodded towards the cloud. 'I could have believed it was the middle of summer a moment ago but now I can certainly believe it'll be November on Tuesday.'

'Fancy a walk?' I asked.

'Sure.' She squeezed my hand. 'Is it time?'

I nodded. 'It's time and I'd like you with me.'

We walked down the steps in front of The Surf Shack and onto the beach. I took a deep breath.

'Are you okay?' Jemma asked.

'I think so. I'm glad you're here.'

'After everything you've done for me, I wouldn't be anywhere else.'

We wandered along the beach in silence. I could do this. I could stand there and not break.

My pulse raced as the rock pools came into sight in the distance. The sky darkened another shade and so did my mood as I re-lived our last moments together.

I felt a tug on my coat sleeve. 'You don't have to do this,' Jemma said. 'You've already faced a lot of memories today. If this is too much...'

Was it? I ran my fingers through my hair and interlinked them at the back of my head, holding them there with my arms pressed against the sides of my face and my head lowered. I took another deep breath then lowered my arms. 'No. I can do this. I *need* to do this.'

We continued towards the rock pools in silence.

'Where was it?' Jemma whispered.

The sky darkened further as I pointed to a patch of beach a few feet away from the first rock pool.

'I'll wait here, shall I?'

I nodded. Another deep breath. On shaky legs, I strode the last ten metres or so to the spot. I don't know what made me do it but, when I got there, I looked up towards the sky and, at that exact moment, the clouds parted. A shaft of sunlight beamed down right on me and a feeling of calm flowed through me. 'Nikki,' I whispered, as the sun warmed my cheeks. 'You're here.'

I turned in a circle with my arms spread wide, soaking up the sun. I could see Jemma where I'd left her with her hand over her mouth, staring up at the sky.

'Goodbye,' I whispered, completing my circle and squinting into the light. 'You go and catch some waves. Don't worry about me. I'm getting there. It's slow, but I'm definitely getting there.'

A few seconds later, the sun disappeared behind a cloud again. She was gone. I stood there for a minute or so more, then returned to Jemma.

'The sunshine...' she said.

'I know.'

'It was beautiful.'

I nodded.

'I don't know what your beliefs are but it seemed like Nikki was there for you.'

I took a moment more, drinking it in, then indicated that we should set off walking back towards Blue Savannah. 'I thought that too. I believe in science but I've seen events – miracles if you like – that medicine and science can't explain so there's a part of me that believes it doesn't just end.'

'I'm the same. I believe in something.'

As we continued along the beach, it became busier, and we were soon in the midst of the activity.

'How are you feeling now that you've visited the place?'

I stopped walking and looked back towards the distant rock pools, before turning to face Jemma. 'Like I've just taken another *enormous* leap forward.'

'That's good to hear. I was worried it could go the other way.'

'So was I! No, it was good. It was the best thing I could have done. I don't know what I was expecting. I've avoided North Bay since it happened and maybe that was the right thing for me at first, but I don't need to do that anymore. We spent so much time here that I keep thinking of all the good times rather than that day. Even on the day it happened, I can think of good memories because...' I glanced back down the beach, thinking about the events of that morning.

'Because what?' Jemma asked.

I turned back to her. 'Nothing. Ignore me. Anyway, it was thanks to you that I came here today.'

'Me? I didn't do anything. You'd already decided to come. I pretty much gate crashed it after my crisis with Mum.'

'It was the thought of you moving home that made me realise how much I missed this place, which then prompted me to phone my mum. As soon as I'd decided to come home, visiting the rock pools was the obvious thing to do and you gave me the strength to go through with it. Thank you.'

'Stop it! You'll make me cry again!'

I put my arms out towards her and Jemma eagerly accepted the hug. She wrapped her arms round my waist and put her head against my chest. 'You did an amazing thing today,' she said.

It genuinely felt as though I'd been trapped in a dark tunnel and had finally made it to the light at the other side, thanks to Jemma. I gently kissed the top of her head, and closed my eyes as I held her closely. She tilted her head back and looked up at me. My heart started to race as I gazed into her hazel eyes and...

'Well, well, well. The delectable Dr Jones has finally come home.' My head snapped round at the sound of her voice. 'Hello, gorgeous.'

'Kirsty,' I said through gritted teeth. Why hadn't I thought about it? It was Sunday morning and Kirsty always walked her Nana's poodle along the beach on a Sunday when she wasn't working. Bloody typical that I'd bump into her.

'Aren't you going to introduce me to your friend?' she purred, pawing at the dark-haired man next to her while the poodle yapped and tried to jump up at me.

Jemma had moved out of the hug but I kept my arm round her shoulders, feeling as though I needed to protect her from the viper in front of us. 'Jemma, Kirsty. Kirsty, Jemma.' I wasn't going to expand on it.

'Ah! So you're Kirsty,' Jemma said. 'You're not at all how I imagined you. I thought you'd be wearing doggy ears, a collar and a lead.'

The smile slipped from Kirsty's bright red lips for a brief moment and, much as I wanted to laugh and cheer at Jemma's witty comment, I knew that Kirsty was about to fire back with something bitchy.

Turning her attention to me, Kirsty grinned. 'After you ran away to London like a scared little boy, we all thought you were going to pine for surfer girl forever. Looks like we were wrong. You obviously didn't give a shit about her after all, given that you've moved onto a new one so quickly. What would Nikki say, knowing that you were being unfaithful to her memory so soon? Tut tut.' She shook her head. 'Don't think much of the replacement either, but you never could handle a real woman, could you?'

She was clearly waiting for a response but I wasn't going to rise to it. She looked Jemma up and down and sneered, then threw a seductive look at me. Pathetic. I turned away, making her tut.

'Bye, losers.'

'I'm so sorry, Sam,' Jemma said, as my arm slipped off her shoulder. 'I shouldn't have said anything.'

'You weren't to know how she'd respond.'

'I could have guessed based on what you'd told me. After this morning's incident, you'd think I'd have learned when to keep my big gob shut and... and now I'm wittering again instead of shutting up. Sorry.'

I twisted round and looked back down the beach towards the rock pools. Bloody Kirsty. Five minutes ago, I'd felt so elated. But now...

I turned back to Jemma. She looked up at me with those big innocent eyes of hers and I swallowed hard. 'I'd better get to my brother's for lunch before they send out a search party. Do you need a lift anywhere?'

She didn't answer for a moment and I knew my brusque tone had hurt her, but I couldn't say it was all right because it wasn't. Maybe I could have laughed it off but the problem was that Kirsty had been so close to the truth. As I'd gazed into Jemma's eyes, I'd imagined kissing her. It had been just for a fleeting moment but, in that moment, Nikki was nowhere in my thoughts. It hadn't even been a year and I was already thinking about kissing someone else on *our* beach. How could I do that to Nikki?

'I might stay here on the beach for a bit longer,' Jemma said. 'I can't face going home just yet. Thanks for the offer, though.'

I should have insisted she let me take her home, maybe even go inside with her and make sure her mum wasn't going to have a go at her again. But I couldn't. I needed to get away from her and make sense of the turmoil of emotions inside me.

'If you're sure?'

'I'm sure. Enjoy your meal.'

I headed towards the steps by The Surf Shack.

'Hey,' Jemma called.

As I turned round to face her, the clouds broke again and the sun shone down, reflecting off her hair and face. She looked absolutely stunning at that moment and my heart raced as I stared at her.

'You did an amazing thing today,' she said. 'Don't let what Kirsty said overshadow that giant leap you took.'

It took every ounce of strength I had not to run back to her and take her in my arms. Instead, I nodded then turned my back on her and did my usual trick: I ran away.

30

JEMMA

I watched as Sam disappeared into the distance, swamped by the throng on the promenade. That went well. Not.

Well, I couldn't stand in the middle of the beach forever but I couldn't go home either, unless... I checked my phone. Nothing from Mum. No texts. No missed calls. Nope, I definitely couldn't go home.

Wandering up to the serving hatch of the ice-cream parlour wedged between Blue Savannah and The Surf Shack, I ordered a take-away coffee, then sat on the wall overlooking the beach. I removed a piece of fabric, a needle and some thread from a make-up case in my bag. Some people always had an eReader on them and others were practically welded to their phone, digging it out at any moment of downtime. I always had a project with me. Hand-sewing the tiny limbs of a bear never failed to de-stress me and I seriously needed de-stressing right now.

Ten minutes later, my phone rang and my pulse raced. Mum? Sam?

'Hi Leah,' I said, trying not to sound disappointed.

'How's it going? Do you miss us?'

'I miss you loads and it's a disaster.'

Adjusting my position on the wall so that I could lean against a pillar, I sipped on my coffee and told Leah what had happened with Mum and then with Sam on the beach.

'Sounds like Dr Jones has the hots for you and that evil ex of his scared him off.'

'No. I don't think he sees me as more than a friend, although I think you're right that her comment scared him off. He's still grieving for Nikki. The suggestion that he was seeing someone else really hurt him.'

'How do you feel about him?' she asked.

'He's a good friend. A *really* good friend.'

'But could he be more than a friend? The pair of you are so cute together.'

'Leah! Give over with the match-making. I'm still trying to get over Scott. I'm not sure I'll be able to trust anyone again after that. With that and everything going on at home, a new relationship isn't exactly in my top ten of priorities at the moment. I'd say it's not even in my top one hundred. And even if I was in a place to start seeing someone again – which I'm absolutely not – Sam's still grieving for his fiancée so nothing about him screams potential new boyfriend. And, even if he wasn't grieving, he lives in London where I don't live anymore. Although, if things don't improve with Mum, I might be begging you for my room back and Owen for my job back.'

'It won't come to that. Your mum and you will be best friends again in no time. She just needs handling carefully and you admitted yourself that you did exactly the opposite of that.'

* * *

Rachel opened the door a couple of hours later. 'He's had his dinner and he's excited about, and I quote, "thrashing Jem at bowling because she's rubbisher than a three-year-old". Sounds like a fun afternoon.'

I rolled my eyes. 'I have no defence. I *am* rubbish. It's an inconsistency thing. I'll get a strike and then I'll miss every pin on my next few turns or only knock a couple down. Yet I swear I'm not changing my technique. Would Eden like to join us?'

'I'm glad you asked because Logan's already invited her. You're sure you don't mind?'

I smiled. 'It's the least I can do. I should have asked her earlier. Sorry.'

Rachel looked serious. 'Any news from your mum?'

'No. I texted her to say I'd taken Logan out and that I was sorry but I haven't heard anything in return. I don't know wha—'

With squeals of excitement, Logan and Eden thundered down the stairs, ending the conversation. They bounced up and down, each begging to go first.

'I'll toss a coin for it,' I said. 'Or you can play rock, paper, scissors in the taxi.'

'Taxi?' Rachel peered round me towards the waiting car as Logan and Eden raced each other down the drive. 'You should have said. I'd have picked you up. I assumed you were in your mum's car.'

'I didn't dare take it after this morning's incident. Thought it might be my turn to be accused of theft.'

'Oh, Jemma. I'll go round to see her while you're out with the kids.'

'Anything you can do to calm her would be forever appreciated.'

* * *

I'd like to say that I did myself proud at Bay Bowling but I was completely thrashed by two kids. Embarrassing. It was exactly the distraction I needed, though. Listening to their incessant chatter was so refreshing and it warmed my heart to see how close the pair of them clearly were. I wondered whether their friendship would turn into something more as they got older. If it did, I hope it lasted. Good friends were a precious find.

With friendship on my mind, I thought about Sam earlier. I was so proud of him for what he'd done. It couldn't have been easy. I'd looked up at him to ask how he was feeling and then Kirsty had appeared and things had turned sour. Why had she had to appear at that point? I pictured us just before, arms round each other and, suddenly, I imagined him cupping my face then kissing me. Where on earth had that come from? Leah! It was her fault for questioning our relationship. I'd never have thought of it if she hadn't planted the seed.

While Logan and Eden played on the penny falls machines before we left the arcade, a text arrived:

✉ From Rachel
I'm at Bear's Pad. Your mum's OK. She's more mad with herself than you. Do you want to bring the kids back here? xx

* * *

Logan and Eden spent most of the taxi journey to Bear's Pad debating whether it was better to have the highest overall score like Eden or the most strikes like Logan. I spent most of the taxi journey trying to control my nausea. I genuinely had no idea what was going to happen with Mum. Rachel had obviously smoothed the waters but I wasn't sure what the future held or if I was strong enough to cope with it if the incident this morning was an indication of how things were going to be.

They were in the lounge when we got home. It was all a bit awkward at first. Logan and Eden immediately launched into telling Mum and Rachel every miniscule detail of our game. All the while, I loitered in the doorway, watching as Mum laughed in the right places, feigned interest, and seemingly did anything to avoid eye contact with me.

'How about you take Eden into the kitchen to get a drink?' Rachel said to Logan when they moved onto the details of their games in the arcade.

'What do you want to drink?' Logan asked Eden.

'Take her into the kitchen and let her pick,' Rachel said firmly.

'Then you can take your drinks up to your bedroom and play Minecraft again.'

Logan shrugged. 'Come on, Eden.' They ran out the room, giggling.

'Why don't you sit down, Jemma?' Rachel suggested. 'Julie's got something she wants to say to you.'

Obediently, I perched on the nearest armchair and waited.

Mum cleared her throat. 'When I was Logan's age, I had a really bad case of the chicken-pox. Spots were everywhere – on my eyelids, in my ears, in my mouth and even in my, er, lady bits, shall we say? I'd barely had a day's sickness until then and I didn't cope well with being so poorly. Apparently I worked myself into a frustrated frenzy, shouting, crying, hurling myself around which heated my body up and made the itching worse, making me even more frustrated and upset. My mum couldn't cope. I actually made her ill and she had to send me to my grandma's after a few days. Thankfully I've been pretty healthy ever since. Then I got diagnosed with Parkinson's and I've felt like that frustrated ten-year-old all over again, hating what's happening to me, but powerless to do anything about it.' She sighed and shook her head. 'I'm not coping well with this diagnosis. I thought I was the sort of person who could take anything that life wanted to throw at me. I thought I was really strong. I thought I was a fighter. But that's obviously not the case.'

'You *are* strong,' I insisted. 'You're the strongest person I know. I've always wanted to be more like you.'

'Oh, Jemma-bear. You don't want to be like me. Or at least not the me that I am at the moment. I'm angry, I'm bitter and I want to lash out. Right now, I feel as though I hate the world and everyone in it. I especially hate that Dr Steadman for being such a useless imbecile. I'm scared that I turned up at our old house, I'm scared that I left the shop unlocked, I'm scared that I shouted at Logan and accused him of stealing money that I'd forgotten I'd spent, and I'm scared that I yelled at you and threw a mug at the door which could easily have hit you. None of that is normal behaviour yet all he can say is that his investigations are "inconclusive". What the bloody hell is "inconclusive" when it's at home? Yet that stupid prick doesn't seem to think I need a further appointment to get something that *is* conclusive. Where does that leave me? I just want to know what's wrong with me because I'm worried that, as well as the Parkinson's, there's something else going on.'

Rachel and I exchanged looks. 'What do you think might be wrong with you?' I ventured, hoping it was the right thing to ask.

Mum shrugged. 'Losing my marbles. Going doolally. It would be just my luck to have sodding dementia too.'

I glanced across at Rachel again but she widened her eyes and shook her head. I agreed. Mum was joking. It wasn't up to me to suggest that perhaps she'd hit the nail on the head. I'd leave that to a medical professional. Like Sam.

'Would you like a second opinion?' I asked tentatively, scared she'd bite my head off again.

'God, yes! Do you happen to know anyone who's an expert in these matters?'

I paused for a moment. 'Actually, I do...'

I've never picked my words so carefully in my life as I told her about Sam's expertise. The last thing I wanted her to know was that I'd only met him in the first place because I was worried about her, or that we'd already discussed him doing an off the record consultation. I just hoped he was still willing to do that after he'd rushed off earlier.

Mum loved the idea. I left it that I'd call Sam later, telling Mum that there was no guarantee he'd be able to see her, but I'd do my best to arrange something.

After that, she apologised and said she was going to get some counselling to help her manage her anger. One of Rachel's regular travel clients was a counsellor so Rachel was going to find out her areas of specialism. If she didn't specialise in what Mum needed, they'd find someone else. Quickly.

'I *am* going to need to take a step back at work,' Mum said. 'You're absolutely right about that. I've known it for a while but I haven't wanted to accept it. I refuse to let Parkinson's completely change my life but I do accept that I'm going to have to make a few adjustments.

Parkinson's or no Parkinson's, I've always known that, at some point, I'd have to slow down because nobody can sustain my work level forever, especially with all the travel that's involved. I guess I wanted to make that decision for myself rather than have the decision imposed on me but we don't always get what we want, do we? I've composed resignation letters for both the valuation roles but I wanted to see whether you wanted to be considered for either or both roles before I send them. I could put in a good word if you do.'

I wasn't sure whether Mum wanted me to respond, but I couldn't give her a decision until I knew whether I had a job in Bear With Me or whether I'd be moving back to London.

After a slight pause, Mum continued. 'I need to step back from Bear With Me too, but I refuse to do that completely. It's my business and it's such an important part of my life that I don't think I could cope without it—'

'I wasn't trying to push you out,' I interrupted. 'I handled the conversation really badly.'

Mum gave me a weak smile. 'That makes two of us. I know you're not trying to push me out but the truth hurt earlier. Things *are* slipping. I'm behind with the accounts, I'm making a mess of the ordering and I double-booked a workshop last week. I had five people turn up to learn how to make bears and another four for a basic sewing class half an hour later. Neither of the workshops were in the diary. I'm making a Ju-Sea Bear at the moment but I don't know who it's for. I've got the brief written down in the order pad but no customer name or phone number. I'm going to have to hope that the customer phones up to ask if the bear's ready. I still want to work in the shop. I *need* to work in the shop. If you're willing, though, I'd like you to take on the management side by which I mean the accounts, orders, bills, marketing, workshops, events, and so on. I'll still manage the team but I'll step away from the behind the scenes stuff which I'm messing up. You can work in the shop too if you want. I never got around to replacing Gillian after she left in May. Liv's been covering those hours but she's more than happy for you to take them. With those shop hours and the behind-the-scenes responsibilities, I reckon you could have a reasonably full-time job, but you might want to take on one or both valuation roles for a bit more excitement.'

'Thanks, Mum. It sounds perfect.' I felt quite tearful with relief and so grateful to Rachel for whatever she'd said to help Mum reach this conclusion. The combination of roles actually sounded really exciting but the main thing was that I had a role and I could stay.

'Not as good as being a museum curator, I'm afraid,' Mum said.

'Being here for you and Logan is more important than that.'

Mum nodded. 'I know I told you to leave earlier but I didn't mean that. You've made a big sacrifice for Logan and me and I really do appreciate it. It's going to make a massive difference to us both and to the business having you around. It's not going to be easy, though. I'm going to get counselling and hopefully a second diagnosis if your friend can do that but the anger and frustration isn't going to go away overnight. We've got some tough times ahead. You do know that, don't you?'

'I do.'

'Your mum's going to get a cleaner in too,' Rachel said.

'You don't have to do that. I can do it.'

Mum shook her head. 'No. If you've moved back home for good, you need to have a social life instead of spending every non-working hour cleaning.'

'I don't mind helping.'

She shook her head again. 'You don't need to. It's already arranged. Someone in the village has a cleaning company. She's going to send one of her team round every Friday to clean and every Tuesday to do the ironing. All we need to do is keep on top of the washing. When we get to the spring, we may need a gardener too. Logan's keen but it's too much for him on his own. We're fine for now, though. So how does that all sound?'

I moved across to the sofa and hugged Mum. 'It sounds great. Thank you.'

She held me tightly and whispered 'sorry' into my ear but I told her to forget it and that I understood. And I did understand. For a young, fit, healthy woman, this was one hell of a shock and I could see why dealing with it was such a struggle. I just hoped that the counselling would help her control her temper and get her to see us as allies instead of the enemy. I also hoped that Sam would still be willing to give that second diagnosis.

I had Sunday lunch at Jack and Millie's and tried to join in the laughter and banter but my mind was still on the beach. All I could focus on was that brief moment where I'd thought about kissing Jemma then Kirsty's bitchy comments about how quickly I'd moved on. She'd wanted to hurt me and she'd succeeded. The guilt lay heavy on my heart.

As I drove Thor back to London, I kept replaying the morning's events over and over in my mind. How could I do that to Nikki's memory? How could I visit the rock pools, full of love for Nikki, then wrap my arms round another woman and think about kissing her?

By the time I arrived back at my flat late that night, a text had arrived from Jemma:

⊠ From Jemma
The good news is that I don't need to book a return removals service. Yay! Mum's calmed down, we've both apologised, I'm staying, and I've got a job in the shop plus she's recommended me for her valuing jobs. The bad news is that Mum isn't coping well and she now thinks there's something wrong other

than the Parkinson's. She's even mentioned dementia
although she was joking so I kept quiet about that.
Have just fired off yet another complaint email
about Dr S and his inadequacies. Anyway, she'd love
a 2nd opinion and if you're able to come home next
weekend and can fit in an off the record consultation, we'd both be really grateful 😊 xx

I couldn't do it to Nikki. I had to step away from Jemma before
anything happened and we both got hurt. There was only one way to
do that. I quickly typed in a response before guilt consumed me about
letting Jemma and her mum down:

✉ To Jemma
Great news that you've sorted things out with your
mum. Really sorry but I may not make it up north
again next weekend

She must have still been awake as a reply came back moments
later:

✉ From Jemma
That's OK. I understand. It's a long drive 2 weekends in a row and I know it's probably awkward for
you when she's not officially your patient. We'll
hopefully sort something else out as she hates Dr
S. We might go private. Thanks for all your help so
far. You've been a true-life superhero x

How big a shit did I feel? She was obviously trying to make excuses
for my inadequacies and feelings of guilt. I couldn't cut her off
completely. It wasn't fair.

✉ To Jemma

I still want to help. I'll definitely be home again
before Christmas. I'll let you know when I've got a
date and I can meet your mum then

⌧ From Jemma
Mum can't wait that long. It's fine. As I said,
we'll sort something else out. Thank you

I scrolled through the series of texts. Jemma's had gone from two
kisses to one to none. That said more to me about how she felt than the
actual words. I'd massively let her down yet she was still being kind to
me. As if I deserved that. If I'd felt like a big shit after my response to
the first text, I felt like a sewer-full of the stuff reading her final reply.

'I'm sorry, Jem,' I muttered, switching my phone to silent. 'I'm no
good to anyone.'

I'd offered her friendship and support then had snatched it away
the minute there was a suggestion of something more than friendship.
Yet where had that suggestion come from? Kirsty bloody Griggs! It
wasn't like Jemma had been flirting with me or that she'd given me any
indication that she wanted to be anything other than mates. It was
Kirsty who'd planted that idea and my own guilt that had given it
wings. What was wrong with me? I'd craved friendship, I'd got it, and
I'd thrown it away. Idiot!

I sat on the sofa with the phone beside me, debating whether to
text her again and tell her to ignore me and of course I'd go home next
weekend and meet her mum. An hour later, I was still going round in
circles about whether or not it was a good idea when my phone illumi-
nated with another text:

⌧ From Jemma
I may be way off the mark here so sorry if I am but
I have to 'say' this. I really like you, Sam, and I
know that you like me too. You don't go over and
above like you've done for someone you don't reckon

much to. I know you felt that instant connection
when we met and we've both said it feels like we've
known each other for ages. We may only have met
recently but we've been through some intense times
together. I value your friendship and I value your
counsel and I'm pretty sure you feel the same about
me. This morning was another great example of us
supporting each other through tough times and I was
looking forward to continuing to be there for you.
Then your vicious ex appeared and started spouting
her crap. I don't know which part of it hit a nerve
or whether it all did but you need to know that
what she said this morning wasn't worth the breath
it took for her to say it. If you're pulling away
because I've asked too much of our fledgling
friendship and you need some time to yourself, I
understand. I have been pretty needy. But if you're
pulling away because of that absolute bollocks that
Kirsty said, I urge you to think again. I know
you're not ready to move on from Nikki and I'm not
asking you to. I'm still trying to get over Scott.
Neither of us is ready for a relationship with each
other or with anyone else. But I didn't think
that's what we were building up to. You never gave
me the impression you wanted more and I hope I
didn't either. I thought we were building a friendship. If that's what you still want, please stay in
touch as you may be my newest friend but you're
someone I want to keep in my life xx

How was I supposed to respond to that?

* * *

The following Saturday, I sat in the campervan at the same services I'd stopped at with Jemma a week ago. Pretty much the same parking space too. I stared out of the window, half-expecting her to bound down the steps with a McFlurry in each hand and a packet of wine gums dangling from her teeth. Had it really only been a week ago? Seemed longer.

Digging my phone out of my pocket, I scrolled through the text conversation I'd had with Jemma on Sunday night, reading and re-reading every message.

I hadn't replied to that final long one. I hadn't known what to say. I'd decided to sleep on it and hopefully get my thoughts in gear. Yet I wasn't any clearer on how to respond by Monday night so I slept on it again.

By Tuesday morning, it seemed too late to reply. Action was needed instead. My manager wasn't impressed at the short notice of my leave request. I hadn't wanted to pull a guilt trip on him but when I let it slip that the following Friday would be the one-year anniversary of Nikki's death and her parents had arranged a memorial gathering, he couldn't sign the authorisation quickly enough.

Knocking back the last drops of coffee in the services car park, I wondered whether to send Jemma a text to say that I was on my way home and wanted to meet up with her. It seemed so inadequate after nearly a week of silence. No. I'd wait until I was home instead and could see her face to face. If I hadn't completely blown it already.

Thor and I re-joined the motorway and headed north. I was going to have to confess everything. Kirsty had hit a nerve because she'd been right about Jemma. Five days without contact with Jemma had proved to me that I *had* moved on. Less than a year after my fiancée died, I'd developed feelings for someone else. Strong feelings. I didn't expect anything in return but I needed to explain why I'd reacted the way I had. If I'd learned anything from my relationship with Kirsty and if Jemma had learned anything from her relationship with Scott, it was the importance of trust and honesty. If we were to have any sort of friendship and perhaps something more one day, it had to be built on both of those things.

* * *

I lay on the bed in my old room at Mum and Dad's a few hours later and, with fumbling fingers, tapped in a text:

✉ To Jemma
Hi. I'm sorry for the lack of contact this week. I started a reply to your message so many times but could never find the right thing to say. I thought it would be easier to say it in person. I've got the week off and am back home again. If you have any time tonight or tomorrow to hear my pathetic excuses, I'd like to try and make it up to you xx

It was three hours before a reply came back. Three agonising hours where I cursed myself for running away again and not facing up to my feelings.

✉ From Jemma
Hello stranger! Thought you'd disappeared off the face of the earth. I'm at Bear With Me and it's been manic. I've only just seen your text. I'm going to South Bay tonight with Mum and Logan to see the bonfires and fireworks. I'd invite you to join us but Mum will get stressed and want an instant diagnosis. I can meet you on the seafront afterwards if you like. Say 8pm?

✉ To Jemma
Sounds good. Thank you xx

✉ From Jemma
What for?

✉ To Jemma
For giving me a second chance xx

✉ From Jemma
Surely you know by now that I'm a sucker for a sob
story and I ALWAYS give people second chances ;-)
Now stop texting me. I'm very busy and important
and have lots of bears to hug. See you tonight xx

* * *

'You look very smart, Sammy,' Mum said, watching me as I sat on the stairs and pulled on my walking boots. 'I'm not so wild about the footwear, though.'

I wrinkled my nose. I'd gone for some dark blue jeans and a short-sleeved shirt instead of my usual ripped jeans and T-shirt combo but the footwear fell short. 'I don't have much choice. I screwed up on the packing. I've only got my knackered Converse and these.'

'Shame your dad's two sizes smaller than you or you could have borrowed some of his.'

'Such a shame! Because loafers or brown sandals are so my thing.'

Mum laughed. 'Cheeky. It's good to see you smiling again, Sammy. Especially with this Friday being—'

I stopped tying my laces and looked up. 'You can say it, you know, Mum. Friday's the one-year anniversary of Nikki's death. One whole year.'

'Will you be okay?'

'For the first time, I really think I will be. It's been a very dark twelve months but I can finally see light.'

'Because of this Jemma who you're meeting?'

I chuckled as I resumed tying my laces. 'Stop fishing, Mum.

Jemma's a friend and she's been very clear that friendship is the only thing on offer, which is fine. She's helped me, though. She got me to open up about Nikki, she got me to confront my demons by visiting the spot where it happened, and she's given me hope for a future without Nikki, whether that's with her, someone else, or just on my own. Thanks to Jemma, I've started thinking about the future instead of agonising about the past.'

'She sounds wonderful, Sammy.'

I stood up and hugged her.

'Enjoy your evening,' she whispered. 'You deserve it.'

* * *

I made it down to South Bay a little after 7.00 p.m. I was an hour early but I wanted to see the bonfires and fireworks first. It was something Nikki and I had always enjoyed doing.

Low tide meant a long, wide stretch of sand, perfect for Bonfire Night revellers to spread out and enjoy the evening. A trail of bonfires stretched round the bay. Some were small with a family or a few friends gathered round them. Others were large with up to fifty or sixty people seated, standing, or even dancing round them. Children and adults waved sparklers, and fireworks banged and squealed overhead. I leaned on the metal railings by the lifeboat station, taking it all in. Jemma and her family were likely to be on the beach so I was going to stay on the path and give them their family-time.

I shoved my hands in my pockets, zipped up my jacket to the top, and slowly meandered along the seafront, thankful that, although it was cold, it wasn't windy.

The aroma from the many chippies facing the sea was too much to resist and I succumbed to a tray of chips although they didn't retain their heat for long in the chill of the night. I licked my salty fingers and looked round for a bin to dispose of the tray and cold remains. Job done, I turned to join the steady flow of pedestrians but I mistimed it and tripped over a buggy, only just managing to stop myself from sprawling onto the pavement.

'Oh my goodness! Are you okay?' a woman said.

'Yes. Fine. Sorry,' I looked up and smiled at her. 'It was my fault. I wasn't looking. I hope I haven't damaged your vehicle.'

She laughed and flicked her long auburn hair over her shoulders. 'I think it's pretty sturdy. We can probably get away with not exchanging insurance details.'

I moved aside to avoid another collision and, as I did, I locked eyes with the man with her. He looked familiar. He frowned as he looked at me and I was sure he recognised me too. An excitable squeal from the child in the buggy broke his gaze and they continued walking.

And then it struck me. That was Stevie. Stevie Barnes. My mate from school who I'd fallen out with. Jemma had said I should get in touch with him and now was my chance.

'Stevie?'

He stopped and turned round, his eyes narrowed as though trying to place me. Then they widened. 'Sam?'

I smiled and nodded.

'Jesus, Sam!' He took a couple of paces back towards me and shook my hand. 'It's been... how long? Since college?'

'About sixteen years. How're you doing?'

'I'm good. Really good.'

The red-headed woman joined him and gave him a playful nudge. 'Sorry. Being rude,' he said. This is my partner, Elise, and our daughter, Melody. We've also got a three-month-old son, Tristan. Elise, this is Sam. Rob and I were great mates at school and then we lost touch because...' Stevie shook his head. 'Stupid reasons actually and all a very long time ago.'

He smiled at me and I knew instantly that the past had been forgiven and forgotten – put down to youth and immaturity. 'So, what about you, Sam? Married? Kids?'

'No. I didn't quite make it up the aisle.' I paused. Deep breath. I could do this. 'My fiancée died a year ago.'

Elise clapped her hand across her chest. 'That's awful. Do you mind me asking...?'

'Aneurism.'

'Oh, mate, I'm so sorry,' Stevie said. 'How do you get over something like that?'

'I'm not sure you really do but I'm getting there a day at a time. So, do you still live in Little Sandby?'

Stevie nodded. 'Yeah. Still there. Same house I bought when I was eighteen although you wouldn't recognise the inside anymore. Complete refurbishment. You?'

'London. I was a neurological consultant at the hospital here but after Nikki died, I needed a fresh start. Probably not one of my finest decisions so hopefully I'll come back soon.'

'Are you just up for the weekend, then?' Elise asked.

'The whole week. I'm going back next Sunday.'

'Then you boys should get together and have a beer.' She looked up at Stevie, no doubt wondering if she'd said the right thing considering she probably didn't know why we'd lost touch.

Stevie was already digging out his phone. 'Good idea. Rob'll be up for it too.'

We connected our phones to exchange numbers.

'Prompt me if you don't hear from me,' Stevie said. 'Tristan has a good old set of lungs on him, which he likes to exercise pretty much every two hours from midnight so my brain is mush. I'd love to catch up, though.'

'Me too. Nice to meet you, Elise, and hopefully see you next week, Stevie.'

'*Definitely* see you next week,' he said as they set off again.

I stood watching them for a moment, smiling. Yet another thing that Jemma had done for me. I'd never have called out his name if it hadn't been for her.

With about fifteen minutes left until I was due to meet Jemma, I wandered further along the seafront, watching the activity on the sand. Fireworks were still being set off. Some revellers had bought boxes of beer and wine onto the beach and were steadily building up a pile of empties.

I paused again, leaning on the railings. A young lad of about ten or so was writing with a sparkler while a girl of a similar age bounced up and down impatiently waiting for a woman in a bobble hat to light her a sparkler too. The second sparkler burst into life and they all squealed. The face of the woman in the bobble hat was momentarily lit up before she handed over the sparkler and my very own set of fireworks burst into life in my stomach. Jemma. She lit another sparkler and passed it to a woman who I assumed had to be her mum.

I couldn't take my eyes off Jemma as she patiently lit sparkler after sparkler. When they were all spent, she chased the squealing girl and boy in circles across the sand, laughing as she repeatedly failed to tag them. Her mum laughed too although she didn't join in.

The game stopped and I heard groans from the kids, presumably because they'd been told it was time to go home. Jemma linked her arm with her mum and began walking up the sand towards me. Not wanting to make things awkward, I moved further along the railings so she wouldn't see me, but I could still see her.

She hugged her mum and each of the kids then watched as they headed along the seafront towards a row of parked cars. Jemma dug out her phone. Moments later a text came through:

⊠ From Jemma
They've gone. Where are you? X

⊠ To Jemma
Take ten steps forward x

I watched her as she looked at her phone, then snapped her head up in surprise. The grin she gave when she spotted me set those fireworks off again.

A voice in my head kept saying: It's not even been a year yet. How could you do this? But I knew that was my own guilt speaking. I knew exactly what Nikki would say about this scenario because we'd actually discussed it. One of the doctors at work had lost his wife after a short battle with cancer and, within four months, he was seeing someone else. A year later, they were married. Nikki came home fuming one evening because several of her colleagues had made cruel suggestions that he obviously hadn't loved his wife if he could move on so fast, or that he must have already been seeing the new girlfriend while his wife was dying.

'You can't put a time on these things,' she'd cried. 'I don't think anyone will ever get over losing someone they love, but they shouldn't be expected to grieve forever, especially if they're still really young when they lose that person. Nobody has a right to say that four months is too soon. If he'd found someone he cared about after four days, four weeks, four months or four years, that's his business. It doesn't mean he didn't care about his wife or has forgotten about her. It simply means another opportunity for love has come along and he's grasped it with both hands.'

I'd massaged her shoulders and told her how much I loved her feistiness about these things. 'I'm serious,' she said. 'If I drop dead tomorrow, you must *not* spend months or, even worse, years grieving for me. It serves no purpose. It's not going to bring me back and you still have a life to live so live it.'

I'd laughed and reminded her that, statistically, women lived longer than men so it would be her finding someone new, not me. 'I mean it,' she said. 'I'll come back and haunt you if you don't.' I'd forgotten about that conversation until now. Nikki would not have been impressed at me spending the past year grieving for her.

'We meet again, Dr Jones.' Jemma smiled up at me. 'I think you owe me a drink.'

'I think I owe you an explanation.'

'You do indeed, but it'll have to wait because I'm freezing so a warm pub is my priority right now.'

I looked along the seafront. The pubs would be packed and we might struggle to talk. It was too much of a trek to the top of town but there were a few pubs on the way.

'The Sea Dog?' I suggested.

Jemma nodded. 'Lead on.'

As we walked, Jemma chattered about her evening on the beach, how great it had been to see her mum laughing, and how exciting it had been to have so many fireworks going off round them.

The fireworks continued to explode in my stomach. Exciting? I wasn't so sure. Bloody terrifying more like. I could do this, though. I could tell her. I could move on. But was she ready to move on from Scott? She'd said in her text that she wasn't, but had that been a defence mechanism? I'd soon find out.

32

JEMMA

'This is Gunpowder Plot.' Sam placed a pint in front of me. 'I've got Rocket Release or something like that. We can swap if you don't like yours.'

I eyed the dark ale then took a sip. It absolutely hit the spot. I'd got out of the habit of drinking real ales since moving down south, but I'd realised I had a craving as soon as we'd walked into the pub. 'Ooh, lovely. Bit like Old Peculiar. The boy chose well. Can I try yours? It looks a bit lighter.'

'It is. Similar percentage, though.'

He handed it over and I took a sip. 'I like it but I prefer mine. Thank you.'

Sam pulled out a stool and sat down opposite me.

'You're not one of those men who hates women drinking pints, are you?'

He shook his head. 'I don't know why some men have an issue with it. Or some women. Nikki sometimes drank pints too, although she was more of a fan of bottled lager than real ale.'

I studied his face. That wistful look and the glint of tears had gone when saying her name.

'Have I got a beer moustache?' Sam rubbed across his lips.

'No! Nothing like that. I noticed that it seemed easier for you to talk about Nikki just now. Have you had a breakthrough?'

'I have. On North Bay last Sunday, thanks to you. In fact, I had two, but one of them came later.'

'I'm assuming visiting the spot where it happened was one of them.'

He nodded. 'I faced my past and it wasn't as hard as I expected. That moment when the sun appeared was amazing.'

I could picture it vividly. 'It was stunning. I feel quite privileged to have seen it.'

Silence.

Either I was going to have to ask or he was going to have to tell me. I sipped on my pint. Damn. I knew I'd break first. 'And the second breakthrough...?'

His eyes held mine with a look so intense that my stomach did a flip. He had the most beautiful eyes. Deep blue with flecks of grey, like the ocean after a storm.

He broke eye contact and glugged down at least half of his pint in one then chewed on his lip. He seemed nervous and I couldn't think why.

'Did it have something to do with what the delightful Kirsty said?' I prompted.

'She has a way of getting under a person's skin. She knows the exact buttons to press to make someone fall for her or to hurt them like hell. When she suggested that I hadn't loved Nikki and had moved on already, she knew what she was doing.

'But you hadn't moved on. We were – are – just friends.'

Sam took another glug on his pint. 'I felt so guilty when she said that which was, of course, exactly what she wanted. And the reason I felt so guilty was because it's true. Unexpectedly, I have moved on. I'll always love Nikki and I'll never forget her but I've met someone else recently and I can't stop thinking about her.'

My stomach flipped again and I felt my heart race. I didn't mean to say it, but the word just popped out. 'Who?'

That intense look was there again. 'You, Jemma.'

I knew that's what he was going to say. Hoped, even.

Time seemed to slow down. The chatter, laughter and clinks of glasses faded into the background and it felt like there were just the two of us in a bubble on our own as he waited for my reaction, an expression of hope tinged with fear in his eyes.

Like a movie montage, key moments from our brief acquaintance flashed through my mind – the first time I saw him in The George and Dragon, huddled over his pint and looking lost, his kindness in reassuring me about Mum, his calming influence when Mum went AWOL, his welcome presence when Drew lost it over Luukas, and laughing hysterically as he drove me home in the campervan.

The butterflies in my stomach swooped and soared as I imagined all the times he'd held me and how safe I'd felt in his arms. And I thought about that moment on the beach before Kirsty appeared and that daydream I'd had of him kissing me – the one that had continually nudged at me until I'd admitted to myself that I hadn't just looked up to ask him how he was feeling.

But he'd run off. He'd got spooked. How could I be sure he wasn't going to do that again if I admitted I had some tentative feelings for him too? Then where would I be? Last Sunday had been bad enough. I wasn't daft. I knew exactly why he'd fled. There'd been a definite moment of chemistry and, if Kirsty hadn't appeared, the kiss would have been reality instead of a daydream.

It took nearly an hour to compose that enormous text to him. I'd wavered between admitting I'd felt something and running a mile from it before settling on the path of least humiliation and emphasising that we were just friends. My main objective had been not to lose him from my life. And not just because of Mum.

'Say something. Please,' he urged.

I knew how hard it would have been for him to put himself out there because I felt the fear too. I needed to understand what he wanted from me. He didn't strike me as the sort who'd rush into a rebound relationship but, after Scott, I was hardly an expert on how men behaved.

'Why me?' I asked, stalling for time. 'We're just friends.'

'Why?' He looked amused. 'Do you want me to list the reasons?'

Yes! Convince me you're not going to break my heart too! But then I thought about Scott turning up at the flat after ghosting me and everything he said and did to convince me to try again. I pictured him telling me how I'd mesmerised him and he simply had to be with me but it had just been a line. One last line for one last shag before he went back to his cosy family life and left me alone and broken once more.

Panic rushed through me. I couldn't let Sam do that to me. I didn't want to hear it. Picking up my drink, I glugged on it, just like Sam had done with his moments before.

'It's not real,' I said eventually. 'You only think we're more than friends because I've helped you with Nikki. You're grateful. That's all. You've come out of the dark and you're confusing gratitude for something else.' I have no idea how I managed to sound so convincing. Maybe because I was trying to convince me as much as him.

'It's not that.'

'It is.'

'I promise you it isn't. I wondered that myself at first. I've spent all week thinking about you and the possibility of us. I *am* grateful for everything you've done to help me move on, but somewhere in the midst of that, the truth is I started to fall for you.'

'Shit!' Falling for me? Falling in love? This was serious. This was way beyond a few tentative feelings.

He wrinkled his nose. 'Am I that repulsive?'

I gaped at him and clapped my hand across my mouth as I realised I hadn't sworn in my head. 'No! Sorry. I didn't mean to say that aloud. I'm... I don't... Oh my God, Sam. Falling for me? I completely didn't see this coming. I really didn't. I don't know what to say.'

'That somewhere in the midst of it all, you've fallen for me too?' He shook his head. 'I'm joking. Bad joke, obviously. Never was my strong point. Look, Jem, you don't have to say anything. I'm not expecting any declarations of undying devotion. I'm not even expecting you to say that you maybe *could* see me as something more than a friend in the future, but I promised you an explanation as to why I ran off on—'

'Ran off and ignored me for a week.' I didn't normally use humour as a defence mechanism but I couldn't help myself. I needed to lighten things up. I needed to think.

Sam smiled and the twinkle in his eyes set my stomach fizzing.

'Yes, an explanation as to why I ran off and ignored you for a week like the idiot I am. I would love nothing more than to take you out on a date and to kiss you goodnight and see where this takes us. I do, however, realise I'm not the only one who's been hurt. Just because I'm ready, it doesn't mean that you are and, even if you were, it doesn't mean I'm the one for you either.' He released a deep breath and looked at me hopefully. 'So there it is. Cards on the table.'

I nibbled on my thumbnail, wondering how to respond.

Sam stood up. 'How about another drink?'

'Yes please!'

'You won't run away while I'm at the bar, will you? A kind of revenge scarper?'

I smiled. 'It's tempting, but another pint of that Gunpowder Plot is even more tempting so I promise to stay put. Besides, running away is *your* speciality, Dr Jones. Your superhero superpower perhaps?'

'Ooh, harsh. But fair.'

While Sam weaved through the revellers towards the bar, I downed the remnants of my pint. Wow! I had completely not seen that coming, even after Leah had suggested he had the hots for me. I'd thought it was just a moment of attraction that was worth exploring – not a case of him actually falling for me. How had I missed it? Probably because I just assumed that he was grieving for Nikki and would continue to do so for a long time, so there was no way he'd want to move on.

I watched him leaning on the bar. He was side-on to me and must have registered that he was being watched because he turned round and gave me the most dazzling smile. My stomach flipped again and I quickly looked away. When I turned back, Sam was placing his order. I drank him in and, for the first time, it struck me that he wasn't just easy on the eye as I'd originally thought; he was seriously hot. He was certainly attracting admiring looks from several women. After what happened with Scott, could I risk letting anyone in again? And so soon? I was still grieving the loss of my fiancé, friend, and future. Was I ready for a new future? With Sam?

'Another Gunpowder Plot.' Sam handed me the fresh pint. 'I went for the same as you this time.'

'Sam, I—'

'You don't have to say anything.'

'I want to. You've been honest with me and I want to be the same. I'm really flattered and I know that this is a huge step for you...' Looking at his eager expression, I hesitated. I couldn't do it. I wasn't ready to risk getting hurt or to hurt him. Not yet.

'But...?'

'I'll admit that I felt something on the beach. We had a moment and, if Kirsty hadn't turned up, something might have happened. But that's all it was for me. A moment. I'd had a difficult week and you were there for me every step of the way and I was so grateful. Then you took a huge step in going to the rock pools and there was that shaft of light. It was intense and emotional and I think we both got swept up in it all. Now you're saying you feel something more than friendship and I don't know what to do with that.'

'I'm not expecting you to do anything with it. Like I said, I owed you an explanation and Nikki taught me always to be honest about my feelings. I didn't know how I felt last weekend. It had kind of crept up on me.'

I sipped on my beer while trying to find the right words. 'I really like you, Sam, but I haven't thought about you in that way. I don't know if that's because I'm still in love with Scott, or whether it's because I never let myself think of you like that because I thought you were still in love with Nikki. I can't believe I just said that. Of course you're still in love with Nikki. You always will be. That's not what I meant. Oh God, I'm making such a mess of this.'

Sam placed his hand over mine and looked into my eyes. I felt instantly comforted. 'I know what you mean,' he said. 'You didn't think I was ready to move on so it's as though I was off limits. Like looking at a married man and knowing you can't go there. Unless you're Kirsty, of course, in which case you see that as an exciting challenge.'

I smiled. 'You always say the right thing.'

'Not always. I don't know if telling you how I feel was the right thing.'

His hand was still holding mine. I squeezed it, trying to ignore the fizzing in my stomach. 'You did the right thing.'

'Just at the wrong time?'

I shrugged. 'You ran away when you realised you had feelings for me. You've had six days to get your head round this, to fight the guilt and to think about what you want. What have I had? Six days of radio silence, wondering if I'll ever hear from you again. And now here you are, more relaxed and focused than I've ever seen you, putting yourself out there without expecting anything in return and I don't know how to respond.'

He brushed his thumb over the back of my hand, sending a tantalizing fizz shooting up my arm. 'Just be honest with me. I know you need time to think but, if it's a categoric no, never, not any time, you can say. I can take it.'

His tentative smile melted my heart. 'It's not a no but it's not a yes, either. It's definitely a possibility.'

He lifted my hand to his lips and gently kissed it, sending tingles along my arm and through my body. 'Thank you.'

Time. That's what I needed. I also needed to change the subject before I lunged across the table and kissed him. 'So, how long are you up for?'

'A week. Which means I can meet with your mum if she's still up for it.'

'You'd still do that? I got nowhere with the hospital and I've been that busy sorting out the mess at the shop that I haven't been able to chase it again.'

We chatted about my first week as Deputy Head Bear-Keeper at Bear With Me, what happened with Mum when I'd returned to Bear's Pad on Sunday afternoon, and how much Tiff, Leah and Drew were missing me. Apparently Tiff and Drew had demanded that Sam join them for an after-work drink on Wednesday and all they'd talked about was how empty the flat was without me and how they couldn't wait to come up and visit.

'Aw, I miss them too,' I said. 'Please send my love next time you see them. I FaceTimed Leah on Tuesday and she insisted I make her a Ju-Sea Jem Bear so she can always have part of me close-by. I was making two for my boss, Owen, so I've paused those and I've started on Leah's. I should have it finished before you go back so you could maybe deliver it for me.'

'Removals, courier, relationship advice. So many businesses to run. I had no idea Thor would turn out to be such a versatile campervan.'

Picturing Thor, I said, 'Will you manage to get much surfing done while you're here or is it too cold?'

'Cold? It's never too cold for a true surfer. We have to say that because, to be honest, the North Sea's always bloody freezing, summer or winter. We just need thicker wetsuits in the winter and shorter stints. Hopefully, yes, although the sea was really calm today so would have been rubbish. If the swell gets up later in the week, I'll get out. You should come with me.'

'Er, no! Have you seen the temperature forecast for this week? If I'm ever getting on a surfboard, it will not be in minus figures. Other than surfing, what do you have planned?'

'Meeting up with Stevie Barnes and Rob Harris hopefully.'

'You got in touch?'

Sam told me about running into Stevie on the seafront earlier. I was so pleased for him to have an opportunity to face up to his past again.

A taxi arrived for us shortly after eleven and, as I stood up, I wobbled unsteadily. How many pints had I had? Three? Four? Oops. Sam put his arm round my shoulder to steady me and I snuggled into his chest, breathing in a manly mixture of shower gel, deodorant and bonfires.

Out of the taxi window, I watched fireworks illuminating the blackness while Sam dozed beside me. I keep sneaking sideways glances at him, wondering what it would be like to kiss someone who wasn't Scott. Sam's lips twitched slightly as his head lolled to the side. I imagined my lips touching his and a shiver of pleasure rippled down my spine. *Stop it! It's the drink.*

When the taxi pulled up outside Mum's cottage, Sam awoke with a jolt. 'Where are we?'

'Bear's Pad.'

'Can you give me five minutes?' he asked the driver, letting himself out of the car and rushing round to my side.

'What are you doing?' I asked.

'Walking you to your door.'

'It's Little Sandby. I don't think I'll get held up by knifepoint walking up the drive.'

'You might get spiked by a hedgehog or stared at by a fox.'

I wasn't going to win the argument so I indicated that he should follow me.

Keys at the ready, I stood on the doorstep and turned to face him. 'Safely home. You were right. It was a perilous journey full of spiky hedgehogs, intimidating foxes, and stroppy badgers. Barely made it past them alive.'

Sam smiled. 'That last badger nearly got you, you know. If I hadn't been here to protect you...'

'Aw. My superhero again.'

There was silence for a moment. I knew I should turn round, unlock the door and say goodnight, but my feet were rooted to the spot.

'I'll send you a text about seeing Mum,' I said.

'I'm pretty flexible. The only day I definitely can't do is Friday.'

'Okay. She'll really appreciate it. Thank you.'

The keys were digging into my palm yet I still couldn't seem to bring myself to turn round and go inside.

'I'd better go,' Sam said. 'Might take some time to battle the night creatures and that taxi driver's probably getting impatient.'

'Okay. Off you go.'

'I'm going.'

'Go on, then.'

'Night, Jemma.'

'Night, Sam.'

And then it happened. He leaned across and brushed his lips against mine in the softest of kisses. I closed my eyes for a moment, my heart pounding, every part of me fizzing. He barely moved his lips – it was little more than a prolonged peck – but I was breathless and light-headed when he pulled away.

We gazed at each other and I could feel the atmosphere between us sparking like the fireworks in the night sky. I wanted him to kiss me again. I wanted to feel those strong arms round me. I wanted...

A firework exploding above us broke the moment. We both looked up at the sky then back to each other.

'My cue to go.' Sam stepped back onto the drive. 'Sleep well.'

He waved as the taxi pulled away moments later. I waved back then found myself touching my lips where I could still feel that soft kiss. Could I trust him with my heart? Could he trust me with his? I had a hell of a lot of thinking to do.

33

SAM

'How did it go last night?' Mum asked over breakfast the next morning.

'Not as good as I hoped, but better than I expected.'

'That sounds a bit cryptic.'

I pushed my empty cereal bowl aside. 'I told Jemma that I've got feelings for her.'

'You do? Oh, that's wonderful, Sammy.'

'You don't think it's too soon?'

'Who can predict when love will knock on the door again. You can't put a timescale on these things. What did she say?'

'She's not sure yet. She was in a relationship. He asked her to marry him and then she found out that he was already married with twins. She's had a tough few months.'

'The poor girl. Why do people do things like that?'

I shrugged. 'I asked Kirsty that and she just said, "because I can". I guess some people have a different moral compass from the rest of us.'

Mum curled her lip. 'I never did like that one. How did you leave it with Jemma?'

'She needed time to think.'

'She's probably scared of getting hurt again.'

'I know. And she's probably worried that it's a rebound thing for me.'

'But it isn't?'

'No, it isn't. I spent all week asking myself that.'

Mum reached across the table and patted my arm. 'I'm so happy for you, Sammy. Even if Jemma isn't in your long-term future, I'm glad you're in that place now where you can think about someone new. I was worried about you. We all were.'

'I know. You don't need to be worried anymore. I'm doing okay.'

She sipped on her coffee. 'You don't have to go to Jack and Millie's for lunch if you'd rather see Jemma.'

'That's not exactly giving her time, is it? She knows where I am. When she's ready, she'll get in touch.'

I took my bowl into the kitchen and paused for a moment, hands on the sink, looking out towards the garden. Had I done the right thing in being so honest with Jemma? I hadn't scared her off so that was at least something. She hadn't said no. And, when I kissed her last night, there was definitely a spark between us and it was obvious she felt it too. Whether she was ready or willing to do something about that spark was another matter but the ball was in her court now. I had to give her time and space.

* * *

Sunday lunch at Jack and Millie's was loud, frantic, and messy. Isla kept trying to wriggle free from her booster seat and seemed to think that grabbing handfuls of peas and hurling them across the table was hilarious. Actually, it was, especially when they kept disappearing down Millie's cleavage. Saffron banged noisily on the tray of her highchair and managed to wear more food than she ate, although Isla was pretty messy too.

I realised guiltily that Sunday lunch the week before had been a very sombre affair, thanks to my dark mood. I'll bet nobody had wanted to say anything in case I had a strop, sped back to London, and stayed away even longer next time.

We moved into the lounge for coffee while Jack and Millie disappeared with a child each to clean and change. While they were gone, my phone beeped, setting my pulse racing. Jemma? But it wasn't her.

✉ From Stevie
If you're free tomorrow night, do you fancy meeting Rob and me at The White Horse? About 7.30?

✉ To Stevie
No plans. Look forward to it

'Was that Jemma?' Mum asked.

I shook my head. 'No, but it was good news.' I put the phone down on the chair arm while I told her and Dad about bumping into Stevie.

'That's wonderful news,' Mum said. 'It was such a shame when you all lost touch. I suppose going away to university can do that to friendships.'

I'd never told my parents why we'd fallen out but it was time to come clean.

'We all say things we wish we could un-say,' Mum said when I'd finished. 'Which is why it's a good thing that Jemma didn't promise you anything yesterday when she wasn't sure if she could keep that promise. I like her already.'

'Like who already?' Jack asked, returning to the lounge with a clean Isla wedged under his arm.

'My friend, Jemma. Long story.'

I was saved from explaining it by Isla squealing and begging to be put down.

'If I put you down, do you promise to stay clean for at least an hour?' Jack asked her.

'Put me down!'

'Not until you promise.'

'Promise.'

He put her down, but only after he'd dangled her upside down by her ankles first, resulting in more squealing.

Millie appeared with Saffron. 'Who's being murdered in here?'

'Daddy made me downside up,' Isla shouted.

'Ooh, naughty Daddy,' Millie said, playfully bobbing him on the arm with Saffron's feet.

'Look at me!' Isla cried. She stuffed a cushion up her dress and wandered round the lounge patting it. 'I'm Mummy.'

'Stop it, Isla,' Millie snapped, lunging for her daughter.

Isla was too fast and ran to the other side of the room. 'I'm Mummy, I'm Mummy,' she chanted.

'Isla! Stop it now,' Jack said, a sharp edge to his voice.

Mum stood up, grabbed Isla and removed the cushion, giving her a stern look.

'What's going on?' I asked. 'She's only playing.'

'I want a brother this time,' Isla said, stamping her feet.

Oh! So Jack had got what he wanted. 'You're pregnant?' I asked, looking from Millie to Jack, then back to Millie.

'I'm sorry, Sam. We were going to tell you.' Millie's cheeks were flushed bright red and she looked mortified.

'Congratulations.' I hoped I looked and sounded genuinely thrilled for them. 'Am I missing something? Isn't this good news?'

'Yes,' Millie said. 'Well, no, actually, because I didn't want another so soon, but I've got used to the idea. It's just that...'

Jack squeezed Millie's hand. 'It's just that... well... this Friday... you know.'

'No! Jesus! What are the pair of you like? Yes, it's the anniversary of Nikki's death, and yes it's going to be a difficult day – especially with the memorial thing – but life goes on. Quite literally in your case. You don't need to hide stuff like this from me.' Again, I hoped I sounded convincing. My heart was thumping and my stomach started churning.

Millie wiped at her eyes. 'You're sure it's not insensitive talking about our new life when... you know?'

'Honestly, Millie, it's fine. Really exciting. When's number three due?'

'21st May.'

My heart raced even faster. 'What date was that?'

'21st May,' Jack said. 'Are you okay? Sam? You don't look so good.'

'21st May,' I muttered. '21st May.'

I was aware of them all staring at me, questioning the relevance of the date. Because they didn't know. Nobody knew. I hadn't told anyone and I should have done. They'd had a right to know.

I scrambled to my feet, swallowing down the rising nausea. 'Sorry, I need to go.'

'Sammy! What is it?' Mum cried.

'Uncle Sammy!' Isla shouted.

But I was already at the door. Slamming it closed, I sprinted down the street. I didn't know where I was going but I needed to get out of there. The news was hard enough but that date? Three hundred and sixty five days in a year. Three hundred and sixty fucking five days. And it had to be that one.

34

'It's the right decision,' Karen assured me as I re-read my text again and again. It was Sunday afternoon and we were in the kitchen diner at Bear's Pad, catching up over lattes and a sneaky shortbread or three.

'It's not too soon?'

'What's time got to do with it? Scott cheated on you, abandoned you, begged forgiveness, then abandoned you again. If you'd started seeing someone that very evening, it wouldn't have been too soon. Just send it, will you? Or I will.' She tried to snatch the phone off me but my reflexes were too quick.

'Seriously, Jem. It's a no brainer. I can tell you really like him and he's obviously besotted with you. And he's honest. He's told you how he feels about you with no pressure to reciprocate it. You know he's got no girlfriend hidden away. Send it!'

I read the message once more, then grinned at Karen. 'It's gone.'

'About bloody time too.'

To Sam
How does Tuesday at 6pm sound for a consultation
with my mum? And how does tonight at 7pm sound for
a date with me? A proper one. I'm a bit scared at

the thought of a new relationship but I know I can
trust you not to hurt me like Scott did. I may be a
little cautious and want to take it slowly, but I
think there's the potential for something that will
be worth the wait xx

An hour later, Karen had to go but I hadn't heard from Sam.

'He'll get in touch,' Karen said, hugging me at the door. 'Stop worrying. He won't have changed his mind overnight.'

'He was going to his brother's for Sunday lunch.'

'There you go, then. He's with his family. He'll reply when he can.'

I cleared away our mugs and made a cup of tea for Mum, which I took up to her workshop where she was finishing off the Ju-Sea Bear for the unknown customer.

Logan was sprawled on his bed, game controller welded to his hands, and didn't even glance at me when I opened his bedroom door. It was good to see him so relaxed. As horrendous as the confrontation had been with Mum last Sunday, it had managed to clear the air. Rachel's client had been able to meet Mum's needs and she'd already had her first counselling session. She'd returned home with a big smile on her face, saying that she thought it was going to make a huge difference.

I'd deliberately left my phone in the kitchen in the hope that Sam would reply if I wasn't constantly watching it. I curled up on the sofa and flicked through one of Mum's teddy bear magazines but I barely registered the pictures. Sod it. I'd have to check.

My heart leapt when I saw that my tactic had worked. There was a text message and a couple of missed calls from Sam's number. I clicked on the text first:

✉ From Sam
Hello Jemma. This is Sammy's mum, Carole. I don't
mean to worry you but something happened after

lunch and he ran out, leaving his phone behind.
He's not with you, is he?

Oh my God! What on earth could have happened? Pulse racing, I
dialled his phone, which his mum immediately answered. She filled
me in on the news that Jack and Millie were expecting another baby
and how Sam had seemed fine until they'd told him the due date.

'I swear it was like he'd seen a ghost,' she said. 'Next minute, he was
out of the door and sprinting down the street.'

'What was the date?'

'21st May.'

'Does that mean anything to him?'

'Not that I'm aware of. Nikki died in November and the wedding
would have been June.'

'Didn't he meet Nikki in May?'

Carole sighed. 'Sorry, love, but I can't remember.'

'I'm pretty sure he met her about the time my dad died. Mind you,
even if it was the date they met, why would that cause him to run out?
It doesn't make sense.'

'Nothing makes sense at the moment. Jack and David – Sammy's
brother and dad – have taken the car and have been driving round the
streets but he could be anywhere.'

I could hear the panic in Carole's voice and tried to keep mine
calm. 'Have they tried the beach?'

'I don't know. Do you think he'll be there?'

'He might be.'

'Oh, hang on, love. They're back. One second.'

I heard the sound of car doors banging and muffled voices.
Jamming my phone between my ear and shoulder, I pulled on my
boots and coat.

'Jemma, love, are you still there?'

'I'm still here. Any news?'

'No. He's taken the campervan but he hasn't taken any of his stuff.

They can't drive round forever. David and I will head home. Hopefully he'll turn up there or at Jack's soon.'

'I'm going to the beach,' I said. 'I'll let you know if I find him.'

'Thank you. And I'll let you know if he comes home in the meantime.'

* * *

Mum said I could take her car, which reminded me that I hadn't done anything about finding my own. Must rectify that.

The light was fading as I approached North Bay. Another fifteen minutes or so and it would be in full darkness. The upside was that there were loads of parking spaces. I pulled into one, got out, and glanced along the stretch of spaces. The only campervans I could see were modern ones. My stomach sank, but I crossed the road anyway and headed towards North Bay Corner. Just because Sam hadn't parked in the same place as me, it didn't mean he wasn't at the beach. There were plenty of other places he could have parked.

I looked towards the sea. High tide. He wasn't going to actually be *on* the beach, then.

Pulling my bobble hat down over my ears, I hurried past Blue Savannah, the ice-cream kiosk and The Surf Shack. There were a few people out for a walk, some with dogs, but the promenade was predominantly deserted. I smiled to myself as I spotted one family brazening it outside a bright yellow beach hut, huddled on deckchairs, wrapped in blankets. Talk about making sure you got your money's worth.

I reached the end of the beach huts. On the beach below, the rock pools started shortly after the huts ended, but they'd have been engulfed some time ago by the rising tide so he couldn't be down there.

A cyclist whizzed past me in the opposite direction and then I was alone. The path widened and curved round a grassy area with some benches on it but they were deserted. Crap. I'd been so sure that he'd head for the beach and, unable to get down to the rock pools, would have been on one of the benches.

It was properly dark now although there was thankfully good lighting. I'd go as far as the corner by Sea Rescue Sanctuary and, if there was still no sign of him, I'd have to go home and wait it out.

Feeling increasingly uncomfortable being alone in the darkness, I made my way to the corner, but to no avail. With a heavy heart, I started to re-trace my steps. The sea wall was quite high at that point but there were stone steps going down to the sand, running alongside the wall. I'd only seen the entrance to the steps on my way out, but I could see the steps descending ahead of me on my return trip. About six steps down, with his back against the wall, staring out to sea, was a lone figure. My heart leapt. Sam.

I watched him for a moment, wondering if he'd become aware of me, but he was clearly lost in his own world. Would he appreciate me invading his thoughts? Tough. There was no way I could leave him there. It was dark and cold and, although the sea wasn't rough, it wasn't safe.

Clinging onto the handrail, I descended a couple of steps then sat down, shivering as the coldness of the concrete steps immediately permeated through my coat.

Sam looked up, his eyes wide. 'Jemma!'

'Looks a bit cold for a swim.'

'I've surfed in colder.' He looked out across the gentle waves then turned back to me again. 'What are you doing here?'

'You left your mobile at your brother's and your mum rang me. She was worried about you and wondered if you were with me which made me worry about you, so I drove down here hoping to find you.'

'I'm sorry. I didn't mean to panic everyone.' His voice was strained and, although the gentle glow from the streetlight only partially lit his face, I could see the anguish in the crease of his forehead and slump of his shoulders.

'Was it something to do with the new baby's due date?'

He nodded.

'What happened on 21ˢᵗ May?'

He sighed and tossed a stone into the sea. 'Nikki always told me to be honest but I haven't been honest with you. Or anyone else.'

My heart skipped a beat. No! Not another one! Surely he didn't have a family hidden away somewhere. I quickly dismissed my fears. He wasn't Scott.

'Go on...' I encouraged.

He continued to stare into the darkness. 'The day it happened, I told you – and everyone else – that we were walking along the beach, chatting about our plans for the future. I told people we were talking about the wedding and some home improvements. That's all true. We *were* talking about those things, but I never expanded on what the home improvements were and why. Nobody asked. Why would they? Who cared if we were upgrading the double-glazing or putting in a new kitchen. Except that wasn't what we were planning. We were planning changes to the second bedroom.'

Sam turned to me and I suddenly knew what he was going to say. No! That wasn't fair.

'She was pregnant,' he said, confirming my suspicions. 'We'd had our first scan that morning. I didn't just lose Nikki that day.'

His voice cracked and he crumbled.

'Oh, Sam! I'm so sorry.' I shuffled down the steps and wrapped my arms round him, holding him close as he sobbed in my arms and icy tears rained down my cheeks at the tragedy of it all.

When the worst of his grief subsided, he loosened his hold but kept one arm round me as he sank back against the sea wall, staring out across the sea once more. I squeezed his shoulder and he rested his head against mine.

'I didn't tell anyone. I couldn't. It was so hard losing Nikki without losing a baby too. The staff at the hospital were sworn to secrecy. How could I tell her parents that they'd lost a daughter *and* a grandchild that day? So I put it in a box and closed the lid and have refused to think about it until today when they said the due date for Jack and Millie's baby.'

'Your baby would have been born on 21st May too?'

'Of all the dates, it had to be that one. It was like the lid sprung off the box and the grief started pouring out again. I had to get out. I never paused to think about how worried they'd be.'

'They'll understand but you're going to need to tell them. You know that, don't you?'

He sighed. 'I know. Nikki and I met on 21st May too. It seemed like the perfect date for our baby to be born. Just like having our wedding on her thirtieth birthday.'

'The day you met was the day of my dad's funeral. And the day you would have married was the day after my twenty-eighth birthday and Scott's proposal.' I don't know why I said that. It probably had no relevance but, to me, it felt like another connection we had.

'We'd been trying for two years and we'd pretty much given up hope of it ever happening. Then, suddenly, we had our little miracle and they were both taken away from me.'

I tried to pull him fully back into my embrace but he didn't respond. He didn't move his arm from round my waist but he now seemed stiff and uncomfortable instead of relaxed. We huddled awkwardly on the steps, both staring into the water until the wind picked up and I shivered.

'You're cold. We'd better go.'

I wasn't going to argue. I was freezing and he had to be too.

'I didn't see your campervan,' I said, when we'd made it back onto the promenade.

'I parked at the Sea Rescue Sanctuary. It's closer. Are you on the seafront?'

I nodded. An awkward silence settled round us and, for that brief moment, we felt like strangers.

'I should probably get home so they stop worrying about me,' Sam said.

'Yeah. Me too. Sort some tea out for Mum and Logan if they haven't had it yet.'

'Can I walk you back?'

'Don't be daft. It's not like it's the dead of night. There's lots of lighting and there are plenty of people around once I get to the corner.'

'Then I'll walk you to the corner.'

So he did. In silence.

My stomach tensed with each step. He hadn't needed to say it. I knew that this changed things between us. He'd regressed. He wasn't ready. He'd probably been kidding himself that he ever was.

'Thanks for coming to find me,' he said when we reached the end of the promenade.

I nodded. 'I'm so sorry, Sam. Losing Nikki must have been devastating, but losing your baby too... I can't begin to imagine what you went through that day and what you've been going through ever since.'

'I thought I was okay. I really did.'

And there it was – what I suspected conveyed in words. Too much, too soon. 'I know you did. I guess that box was never going to stay closed forever, was it?'

'I'm sorry.' He raised his arm as though he was going to reach out and touch me, but he dropped it to his side again. 'I didn't blank it out, you know. I just... I don't know. I don't understand what's happened today.'

He looked broken. I longed to kiss him and try to take his pain away but I knew I couldn't. 'Go on. Get home. Tell your parents. Bye, Sam.'

'Bye, Jem.'

I turned away, feeling like I'd just lost him. Shit! The text.

'Oh, Sam.' He stopped and turned round, his shoulders slumped. 'I sent you a text earlier. Ignore it. Don't read it. Please.'

'What did it say?'

I shook my head. 'It doesn't matter. Just ignore it.'

Then I turned away and hurried back to Mum's car, my heart breaking for him and everything he'd gone through and still was going through. What a tragedy.

I sat in Mum's car with the heating on full blast, tears dripping onto the steering wheel. It was over. It hadn't even started and it was already over. He wasn't ready after all, understandably so, yet I'd gone and taken that scary leap. He'd been so adamant it was what he wanted and, after that brief kiss on Mum's doorstep, I hadn't been able to deny that it was what I wanted too. I'd let my guard down and let him in and look where it had got me. Alone and heartbroken yet again. I should have stayed strong. I should have said no.

35

SAM

I sat in Thor for a while, with the heating on full pelt, trying and failing to take the chill off my bones. I hadn't been aware of the cold for the couple of hours I'd been on the steps, but now I was. My hands were blue, my feet were numb and I couldn't stop shivering.

Jemma must have texted Mum and Dad to say she'd found me because they were waiting on the doorstep as I pulled onto their street.

'I'm sorry,' I said as I got out.

Mum rushed forward shaking her head. 'Explanations later, Sammy. I've run you a bath.' She grabbed my arm and ushered me inside where the central heating blanketed me. 'I know you prefer showers but I think you'll need the heat. You must be frozen.'

'I am. There's something I need to tell you, though.'

'Whatever it is, it can wait. You need to warm up. Then we can talk.'

* * *

She'd been right about the bath. As my skin turned from blue to pink, I felt life seep back into me. I sank under the bubbles. Jesus! What had I been thinking of? Why hadn't I told anyone? It was always going to come back and bite me on the arse in spectacular style.

Instead of spending the past year grieving for Nikki and our baby, I'd spent the time grieving only for Nikki and now I needed to come to terms with the second life that had been lost that day. As I'd said to Jemma, I hadn't blanked it out or anything like that; I'd just refused to dwell on it. Why? Maybe the pain of losing Nikki was so acute that I couldn't cope with the loss of my son or daughter too.

There'd been moments, like on the beach in Kent with Jack on what would have been our wedding day, and last Sunday on the beach with Jemma. On both those occasions, it was as though I'd lifted the lid of that box and peeked inside, then snapped it shut again. What a mess. *And so it begins again...*

* * *

Mum cried when I told her about the baby, but insisted that, whilst she was sad about the loss of her grandchild, she was more upset that I'd faced it alone.

'You'll have to tell Zack and Hailey.'

Nikki's parents. She was right, but the thought was terrifying. 'They'll hate me for keeping it from them.'

'They'll be hurt but they won't hate you.'

'Do you think I should tell them before the memorial?'

She pondered for a moment. 'No. Let them have the evening they planned. They want it to be a happy occasion celebrating their daughter's life. They might not be able to do that if they knew about the baby and they could resent you for that. Tell them afterwards, before you go back to London.'

* * *

As I was getting ready for bed that night, I realised that I hadn't looked at my phone. There were three texts from Jemma. I read the most recent first and scrolled my way up:

✉ From Jemma
I can't tell you how sorry I am for your loss.
Don't forget to ignore that text. Please, please,
please. You know where I am if you need me xx

✉ From Jemma
Hi Carole. I found him at North Bay. He's on his
way home now. He'll be frozen. Take care of him for
me x

My finger hovered before scrolling up to the final message. She had
to know that I was going to read it.

✉ From Jemma
How does Tuesday at 6pm sound for a consultation
with my mum? And how does tonight at 7pm sound for
a date with me? A proper one. I'm a bit scared at
the thought of a new relationship but I know I can
trust you not to hurt me like Scott did. I may be a
little cautious and want to take it slowly, but I
think there's the potential for something that will
be worth the wait xx

Oh crap! She'd trusted me not to let her down and what had I
done? There was no way I couldn't respond. It wasn't like my feelings
for Jemma had changed. It was just that the timing was wrong.

✉ To Jemma
Sorry but I read your text. I couldn't help myself.
Last night you asked me to give you some time
because I was ready and you weren't. Now we've
swapped positions and I'm hoping you won't give up
on me while I have some more head space. I really
do care about you and I agree that we could have

something amazing together. You have no idea how much I want to take that final step but I have to come to terms with losing the baby before I can do that. Sorry seems so inadequate. You trusted me not to let you down yet I've done just that. I won't let your mum down, though. I still want to meet her and I'd like you to be there but I understand if you'd rather I give you some space. Tuesday at 6pm is fine by me and I can come to your house. Thanks for this afternoon. I can't tell you how grateful I was to have you there which makes me feel all the shittier for letting you down. Sorry again xx

I read my text over and over. It really was inadequate. Massively so. But it was all I could offer her right now.

36

I stared at Sam's text. It was what I'd expected. In fact, it was probably better than I'd expected and my heart melted that, despite his turmoil, he still wanted to be there for Mum.

The relief on Mum's face when I said I'd secured a consultation for a second opinion negated any awkwardness I might feel at seeing Sam again. I'd be fine. Nothing had happened between us. We were still friends, exactly the same as before, and there was therefore no need for Mum to know about my feelings for him. I wasn't ignoring the 'no secrets' pact; I was simply choosing not to talk about something that hadn't happened. Or something like that!

✉ To Sam

Yes please to meeting Mum. I'll be there but she doesn't know what's happened — or not happened — between us this weekend so please don't say anything. Not that you would. I just need to say it, though. Feeling a bit embarrassed about the content of my text. Please forget about what I said and just focus on you and what you need right now. I hope you're able to get some sleep tonight and

that your family can give you the support you need.
See you on Tuesday but you know where I am if you
need me in the meantime. I'm still your friend
assuming you want me to be xx

From Sam
Please don't be embarrassed about what you said. I
loved reading it. I wish we could have been on our
1st proper date tonight but it wouldn't be fair of
me to start a relationship with you when I haven't
yet come to terms with the past, much as I want to.
I'll see you on Tuesday. Take care xx

* * *

I felt sick on Tuesday. All day. Every time I thought about Sam – which
was pretty much most of the day – my heart raced and I imagined that
soft kiss on the doorstep turning into so much more. Which was ridiculous given that nothing was about to happen between us anytime soon.

It was one of my days serving in the shop alongside Mum but, after
I'd tried to charge a customer £1000 for a £100 collectible bear, had
knocked over an entire display of plush teddies, and had created
carnage in the shop window by causing a domino-effect bear tumble,
Mum suggested it would be a good idea for me to be where customers
and bears weren't. I wasn't much use with the paperwork either,
managing to spend an hour working on a document before closing it
without saving it.

'Are you okay?' Mum asked as we closed and locked up the shop at
the end of the day. 'You've not been yourself today.'

There were two reasons to be anxious about Sam's visit and I could
certainly share one of those with her. 'I've got myself a bit worked up
about your consultation with Sam. What if his verdict is inconclusive
too? Or if it's bad news.'

Mum shrugged. 'Then we'll cross that bridge together. I don't think it will be inconclusive, though. According to my friendly stalker's sister, your friend Dr Jones is a far better doctor than Dr Steadman. She was gutted when he left. If it's bad news, then at least we know what we're dealing with. At the moment, we haven't a clue.' She linked my arm and steered me towards the car park. 'Of course, if it *is* bad news, I'll have to shout and scream and throw a few vases at you and Logan, but then I'll be fine.'

I was glad she could laugh about it now. She'd had another counselling session last night and had come home on a high again. Meeting up with her friendly stalker's sister had also been invaluable. It had shown her how it was possible to have Parkinson's, still work, and still have a busy social life.

* * *

The knocker sounded shortly before six, setting my pulse racing. I opened the door and nearly melted. He was in a suit! And he looked even better in one than Scott had. OMG! Swoon!

'Sorry about the outfit,' he said, catching me staring. 'I had an appointment which ran over. I could either change and be late, or be on time in a suit.'

'I love a man in a suit,' I said, still drinking him in.

Sam laughed and I snapped out of my trance, placing my hands on my burning cheeks. 'Did I just say that aloud?'

'Yes. I'm glad I meet with your approval.'

'Oh, Sam, you know you do. And now you've just gone and ticked another box.'

That intense look was in his eyes again. He reached out his hand as though he was going to touch my face or my hair. Too intimate. I quickly stepped back into the hall. 'Come in. I'll introduce you to Mum.'

Sam followed me through to the kitchen diner. 'This is my mum, Julie. Mum, this is Dr Sam Jones.'

Mum stood up and shook his hand. 'Thank you so much for doing this. You do realise that you're now trapped here until you give a conclusive diagnosis.'

Sam smiled. 'I'm sure I can help you but I might have to pretend I can't so you can trap me here forever.' He looked at me as he said that and my stomach fizzed. 'You have a lovely home, Julie.'

'Thank you. I like you already. Please take a seat. Jemma was about to make drinks. Tea? Coffee?'

'I'll be bouncing off the walls if I have any more caffeine today. Just some water for me, please.'

The smile he gave me made my legs feel like water. I'd gone and done it, hadn't I? Instead of pushing any fledgling feelings aside while he came to terms with his grief, I'd done the opposite and fallen for him big time. Trust me to pick someone emotionally unavailable this time instead of physically unavailable. It wasn't like it was forever, though. I just needed to give him some time and, if the looks he was giving me were anything to go by, he was definitely keen; just not ready. I could wait.

Sam placed his pad, a pen and various other documents on the dining table. 'Jemma's told me about your diagnosis but I'd like to start completely afresh if that's okay. Imagine I know nothing about you so that we don't miss anything.'

'Fine by me,' Mum said.

'The best starting point is to ask you what you hope to get from this session with me.'

'Some clear direction. I've been diagnosed with Parkinson's and, while I don't like Dr Steadman, that side of it seems to be okay, but there've been other things. Let's call them incidents. I don't know whether they're related to the Parkinson's or if there's something else going on, but he's been as much use as a chocolate teapot. I'm hoping you can give me some clear answers so I can move forward and work out how to live my life, even if that means there's something else going on that I need to face.'

Sam nodded. 'Sounds reasonable and I'm sure I can help you there. What I need to do is explore your full medical history, including your diagnosis, and then we'll talk about the "incidents" you refer to. It may take some time to make sure we cover everything so please do say if you want a break, some air, another drink and so on. I want you to be comfortable. We'll also do something called the MMSE. That stands for Mini Mental State Examination.' He smiled reassuringly at Mum. 'Sounds scarier than it is. It's basically a pen and paper exercise that will take about ten minutes or so. Nothing to worry about but I'll explain more about it when we get to it. Are you ready to start?'

'As ready as I'll ever be.'

I squeezed Mum's hand beneath the table. 'Thanks for doing this, Sam,' I said.

'Any time. I'm only sorry that you both don't feel that you're getting the support you need at the hospital. Right, let's make a start...'

* * *

Sam was amazing. Where Dr Steadman's approach was cold and clinical, Sam's was warm and informal, showing empathy where appropriate, and making Mum laugh at other times. He couldn't have done more to put her at ease. Although he knew a lot of the information already from our discussions, he didn't let on that he knew it, exploring each "incident" as though it was the first time he'd heard about it. I added in a few bits here and there but it was mostly Mum who did the talking. He insisted we take a break before moving onto the test.

'Oh, Jemma, he's wonderful,' Mum said as we stretched our legs on the deck, thankful for the dry evening.

'He is, isn't he?'

'It's a shame you two are just friends. He'd make a fabulous boyfriend.'

I had to turn away so she couldn't see the tears glistening in my eyes. 'He probably would but neither of us are in the right place to consider a relationship right now. Who knows. Maybe the friendship will grow into something more.'

When we returned to the dining table, Sam explained more about the test – a series of verbal questions before moving onto the pen and paper test.

He asked her what day of the week it was, what date, what year and I realised I'd been holding my breath while she answered each question quickly and, thankfully, accurately. After the incident with our old house, I'd half-expected her to give a date of a decade earlier.

He gave her the name of a man and the first line of his address, asked her a couple more questions, then asked her to tell him the name of the man and his address. She reeled the information off without hesitation.

He asked her to spell the word 'world' backwards, which she did quicker than I managed in my head. He then asked her to count backwards from one hundred in sevens. We laughed when Mum admitted that her seven times table had been her nemesis at school and why couldn't he have asked her for her fives. But she did it.

When they moved onto the pen and paper test, Sam handed me a copy of the questions so I could see what Mum was going to answer. It contained more questions along the lines of what he'd already asked, plus some shapes for her to copy. It didn't take long before she handed the completed test back to Sam.

'Do I get my degree now?' she asked.

He smiled. 'I can print you a fake one off the internet if you like. Give me a couple of minutes to look at this.'

I squeezed Mum's hand again.

A few minutes later, Sam nodded and put the test aside. 'Dr Steadman *definitely* didn't do any of these tests with you?' he asked.

She shook her head. 'No. Nothing like that.'

'I can't understand why he didn't do this. Sometimes it's helpful to do tests like this to point towards a diagnosis around memory problems, such as dementia, but it can be equally helpful to do them to rule out something like dementia. In your case, Julie, I have a really clear diagnosis...'

I nibbled on my thumbnail as I waited. *Please don't say dementia. Please don't.*

'From our conversation this evening and from these tests, it's my professional opinion that you do *not* have dementia.'

'Not?' I asked, feeling weak with relief.

'Not.'

'Well, that's a relief,' Mum said.

'You're sure? I don't mean to doubt you, but...'

'I'm sure. If Julie had dementia, she wouldn't have got a near enough perfect score on the tests.'

'But there've been some pretty major incidents,' I said. 'Particularly the turning up at the wrong address.'

Mum nodded. 'She's right. If it's not dementia, what is it as that's not normal behaviour?'

'There are a couple of possibilities,' Sam said. 'One is that there's something else going on that we can only detect with a CT or MRI scan. Have you had either of those, Julie?'

'No.'

'Obviously that's not something I can arrange for you but you can insist that Dr Steadman does. However, my personal opinion is that it's the other possibility. Stress.'

Mum frowned. 'Stress? Are you being serious?'

'Very serious. Look at you, Julie. You're a single mother running your own business, which is open seven days a week for a significant part of the year. In addition to that, you make bears, you run workshops, and you value bears for two different companies – a role which sees you travelling extensively. That's an enormous workload that a normal person would struggle to maintain for a few months. You've been doing it for years and it's bound to have taken its toll. Although you were divorced, the death of your husband will have affected you, even if you didn't realise it at the time. Throw in a Parkinson's diagnosis, and I think that's tipped you over the edge.'

I looked at Mum and she shrugged. 'I've *always* been busy at work. I'm used to it.'

'She has,' I agreed.

'And I'd suggest that it's now caught up with you,' Sam said. 'I can tell that neither of you are convinced. Stress, unfortunately, is one of those words that gets overused. People who are a bit busy say they're stressed and there have been loads of cases of employees claiming to be off sick with work-related stress who are really trying it on. Stress – *proper* stress – is a very serious condition with dangerous repercussions.'

Sam went on to explain that some people under severe stress could have cognitive symptoms such as memory problems and difficulty in concentrating, emotional symptoms such as agitation, moodiness and anger, physical symptoms such as aches and pains, nausea, rapid heart rate, and behavioural problems such as eating more or less, sleeping more or less and neglecting responsibilities. We could put a tick against most of the symptoms under each of those four areas.

'So you're saying that all of those incidents could have been reactions to stress?' Mum asked.

'Yes.'

'And turning up at Fountain Street? I mean, that's a huge thing.'

'That as well, although I'd suspect that something happened that day to trigger it. Did anything unusual happen?'

'Typical day in the world of retail,' Mum said. 'Let me think. Lots of lovely customers, an argumentative woman who didn't get why collectible bears are expensive. And I found out—' She stopped and looked at me, eyes wide.

My stomach churned. 'You found out what?'

'Oh, Jemma, I'd completely forgotten.' She pressed her fingers to her lips. 'I promise I wasn't keeping secrets.'

My heart started racing. 'What?'

Mum's shoulders slumped. 'Eddie Holmes.'

I stiffened at the mention of his name. Murderer. The drunk driver who killed Dad. 'What about him?'

'There was an article in The Bay News. He was drink driving again and he hit a young girl on a zebra crossing.'

My stomach lurched and I thought for a moment I might be sick. 'Did he kill her?'

'Thankfully no. She was hurt, but nothing life-threatening.'

The nausea passed and I slumped back in my chair, shaking my head. 'He should have been locked up for life.'

'I know, sweetheart. I know.' She looked at Sam. 'He was the drunk driver who killed Jemma's dad. Don't even get me started on what I think of the justice system for the ridiculously short sentence they bestowed on him. First offence, my arse. Pleaded guilty so they're more lenient, my arse. Ooh, and a driving ban. Like that was going to make any difference when he was already banned for having too many points and had no tax and insurance anyway.'

'I'm sorry. That must have been so hard on you all. It sounds like that news was the straw that broke the camel's back, Julie. I'd suggest that, on autopilot, you headed for what had once been your sanctuary – your home before Eddie Holmes took Jemma's dad away from you all.'

It didn't surprise me that he'd hurt someone else. It was inevitable when he hadn't been banged up for life. Why had they let him out? Why had he been able to return to life as he'd known it, barely impacted by the carnage he'd left behind?

I pushed my angry thoughts out of my mind and focussed on what Sam was saying. The more he talked about stress, the more it made sense. He advised Mum to make an appointment with her GP to have her blood pressure monitored and explore stress and depression. He approved of the decisions she'd already made around resigning from the valuation work and having me supporting in the shop. He advised her that, whilst she probably wouldn't notice an immediate impact because she'd no doubt be stressed about the adjustment to her routine, she would notice it soon enough.

Sam looked at his watch. 'It's nearly nine. I've been interrogating you both for the best part of three hours. You must be exhausted, Julie.'

'I am actually. But it was worth it. I can't thank you enough, Sam.' Mum yawned and stretched. 'I need to go to bed. Are you okay if Jemma sees you out?'

'Of course. Good night, Julie. Please get in touch if you have any other questions.' He handed her a business card. 'Definitely get in touch with your GP though.'

'I will. I promise.'

I cleared away the empty glasses and mugs while Sam packed away his paperwork. When I heard Mum's bedroom door close upstairs, I turned to him. 'She definitely doesn't have dementia?'

He stopped what he was doing and smiled. 'Definitely. I wasn't just saying that stuff about stress to deflect her. I'm absolutely certain that's what it is, possibly accompanied with depression. She's likely been stressed for years but has just been one of those powerhouses who's pushed through it. I suspect your dad's death was the catalyst for it becoming a bigger thing.'

'But she didn't even like him. She wasn't upset when he died.'

'She doesn't have to have been. She might not personally have been affected by his death but she'd have been aware that you and your brother were going to be and that her role was now as mum and dad to you both. Consciously or not, she'll have created that extra role for herself, adding even more stress. Hey, don't cry.'

'Sorry,' I wiped at my tears. 'It's just such a relief to hear you say that it's only stress.'

'Don't underestimate stress. It's dangerous.'

'I know. It's just that I'd rather it's stress which she can do some-thing about by reducing her workload and having me here to help with Logan, as opposed to dementia which she can't do anything about. I thought we were losing her, Sam.'

Next minute, I was in his arms again. He held me, stroked my back, whispered soothing words as the worry of the last few months poured out of me.

When I'd stopped crying, he loosened his hold slightly and looked down into my eyes.

'I think someone else is suffering from stress too and I don't think I've helped, have I?'

'You couldn't have predicted what happened.'

'I know, but... You have no idea how much I want to kiss you right now.'

My already racing heart skipped a beat. 'I wouldn't push you away.'

'I can't. I want to, but I can't. I'm going to this one-year memorial for Nikki on Friday. Her parents own one of the beach huts on North Bay and they're having a few drinks for close friends and family. I need to focus on that and then, on Saturday, I'm going to tell them about the baby. Maybe we could meet up on Saturday night and talk?'

I held my breath as he brushed a strand of hair behind my ear. 'I'd like that.'

'So would I.' He shook his head. 'I have to go before I do something I know I shouldn't.'

I nodded, although I wanted to scream: 'Just do it!'

As we stood by the door a few minutes later, Sam said, 'I know I'm probably confusing the hell out of you at the moment but I've never been anything but honest with you. Let me get through Friday and past telling Nikki's parents. I don't know whether I'll need days or weeks or months after that but I'll continue to be honest with you. I promise.'

He leaned forward and gave me a soft kiss on the lips then ran down the drive to his campervan, leaving me touching my lips yet again, longing for more.

37

7.10 a.m. North Bay. Friday 11th November. One year on.

I sat cross-legged on the cold sand next to my surfboard, eyes fixed on the horizon. Sunrise was due any minute.

To my left, way down at the other end of the beach, were the rock pools where I lost her. I could just about make out the shape of the Sea Rescue Sanctuary but the beach itself was in darkness.

I turned my gaze back to the sea. I'd expected to feel tearful but, as the sun peeped over the horizon and became a growing arch of orange, I felt hopeful. New day. New start.

Standing up, I grabbed my board then ran towards the sea. 'This is for you, Nikki,' I whispered. 'And our baby.'

The unmistakable aroma of bacon and eggs hit me as soon as I opened the door to Mum and Dad's, making my stomach growl appreciatively. I found Mum in the kitchen filling the teapot. She tried to dab her eyes with a tea towel but she wasn't quick enough. 'Sorry, Sammy. I didn't want to cry but I can't help it. I miss her.'

I hugged her. It was easy to focus on the pain I'd felt during the past year and forget that Mum and Dad had lost their surrogate daughter too. 'I miss her too.'

'How was the surf?' she asked, pulling away and reaching into the cupboard for some mugs.

'Perfect. I think Nikki would have approved. She wouldn't have wanted me to spend the day moping about.'

'I think that Nikki would approve of *anything* that makes you happy.' She looked at me pointedly and raised her eyebrows.

'Why do I get the impression that you're not talking about surfing?'

She shrugged. 'I've no idea what you mean.'

'Yeah, right. Have I got time for a shower before breakfast's ready?'

'I can keep it warming. Off you go. You've got sand in your hair as usual.'

An image of Nikki on the evening I met her, sand in hair, flashed into my mind, making me smile.

A text was waiting from Jemma when I'd finished in the shower:

✉ To Sam
Thinking of you today as you remember Nikki and the baby. Hope the memorial is everything you hope for xx

I sat on the edge of my bed, wrapped in my towel, as I re-read her text. How was it that she was so thoughtful? Things hadn't been awkward on Tuesday when they so easily could have been. She'd been so understanding. When I'd said that I needed time, she hadn't whined and she hadn't pushed. But she hadn't pulled away either. She'd have let me kiss her. She said so. I wished I had.

I hadn't been able to stop thinking about her since then. I'd picked up my phone to call or text on countless occasions but kept reminding myself that I had to keep my focus and get through the anniversary and memorial drinks before I could even think about picking things back up with Jemma. I should have done that in the first place – waited until the anniversary had passed before I'd opened my big mouth, then we wouldn't be in this situation. We'd still have been friends and I could have let it grow naturally instead of diving straight in and wiping out. I hoped I hadn't destroyed her trust in me.

My thoughts turned to the evening plans at Hailey and Zack's beach hut. I was dreading it because, from a conversation I'd had with Hailey yesterday, it was obvious it was no longer the small, select gathering they'd originally suggested. I didn't like huge parties and neither had Nikki. She'd have hated knowing her parents had invited so many people. It would be easier to face if Jemma was with me but that was hardly appropriate. Even if I introduced her as a friend, there'd be whisperings and assumptions.

I read Jemma's text once more. I wanted to see her. I wanted to talk to her. But it wasn't fair. So I typed in something friendly but completely non-committal and shook my head in disgust as I sent it:

✉ To Jemma
Thank you. It was meant to be a small gathering but I think their definition of small may be my definition of huge so not looking forward to it xx

* * *

'What are you doing today?' Mum asked over breakfast.

I shrugged. 'Stevie and Rob offered to meet me at lunchtime or this afternoon for a pint but I haven't confirmed anything.'

'That sounds nice. Will you do it?'

Would I? Sod it! I had nothing else planned and it was good of them to offer.

'I'm so pleased that you're back in touch with them,' Mum continued. 'They were such lovely boys when you were at school together. And you did say you had a good evening with them on Monday.'

I had. I'd expected it to be awkward and, when I'd walked into The White Horse and spotted them laughing together, I'd almost lost my nerve. Then I'd noticed the third pint on the table. Stevie clocked me at that point and waved me over. 'We remembered you used to love real ale. We're hoping you still do. If you do, it was my idea. If you don't, it was Rob's!'

After that, it had been easy banter all the way. I decided to wipe the slate clean immediately and apologise for my stupid comments about Maddy. Stevie laughed and said that he could have saved himself a lot of pain if he'd actually listened to me instead of being so stubborn. He said that, if I could forgive him for not inviting me to the wedding, we were evens.

We chatted about their lives since college. Rob had gone away to Bristol University and stayed down there, only returning home a couple of years ago when he'd split up with his girlfriend. He said he was bi-sexual and was now living with a bloke called Gary who happened to be the ex-husband of Stevie's partner, Elise. I certainly hadn't expected a revelation like that.

The subject then moved onto Nikki. I didn't tell them about the baby or about Jemma. I'm not sure why.

It turned out that Rob had known Nikki, although he hadn't seen her for years. That was the thing about Whitsborough Bay; everyone seemed to know everyone.

'You know what, Mum?' I said, tucking into my second butty. 'I think I will meet them.'

'That's the spirit.'

38

JEMMA

I couldn't believe it was Friday already. Wednesday and Thursday had whizzed by. Mum had woken up on Wednesday morning with a new lease of life, making an emergency appointment to see her GP that afternoon and another appointment with her counsellor to explore the new information.

I organised test drives for three cars on the Thursday afternoon and made a speedy decision as to which I liked best, placing an order on the same day. My very first car.

Mum spent Friday morning in Bear With Me but agreed to have the afternoon off to de-stress. Rachel had booked them both in for a pampering afternoon at a local spa and they were planning to end their day with a film and a takeaway at Rachel's. Billy Thomas had invited Logan for tea, the cinema, and a sleepover, which meant I'd be on my own for the first time since I'd moved home.

Some me-time would be welcome but how would I spend it? Thinking about Sam and convincing myself that, if he ever felt ready to move on from Nikki and the baby, he wouldn't still be interested in me. And dwelling on the revelation that Eddie Holmes nearly killed someone else when he should still have been behind bars, paying for what he'd done to Dad.

I was in the staffroom catching up with the accounts when there was a knock on the door and Annie pushed it open. 'Sorry to disturb you but there's a woman downstairs asking for you.'

'For me? Not Mum?'

'No. You.'

'Did she give her name?'

Annie grimaced. 'I never even thought to ask. Sorry.'

'That's okay. Let me save this spreadsheet then I'll be down.' I'd been in touch with The Bay News about running some adverts and a promotional piece so I assumed it was a journalist or sales rep from there.

Annie pointed towards a woman with dark bobbed hair peering into a glass cabinet containing some vintage bears, lovingly restored by Mum.

'Hi, I'm Jemma,' I said, approaching the woman. 'You wanted to see me?'

She turned round, straight-faced, and looked me up and down, which unnerved me somewhat. 'Is there somewhere private we can talk?'

'We've got a staffroom. Can I ask your name?' She looked familiar but I couldn't place her.

'Fiona,' she said. 'Fiona Hannigan. It's about my husband, Adam. Although I think you know him as Scott.'

Shhhiiiiiiitttttttt!!!!!!!!! I stepped back into a display table, knocking over a couple of bears. No wonder she looked familiar. I'd seen all those photos of her on social media.

'Are you okay, Jemma?' Annie called from behind the counter.

'Erm... Yes. Fine. Lost my footing.' I cleared my throat and hoped I sounded in control. 'We're going upstairs. Are you and Liv okay on your own?'

Annie gave me a strange look but stopped short of reminding me that there were usually only two staff serving and I'd been upstairs all afternoon anyway. 'We'll be fine. You take your time.'

I tried to sort out the bears but knocked another one over. Liv appeared by my side. 'I'll sort these out. You see to your visitor.'

My stomach churned as Fiona followed me up the stairs. She didn't look like the sort of woman who'd throw a punch but she'd probably be justified if she did.

'Tea or coffee?' I asked.

'Tea please. Milk, no sugar.'

I pointed to the table. 'Have a seat. I won't be long.'

For the first time ever, I was thankful for the world's noisiest kettle as it meant we couldn't talk. Which meant I could calm down a bit first. Except that I felt anything but calm.

Drinks made, I approached the table, my stomach in knots, and handed Fiona her tea. I sat down and waited for her to speak as I had no idea what to say as an opener.

'You're probably wondering why I'm here.'

I could guess. 'Presumably Scott... Adam told you about me.'

'Not exactly.' She twisted a lock of hair round one of the fingers of her left hand. I noticed the absence of a wedding or engagement ring. They'd split up?

'I found out about you,' she said flatly.

'I'm sorry. That must have been hard.' Didn't I know it?

'It was...' She paused as though searching for the right word, '... well, it was one of those things you hope you'll never discover.' She held my gaze. Awk-ward.

'I have some questions,' she said. 'Some of them may seem strange, so please bear with me. Do you mind?'

'Go ahead.'

She took a deep breath. 'When did you meet him?'

'January last year.'

'So it was going on for...?'

'About eighteen months.'

'When you met him, did you know that he was married?'

I shook my head. 'God, no! I know you don't know me but believe me when I say I'm not the sort of person who'd do that. If I'd thought for a second that he was married when we met, or even that he had a girlfriend, nothing would have happened. I promise you.'

Holding Fiona's gaze, I noticed how exhausted she looked. Her grey eyes glistened with unshed tears and she had dark shadows beneath them which she'd attempted, but failed, to cover with concealer.

'How and when did you find out about me?' she asked. 'Did he come clean?'

'I wish. No. He ghosted me in June. I didn't understand why he'd dropped out of my life like that. I thought we were h...' I stopped. She didn't need to know that we were happy. I didn't want to rub it in. 'My flatmate and I did some investigating, found out where he worked, and discovered he'd given me a false name. I emailed him to let him know he'd been sprung. An out of office message came back saying he was on paternity leave and that's when I found out that he'd been living a double life.'

She winced. 'Oh my God! That's really how you found out?'

I nodded. 'As I said, if I'd had even the slightest inkling before then... I'm not the sort of person who'd do that to another woman.'

Fiona held my gaze as though deciding whether she believed me or not. 'Did he tell you why he gave you a false name?'

'It was some sort of game that the two of you played. Scott Hastings is a character out of a film. *Strictly Ballroom,* I think.'

She gasped and smacked the palm of her hand against her forehead. 'Of course he is! How stupid am I? It's one of my favourite films and I never even registered the name.'

I wrapped my hands round my mug, for comfort as much as anything. 'Why are you here? I don't mean that in a rude way. I just don't understand why you're asking me about Scott... Adam... when you could have confronted him about it. He'd have more answers than I do because, to be honest, I still don't fully understand what happened or why.'

Fiona looked down into her tea and shook her head. 'I can't confront Adam.'

'Why not?'

She looked up and straight into my eyes. 'There's no easy way to say this. I'm sorry, Jemma, but Adam's dead.'

39

SAM

'Tough day?' Stevie asked that afternoon, joining me in a booth in The Lobster Pot, a pub on the seafront overlooking South Bay's harbour.

'Not too bad so far. This thing at the beach hut tonight could tip it the other way, though.'

Rob took a seat next to him. 'My parents are going. The invitation included me too.'

'And you haven't seen her for years?' Why had they gone so overboard with the invites?

'We were maybe fourteen or fifteen last time,' Rob said. 'We weren't friends. Not that she wasn't a lovely girl. It's just that we didn't know each other well enough to be mates.'

'It's fine. I knew what you meant. Balls. It's going to be full of people I don't know who probably barely knew Nikki too but they'll all be looking at me. I can't stand all the sympathetic looks and whispers.'

Stevie raised his pint. 'Then you're going to need several of these to psyche yourself up.'

That sounded like a brilliant plan.

Some people make out that men don't talk, or at least they don't talk about difficult subjects and feelings, but the three of us talked non-stop that afternoon, really setting the world to rights.

We discussed Nikki's death, the baby, and how running away to London hadn't been the answer. We talked about how Stevie had dealt with losing his baby and how Maddy had screwed him up so badly that he'd thought he'd never be able to commit to a long-term relationship again.

Rob shared how he'd felt when he realised he was attracted to men as well as women, and how messed up he'd been after he'd split up with his girlfriend in Bristol after she found out that he'd dated men before but hadn't told her.

And I told them about Jemma.

'Seriously, mate, you should be with her,' Stevie slurred, pointing his finger at me and swaying slightly.

How many pints had we had? Six? Zack and Hailey weren't going to be impressed. Better not have any more.

'Another beer?' Rob asked, indicating the empties obliterating the table.

'Go on, then.' What difference would one more make?

Rob headed off towards the bar, ricocheting off a table he'd misjudged on the way.

'You think so?' I asked, returning to Stevie's comment.

'She sounds lovely. D'you love her?'

'Yeah. Didn't think I'd love anyone again after Nikki. Didn't think lightning would strike twice.'

'Then tell her. Don't lose her.'

'Only been a year,' I said. 'Too soon?'

'Noooooo! Just a number. Nikki'd want you to be happy, yeah?'

'Yeah.'

'Jemma makes you happy, yeah?'

'Yeah.'

'Bollocks to everyone else, then. Took me...' He squinted and started counting on his fingers but the maths was obviously too hard with six pints inside him and he couldn't coordinate his fingers either. He gave up. 'Took me fourteen years or summat like that to find love again. If you've found it, grab it. Might not happen again.'

'What if she wants to stay friends instead?'

'Then it wasn't meant to be. Move on.'

'What about the baby?'

Stevie shrugged. 'What *about* the baby? Nikki was pregnant, Nikki died, baby died, but *you're* still alive and you need to live your life. You say you haven't grieved for the baby but you have. You've grieved for Nikki and the baby was part of her. You don't need to start again. They're both gone, but you're here and you've found someone you love and, if she loves you too, you might have your own babies one day. When Maddy and I lost Rebecca, it was horrendous but I got over it. Rebecca was one of those babies who wasn't meant to make it, just like yours. Now I have two babies of my own. Melody's not mine biologically but she's still as much mine as Tristan is. I'll never forget Rebecca and neither of them are replacements for her. It's just how life is. You can ride the waves or you can get caught in the riptide. Which do you choose, Sam?'

'The waves.'

'Then you choose life. You choose the future. You choose Jemma.'

'I choose beer,' Rob said, placing three pints on the table.

'Me too!' I said, laughing.

'And me!' Stevie added.

We clinked our pints together. 'To Nikki and the baby,' I said.

Stevie grinned at me. 'To the waves, to life, to the future, and to Jemma.'

And to Jemma. The future with Jemma. I liked that.

40

I stared open-mouthed at Fiona. Scott was dead? He was actually dead? He couldn't be. How? When? It didn't make any sense.

'It was a massive heart attack,' Fiona said gently.

I clapped my hand across my mouth. 'What? But he was only thirty-two.'

'I know. It's no age, is it? He was away at a convention at the time. He'd been complaining about chest pains to one of his colleagues and they both assumed he'd pulled a muscle putting up the stand. At his age, you wouldn't imagine it to be something more serious. After lunch, he said he didn't feel right. Twenty minutes later, he collapsed.' She took a deep shaky breath. 'By the time the ambulance arrived, it was too late. Gone.'

'But he was fit. Healthy.'

'They had to do a post-mortem with it being a sudden death and they found a congenital heart defect that had gone undetected. He'd been a ticking time bomb and he hadn't known it.'

I shook my head, waiting for some sort of punchline to a sick joke. But there wasn't one. This wasn't a joke.

'When?' I whispered.

'Friday 15th July.'

Oh my God! That was the date he stood me up in La Vecchia Scuola. The staffroom started to spin and I thought for a moment that I was either going to faint or throw up. Fiona pushed a glass of water to my lips, ordering me to sip it. Gradually everything returned to focus.

'I'm sorry,' she said. 'I shouldn't have just blurted that out. I know he was meant to meet you that night because he was finally going to leave me.'

'No. He couldn't do it. He didn't turn up. He chose you.' I grabbed a tissue from the box and wiped my cheeks. 'He sent me a text that night to say...' I stopped and stared at Fiona, open-mouthed. 'You said he collapsed after lunch. That text came through around 11.00 p.m. That would mean... Was that you? Did you send the text from his phone?'

She lowered her eyes, colour flooding her pale cheeks. 'I'm sorry. I was angry and I know I had no right to be after what I'd done but I couldn't help it. I had to lash out and that was the only way I knew how.'

When she looked up again, guilt was plastered across her face. 'They gave me this bag, you see. At the hospital. This see-through plastic bag with his belongings in it. His watch, his wedding ring, his wallet. And there were two phones. I remember holding the bag up and staring at them, wondering why he had two when the one he used at home was his work phone. His boss and one of his colleagues were still at the hospital. I asked if they were both work phones but his colleague joked about one of them being Adam's "private" phone which he was always phoning and texting me on.' She sighed and shook her head. 'Standing in that hospital corridor staring at that unfamiliar phone confirmed what, deep down, I'd known for a long time. He'd met someone else. You'll probably think I'm awful for fixating on it when my husband was only just gone but I had to find out who you were and that phone was going to give me the answer.'

'I'm sorry. As I said before, I honestly didn't know he was married.'

'I know. I read your messages. My sister, Dawn, has this boyfriend who has a heart of gold but, for some reason, he knows how to do some dodgy stuff. Dawn told me that no good would come of unlocking the mystery phone and discovering the secrets it held but I couldn't help myself. It was like an obsession. So her boyfriend unlocked it for me and there you were – the woman my husband loved. Texts, photos, emails, a Facebook account. A whole new life for someone called Scott Hastings.'

She explained how she'd read the most recent texts, which made it clear that Scott was planning to leave her to be with me. At that point, anger took over and she sent the text telling me that he'd picked her instead. She'd then worked back through the texts, seeing my discovery that he had a wife and twins, the 'where are you?' texts when he ghosted me, and as far back as the proposal.

'Dawn took the phone off me at that point and wouldn't give me it back. She said that Adam wasn't around to justify or explain what had happened and that I'd only work myself into a frenzy going through every single text and Facebook post if she let me keep the phone. I had to remember him as the good husband and father I'd thought he was earlier that day and leave it there. She said I'd regret sending the text to you and she was right. I had no right to lash out like that and I had no right to keep the news of his death from you. She may be younger than me but my sister's a hell of a lot wiser.'

'So what made you tell me now?'

'Adam's office forwarded me an envelope containing a blank cheque for £500. You hadn't signed the note but your name was on the cheque. I didn't know what to make of it so I told Dawn. She'd been keeping an eye on Adam's phone and said that you'd sent him a text saying you wanted the money to go to the hospital or the twins. It was obvious that you were a decent person and not the husband-stealing bitch I wanted to believe you were. She said I definitely owed you the truth so here I am. I donated the money to the special care baby unit, by the way.'

I sipped on my water, trying to take it all in. Scott was dead. He hadn't stood me up. He'd been laid out on a mortuary slab instead. I shuddered at the thought.

'It's a lot to take in, isn't it?' Fiona said. 'I often have to remind myself that he's not just away on another business trip. He's never coming home again.'

We sat in silence. The tears started again as I thought about how hurt I'd been after that last text from him and how much I'd hated him at that moment. And he hadn't even sent it!

'Did he tell you that I tricked him into marrying me?' she asked. 'I'd always longed for children and I saw Adam as my chance to have a normal loving family. I'd been badly hurt – physically as well as emotionally – by the one man I fell in love with. Adam had never shown me anything but friendship and kindness. I thought it would be enough for us to make it but I began to feel him slipping away from me and, with him, my chance to have children. There was no way I could trust anyone else after what Begsey did to me. It was so wrong of me but I was desperate. I told Adam I was pregnant knowing that he'd ask me to marry him because that's the sort of man he was. I lay awake each night, haunted by feelings of guilt. I kept psyching myself up to tell him the truth but I couldn't face losing him. A couple of weeks later, I discovered I really was pregnant. I convinced myself that it was a sign and Adam and I were meant to be together. I had this little fantasy that we'd properly fall in love with each other when we became a real family. It was a quickie wedding with a handful of guests but we lost the baby at eight weeks. I knew then that I should let go of Adam too but I couldn't. I was too scared.'

She swiped at the tears trailing down her cheeks as her voice cracked. 'I should have let him go. I know that now. There were so many occasions when he came home and I knew he was building up to telling me it was over but I never let him come out with it. I pulled a guilt trip on him every time. There'd never been much passion between us. We were, after all, just really good friends. But if we weren't sleeping together, I was never going to fall pregnant so I...' She paused and shook her head. 'You don't need to know the details but let's just say I took advantage. When I fell pregnant with the twins, I was under strict orders to avoid any stress so I knew I could keep Adam. For a while anyway.'

I was in shock and had no idea what to say. My mind was racing. Everything he'd told me that final time together about neither of them being in love with each other, about Fiona only being with him to have children, about him going home to end it so many times had all been true. He'd said that he'd never lied to me about any other aspect of his life and his wife had just confirmed that.

Fiona exhaled deeply then lifted her bag onto her knee. 'I've got something for you. Dawn and I weren't sure how you'd feel about this so you can say no if it's too much.'

She reached into her handbag and took out something wrapped in a carrier bag. 'We had Adam cremated. It felt wrong to scatter his ashes near me when I wasn't the keeper of his heart.' She placed a wooden box on the table. 'I think he'd want his resting place to be near you, especially as he'd have been with you for real now if he hadn't died.'

My hand shook as I slowly reached out and touched the pale wood. My fingertips rested on the box for a moment then I withdrew my hand.

'He might not have gone through with it. He'd been seeing me for eighteen months and he'd never left you during that time. He might still have stood me up. He might still have chosen you.'

She shook her head. 'He loved you. Not me. Not in that way. One day he was always going to fall in love for real and I only hoped that, by the time that happened, we'd have had the children I desperately wanted. He chose you, Jemma.'

'You don't know that. He'd already ghosted me once. He could have done it again.'

'He could have but he wasn't going to.' She took a phone out of her bag. I recognised it immediately as Scott's. She tapped a few buttons then passed it to me. It was open on his emails and, specifically, confirmation of an appointment with a divorce lawyer.

I looked up at Fiona, biting my lip.

'Now click on the Notes app.'

I did as instructed and saw calculations for how he could financially support his family and still put money away for our wedding. There was also a list of items he could sell to raise more money.

I handed the phone back to Fiona. He'd told me on the evening we got back together that he'd done both of those things and, once again, he'd been telling the truth. 'I'm sorry. If I'd known about you...'

'It's not your fault. You didn't know. I caused this and I'm here to put things right.' She pointed at the phone. 'I don't think it gets much clearer than all of that, does it? He chose you and, strange as it may sound, I'm glad he found the real thing before he died, even if it wasn't with me.'

41

'You're sure you don't want to join in?' Karen asked me early that evening, putting her right foot up on the bench beside me and tightening the laces on her trainers.

I shook my head and indicated the grey woollen dress and boots I'd been wearing for work. 'I'm hardly dressed for it.'

'This is true. Cute dress, though.'

'Thank you.' Shivering in a sudden gust of wind, I fastened up my coat. 'I'll sit on this bench and watch you work your magic. Well, what I can see in the streetlights.'

'Okay. I'll be about an hour then you have my undivided attention.' She put her foot down and sighed. 'I'm sorry, Jem. I wish I could talk now because I can tell that something's upset you big time.'

Tears threatened to break loose again. 'Go! I'll be fine. Your clients need you. I think that's one arriving now.'

'Crap! Laters.' Karen picked up her clipboard and backpack then bounded across the grass towards the sea wall where a woman in her fifties encased in fluorescent pink lycra was waiting. Wow! I didn't need the streetlights to see her!

I leaned back on the bench and looked past Karen and her client towards the sea, then down the promenade. Watching a group of women in their fifties working out wasn't how I'd envisaged spending my evening but I couldn't face being at Bear's Pad alone after Fiona's surprise visit and shock revelation this afternoon. I still couldn't believe it.

Another gust of wind made me shiver and wrap my arms across my body for warmth. It was a fairly mild evening, especially compared to Bonfire Night but it certainly wasn't warm enough to be sitting on a metal bench for an hour and a quarter. I glanced at my watch. Karen was only fifteen minutes into her hour-long session. Sitting in Blue Savannah on my own would be even worse than being home alone. I needed to find something to distract me.

I took a walk along the promenade and phoned Leah but it went straight to voicemail. I tried Tiff. Her phone rang for ages and it struck me that 7.15 p.m. on a Friday night probably wasn't a good time to catch anyone. If she wasn't at work, she'd be out at the pub. I was just about to hang up when she answered with a croaky voice.

'Hello?'

'Hi, Tiff. It's Jemma. You sound awful.'

'I'm full of cold. I think I might even be bordering on man-flu.'

'That bad eh?'

'Definitely. How's life up north?'

'Not so good. I had some awful news today...'

'Could she have been lying?' Tiff croaked after I'd told her about Fiona's visit, my voice cracking at regular intervals.

'I don't think so. She had no reason to. I was already out of his life, thanks to the text she sent. Besides, she brought his ashes with her.'

'It could be dust in there and you'd never know. Wait a second.'

'What are you doing?' But it was quiet so I'd have to wait. My eyes strayed towards Karen's small group. They seemed to be doing some sort of relay in pairs. One did burpees while the other ran along the promenade and back, then they swapped. I felt exhausted just watching them.

'I'm back,' Tiff said. 'Sorry, Jem, but she's telling you the truth.'

'Have you consulted your crystal ball?'

'Yes. It's called Google. I found an obituary in the local paper, a couple of articles about him, and a tribute on his company's website. He's really gone.'

The tears started again. 'I didn't get to say goodbye,' I squeaked.

'I know. I'm so sorry. He was far too young. It doesn't seem fair.' She paused for a coughing fit. 'Sorry about that. What happens now?'

'I honestly don't know. I've spent the last four months getting over him while believing he was the bad guy who'd broken my heart and let me down yet again. Turns out it was really *his* heart that was broken and had let *him* down instead.'

* * *

Karen stared at me later, eyes wide, shaking her head. 'I can't believe it! When you turned up tonight, I knew something had happened but I thought your mum had maybe had a setback. Shit, Jem, I'm so sorry.'

Tears filled Karen's eyes and she quickly swiped at them. 'Look at me. I barely knew the guy and it's set me off. How are you feeling?'

I shrugged. Glancing round Blue Savannah at the laughing couples, families and groups of friends, my eyes rested on the booth where I'd introduced Scott to their full English breakfast. I could almost see him sitting there, smiling at me, telling me he loved the breakfast but he loved me more. He was always saying things like that.

I turned back to Karen. 'I'm a bit numb at the moment.'

'Will you scatter his ashes?'

'Yes, but not yet. I don't think it's healthy to have a box of someone's ashes sat at home like some sort of shrine. I don't know where I'll do it, though. He really liked Whitsborough Bay but he'd only been here three times so we didn't have a special place as such. I'll need to think.'

'You know I'm here for you if you want company when you do it,' Karen said.

'I know. I appreciate it.' I sipped on my pint.

'A toast?' Karen suggested, raising her glass of tonic water.

I raised my glass. 'To Scott, taken far too soon.' My eyes blurred as I took a sip. The lump in my throat was so big, I could barely swallow.

'Have you told your mum?' Karen asked.

'Not yet. I wanted her to enjoy her relaxation day. I'll tell her tomorrow.'

'When I was doing yoga with her on Wednesday, she was like a different woman.'

At least I could smile about that. 'All thanks to Sam. Another strongly worded complaint has gone to the hospital about that idiot Dr Steadman. I can't believe he didn't do that dementia test on her after the Fountain Street incident. If it hadn't been for Sam going completely out of his way to help her, I don't know where we'd be.'

'What's next for you two?'

'Sam and me? I don't know. Still friends. Perhaps.'

Karen frowned. 'Why do you say "perhaps"?'

'We met in the first place because I needed advice about Mum but I don't need that anymore as he's diagnosed the problem. If I'd still been living in London, we could have met up regularly. We could have scoured London together for decent real ale establishments and seen what developed. Now that I'm living here, things will probably just peter out.'

'Bollocks!' Karen cried, drawing attention from the tables round us.

I sank down in my seat. 'Karen!'

'Well, it is. You're smitten with him. Every time you talk about him, your whole face lights up. You want to rip off his clothes and bump uglies with him.'

'I do not! Okay, I did, but how can I even think about that after the news I got today?'

Karen ran her fingers through her hair and sighed. 'Sorry, Jem, but I'm going to have to say this. If I word it badly, I'm sorry. You're better with stuff like this.'

'Do I need another drink?'

'Yes. I think so. I wish I wasn't driving so I could have one too.'

'You're making me nervous,' I said.

I returned from the bar with another round of drinks. 'Hit me with it.'

'Please don't get mad at me, but the Jemma I know and love would *not* have let her fiancé abandon his wife and babies to be with her, no matter how much she loved him. Come on, Jem, you know I'm right. I know you loved Scott and I know how devastated you were when you found out about his other life but you said yourself that you couldn't be with a liar and a cheat. I get why you wanted to talk about giving him a second chance. As I said at the time, I'd have struggled not to do the same for Ryan. But if Scott hadn't died that night, I'm not sure you would have agreed to try again because of the kids. If you had gone for it, I don't think your relationship would have lasted. You couldn't have done it to them or to yourself. You're not like that. The guilt would have eaten away at you and destroyed your love for Scott.' She grimaced. 'Sorry. I wouldn't be your best friend if I didn't say that.'

I sipped on my drink, thinking about what she'd said. 'Oh my God,' I muttered.

'"Oh my God", you're a genius and you know me better than I know myself, or "oh my God", you're a bitch for bringing this up when I've just found out he's dead.'

I had to laugh at that. 'The former.'

'Really?' Karen visibly relaxed. 'Thank God for that.'

We had no way of knowing what the future would really have held for Scott and me, but Karen knew me well. It *would* have eaten away at me to the point where I'd have pushed him back to Fiona, even if he hadn't wanted to go, because I couldn't live with the guilt.

We chatted more about where this left me, then we moved onto cheerier subjects like how Ryan's and Steff's marathon training was going, and how rapidly their bootcamp business was growing. It was lovely to see my friend so animated about her business success. I remembered the long hours and hard work she'd put into getting it off the ground, but it was clearly paying off now. But overshadowing the excitable discussions was a voice in my head repeating over and over: *Scott's dead. He didn't intentionally abandon me. He died.* And I had no idea how I should feel about that.

42

SAM

Walking round The Headland from The Lobster Pot on South Bay to Zack and Hailey's beach hut on North Bay had seemed like a good idea. Thing is, I could barely walk. I certainly couldn't walk in a straight line. Not that The Headland was straight; it was a steady curve. Maybe that was the problem – I was trying to walk in a straight line but kept bumping into the sea wall instead. My legs and knees were going to be so bruised, but at least I'd have sobered up by the time I got to the beach hut. A bit.

My phone rang. 'Mum?'

'Sammy? Where are you? We've been here since five.'

'What time is it now?'

'6.45.'

Was it? Hadn't meant to stay in the pub that long. 'I'm walking round The Headland now.'

'People are asking after you.'

'I'll be there soon.' I hung up before she had a chance to say anything else.

So it had started and I wasn't even there – the talking, the whispering, the sympathetic looks. I knew it.

I've no idea how long the walk took me, but I finally made it round to North Bay. I heard them as soon as I rounded North Bay Corner; voices and music drifting towards me. I imagined the laughter and chatter stopping as I approached and shuddered at the thought.

My pace slowed as I stepped onto the promenade, moving aside as a couple of women who appeared to be in their fifties jogged past me. I squinted. One of them looked like she'd been involved in an explosion in a pink lycra factory. My eyes!

Mum had to have been watching out for me because she stopped me some way from the beach hut. My unsteady approach must have shown clear signs of inebriation because the first thing she said was, 'Oh, Sammy, I thought you might have only had a couple of pints with your friends.'

'I did. And then a couple more. And a couple more. And a couple more after that.'

She sighed and I waited for a lecture but she looped her arm through mine instead and slowly pulled me along the promenade. 'I suppose you have a good excuse but I wish you'd waited until you got here before drowning your sorrows.'

'Sorry. It helped.'

'Good. Fortunately, Hailey and Zack are well-oiled too so hopefully they won't notice the state of you.'

'Where's Dad?'

'Roped into barbeque duty.'

'There's a barbeque? In November?' I sniffed the air and realised I could smell sausages and burgers.

She rolled her eyes. 'Five of them. It's all got a bit out of hand if you ask me but she was their daughter so it's up to them how they recognise the year's anniversary.'

There must have been about sixty or seventy people milling round in front of the beach huts, on the promenade, and on the beach. Small gathering my arse.

'I need a beer,' I said.

'I could do with one myself but I agreed to drive. Being drunk is probably the best way to get through these shenanigans.'

Hailey spotted us and made a beeline for me, arms outstretched. 'He's here!' she cried. 'Everyone! Sam's here!'

Cue sympathetic looks from every direction. Nudging. Whispering. Arse!

'Would you like a drink?' she asked, releasing me.

'Yes. Definitely.'

A woman I've never seen before thrust a lager into my hand, then Hailey grabbed my arm and proceeded to parade me around, introducing me with the same cringeworthy statement: 'This is Sam, Nikki's fiancé. He was so grief-stricken, he had to leave Whitsborough Bay.' Cocked heads, sympathetic smiles, watery eyes. I couldn't bear it. Out of respect to Nikki, though, I let the charade continue and repeated to stranger after stranger, 'It's been a difficult year.'

Someone pressed a plastic cup into my hand. I turned round. 'Dad?'

'Vodka and coke,' he said. 'Thought you might need something stronger to get through this.'

I nodded then knocked it back in one. Thanks to the long walk, the beer buzz had faded and I needed something else to take the edge off.

'She's introduced you to the world and his wife now,' he said. 'I think you're safe.'

'It's hideous,' I whispered.

'I know. Another?'

'Hell yeah!'

He returned with another and I knocked it back in one, coughing. 'What was that? Paint stripper?'

Dad laughed. 'I might have been a bit generous with the vodka but not the coke.' He winced when Zack shouted his name. 'Barbeque duty calls. Yippee! Drinks are on a table outside their beach hut if you want another.'

'I'm good for now. Can you take this?' I handed him my empty cup. 'Do you think they'd notice if I left?'

He shrugged. 'I think Hailey's done her bit with you but I reckon you should stick it out for a bit longer. If you can cope with it.'

Dad headed off to flip burgers and I headed towards the drinks table. Sod it. I'd regret it in the morning but I needed one more drink. Maybe not a triple vodka, though.

Bottle of lager in hand, I weaved my way through the throng to the edge of the promenade and, now past the crowd, slowly lowered myself to a seated position with my legs dangling over the edge.

'Sorry, Nikki,' I whispered into the darkness, holding my bottle up to the sky. 'You'd have hated this. We drank to you in the pub, though. You'd have liked that.'

The afternoon had been spot on. Great company, great beer, great conversation. They'd both loved and lost but they'd bounced back and were happy with their new lives. I could be happy with mine. Hopefully Jemma was still on for seeing me tomorrow night so we could talk and I could apologise for been such a tosser over the whole baby business.

A pair of cold hands covered my eyes from behind and a female voice whispered, 'Guess who?'

My heart raced. 'Jemma?'

'You can call me that if it turns you on.'

Shit! I shrugged her hands off me and spun round. 'What the hell are you doing here?'

Kirsty giggled as she sat down beside me, bashing into me as she did so. Obviously drunk. Like me. She moved closer so that her thigh pressed against mine. I shuffled along. So did she.

'Quit it!' I hissed. 'Why are you here? You weren't friends with Nikki.'

She giggled again. 'What's *she* got to do with it? Jeremy invited me.'

'Who's Jeremy?'

'New doctor. Moved in next door to Nikki's parents. They invited him to the party and he invited me.'

'It's not a party.'

She looked over her shoulder towards the throng of people in front of the beach hut. 'It's doing a pretty good impression of a party if you ask me.'

'Well, it's not *meant* to be a party. It's meant to be a small group of friends and family celebrating Nikki's life.'

'Oh yes, it's the anniversary today, isn't it? One year. Are you sad?' She reached out to touch my cheek.

'Get off me!' I dropped down a foot or so onto the sand but Kirsty did the same.

'What do you want?' I snapped.

'Isn't it obvious?'

'No.'

'I want the same thing I've wanted since the Christmas party five years ago. I want you.'

'Jesus, Kirsty, what's wrong with you? You had me, remember but I wasn't enough for you. You wanted others too.'

She stroked my arm but I shrugged her off and moved away, staggering on the uneven beach.

'Don't be like that, babe. I've learned from my mistakes. I wouldn't do that again.'

'I'm not your babe and have you heard yourself? You're here with some bloke called Jeremy. You were with someone else last time I saw you and now you're giving me the come on.'

'They don't mean anything to me. It's you that I want. Please, Sam. Give me another chance.'

I strode away from her and away from the party, feeling very sober all of a sudden. 'Go away, Kirsty.'

'Sam!' She ran after me. 'Please!'

I continued walking. 'I'm not interested.'

'Then what about a quickie for old time's sake? You know you loved it when I let you put your—'

'Stop it!' I spun round. 'Seriously, Kirsty. You've got to stop doing this. It's not all about sex, you know.'

'It should be.'

'No it shouldn't. Stop hurling yourself at a different bloke every night. You're degrading yourself.'

She planted her hands on her hips. 'What's so wrong with enjoying sex?'

'Nothing. But you're shutting yourself off to everything else.'

'You're a fine one to talk,' she cried. 'My fiancée's dead, boo hoo. I can't cope, boo hoo. I'm running away to London, boo hoo.'

I stared at her wondering what the hell I'd ever seen in her. At that moment, she disgusted me. There wasn't a single caring or compassionate bone in her body. She was nothing like Nikki or Jemma.

'Go back to your new fuck-buddy.' I turned and strode down the beach again.

She ran after me and shoved me from behind. 'Nobody turns me down.'

'I think you'll find they just did.'

'You think you're so high and mighty, Dr Jones, but you're nothing special, you know. You and Nikki? I'd have given it another year then she'd have seen what a boring piece of shit you are. All looks and no substance.'

I turned to face her again. 'Then why are you so desperate to have me back?'

'I like a challenge. Come on, Sam. So you don't love me anymore but even you can't resist me.' She unzipped her jacket.

'You're right about one thing but not the other. I don't love you. But I *can* resist you.'

'No you can't.' She swiftly unbuttoned her top and pulled it aside. She had no bra on, which didn't surprise me. She'd often gone out braless or commando, saying it gave her a thrill. And in the early days, it had given me a thrill too. Not anymore.

'Put them away, Kirsty.'

She ran her hands over her breasts and down her stomach. She had an incredible figure, but it no longer turned me on.

'You know you want me really,' she said, rubbing her fingers over her nipples.

I shook my head. 'I don't. Put your clothes back on, Kirsty.'

Without warning, she lunged at me. I stepped backwards and

tripped over something – an abandoned sandcastle perhaps. Next thing I knew, I was sprawled flat on my back, winded. I tried to catch my breath but Kirsty saw her chance and straddled me. She grabbed my hands and cupped them over her breasts. I yanked them away.

'Screw me, Sam,' she whispered. 'Right here on the beach.' She grappled with my belt, pulling it loose from the buckle.

'Get off me!'

'Nobody needs to know. It'll be our secret.'

She pressed against my chest and started kissing me. I cringed at the touch of her lips. Finally getting my breath back, I managed to roll her over so that she was laid on her back and I was on all fours on top of her. She let out a little squeal of excitement and arched her back as though this was part of the foreplay.

'Listen to me carefully,' I hissed. 'I don't need you, I don't want you, and I have zero respect for you for hurling yourself at me on the anniversary of Nikki's death on the beach where she died. You need to get yourself dressed, go back to your doctor friend, and stay away from me forever. Do you hear me?'

'Ooh, I love it when you're all angry like this.' She licked her lips and arched her back again, thrusting her breasts into the air.

I scrambled to my feet and re-fastened my belt as Kirsty lay on the sand, watching me. 'Are you sure I can't tempt you?'

'I've never been more sure of anything in my life. Get up and go home.' I reached out a hand to help Kirsty to her feet but she ignored it.

Propping herself up on her elbows, she purred, 'Last chance.'

'It's over. It was over before I met Nikki and it will *never* start again. Go home, Kirsty. Leave me alone. Please.'

Kirsty sulkily pulled her top across her breasts. 'You'll regret turning me down.'

'I'll learn to live with it.'

43

JEMMA

Leaving Blue Savannah later that evening, we set off along the promenade as Karen had parked at the Sea Rescue Sanctuary.

'It's busy down here tonight,' Karen said, nodding towards a large group of drinkers congregated in front of some of the beach huts. She sniffed. 'Is that a barbeque? In November?'

I stopped and grabbed Karen's arm. 'Crap! That'll be Nikki's memorial thing. I thought it would be finished by now. Sam wanted space. If I walk past, it'll look like I'm ignoring that.'

Karen linked my arm and we wandered along the beach instead, taking it steady to avoid abandoned sandcastles and ditches. There was just enough light from the promenade to illuminate our way, aided by an almost-full moon.

We sped up as we passed the group. Sam had been right – not a 'small' gathering by any stretch of the imagination. There had to be at least sixty people there. Poor Sam. He'd have hated it. I found myself wondering if he was still there or whether he'd managed to make his excuses to slip away.

'Ooh, domestic,' Karen said a few minutes after we'd passed the group. Some way ahead of us was the dark silhouette of a tall man striding down the beach away from a woman. He kept stopping, turning round, saying something to her, then walking off, but she chased after him every time.

'Shit! Did you see that?' Karen said. 'I think she pushed him over.'

The man lay flat on his back on the sand and, next moment, the woman straddled him.

I grabbed Karen's arm and pulled her to a stop. 'I hope they're not about to have a quickie. What should we do?'

'Take photos and post them on Twitter?' she suggested. 'Kidding!'

The next set of steps off the beach were a little way past the couple. The ones behind us were unapproachable thanks to a large pool of water at the bottom of them.

'We'll have to creep past them,' I whispered.

The man flipped the woman over and straddled her instead. She let out an excitable squeal. His voice carried on the wind but not clearly enough to make out any words. Moments later, he stood up.

'Either that was super quick or he's not interested,' Karen whispered.

I stifled a giggle.

He put out his hand to her but she lay on the sand, propped up on her elbows.

We were close enough now to make out their conversation.

'Last chance,' she called to him.

'It's over,' he cried. 'It was over before I met Nikki and it will *never* start again. Go home, Kirsty. Leave me alone. Please.'

My heart raced. Oh my God! Sam and Kirsty.

'You'll regret turning me down,' she shouted.

'I'll learn to live with it.'

He turned away, looking down the beach... straight at Karen and me.

44

SAM

I blinked my eyes and stared again at the two women standing a couple of feet away from me.

'Jemma?'

She nodded uncertainly and I watched her eyes flick to the side. Shit! Kirsty!

'It's not what it looks like.' I cringed as soon as the words left my lips. Isn't that what everyone says when they get caught in an uncompromising position?

'Aw, isn't this lovely?' Kirsty appeared by my side. 'New girlfriend meets ex-girlfriend again at the shrine to the dead girlfriend.' She placed her hand on my shoulder but I pushed it off.

'Jesus, Kirsty! Leave me alone.'

'You weren't saying that five minutes ago,' she purred.

'Yes I was.' I faced her and my heart sank when I saw that she still had her top undone. I shook my head and looked at Jemma again, my stomach churning at the look of disgust on her face. 'I can explain.'

'There's no need.' She sounded weary.

'There is! We haven't... I wouldn't... She threw herself at me.' I realised I sounded like a little kid caught with his hand in the sweetie jar.

'I know,' Jemma said gently. 'We saw what happened and, even if we hadn't, I know you, Sam. You're not *that* bloke.' She turned to Kirsty and her voice hardened. 'You, on the other hand, are *that* woman. I have no idea what Sam ever saw in you and after tonight's little episode, I bet he doesn't either. You should be ashamed of yourself. Have you no respect?'

Kirsty, top still unfastened, brazenly planted her hands on her hips. 'You don't know me.'

'No, and I never want to.' Jemma grabbed her friend's arm. 'Come on, Karen. Bye, Sam.'

They stormed past us towards the steps.

'Thanks a lot,' I said to Kirsty.

'You're welcome.' She grinned as though she'd done me a big favour.

'You don't get it, do you?'

'Get what?'

'Any of it.'

She pointed towards Jemma. 'What I don't get is why you'd choose her over me. What's *she* got that I haven't got?'

I put my fingers out, about to reel off a list, when it struck me. What the hell was I doing? The woman I loved was walking away from me and I was wasting time with a woman who I despised.

'Me,' I said, turning away from Kirsty. 'She's got me.' And if I'd blown it, I'd do whatever it took to make up for it. I sprinted along the beach without giving Kirsty a backwards glance.

Jemma and Karen had reached the top of the steps and were heading along the promenade in the direction of the Sea Rescue Sanctuary.

'Jemma!' I cried, taking the steps two at a time. They both turned round. 'I'm so sorry.'

She shook her head. 'It's not your fault. I could tell what she was like the first time I met her and I know this was all her tonight. Forget about it.' She gave a weak smile then turned away again.

'Jem! I need to talk to you.'

She turned to face me once more. 'Not tonight, eh, Sam? It's been a tough day for us all.'

Her shoulders were slumped and she looked so sad. Something else had happened – something bigger than witnessing Kirsty's pathetic little seduction routine just now. 'Has something happened with your mum?'

Jemma sighed. 'No. It's not Mum.'

I took a step closer to her, fighting hard against the temptation to throw my arms round her and protect her from whatever new pain she was facing. 'What is it?'

Jemma opened her mouth to speak, then shook her head. 'Nothing. Just some unexpected news but it's not important at the moment. This is Karen, by the way.'

We exchanged polite hellos. Then silence. Jemma kept her eyes down, kicking at a piece of seaweed with the toe of her boot.

'Well, this has been lovely, but Jem's keen to get home to her mum,' Karen said. 'Maybe you could give her a call tomorrow, Sam?'

'Yeah. Of course.' My arms twitched but I held them by my side. It wasn't the right moment. 'I'd better let you go. Sorry again. About everything.'

Jemma nodded before walking away with Karen.

I sat down heavily on the top steps. What an evening. While the memorial 'party' had been grim, the episode with Kirsty and the situation with Jemma had just eclipsed it. Why was everything always so complicated? And what 'unexpected news' could Jemma have received to make her so low?

* * *

On my way home in a taxi a little later, I dug my phone out of my pocket to send Jemma a text but she'd beaten me to it:

✉ From Jemma
I know today will have been tough for you and I

don't want you to end it thinking I'm angry with
you. Although I wish I hadn't seen what I saw on
the beach, I know it was all Kirsty and you were
trying to get away from her. I'd like to see you
before you go back to London. I'm working at Bear
With Me tomorrow but I can nip out after lunch. Can
you meet me in Castle Park at 2pm?

We'd talked about meeting tomorrow night to talk. Clearly she
didn't want to do that anymore and I couldn't blame her. I wanted to
call her back or ask more questions but I could feel the exhaustion
from the tone of her text. All she needed from me right now was a yes
or no.

✉ To Jemma
I'll be there xx

With a heavy heart, I made my way slowly back to Mum and Dad's,
unable to shake the feeling that I'd lost Jemma. Not because of what
had happened with Kirsty but because of all the false starts. I should
never have told her how I felt. I should have let the friendship build, I
should have been there for her, I should have let the anniversary pass,
and I should have taken those baby steps I'd been taking since the
wedding that wasn't, instead of that stupid great bloody leap of faith.

As I lay down to sleep, all I could picture was Jemma's sad, weary
face.

45

Bear With Me was busy. Saturdays generally were but this one was extra busy thanks to the start of the Christmas season.

The Christmas lights had been put up around town ready for the official switch-on next weekend. During the week, Annie and Liv had decked out the shop with a tree and strings of fairy lights. We'd taken delivery of a range of Christmas-themed bears and they had pride of place in the window displays and on a tiered display in the centre of the shop. People were definitely starting to shop for Christmas. Fortunately, the steady stream of customers kept my mind off the conversation I needed to have with Sam.

Mum squeezed my hand and wished me luck when I left Bear With Me shortly before 2 p.m. I stepped out onto the cobbles of Castle Street and took a deep gulp of sea air. Sarah opened the door to Seaside Blooms at the same time, her arms full of small bouquets of flowers. She smiled and nodded at me across the throng of shoppers. It was so tempting to cross the cobbles and strike up a conversation with her instead but I couldn't keep Sam waiting. Things needed to be said.

With a flutter of butterflies in my stomach, I turned right to head to the small park at the end of the street. What a gorgeous day. If it wasn't for the slight nip in the air, I could have believed it was the middle of summer thanks to the cornflower blue sky with wispy clouds that floated lazily towards the sea.

Sam was there already, sitting on one of the benches, staring out towards the sea below. My stomach fizzed and my heart sang at the sight of him, his blond hair being tousled by the light breeze. He turned round and smiled warmly. 'Jemma! Hi.'

'Hi, Sam. How are you?'

He indicated for me to sit beside him. 'Better for some fresh air,' he said after I sat down. 'I might have drunk too much yesterday and I paid for it this morning.'

'You didn't seem drunk when I saw you on the beach.'

'There's nothing like your psycho ex trying to seduce you to sober you up.' He shook his head. 'I'm so sorry that you saw that. You do know that nothing happened, don't you?'

I nodded. 'I know. She's a beautiful woman, though. Must be pretty hard to say no to her.' I bit my lip. I hadn't meant to say that. I sounded jealous.

Sam laughed. 'Believe me, saying no was easy. Getting her to hear and accept it? Not so easy. Besides, she's only beautiful on the outside. Not like you.'

My heart raced as he gazed at me intently. I felt my cheeks colour and had to look away.

'Aside from Kirsty-gate, how was the anniversary? Was it sad?'

He was silent for a moment. 'No. Not sad. Until the beach hut thing, it was a great day that Nikki would have loved.'

He told me about his sunrise surf, his relaxing morning with his mum, spending the afternoon in the pub with Stevie and Rob, and then the awkwardness of the party, being paraded round a load of strangers.

'Sounds horrendous,' I said. 'I wonder why they invited so many people, especially when you didn't know any of them.'

He shrugged. 'I think it got a bit out of control and they lost sight of the bigger picture. Do you know what I kept thinking the whole time I was there?'

'I'm a neurologist, get me out of here?'

He laughed loudly. 'Stevie, Rob and I talked a lot of gibberish in the pub yesterday, but we had some really good conversations too about our pasts and bad things that have happened. Steve pointed out that Nikki and the baby are dead and nothing's going to bring them back, and I should stop acting like a part of me died with them. What I actually kept thinking about last night was how much I wished *you* were there with me.'

I raised my eyebrows at him, surprised at the suggestion. 'I don't think that would have been very appropriate.'

'Who says? Where's the rule book that dictates how long you have to grieve for and when it's appropriate to introduce the woman you love to your friends and family?'

Oh. My. God! Had he just said he loved me?

My heart soared and I checked myself. It made no difference. It couldn't. I still had to tell him what I'd planned to tell him. Was it possible to feel both elated and sick at the same time?

'Did you hear what I said, Jem? I know I've screwed things up with us, telling you I cared then running away again. I keep doing that. Things get tough so I run away instead of facing them. Nikki would have been disgusted with me. We used to play this game called, "What would Thor do?" If we had a problem or a challenge, we'd ask that question. The idea, of course, was to come up with something crazily superhero-ish but there'd be some sensible suggestions in there too. In this case, Thor would have accepted that love and life can be snatched away in the blink of an eye and that, if we're fortunate enough to find love again and an opportunity to live again, we should take it.'

'What are you saying, Sam?'

'I'm saying that I've treated you badly and I can't even begin to find the words to tell you how much I regret that. I promise that I'm not about to have another wobbly. I promise that I've come to terms with losing Nikki and the baby. I promise I'm not going to run away again. I love you, Jemma. Will you give me another chance?'

I closed my eyes and breathed in and out deeply.

'Jemma? Was it too much?'

I shook my head. 'It was lovely. It really was. But the answer has to be no.'

Sam stared at me for a moment before nodding. He looked out towards the sea again. 'Did I screw up that badly?'

'No! It's not that at all. I want to say yes. I really do. It's just that... Well, there are practicalities for a start. I live here and you live in London. I know you don't like it there but you yourself said that your job is there and there aren't any vacancies up here. I spent eighteen months having a distance relationship with Scott. It was really hard but I did it because I loved him and trusted him. Then I found out he was married. It was too easy for him to lead a double life when geography and work kept us apart. I trust you, Sam. I really do. Even if I hadn't seen you walk away from Kirsty when she was half-naked and throwing herself at you, I'd have still trusted you and I'd trust you if we had a distance relationship. At first. But then the doubts would creep in. What's Sam doing during this week? Who's he out with? Are they really *just* friends? I don't want to become that person. I *can't* become that person. It would break us apart. I've never been the jealous suspicious type but I think I would be now, thanks to Scott. You know what it's like getting over your partner's infidelity. You had that with Kirsty. You knew you couldn't get back with her because you'd be asking those same sort of questions.' I chewed on my thumbnail. 'I'm sorry, Sam, but I can't do it.'

A sudden gust of wind whipped my coat hood up over my head. Sam leaned forward and gently pushed it down again. I held my breath and closed my eyes as his hand brushed past my cheek. I wanted to turn my head into his palm and kiss his hand but I had to stay strong. I had to finish this.

He lowered his hand again and I released my breath. 'Thank you.'

'You're welcome. I can add hood lowering to my list of services.'

'You're very good at it.' He held my gaze and my stomach fizzed again. Damn it!

'Am I right in thinking that, if I didn't live in London, you'd give me a chance?'

'It's not that simple.'

'It could be. You know I want to move back so I'll keep looking for jobs and I'll return eventually.'

'Eventually could be years away. And, well, the thing is...' My voice caught in my throat.

Sam turned his body round so he was fully facing me. 'What aren't you telling me, Jem?'

My bottom lip started to wobble and tears pooled in my eyes.

'Come here.' Sam put his arms round me and held me while silent tears rained down my cheeks. 'It's okay. I'm here for you,' he whispered into my hair.

When I'd calmed down enough to speak, I remained cuddled up to him. 'I had an unexpected visitor yesterday. Scott's wife.'

'Shit! What did she want?'

'To tell me that Scott's dead.'

Sam pulled me closer to him as I told him about Fiona's visit. We sat huddled together, staring out towards the sea, both of us knowing exactly how it felt when someone you loved died. Brutal. Absolutely brutal.

I don't know how much time passed. Ten minutes? Fifteen? I reluctantly sat up. 'I have to get back to the shop so Liv can go home.'

I stood up and Sam did too. 'You see why it's not that simple?'

He nodded. 'I'm so sorry, Jem. I bet you don't know what to think anymore.'

'If I'm honest, I'm trying *not* to think at the moment. Have a good journey back tomorrow.' I dug into my bag and handed him a package. 'Can you deliver this to Leah for me? It's the Ju-Sea Jem Bear she wanted. And send them all my love.'

Sam took the bear. 'Okay. I'll be back soon.'

I nodded. 'Look me up when you are. I'll miss you.'

'I'll miss you too.' He leaned forward and gently kissed me on the lips, lingering for a moment. Electricity zipped through me as I reached my hands up to his face. Our eyes connected for a moment and then our lips joined again, my hands in his hair, his in mine. Oh. My. God. His tongue teased mine and I pressed my body closer to his, my heart racing like mad. It was everything I'd imagined and so much more.

But I had to stop it. I slowed the kiss and gently pulled away. 'Sorry. I shouldn't have done that. Call it a goodbye kiss for a very special friend.'

Sam smiled. 'I hope you don't kiss all your friends goodbye like that.'

I smiled too. 'Could you imagine Drew's face if I'd done that to him when I left London? Take care of yourself, Sam.'

'Don't leave.'

'I have to. I'm sorry.'

Then I turned and dashed up Castle Street, tears raining down my cheeks once more as it struck me how deeply I'd fallen in love with Sam. I had to stay strong and keep walking. I couldn't do the distance relationship thing with him because I knew, without a shadow of a doubt, that it would destroy us both.

46

I stood on the same spot, staring down Castle Street, until the crowds of shoppers swamped Jemma and I couldn't see her anymore. I touched my fingers to my lips. What a kiss. What a way to say goodbye. Except I didn't want to say goodbye and, judging by the passion in that kiss, neither did Jemma.

I wanted to talk to her about Scott and how she felt about it. I wanted to share our experiences of grief. But I needed to leave her be so that she could do that in her own time with whomever she chose. She had some great friends in Karen, Tiff, Leah and Drew. She was close to her mum. They'd all be there for her. I was a distraction and I'd slow down the grieving process if I was around. Which I wasn't. And that, in itself, clearly presented one of the biggest barriers to making a go of things with Jemma. It was time to do something about it.

✉ To Jack
Are you and Millie around this afternoon or this evening? I need to talk to you. And to apologise

✉ From Jack
We're in now. Isla's just removed Saffron's nappy

and swung it round her head in the middle of the
lounge. Couldn't have timed it better as Saffron
had just taken a dump. You can join in the cleaning
effort. Sounds like a great way to apologise!

⊠ To Jack
I told you before that you needed to work on your
sales technique! I'll be there in 15 mins with my
surgical mask and gloves!

47

JEMMA

Six weeks later

'Mum! Jem! Mrs Denholm's moving out.'

Joining Logan at the lounge window, I peered out as two men exited the cab of a small removals van and walked towards Mrs Denholm's front door.

Well into her nineties, Mrs Denholm had lived in that cottage for decades and had always been a lovely neighbour – the sort who'd do anything for you without expecting favours in return. She was fit as a fiddle but her eyesight was failing. She knew she'd have to give up driving soon and the bus service to Little Sandby didn't run regularly enough to be a viable alternative. Faced with becoming isolated in the village or moving into Bay View Care Home in town where she had several friends, she'd realised there was only one sensible decision to make and had put her name down on the waiting list some time ago.

I returned to the sofa. 'I didn't think she'd move out so quickly. I thought there were no places at Bay View.'

Mum pulled a face. 'There weren't but someone died and she was top of the list.'

'Oh. That's sad. But good for her.'

'Will another old lady move in?' Logan asked, still watching the removals workers.

'I've no idea,' I said. 'It would make a great first home so it might be a younger person or a couple.' The décor hadn't been changed since the 1970s so it needed completely gutting but it was a lovely cottage full of potential for someone willing to take on a project.

Logan turned round, his face animated. 'Ooh, what about a family with a boy my age?'

'Maybe. It's only got two bedrooms so it's not really a family home although there's room to extend.'

'It'll be months before we get new neighbours,' Mum said. 'It isn't even on the market yet. Mrs Denholm said she wants to settle in at Bay View first.'

I stood up and stretched. 'Right, time to go. Are you both ready?'

Mum nodded. 'Quick wee and I'm good.'

'I just need my bag and my trainers.' Logan ran out the room and thundered up the stairs.

'Why's Dr Steadman suddenly decided to see you again two days before Christmas? And why does he want me to go with you? He's barely acknowledged my presence before.'

'I don't know. I just do as I'm told. Don't worry. Annie and Liv will be fine opening the shop and we'll be there before it gets too busy.'

I pulled on my coat and boots while they both sorted themselves out, smiling at the change in Mum over the last month or so. She had a new mantra: *Parkinson's does not control me. I control Parkinson's.* And it seemed to work. She was exercising regularly with Karen, attending counselling, and she was seeing her GP for stress management and depression.

She'd taken a massive step back from the business and the suggestion that Annie and Liv would be fine without us showed me how far she'd come as she'd have normally been worried about queues and replenishing stock so close to Christmas. She'd also met up with her friendly stalker's sister every week, who'd introduced her to a few other locals with Parkinson's and the opportunity to discuss shared experiences seemed to really help her.

For me, the weeks had passed by ridiculously quickly. I'd steadily taken on more responsibility at Bear With Me, including running a couple of bear-making workshops, which I'd loved.

I'd been interviewed for Mum's valuation jobs and had secured both. I wouldn't officially start the local role until the New Year but there'd been an auction in early December in London so I'd started working for that auction house immediately so I could attend it. I'd stayed with Leah, Tiff and Drew for the three nights. They'd been true to their word and hadn't looked for a new lodger so it was lovely being back in my old room although strange being there without any of my belongings round me.

While down in London, I'd also visited Owen and delivered the pair of Ju-Sea Jem Bears he'd requested, although we'd put a date in the diary for him to visit Whitsborough Bay in January as he was still dying to see the shop and meet Mum.

Sam and I kept in touch by text and WhatsApp but we never spoke. He'd called me a few times but I didn't return his calls. I couldn't bear the thought of an awkward conversation tinged with regrets.

When I first knew I was going to London, I nearly called him so many times but had to stop myself. Once in London, the pull to call him, to see him, to hold him was almost unbearable, but I needed to stay strong. If I saw him, I wouldn't be able to resist him.

He hadn't been home since our goodbye kiss but he'd messaged to say he was taking some leave and would be home for Christmas. Instantly, an image of the two of us below the mistletoe sprang into my mind and wouldn't leave.

I longed to see him, to talk to him, to laugh with him and, yes, I longed for a future with him. Alone in bed at night, I repeatedly kicked myself for letting him go and worried that I'd made the biggest mistake of my life. But I knew that a distance relationship would have been a mistake too as my paranoia would have torn us apart. I'd just have to keep hoping that a job opportunity would eventually arise, he'd move back to Whitsborough Bay, and we could finally go on a proper date and see where it took us.

* * *

I dropped Logan off at Rachel's before driving Mum to the hospital in my shiny new lease car. Rachel was taking him and Eden for lunch then to see the latest Disney release at the cinema on the seafront at South Bay.

'You grab a seat,' Mum said, approaching the reception desk. 'I'll tell them we're here.'

A few minutes later, she sat down beside me.

'I wonder if Dr Steadman knows that I've put in all those complaints about him,' I said.

'Aren't they meant to be confidential?'

'Yes but I'd like to think they investigate the complaints and, if they do, he'll know it's me.'

'Maybe that's why he's called you in today, then, to tell you what he thinks of you.'

Mum laughed at my shocked expression. 'I'm joking. I expect that, in the absence of a spouse, he just wants to find out how *you* think I'm coping with things.'

'Julie Browne?' the receptionist called. 'You can go through.'

Mum stood up and shuffled down the corridor. She was having what she now called a 'slow day' rather than a 'bad day'. She knocked on a door and pushed it open. I followed her in, closing the door behind me as she sat down, already feeling prickly about facing that idiot, Dr Steadman.

'Morning,' he said. I turned round with a fake smile plastered on my face. But it wasn't him. It was...

'Sam!' I looked from him to Mum and back to him again. 'What are you doing here?' My heart raced as I stared at him. He looked amazing. He'd had his hair cut and there was colour in his usually pale cheeks. And, of course, he was wearing a delectable suit.

He smiled and those gorgeous blue eyes twinkled. 'It turns out that there've been several complaints about Dr Steadman and, when my brother, Jack, mentioned to the Head of Department that I might be interested in having my old job back, he was straight on the phone to me, asking how quickly I could return.'

'Did my complaints get Dr Steadman sacked?' I hadn't liked him, but I didn't like the idea of being responsible for someone losing their job.

'Don't worry. You were one of many.'

'So you're back in Whitsborough Bay? For good?'

His smile widened. 'For good. London wasn't for me. I guess old habits die hard because I ran away. Again. But for the last time.' He held my gaze while fireworks exploded in my tummy, then he turned to Mum. 'So, Julie, how's it going? I've been looking through your notes and I see that Dr Steadman did sort out that MRI scan but nothing came up on it so...'

I couldn't focus on what he was saying to Mum. I just sat and stared at him with what I'm sure was a stupid grin on my face. He'd come back. For me? I hoped so. He asked Mum lots of questions, and she told him lots of things, but I have no idea what either of them said. My mind was in a whirl. Sam was here. In Whitsborough Bay. For good.

The consultation had obviously finished because Mum had stood up and was pulling her coat on and thanking Sam for his time. It was over?

In a daze, I pulled my coat on too and followed her out of the door, grinning at Sam who signalled that he'd phone me.

'My scarf!' I said, touching my neck.

'As if you didn't do that deliberately,' Mum said.

'I didn't.' Well, not consciously anyway.

I knocked and entered Sam's office again.

'I think you've forgotten something.' He held up my scarf. 'Can't have you catching a chill out there.' He placed it over my head but kept hold of it and gently pulled me towards him. 'I thought it was customary for you to give a goodbye kiss to your special friends.'

He didn't need to pull me closer. I was there already, my lips caressing his, my body pressed against him.

'Your next patient's here,' a voice said, startling me and breaking our kiss apart far too soon.

Sam pressed a button on his desk phone. 'Two minutes, thanks, Pam.' He looked at me with longing in his eyes. 'Sorry. Work calls. Are you doing anything tonight?'

I shook my head. If I had been, I'd have cancelled it in a heartbeat.

'I promised I'd take you out for a meal and I never did that. Can I pick you up at seven and take you for dinner someplace special?'

'Where?'

'It's a secret, but I think you'll like it. Plus, I have a Christmas gift for you.'

'Just as well I've got you something too or that could have been awkward.'

He leaned forward and gave me another breath-stealing kiss. 'Till seven, then.'

* * *

'You look absolutely gorgeous,' Sam said, taking my hand as we headed down Mum's drive towards Thor that evening.

Picking an outfit had been a bit of a nightmare. I didn't want to get dressed up if he was taking me to Blue Savannah but I didn't want to be too casual if he was taking me somewhere more sophisticated. In the end, I settled for a petrol blue A-line dress with short sleeves and a fitted waist, opaque tights, and boots.

'Thank you,' I said, taking in his dark jeans and purple shirt. 'So do you.'

He pointed to his smart black shoes. 'No footwear disaster this time.'

I placed his Christmas gift in the back of the campervan, then climbed into the front. 'Where are we going?'

'A little way down the coast.'

'Are you going to be more specific?'

He grinned at me as he started the engine. 'Nope. It's not far so you'll soon find out.'

'I thought we might be going to Blue Savannah.'

Sam shook his head. 'I thought about it but I wanted to take you somewhere that we've both been before but not with Nikki or Scott – somewhere special just for us.'

'Somewhere I've been before?' I frowned. 'Now I'm intrigued. I can't think of any pubs or restaurants I've been to down the coast.'

'Who said anything about a pub or restaurant?'

'Now I'm even more intrigued.'

* * *

Ten minutes later, we pulled into a car park and I looked at Sam with surprise. 'The Starfish Café? I didn't know it opened on evenings. I haven't been here since I was a kid.'

'Same here until recently. Jack and Millie come here often. It's still a café during the day but it's been refurbished and can be hired for private functions.'

'So there's a function on tonight?'

'A private one. Yes.'

We got out. 'Shall I bring your Christmas present with me?' I hadn't seen his gift for me in the back of Thor but it could have been in a cupboard.

'If you like. Yours is inside already.'

A blonde woman who looked to be a few years older than me greeted us at the door. 'Welcome to The Starfish Café. I'm Hollie and I'm your host for this evening. Your table's upstairs.'

We followed her into the café. It couldn't have been more different to how I remembered it. Refurbished and extended, pine tables and plastic tablecloths had given way to a New England seaside-themed classy décor, which I absolutely loved.

'Are we the only ones here?' I asked, aware that I could hear music but no voices.

'We might be,' Sam said.

Hollie led us upstairs and into a function room with stunning views across the sea. It was dark outside but the moon lit up the inky waters and lights from distant ships twinkled in the distance. I'd have to come back during the day to fully appreciate the view.

A table for two was set in the middle of the room. Lights sparkled on a tree in the corner, under which sat a solitary gift. As I propped Sam's present up against the wall and handed Hollie my coat, I wondered if the gift under the tree was from Sam.

'Your drinks are on the table,' she said. 'I'll be up in about ten minutes with your starters.'

'Have a seat.' Sam pulled out my chair. 'Wine?'

'Yes please.' He poured a glass, then placed it on the table and filled his own glass from the jug of water.

'I don't drink and drive,' he said, seeing me watch him. 'Not even a drop. It's not worth it.'

'I feel the same.' My throat tightened. 'Especially after my dad...' I smiled, not wanting to go down that road. 'This is lovely, Sam.' I noticed a scroll tied up with a red ribbon on my side plate. There wasn't one on Sam's plate so it couldn't be a menu.

I held it up. 'What's this?'

He looked at the scroll and wrinkled his nose. 'It's part of your gift. You've probably spotted the other part under the tree. I'm no writer and I'm certainly no poet, but it popped into my head and, well, I've never written anything for anyone before so...'

'You've written me a poem?' Even the thought of it made me go misty-eyed, no matter how badly written or corny it might be. 'Nobody's *ever* written me a poem.'

'And you'll probably be glad of that when you see my effort.'

'Can I read it now?'

Sam's cheeks reddened. 'It seemed like a good idea at the time...'

My fingers paused at the end of one of the ribbons. 'I won't untie it if it makes you uncomfortable. Although I'm dying to read it.'

'Okay. You can read it, but please don't read it aloud.'

I untied the ribbon and unfurled the paper, then started reading in my head:

Worth The Wait

I Thor-t the sky was black and dull and always filled with rain
I Thor-t that when I lost them, I would never live again
I Thor-t that it was too hard here. I turned and ran away
I Thor-t that life was painful as it limped from day to day
I Thor-t that it was my fault, that somehow I was bad
I Thor-t that I could block them out; the things that made me sad

But then I met you, Jemma. You burst onto the scene
Your passion for your family awoke me from my dream
But I was still being haunted by the memories from the past
I needed to get closure if my new love was to last

I knew that I would miss you from the day I left your side
I knew your kiss would linger; that could not be denied
I knew I'd hear your laughter in every single place
I knew I'd long to hold you, and take it at your pace
I knew I had to be there, handing you my heart
I knew I really loved you. I didn't want to part

I Thor-t that I could write a poem. It's harder than it seems!
You're the one I think of, Jem. You're always in my dreams
You didn't want to take a chance with me so far away
I'm in the Bay right here and now and this is where I'll stay
I'll wait for you until you're ready. I know we could be great
Take your time. I know you're hurt. But I know you're worth the wait

Yours always

Sam xx

I don't know at what point in the poem the tears started – probably the first line where he'd expressed so much pain at his loss – but they kept rolling down my cheeks.

'Was it that bad?' he asked, when I looked up.

'Beautiful,' I whispered. 'Absolutely beautiful.' I wiped my eyes with my hands and sniffed. Sam passed me his paper napkin, which I gratefully accepted.

'Did you mean it?' I asked, when I'd pulled myself together.

He reached across the table and took my hand in his. 'Every single word. I want to be with you, Jemma, but I don't want to rush you into anything that's too soon for you or not right for you. I know you've been hurt and I know you've only just found out the truth about Scott so your emotions are going to be in turmoil. I also know how much honesty means to you so I want to be completely truthful about how I feel with no expectations or commitments. If and when you're ready to tell me you feel the same, then I'm waiting. But if you don't feel the same, then I understand and all I ask is that you're truthful with me in return. I've been lucky enough for lightning to strike me twice but, just because I feel that way, it doesn't mean that's how you're going to feel.' He shook his head. 'I'm babbling. Sorry.'

I stroked his hand with my thumb. 'I don't know what to say. I wasn't expecting to see you today or to have any of this.'

'Honestly, Jemma, you don't have to say anything. All I'm asking is for us to spend some more time together and to go out on some dates. Proper dates. We'll take it slowly. Would you be willing to give it a try and see how you feel?'

I smiled at him. 'So, it's removals service, relationship advice, courier, superhero, *and* poet is it? Is there no end to your talents?'

He laughed. 'I'm pretty certain they might have ended with the poetry.'

'It's amazing. It really is. Thank you.' I glanced at the gift I had for him. 'I know you said you had something else for me, but I'd like you to open your present now, if that's okay. It will help to answer your question.' I stood up and passed the large gift to him.

I nervously watched him unfasten the ribbon then peel back the tape. He removed the wrapping, exposing the back of a wooden picture frame. Turning the picture round to the correct side, he gasped. He studied each of the images carefully as I crouched beside him, watching the emotions wash over him, hoping I hadn't spectacularly misjudged how he'd react to it.

He finally turned to me, his eyes sparkling with tears. 'It's... I can't... Jem, I...'

Panic filled me. I *had* spectacularly misjudged it. 'You hate it?'

He looked at me, his eyes so tender I felt like I could turn into a pool of liquid on the spot. 'I love it.'

He gently placed it beside him then cupped my head between his hands and kissed me with the dreamiest, body-melting kiss.

A little cough pulled us apart. 'Sorry,' Hollie said, smiling apologetically. 'I've got your starters. Farmhouse pâté and warm rolls. All homemade.' She placed a couple of plates down and made a swift exit.

It looked delicious but I didn't feel like eating. I had better things to do. Sam kissed me again then reluctantly stopped when his stomach grumbled loudly, making us both laugh.

'Sorry, he said. 'I didn't have any lunch today. Too busy planning things.'

I smiled as I reluctantly returned to my seat. 'Tuck in.'

'Before I do, I have to ask about this.' He picked up the frame and carefully leaned it against the wall so we could both see it. 'Did you draw it?'

'That would be a no. I can draw bears but that's where my artistic talents end. One of Drew's friends, Evan, does this for a living. I sketched him a rough outline of what I wanted to create and he brought it to life. The man's a genius. It's better than I imagined.'

We both looked at the picture. Made up of a series of smaller frames, Evan had created comic book style key scenes from what Sam had told me about his life with Nikki. It started with him in his car on the phone to Jack, telling him that he didn't want to go on the date with Nikki. The next cartoon was him meeting Nikki on the steps while she was in her wetsuit, then him wiping out on his first surfing attempt, and a celebratory drink afterwards. Frame five had him catching his first wave, followed by one of him kissing Nikki on the beach. I wasn't aware of any pivotal moments after that until they got the campervan and he proposed so I'd asked Evan to create a couple of images showing that. Frame eight showed them walking along the beach looking at an image of a scan. I'd agonised over the next image. Should I have Nikki holding her hand up to her head? Sam cradling Nikki in his arms? In the end, I chose an image of Sam on the beach, all alone, looking at the rock pools with his head bowed. The next frame had him packing up the campervan, followed by an arrival in London, driving past a classic London cityscape.

Then *our* story began: him knocking Tiff flying the night they met, him meeting me in The George and Dragon for the first time, rushing home with me when Drew had his meltdown, and rushing home with me again when Mum went AWOL. Frame sixteen showed him looking at the bears for his nieces in my bedroom, then me feeding him wine gums as he moved me back to Whitsborough Bay, followed by him giving me an enormous hot chocolate outside Blue Savannah after my altercation with Mum.

My favourite image was the next one: Sam standing by the rock pools with a shaft of sunlight beaming down on him. I stood nearby, looking up at the sun, an expression of wonder on my face.

Evan captured the run-in we'd had with Kirsty and then Sam running away, leaving me looking devastated. A few more frames captured the beach hut memorial party, Kirsty pursuing him along the beach, then him explaining to Karen and me that it wasn't what it looked like.

The final three images were of us kissing in the park at the end of Castle Street, me disappearing into the crowd as he watched me, then one of both of us looking wistfully out of separate windows, mobiles in our hands, looking lost.

Evan had finished with a big 'What happens next' graphic followed by a couple of blank frames containing large question marks.

Throughout our starters, Sam kept glancing towards the frame and smiling. 'So, what *does* happen next?' he asked after Hollie cleared our plates.

'I think we go on more dates. Proper ones, as you say, and see where it takes us.'

'You're sure you're ready?'

'I think so, but bear with me if I have wobbles. I'm scared, Sam.'

He reached out and took my hand. 'I know. So am I. We've both lost someone we loved and starting again is a huge thing, but I think they'd both want us to. I know Nikki would have liked you.'

'I reckon Scott would have liked you too.'

'I think that's one of the many reasons why we're so perfect together. We understand there's been someone else who was the keeper of our hearts first, but they were taken away from us. You're not Nikki and I don't want you to be. I want you to be you and I want us to have our own memories, like this place which has no memories of either of them. I'm not Scott either and I know you don't want me to be. But Scott and Nikki are very important to us and we should continue to remember them because they're part of who we are today.'

A tear slipped down my cheek. How did he do it? How did he reach into my soul, find the biggest fear I had, and manage to reassure me about it?

'So after I've completely ruined the mood, would you like your other gift?' Sam asked.

I smiled. 'You didn't ruin anything. You voiced one of my fears that I could never compare to what you had with Nikki.'

'You don't need to compare to her. There are things about you that remind me of her, and there are things about you that are nothing like her but it's the whole package that I fell for – not the reminders. It's you I love, Jemma. You.'

'You really are a superhero.'

'Which is the perfect link to this.' He retrieved the gift from under the Christmas tree and handed it to me. 'Happy Christmas, Jemma. This is the keeper of the scroll.'

The box was quite heavy and wrapped in superhero paper, which made me laugh. I swiftly removed the wrapping to reveal a gift box. When I lifted the lid, I grinned. It was a Ju-Sea Bear, dressed in a skirt, cape and breastplate, holding a hammer in one hand. I lifted him out and gazed at his face. 'My very own superhero bear. He's absolutely gorgeous. When did you and Mum conspire about this?'

Sam laughed. 'I couldn't possibly breach patient confidentiality.'

'I love him. I'm sure he'll take great care of the scroll.' I looked up at Sam. 'Are you sure you're okay to give me some time to adjust?'

He lifted up one of my hands and kissed it gently. 'We can take it as slowly as you like. There's no pressure for anything. I know you're still hurting about Scott and I did kind of turn up without warning. After what you said on the day we said goodbye, I knew it was no good promising I'd leave London. Actions speak louder than words so here I am back home in my old job and feeling excited about new beginnings.'

'It's the most romantic thing anyone's ever done for me. I can't believe you gave up your promotion and have returned to your old job so you could be with me.'

'A wise woman once suggested that a choice between a great CV or being surrounded by friends and family was a no brainer. She was right. That day I saw your mum, when I turned up in a suit, I'd been to York Hospital to explore opportunities there. I'd have done the commute for you but they had nothing so I got Jack to put feelers out in Whitsborough Bay. I was lucky that there were so many complaints against Dr Steadman and they were keen to replace him but I'd have moved back here for you, even if I hadn't been able to secure my old job back.'

'Really? What would you have done?'

His eyes twinkled with mischief. 'Thor and I would have toured the North Yorkshire coast offering our removals, relationship advice, courier, superhero, and poetry services of course.'

I laughed. 'You'd have been amazing at it. I look forward to discovering what other talents you have.'

'I'll drink to that.' Sam clinked his glass against mine.

'I've heard a good way to seal a deal is with a kiss. And I do believe I might have just spotted some mistletoe hanging up by that tree.'

We didn't make it to the mistletoe. As I kissed my very own superhero, my stomach fizzed and my heart sang. It had been a very bumpy journey to that point and I was still scared about surrendering myself completely again, but I knew that Sam was worth the risk. I suspected that he wouldn't need to wait for me for very long because I already knew that I loved him and couldn't live without him. And, after everything I'd been through over the past six months, I also knew that I was stronger than I'd ever realised. Yes, I still sobbed at everything from adverts to films to beautiful, romantic poems but Owen had been right; it wasn't a sign of weakness. It was because I cared deeply and that was definitely a good thing.

48

SAM

New Year's Day

'Are you sure you want to do this?'

Jemma took another look at the sea and nodded.

'It's pretty nippy today,' I said.

'You said it's always cold in the North Sea.'

'It is. But today it's also dull and cloudy and the forecast is for rain.'

She looked up at the sky. 'There's some blue sky right over there.'

I squinted into the distance. It was miles away. 'I can pretty much guarantee that it's going to rain before the blue sky hits us.'

'So what if it does? We'll already be wet from the sea. A bit of rain isn't going to make much difference.'

'I'm just thinking about you. It's probably not the best weather for your first lesson.'

Jemma removed a hairband from her wrist and tied her hair back. 'Look, Sam, I want to do this. I know we talked about making our own memories but surfing is part of you – not just you and Nikki – and I want to share it with you. You've done something amazing for me by moving back here so I want to do something special for you. Besides, I've already done the worst part by shoehorning myself into this thing.'

She pointed to her wetsuit. 'I might as well see it all the way through. Lesson one, please, Dr Jones.'

On the sand, Jemma was a natural, but I remembered from personal experience that it was one thing mastering the moves on the stability of the beach, and something completely different trying to repeat them in the sea. She impressed me, though, giggling every time she wiped out. She didn't moan about the cold or how tired she was. When the heavens opened, as predicted, she sat astride her board with her head back, her eyes closed, and her arms outstretched, smiling.

When I insisted we call it a day, she lay her board on the sand and squeezed the water out of her hair. 'That was seriously hard work but I think I almost made it to a kneeling position.'

I hugged her tightly, touched by how hard she'd tried to master it. 'You were amazing. You *are* amazing. Did you enjoy it?'

'Surprisingly, yes. It wasn't as cold as I expected although, now I'm out of the water, I'm frozen.'

'Come on. Let's get changed then do the other thing.'

* * *

The next part of our fresh start to the New Year had also been Jemma's idea. She suggested that I'd already said goodbye to Nikki but not to the baby and I needed to do that. She also needed to officially say goodbye to Scott.

After we'd showered and changed in the facilities at The Surf Shack, we walked along North Bay beach, hand in hand. Jemma held the wooden box containing Scott's ashes and I carried three roses and a long stick we'd found on the beach earlier. She'd done some research and discovered that deep red roses signified love and grief, making them perfect for saying goodbye.

High tide was approaching and many of the rock pools had already disappeared beneath the sea. We'd just have time to do what we planned. At the spot where Nikki had taken her last breath, Jemma took the stick from me and wrote SCOTT in the sand. She kissed the petals of one of the roses, crouched down, and placed it across his name. She handed me the stick and I wrote NIKKI and BABY, kissed the petals of the other two roses and lay them between the two names.

We stood together, arms round each other, watching the tide approach. After a few minutes, it licked the edge of Nikki's name, moving the roses slightly. On the next pass, it took Nikki's and Baby's roses and scrambled their names. I took a deep shuddery breath and swallowed down the lump blocking my throat.

As the tide rolled in again, Jemma opened the wooden box and sprinkled Scott's ashes into the sea where they were taken along with his rose and his name.

I put my arm back round her and kissed the top of her head as we whispered, 'Goodbye.'

A sudden brightening of the sky made us both look up. The clouds had parted and a shaft of sun beamed down on us briefly before the clouds covered the sun again.

'I think they approved,' Jemma said. 'All three of them.'

'I think they did. I'm glad you suggested this. Are you okay?'

'Sad and happy at the same time.'

'Me too.'

We stood for a moment, holding onto each other, until the rapidly approaching tide chased us and we beat a hasty retreat up the beach.

Standing on the promenade, leaning against the sea wall, we watched the tide drawing the sea ever closer until all the rock pools disappeared from sight and the waves lapped against the wall.

I turned my gaze up and down the shoreline, a feeling of content-ment swelling inside me to have returned to where I belonged. It was hard to believe that I'd ever left this beautiful place but it had been the right thing to do. I'd needed the time and space to find myself ... and to find Jemma. How funny that we were from the same small seaside town yet we'd found each other in the third largest city in Europe.

We'd been naïve to think we could keep our fledgeling relationship low-key. It was Christmas after all, which meant lots happening with friends and family. My parents and Jack and Millie adored Jemma and she was an immediate hit with my nieces, especially when she presented them each with a soft teddy bear

It was great getting to know Julie, and Logan already felt like a little brother. When I first met him on Christmas Eve, he announced that I needed to give him and Eden surfing lessons in the summer. On Christmas Day, it had escalated to me taking them away camping in Thor and, on Boxing Day, he declared that I should buy the cottage next door and live there with Jemma. Stomach churning, I'd hardly dared look at Jemma in case all the talk about the future terrified her but she didn't seem fazed by any of it, even when Julie tossed her the keys to Mrs Denholm's cottage and suggested she give me a tour.

'It's worth a look inside,' Jemma said, smiling. 'It's like stepping back in time but you might need to wear sunglasses.'

What an understatement! It was like an assault on the eyes of clashing colours everywhere from the swirly orange and brown carpets to the loud patterned wallpaper, from the avocado bath suite to the moss-green kitchen units. But look past that and what an amazing home it could be.

'What do you think?' Jemma asked as we stood in the master bedroom overlooking the sizeable garden.

'Décor aside, I absolutely love it. It could be a dream home.'

She took my hands in hers. 'Your dream home perhaps?'

'Honestly, Jem, I'd put an offer in today but how would that be fair on you? I promised to give you time and space and me living next door would be breaking that promise. If it's still on the market if and when you're ready, then perhaps it was meant to be.'

She drew me to her and kissed me tenderly. 'Thank you for not pushing. It's not on the market yet so there's plenty of time.'

Across the past week, I couldn't stop thinking about Mrs Denholm's cottage and how it might look with a bit of hard work and vision. Every time I pictured the transformation, I imagined Jemma living there with me. There was no way the house would stay on the market for long once Mrs Denholm put it up for sale but it was too much to hope that Jemma would be ready that soon. I needed to push it out of my mind because no way was I going to say or do anything that might lose her again.

'It's getting chilly,' Jemma said, bringing my thoughts back to the present. 'We should probably head off. Before we do, I've got something for you.' She reached into her bag and removed a green and a red envelope. She passed me the red one. 'I got Evan to send these by special delivery.'

'Evan? Is this what I think it is?'

'This is the next two frames of our story.'

I opened the envelope and took out two more cartoons. The first showed a beach with the three names and three roses across them, with the sea lapping against them. The next showed the two of us holding onto each other on the beach as a shaft of light came down on us.

'I wasn't actually expecting that to happen again,' Jemma said as I stroked my thumb over the drawing. 'But I'm so glad it did.'

'They're spot on. Thank you.'

She held the green envelope to her chest. 'Before you open this and see the final drawing, do you still feel the same way about me as you did when you wrote that poem?'

'If it's possible, spending so much time together over Christmas has made me love you even more.'

'And you don't need more time to be sure how you feel?'

'I'm already sure. I love you and I hope that, one day, you'll feel the same but I'll wait for as long as you need.'

'You don't need to wait. It's already happened. I love you too, Sam. I don't need more time.'

My heart raced. 'You mean that? You're not just saying it?'

'I really mean it and I have the final part of our story to prove it.' She handed me the green envelope and I removed two drawings.

'The top one is option one,' she said.

Evan's drawing was immediately recognisable as Mrs Denholm's cottage. A 'for sale' sign stood in the garden with a 'sold' panel across it. I was standing on the doorstep and Thor was parked on the drive. She wanted me to move in next door. There was only one thing missing on the picture, though.

'Or there's option two.'

I glanced up to see her nibbling on her thumbnail – her tell-tale nervous tick. What did she have to be nervous about? She'd already said she loved me and that had to have taken some courage.

As I flicked over to the second drawing, it all became clear. It was almost the same except Jemma's car was on the drive alongside Thor and Jemma was beside me on the doorstep.

I looked from one image to the next, my heart pounding. 'You know what I think we should do? Go back to my mum and dad's, put these in the frame, then get in touch with Mrs Denholm and make an offer for the cottage.'

Jemma looked at me expectantly, still nibbling on her nail.

'*Our* cottage.' I held up the second drawing. 'Because this is the ending I choose.'

'You're sure I'm not being too forward, inviting myself to move in?'

I shook my head. 'The moment I saw it, I wanted it. And not because of the swirly orange and brown stair carpet, the woodchip wallpaper or the avocado bath suite, gorgeous as they are. Do you know why I wanted it so badly?'

'Cute village? Sea views?'

'They're added bonuses. The real reason I wanted it was because of you. There was something about that cottage that made me picture you and me growing old together there. Maybe it was because I knew you'd rest easy knowing you were right next door to your mum and brother. Everything about it seemed so perfect for us that I knew I had to have it. I'd have put in an offer there and then if I hadn't worried it would scare you off.'

'You can really picture us growing old together?'

I nodded. 'Definitely. Can't you?'

'I can.' Jemma leaned forward and tenderly kissed me. 'Come on. Let's go back to yours and put that offer in. New year. New start. New life together.'

Hand in hand, we made our way down the promenade towards Thor the campervan, chatting excitedly about the future. *Our* future.

Just over a year ago, I'd lost my best friend, my fiancée, and my future. I'd never imagined in the dark months that followed that I could ever let anyone in again but then Jemma Browne blew into my life and changed everything.

When things seem bleak, all you need is love; someone to shine some light through the darkness. Jemma's love and passion for her family and her home reminded me of how important those things were to me too. Thanks to her, I opened my eyes and started living again and I'm so grateful that I could help her do the same.

Our future together, back home in Whitsborough Bay where we belonged, was now filled with exciting promise. It turned out that lightning really did strike twice.

ACKNOWLEDGMENTS

All You Need Is Love was originally published in spring 2017 under the title *Bear With Me*. It was my fifth book but my first independent release after my original publisher ceased trading. I was really nervous about it, not only because it was my first indie book but because it was the first book I'd written outside of my 'Welcome to Whitsborough Bay' series. The series had been really well received but would my readers enjoy a standalone, albeit set in the same fictional North Yorkshire seaside town?

As a keen arctophile myself (collector/lover of teddy bears), I'd always wanted to write a novel featuring a teddy bear shop, especially as I ran my own bear shop for two years during which time I started writing my debut novel. A bear shop setting gave rise to more nerves because I know that the idea of an adult collecting teddy bears may seem a little strange to some. Thankfully, the reviews I received reassured me that readers fell in love with Jemma's and Sam's stories ... and perhaps a little bit in love with bears too.

I was delighted that my amazing new publisher, Boldwood Books, wanted to refresh and re-release all of my back catalogue and it's been a pleasure to revisit this story several years down the line with a fresh pair of eyes and the expert guidance of my brilliant editor, Nia Beynon.

Thank you so much, Nia, for all the fabulous advice on where to trim and where to add more colour.

Early on, I knew that I wanted this story to include either an illness or a life-changing condition. After some research, I settled on Parkinson's, a condition with which my Auntie Jennifer was diagnosed in 2003. When the original version of this book was released, she was seriously ill with dementia too but sadly she passed away in August 2018. My thoughts are with her husband and children from whom a beautiful, vivacious woman was taken far too soon.

I'm very grateful to my mum and dad's next door neighbour, Eveline Haigh, who answered a multitude of questions about her diagnosis and what living with Parkinson's meant for her. An author can conduct masses of research online but nothing quite beats a lengthy conversation with someone about what it's really like. For additional research, I'm indebted to all the invaluable information, guidance and videos on the websites of Parkinson's UK, The Michael J. Fox Foundation, Alzheimer's Research UK, and NHS.

Thank you to my beta reading team for their work on the original version – two exceptionally talented writers and great friends, Jo Bartlett and Sharon Booth, for their encouragement and insightful feedback and to Joyce Williams (my lovely mum), Liz Berry and Susan Hockley for their proofreading abilities, daft mistakes spotting, and extremely helpful comments.

A big, fat, hug of gratitude, as always, is owed to my family – my husband Mark and our daughter Ashleigh. They're so supportive when I drift off into my fictional world and lose the ability to remember anything reality-related!

Although the creation of any of my stories is a solo project, it takes a team to pull the final book together. As well as the input from my editor, I need to thank Sue Lamprell for copy-editing and proofreading. It's been a joy to work with Sue on all of my Boldwood Books. Thank you, Sue, for spotting all the errors and inconsistencies. Thank you also to Debbie Clement for another stunning cover. Isn't it gorgeous? I do need to also thank my husband again here as he designed a beautiful cover for the original version as well as formatting it for me.

If you've listened to this story, I hope you've enjoyed the brilliant narration by Lucy Brownhill and Gareth Bennett-Ryan. Thank you, Lucy and Gareth, for bringing my characters to life, to ISIS Audio for creating the audiobook and to Ulverscroft for distributing it.

Finally, my thanks go to you, my readers and/or listeners. If you've enjoyed *All You Need Is Love* and any of my other books, please spread the word to your friends and family and tell Amazon/ AppleBooks/ Kobo/ Audible by leaving a review. You don't have to write much. You can even just rate the book/ audiobook if you like but reviews are such a great way to thank an author and encourage them to keep writing.

Big hugs

Jessica xx

MORE FROM JESSICA REDLAND

We hope you enjoyed reading *All You Need Is Love*. If you did, please leave a review.

If you'd like to gift a copy, this book is also available as an ebook, digital audio download and audiobook CD.

Sign up to Jessica Redland's mailing list for news, competitions and updates on future books.

http://bit.ly/JessicaRedlandNewsletter

ABOUT THE AUTHOR

Jessica Redland is the author of eleven novels which are all set around the fictional location of Whitsborough Bay. Inspired by her hometown of Scarborough she writes uplifting women's fiction which has garnered many devoted fans.

Visit Jessica's website: https://www.jessicaredland.com/

Follow Jessica on social media:

facebook.com/JessicaRedlandWriter

twitter.com/JessicaRedland

instagram.com/JessicaRedlandWriter

bookbub.com/authors/jessica-redland

ALSO BY JESSICA REDLAND

Standalone Novels

The Secret To Happiness

Christmas at Carly's Cupcakes

Starry Skies Over The Chocolate Pot Café

All You Need Is Love

Welcome To Whitsborough Bay Series

Making Wishes At Bay View

New Beginnings at Seaside Blooms

Finding Hope at Lighthouse Cove

Coming Home To Seashell Cottage

Hedgehog Hollow Series

Finding Love at Hedgehog Hollow

New Arrivals at Hedgehog Hollow

Family Secrets at Hedgehog Hollow

ABOUT BOLDWOOD BOOKS

Boldwood Books is a fiction publishing company seeking out the best stories from around the world.

Find out more at www.boldwoodbooks.com

Sign up to the Book and Tonic newsletter for news, offers and competitions from Boldwood Books!

http://www.bit.ly/bookandtonic

We'd love to hear from you, follow us on social media:

 facebook.com/BookandTonic

 twitter.com/BoldwoodBooks

 instagram.com/BookandTonic

Printed in Great Britain
by Amazon

72271691R00203